Lur

She didn't know

left her husband

peacefully—why s

out at the storm-lashed world.

Then she saw it—a writhing, roiling *blackness*.
Even darker than the stormy night, it was a shifting
mass of negation that held no shape, that one moment
sprouted leathery wings and the next thrust up a
snout full of sharp, snarling teeth. The thing's eyes
glowed a vicious red.

She gasped, whirled, and raced into the baby's
room. She was too late. Her daughter was dead! The
demon had triumphed. . . .

Look for these Tor books by R. R. Walters

LADIES IN WAITING
LILY

LILY
R. R. WALTERS

TOR
HORROR

A TOM DOHERTY ASSOCIATES BOOK

This is a work of fiction. All the characters and events portrayed in this book are fictitious, and any resemblance to real people or events is purely coincidental.

LILY

Copyright © 1988 by R. R. Walters

All rights reserved, including the right to reproduce this book or portions thereof in any form.

A TOR Book
Published by Tom Doherty Associates, Inc.
49 West 24 Street
New York, NY 10010

ISBN: 0-812-52703-8
Can. ISBN: 0-812-52704-6

First edition: July 1988

Printed in the United States of America

0 9 8 7 6 5 4 3 2 1

Prologue

THE STORM HAD RUMBLED PONDEROUSLY EASTWARD, CASTING its blanket of shadow over the Florida peninsula, swamping the summer-parched earth with curtains of rain falling from its sagging underbelly, bringing night early. Now it hung stationary above the coastline, grumbling to itself, regathering its power, piling clouds one on top of the other to become a looming mountain in the nighttime darkness. Deep in its black interior, filigrees of lightning shimmered. Then, with a roar of power gone berserk, it lashed at the coast.

The storm sent whirling dervishes of water along the street in front of a ranch-style house. The lightning spun a web of jagged wounds across the sky and a surging wind, as if trying to escape the searing bolts, howled around the house, whipping two newly planted palm trees in the front yard until they lashed their fronds in agony.

Donna Lazurus drifted into the living room to stand

1

a few moments watching the PBS documentary on polar bears her husband Tony had tuned in. The storm was interfering with the cable reception, so mostly colored confetti flashed in exploding bursts across the screen, and the audio consisted of a snake-pit sibilance of hissing. She moved farther into the room so she could see Tony's face where he was sprawled in the La-Z-Boy chair. His chin was on his chest, his eyes closed, his mouth open in an abbreviated smile. Donna quietly crossed the room and turned off the TV, wondering if it might not be a good idea to unplug it in case of a lightning strike. But she couldn't reach the wall outlet behind it without moving the set, and she didn't feel capable of doing that right now. Her energy level had dropped drastically. Her nerves were flicked with little jabs of cold that made them tingle under her skin. Too tense to sit down, she wandered to the picture window and stood, watching the suffering palms in the front yard.

She folded her arms across her stomach, tightly grasping her elbows, barely managing to keep from shivering. Each breath she sucked into her lungs sent tiny darts of pain through her chest. The cold prickling in her nerves turned into the frigid jabs of icicles. Common sense told her this was a primitive's reaction to the storm, but though she did not delight in walking through heavy rains, she had never before found a storm particularly disturbing. But tonight she was more than nervous. She gnawed at her lower lip, about to turn away from the window, when she saw something moving through the darkness outside. There was no definite shape to it, yet she was aware of form, of contours.

The lightning and the crash of thunder struck simultaneously. Donna stumbled back a step from the window, seeing only streamers of light whirling against the void of darkness. She heard a hissing sizzle, then echoes of the thunder rolling furiously, the window-pane before her rattling as though a spray of hailstones was pelting it. She heard a voice cry out, and realized it was her own. The house lights flared, flickered, went out, then returned to burn with a dimly yellow ghost of light. She thought she detected the faint smell of burnt ozone.

"What the hell—!"

Tony was sitting straight up in the La-Z-Boy. Confusion mingled with shock on his face as he looked questioningly around the room.

"It was a lightning strike," she said. "In the next block, I think."

"Christ, it sounded like Hiroshima."

"I know."

She glanced out the window. The front lawn was empty. Whatever had been out there was gone.

"That's a hell of a way to be awakened." Tony grinned sheepishly at his reaction to the lightning strike.

Donna's heart, which had been thudding much too hard in her chest, began to slow down, and she said, "I'm going to look in on Stevie."

Tony nodded. "I don't hear any crying. Maybe a four-month-old can take this kind of thing better than a twenty-seven-year-old." He pushed himself up out of the recliner. "Going from dreaming of an exciting interlude with my beautiful wife to sitting in the middle of a world blowing itself apart, all in less than a second, can sure as hell jangle one's perspective."

His eyes were soft and suddenly he looked incredibly good to her. In his faded jeans and hueless sport shirt, he was, in fact, magnificent. She crossed the room to him, cupped his face gently in her hands, then placed her lips on his. It was a long kiss; Donna was trying to reassure herself that all was well. Finally she whispered, "Maybe we can make that interlude real a little later."

He ran a hand lightly down her back. "I think maybe we can."

She laughed. "And make it long."

"Long." He gave her a gentle slap on her rear. "I'll be waiting."

She turned on the hall light outside Stevie's nursery. The reflected light would give sufficient illumination without disturbing him.

Apparently the lightning strike had not affected him. He was laying on his stomach. His head was turned, resting on its left cheek, his eyes closed and his mouth opened in a small pouting oval.

Donna hesitated at the doorway, her expression warming as she gazed at her son. Once again she was filled with amazement that her body had formed and nourished and given forth this child who now sprawled so innocently in his crib. She felt an irresistible urge to weep with joy.

Stevie had kicked his covering sheets into a rope that was twisted around his legs. Although the thermostat was set high, Donna feared that the air-conditioned coolness might chill him, so she tiptoed across the room and bent over the crib.

The sheet was more tangled than she had suspected. If she didn't know better, she could easily think it had been deliberately twisted around his short legs. Stevie made no move, gave no sign of disturbance, as his mother undid the sheet. His face remained motionless. Donna pulled the sheet up and began tucking it around him. Still the small body did not react. Suddenly there was an unnaturalness in his immobility. Donna bent over the crib's side, lowering her face to his.

"Stevie? Stevie?"

No response. No sleep-drowned sigh. No twitch of muscle.

In a sort of stupor Donna laid her hand on her son's cheek.

"Stevie?"

The little head stayed as it was, eyes closed, the mouth open in its almost nursing pout. She stared down at him, a horrible apprehension building within her, then held her hand to his mouth. There was no breath.

"Stevie!"

Her hands were no longer a part of her, throwing the sheet back, burrowing under the little body to lift it by its shoulders. The baby's arms hung limp, its head fell back. The oval of the mouth became a terrible empty hole.

"No! *No!*"

Donna clutched the limp body to her breast as something inside her disintegrated. She sank to the floor, still holding the small body to her, only vaguely aware of the looming black walls of the abyss into which she was falling.

A minute later, a horrified Tony Lazurus stood in the nursery's doorway and stared at his wife sitting cross-legged on the floor, rocking back and forth while she hugged the body of their dead son.

1

IT WAS SUNDAY EVENING. THE WEEKEND WAS ALL BUT ENDED.
The wide plain of the sea and the wider dome of the sky
were empty. Along Highway A1A there was the drone
of automobile motors and the swishing of tires on
warm asphalt, but on the beaches only the metronomic
slap, slap, slap of wavelets disturbed the silence.

Three people occupied the emptiness. A man, standing alone, and a couple. The couple, a middle-aged man
and woman, strolled slowly along the line of foam that
marked the ocean's fringe, their heads bent low in an
attitude of what might have been supplication. Every
so often, one of them would stop, bend down to pick up
a shell, and examine it intently before dropping it into
a small bucket or tossing it back to the sea. It was
evening, the time of day when the local population
seldom visited the beach and most of the tourists had
abandoned sea and sand in favor of evening meals at
the local restaurants or fast-food establishments.

Sam Young watched the shell-hunters meander southward, then turned his attention to the ocean. He liked these evening hours. Sometimes, when he was in the mood and the weather permitted, he donned his sweat suit to jog along the beach, feeling comfortable in his aloneness with the ocean and the unending stretch of sand that disappeared into drifting ghosts of sea mist far to the north and south.

He had no desire to label what he felt. Perhaps, he told himself, he did not possess the ability to categorize the sensations he experienced on the beach. But he did feel good after each jogging session—not preposterously healthy, just good—so when he could he jogged four miles, two miles to the south of his beachside townhouse and the two miles back. His was a sedentary job, so he needed the exercise. His greatest physical exertion, as the owner of a public-relations firm, was the manipulation of his desk chair.

Now Sam stood at the southern end of what he called his "jogging course," drawing in lungsful of saline-scented air, wanting a cigarette, yet knowing that if he smoked one when he returned to the townhouse he would negate what he had accomplished with the exercise. The realization somewhat soiled his feeling of achievement, and the thought that he might be able to put off the cigarette until after dinner was but a minor satisfaction. While his breathing returned to normal, he watched a ribbon of darkness widen on the eastern horizon as night crawled up from the other side of the world.

Then, without warning, like a window shade being drawn over the setting sun, the light deteriorated. A shadow inched across the beach, hesitated for a brief instant at the water's edge as if reluctant to leave the firmness of the land, then crept outward over the ocean, staining the purple water a dingy gray. A westerly breeze accompanied. On top of the sand dunes the

slender sea oats nodded their heads in concession to its
passing. The wind carried the smell of dusty, sun-dried
vegetation, fouling the clean odor of the sea. Not too
far inland, thunder rolled. A shiver rippled through the
air and a current of expectation charged the atmosphere.

Sam turned from the ocean and looked inland. Gray
clouds ballooned upward above the dunes, inflated by
the warm air rising from the heated land to the west,
their tasseled edges dyed a silvery-red by the sun they
were erasing.

Irritated at allowing himself to be caught in the open
by one of the summer's convective storms, he began the
two-mile jog home, staying on the path of hardened
sand near the water's edge, knowing it was unlikely he
would get to the townhouse without a drenching.

The smell of rain now rode the air. Still beyond the
dunes, but closer, the thunder was a dull rumble with
no beginnings and no endings, almost subterranean in
the depth of its tone, as if not only were the skies
tumbling, but the foundations of the world were shifting. Sam wanted to increase his speed; however, he
knew that to do so was beyond his capabilities. His
muscles would never answer the demand; so he continued at the pace he had set, legs rising and falling in
mechanical movements like pistons driven by a pre-set
motor.

Off to his right, skimming only a few feet above the
water, a single file of brown pelicans glided south, their
wings occasionally stroking the air like wide-bladed
oars. In the dwindling light, their awkward shapes were
partially silhouetted between the grayness of sky and
sea, and he found it easy to imagine them flying over a
primeval sea. He turned his head and stared until they
were well behind him. When he swung his gaze to the
front he saw the other bird.

It was flying alone. His first impression was of

austerity of movement, of sleekly functional design. The bird was at least twice the size of the pelicans, yet it glided through the slate-hued light with astonishing grace. It's primary color was a dull black. Like the pelicans, it was little more than a silhouette against the gray background, but he received the impression that if the sun were shining, that sooty black would be intensely rich, shimmering with blue highlights. As it trailed along a hundred yards behind the pelicans, Sam tried to remember if he had ever seen a picture of such a bird. He couldn't recall.

The breeze had matured into a young wind. It stirred the sand and rippled the surface of the flat wavelets. A tentacle of it must have touched the bird, because it abruptly ceased its forward flight to hang suspended over the ocean. Its eyes flashed vividly, searching, scanning the ocean and the sand below. Finally it rolled lazily to its left, hung another moment, then plunged downward toward the dark water. Halfway to the ocean's surface, it spread its wings. Sam caught his breath. Never had he seen a wingspan to equal it. He guessed it to be somewhat more than eight feet, and stopped jogging to stare in awe as the wings stretched a diagonal line across the sky. They were, he thought, a combination of sails spread to catch the wind and delicate kites riding the updrafts bouncing from the sea. The bird hung motionless another moment, then turned into the wind. For an instant, there was something welcoming in the way it faced the clouds. Sam could all but feel the affection the great, dark creature directed at the approaching storm, as if the boiling clouds embodied a force within their depths which whispered and beckoned to it like an eager lover.

The huge wings flapped, the bird rose, then very elegantly banked into a sweeping dive, swooping low over the beach. Sam thought he could hear the rushing of slipstream air across the surfaces of the wings. An instant before it would crash into one of the dunes, the bird rose, glided over the crest, then disappeared behind the wind-bowed stalks of sea oats.

Sam stood watching the dune, straining to hear any sound that might carry from behind it. There was only the rattling of the sea oats. Still, he thought it hardly possible for a creature the size of the bird to settle in the coarse dune grass without at least a rustle from the folding of those great wings.

A sudden puff of wind tousled Sam's hair, causing him to look up with a start at the clouds. The storm was now a range of black and white clouds concealing entirely the western sky. At the same time it had expanded north and south, it had moved its leading edge into a position directly over the beach. He looked one last time at the quiet dune, wanting to climb it to satisfy his curiosity, but knew that he was out of time. Reluctantly, he turned away and began to jog homeward.

When he arrived home, he would phone Susan, giving her a description of the bird. She was perpetually interested in things out of the ordinary, and as reference librarian at Sloan Community College, she had easy access to comprehensive files. If her interest was aroused, and he thought it might be, within half an hour she would have an entire biological rundown on the bird. Anyway, it was almost a week since he had talked with her, so this incident provided him with an excuse to phone her. He shook his head, wondering why he needed an excuse to call her.

He had known Susan Rutledge approaching three months. They'd met at a backyard barbeque hosted by a member of the college faculty who sometimes wrote copy for Sam. The initial meeting had not been one of those encounters which explode into a spontaneous relationship. What it had been was an inauguration of a durable friendship, a companionship, perhaps generated by their various experiences in relationships. Between Sam and Susan there were no sexual overtones; in their friendship each found the comfort of knowing there was someone to listen and advise when life began to seem a little dubious.

"Hello!" The voice was no more than a portion of the background babbling of the sea and wind. "Hello! You, down there—hello!"

This time the words found their way solidly into Sam's consciousness. He stopped jogging and looked to his left. Standing beside a sea-grape bush, a woman was looking down at him from the crest of a dune.

Dark-haired, dressed in black clothing, she was, as the pelicans and strange bird had been, merely a distinguishable form in the gray light, without individual details. She appeared tall, though Sam suspected that his low angle of view caused her height to appear greater than it actually was. She wore tight-fitting slacks of some dark material, and a black, long-sleeved garment that resembled a turtleneck sweater, though he could not imagine a person wearing one of those in the summer heat. Her black hair was long and thick and untethered, and it streamed before her like a tattered shroud, tentacles of it whipping across her face to conceal her features.

She raised a hand to brush the hair from her face. "Please," she called, "I wonder if you could help me."

"Perhaps," Sam called back. "What's wrong?"

"Do you have an automobile nearby?"

"At my apartment, a mile or so up the beach."

"Oh, excellent." Holding the heavy mass of her hair away from her face, she started down the slope of the dune. "Then you can help me, I am sure."

Sam watched her, becoming aware, as the angle of his view lost its foreshortening, that the woman actually was tall, very nearly as tall as his own five feet eleven inches. She moved with a sleek resilience, an animal boldness that was both provocative and intimidating.

When she reached the base of the dune, she crossed the beach with long, competent strides, not hampered by the soft sand above the water mark. She halted half a dozen paces from him.

Sam found he was unable to judge her age, but he guessed that maybe she was a year or two older than himself, which would put her just past her middle thirties. Her eyes were delicately almond-shaped and green. In the lee of the dunes, her hair plunged in thick, glossy, blue-black cascades to her shoulders. Bangs partially hid a broad forehead. Within that heavy frame of hair, her face was a combination of stark plains and abrupt angles which sculptured her features into not enchanting beauty but a strong feminine handsomeness. It was the face of a woman aware of her strength. Looking at her with more attention, Sam sensed within her a steaming pulse of emotion. Deep behind the emerald hue of her eyes, he was certain he saw a muted fury.

"Thank you for stopping," she said. There was a huskiness in her voice, and beneath the throatiness, he could hear the suggestion of an unknown accent. "It was kind of you."

"My name is Lily." There was a caress in her voice, like a gentle stroke of hands.

"I'm Sam," he said, knowing he sounded like a jittery pre-teenager meeting the first girl to have stolen his affections. "Sam Young."

"Sam." Her subdued accent gave it a lilt out of proportion to its sound. "It is a good, strong name."

He hesitated, uncomfortably, then asked, "How can I help you, Lily?"

A mischievous glint sparkled in her emerald eyes, but her voice carried no more than potential friendliness. "By saving me from the storm, Sam." She glanced up at the clouds, which had lowered while they talked. "At times I'm set upon by impulses and can do nothing to resist them. This time I was driving along the highway when I suddenly had the greatest desire to wade in the surf; so I drove into the beach access area on the other side of the dune. Somehow I got off the hard packing, and the car became stuck in the loose sand. Oh, it is stuck fine, Sam. Up to the hubcaps. It will take a tow truck to extract it, so I must be taken to a service station, or at least a place where I can phone. Will you allow me to use the phone in your apartment to call for a tow?"

"Of course, but it's unlikely you'll be able to get a truck to come out this late on a Sunday. They're an independent bunch, those service people."

"Still, I will try."

For some reason, Sam felt he had been made "it" in a game he did not understand. Looking at the woman, he remembered the surpressed fury he had initially sensed when she crossed the beach, and began to have the feeling any game in which she was a participant would be played by her rules.

"Maybe," he said, "it would be best if I took you to your home, and you could call from there."

"I don't have a house, at least not yet. Perhaps you could call me an extended-stay tourist. I've been here for more than a month, and I am going to stay in this area, but I am still booked into a motel down the road while I look for a permanent place to live. The tow truck can pick me up at your apartment, and there will be no need for you to go out into the coming storm."

He sensed that the game had begun. He looked pointedly up at the clouds, which were nearly ready to release the rain bulging in their bellies. "Well, whatever. Let's get to my place before the rain comes."

"Should we jog, Sam? I do it now and then too."

"Why not?"

The first drops of rain fell before they'd jogged a

dozen yards. The plump drops plopped onto the sand with an erratic cadence, erupting tiny craters in a random pattern across the beach. Moments later, the downpour hissed over the dunes.

The cold wall of water slammed into the couple, drenching them instantly. Sam's lungs emptied with a rush of breath; his heart hammered, accelerating with a sudden violence. He tried gulping in a mouthful of the saturated air, but the rain filled his mouth and throat, making him choke. Blinking and squinting, he stopped jogging and looked around, trying to locate himself in the intensifying chaos, but the horizons were gone, melted into the gray curtain which shrouded the earth, creating a world without dimensions. Fear stabbed at him.

"Sam, are you all right?" Lily was standing at his side. The heavy mantle of her hair hung in soggy strands about her head, looking like too great a burden for her neck to support. Her emerald eyes peered at him through the rain, and for an instant he thought he saw more pleasure than concern on her face. Then she reached out and took his hand. "Come on, Sam, it can't be far, can it?"

He shook his head, trying to dissolve the strange undercurrent of apprehension that had claimed him. "Only a hop, skip, and jump. Let's go."

Above the beach, lightning gouged fiery streaks through the clouds. Thunder prowled up and down the coast.

They ran, side by side. Around them the gray light dwindled and there was no noise but the hissing of the rain. Sam felt hemmed in. Cold. Rain stung his face. Anger at allowing himself to be caught out in the storm returned. On his left, Lily ran with ease. Her long legs matched his own stride. She held her head high. Rivulets of rain ran down her cheeks, glinting on her tawny skin.

Sam located the wooden stairs that climbed from the beach to the low wall around the communal pool and sodded recreation area of his townhouse complex. Their reddish stained wood was like a scar in the overall gray of the rain. He pointed at them, and shouted, "Over there, up those steps."

Lily nodded and angled across the beach. He followed several feet behind, no longer disquieted. His muscles recovered their normal functioning as the tension left them. At the top of the steps, Sam guided Lily past the swimming pool to the redwood fence which surrounded the tiny private patio of his apartment. He had not locked either the fence gate or the sliding door opening into the townhouse, so they did not break stride as they crossed the patio to enter the dining room.

In their wet clothing, the air-conditioned air struck them a freezing blow. Sam felt the cold whip through him. He hurried to the thermostat to set it at seventy-eight.

"This is a charming place, Sam. You have good taste in furnishings." Lily was standing just inside the sliding door, once again a silhouette, as she had been so much of the time since their meeting. He was just able to distinguish her green eyes. "It's masculine, yet not harshly so. I'm glad that you don't tend toward leather chairs and heavy wood."

"I had help," he said.

"A woman's help, I'd say." She smiled.

"Yes."

"A special woman?"

"She was."

Lily gave a little nod.

He flicked on the dining-room ceiling light. The abrupt flood of illumination startled Lily. She blinked, sucking in her breath, then glanced quickly around the room as if attempting to sort things out and comprehend this new environment. As quickly as it had gone, her composure returned, and she swung toward him.

A long moment passed while they stood looking at one another. For the first time, Sam became fully aware of her. In the light from the overhead fixture, he saw the sheerness of her clothing, so thin that were it of any other color, it would be transparent. Saturated, her garb molded to each thrusting curve and subtle indentation of her flesh, as if she stood behind a veil of dark mist. She was structured generously, her breasts and hips lavish in their fullness, her legs long like a dancer's, strong muscles bulging ever so gently under the clinging material. While he adjusted the thermostat, she had run combing fingers through the mass of her hair, but there remained a wildness in the way it tumbled around her face and clung to her shoulders. Sam had the uncanny feeling that he was standing in the presence of a warrior-woman from some ancient, primitive time when the terrible cries of amazons echoed down mountain valleys.

"I think," he said, "that before any telephone calls are made, you'd better dry off."

Lily considered this for a moment, then smiled, eyes opening to resume their almond shape. "Yes," she said, and again Sam noted the huskiness in her voice.

Much of his restraint fell away. "Come on, I'll direct you to the shower, if you want to take one, and get you a towel."

"Thank you, Sam."

He showed her the upstairs bathroom, then went to the linen closet for a bath towel, and, as an afterthought, hurried into his bedroom to bring a terry-cloth robe from his closet. When he returned, the shower was already running and Lily was undoing the small silver buckle on the belt of her slacks.

She took the robe and slowly ran her fingers in a

caressing motion over the nubby material, then, smiling openly, said, "Sam, you must take a shower too. You are wet and shivery."

"I'll take one when you're finished."

"Why wait, Sam? In those few minutes, a cold might settle in you." He watched her smile change a millimeter at a time, to slowly become touched with sensuality. "If we bathed together, there would be no danger of that."

Suddenly he felt warm. Undefinable currents started to flow through him. Deep inside him, he heard an inner voice telling him to back out into the hallway, that he was on the verge of something over which he had no control. Lily took a small step toward him. He watched the trembling sway of heavy breasts under the thin blouse as she emerged from the thickening mists of steam, and, as before, he had the sensation of a strong and vibrant warrior risen from antiquity.

Lily grasped Sam by the hand. His inner voice made no further protests as she pulled him gently to her. With a guttural purr rippling deep in her throat, she thrust the length of her tall body against him, pushing her loins to his, mashing the fullness of her breasts on his chest. She dropped the robe to the floor and took his other hand, then, stepping back, began to pull him deeper into the steamy mist.

"Come, Sam . . ."

Against the background sound of the shower, he heard her humming a vague tune that was like a whisper of desire. Her hands undid the zipper of his sweat suit. He had never before been undressed by a woman, and he felt uncomfortable, wanting to pull away, but in the heat and the steam the act was somehow unreal, and he felt himself as much an observer as a participant.

Then he was standing naked before her with the

steam eddying warmly around him. Looking into the emerald depths of her eyes, he saw fragments of desire forming into want and greed. He stood unmoving, his awareness expanding. As she pulled the dark blouse up over her head, then pushed the tight slacks down the long length of her legs. Before he could do more than run his eyes up and down the curves of her stately nudity, she slid open the shower-stall door and stepped in, drawing him after her.

Inside the enclosure the hissing of the water jets became thunder in his ears. His mind frantically tried to assimilate all the messages being sent to it, foamy lather on heavy breasts, parted lips and glinting green eyes, the scents of soap and warm flesh, the touch of sensitive fingertips on his body, and the feel of wet skin beneath his palms. Vaguely he realized that he was being taken to a place he had never been before, and underneath the sensations he wondered if he would ever return to what once had been normal, or if he would even want to.

Sam Young stood at the sliding door, looking out at the tiny patio, seeing mostly a dark pool of shadow in the feeble illumination spilling from the dining area's light fixture. The fury of the storm had moved on, but rain still slanted over the top of the redwood fence and drummed on the flagstone flooring of the patio. From out over the ocean, the rumble of the departing thunder sounded like the echoing of a distant train heard through the hollowness of a tunnel. Only an occasional flare of lightning danced in the sky.

Behind him in the kitchen the teakettle, which he had put on the range when he came downstairs, made a squawking, unbalanced noise. It was, he thought, an appropriate sound, because the evening was out of balance. No, not the evening, he corrected himself.

Everything. It was as if all the events in his life, the actions and occasions that had made him what he was, were nullified, turned into insignificant happenings by the fierce passions that had been unleashed in the shower stall. He had passed through an adrenaline storm every bit as fierce as the thunderstorm which had moved through the area, and like the wind-lashed vegetation outside in the dark, his comprehension was frayed. God knew, he wasn't celibate, but the wild, primal sexuality released beneath the water jets was something he had never imagined. He had been torn free of all restrictions.

"I'm sorry to have taken so long, Sam, but women must fuss over themselves more than men."

Startled, he turned too quickly. Lily stood on the far side of the dining table. She had piled her hair on the top of her head, apparently using its thickness and length to tie it into position. The tautness was gone from the angles and planes of her face, softening them into a new entity. Gone was the face of the warrior woman. It had been transformed into the relaxed features of a younger, modern woman with sharpened senses.

For an instant, he felt awkward, then nodded toward the teakettle. "I don't know if you drink it, but I thought a cup of coffee would taste good about now."

"It would. A big mug of it."

He went to a cupboard and brought out a jar of Nescafé. "I only have instant."

"That's fine."

While he put a heaping spoonful of granules in each mug, Lily went to the stove and got the teakettle. He watched her carry it to the table. Even in the cumbersome thick material of the robe, her movements were lithe and provocative. When she passed him, taking the kettle back to the stove, he could smell the faint aroma of her, soap and heat and a deep underlying scent of musk.

After they were seated, he said, "The rain hasn't let up a bit."

She raised her mug with the fingertips of both hands and looked at him over its rim. "It is a big storm, Sam."

"It seems so."

She studied him in silence for what seemed a long time, then asked, "Are you shocked at what happened in the shower?"

He couldn't identify the turmoil of emotions that swept through him. How in hell did one react to the first encounter with untamed, brazen passion? "Maybe a little."

"Are you embarrassed, Sam?" She sat very still, watching him.

"No, I don't think so."

She smiled. "I'm glad, because I couldn't help myself. My whole being suddenly wanted you. I had to have you, Sam. Maybe the charge in the night air, put there by the storm, expanded my consciousness and needs."

Sam's breath suddenly clogged his throat. He returned Lily's stare for a moment, then felt the muscles around his mouth relaxing so his lips stretched into a grin.

"Well," he said slowly, "I think I'm glad you couldn't control yourself."

She laughed. It was a good, rich laugh, before which no doubts could survive, and Sam couldn't help but respond to it. His uncertainties eased.

For no more than the time of a heartbeat, her eyes caught a wayward tint of illumination and gleamed with a deep red glow before she turned away. She looked toward the sliding door, presenting him with a striking profile, and he was not ashamed to stare at the straightness of her nose, the fullness of her lips, and the shadowed hollow of her cheekbones. It was the classic face, determinedly strong, yet sweetly sensual, immortalized by Praxiteles and later by Michelangelo.

"The rain," she said, "makes a beautiful sound, doesn't it? Like music, soft and gentle, mocking the follies of mankind. It's an ageless whisper, Sam, of vanished cultures."

"Where do you come from, Lily?" he asked impulsively. "Where's your home?"

She turned her head slowly to look at him with eyes heavy-lidded once again and smoldering. "I'm sorry, I didn't hear you."

"Your home, Lily. Where do you come from?"

She moved her eyes lingeringly around the room. "No place like this, Sam. Actually, I have no home; so I suppose I'm what you call a vagabond. I like to think the entire world is my home."

"You have no family?"

"No, no more."

"Then you're single?"

"Yes." She dropped her eyes to gaze down at her coffee mug, and he saw a tightness firm up the skin around her mouth and pull at the corners of her eyes. "Once I had a husband, but that was a long time ago, many years ago."

"It can't be as long as you're making it sound. You're not that old."

"Quite some time ago, Sam . . . or so it seems."

He knew he was pressing. "Your husband. What happened to him?"

Instead of taking offense at his persistence, she gave a small, eloquent shrug and, without looking at him, turned to once again stare out the door at the dark patio. For a long time, she was silent—maybe, he thought, listening to the rain—then she said in little more than a whisper, "He . . . divorced me."

"Oh." He had entered some private place in her life, and was ashamed. "I'm sorry. I didn't mean to pry, Lily."

"You didn't, Sam. You showed only natural curiosity. Since the . . . the divorce, I have traveled, and I have met many talented people, some of them in positions of financial power who have shown me how to invest what money I come by; so, by some standards, I have accumulated a small, reasonably secure fortune. It allows me to travel as I wish. The divorce gave me a freedom I would never have known. So do not feel sorry for me, Sam."

He should be satisfied, change the subject, get the cigarette he'd thought about on the beach, offer her one, maybe talk a little of himself in exchange for the scanty information she had given him. But there were still shadows lingering about them, shadows that had to be disspelled, if only for his peace of mind.

He looked directly at her. The tension surrounding her mouth and eyes was gone, but the planes and angles were again delineated. It was a haunted face, reflecting some smoldering turmoil behind it. There was something hostile inside her seeking to escape, and Sam wanted to see it better.

"Are you all right?" he asked.

"Yes, I'm fine." Her green eyes returned his stare with a shiny hardness which he thought could be a prelude to tears. "Mostly I refuse to permit memories to enter my mind, but now and then they push through my barriers and for a short while I wander in a twilight. It passes, Sam. Usually very quickly. You'll have to excuse me."

Again he said, "I'm sorry."

"No, Sam. Don't be. I think you're going to be good for me."

As she spoke, Sam felt the atmosphere in the room

change. Warmth spiced with the scent of blossoms replaced the artificial chill.

He was irritated, but not surprised, at the thickness of his voice when he said, "It sounds as if you plan to stay in the area for a while."

"This is a unique area, Sam. I find it suits me, because of its location. I can live here, where there is still casualness in the lifestyle, but when I want to, I can travel to a number of metropolitan areas in a short time. Miami, Orlando, Tampa, Jacksonville, all are less than two hundred miles away."

"Do you like big cities?"

"I like the anonymity of them." Once more she looked out at the night beyond the door. "One can become merely a silhouette, a shadow, in cities, if that is what one desires."

"Do you want that?"

"At times, yes, Sam." She looked back at him, and her smile became enigmatic. "But I think I've found one more reason why I like it here."

"Dare I ask what?"

"You shouldn't have to, Sam. You should know."

All of his senses suddenly were concentrated on the two emerald eyes looking at him from across the table. There was no calculation in them, no hint of artificiality, in their smoky depths, only a lingering residue of the ardor that had gleamed in them in the shower stall. He wasn't surprised when his response was a similar emotion. In a moment his control would vanish. Resisting, he pushed himself erect in the chair. "I'm afraid it's too late to expect a service truck to come for your car, especially in this rain." He glanced at the clock hanging on the dining-room wall. "I'll take you to your motel."

"I'm in no hurry to leave." Something insubstantial darkened her eyes. "Do you want me to go?"

"No . . . I didn't mean it that way." He had the sudden feeling of a complex emotion forming. "I just thought you might want to get back."

"I'd be alone if I returned to the motel." Her lids lowered, hiding her eyes. "There are times I dislike being alone, Sam, and this is one of them."

"I understand. I have those times too." He asked, "Are you hungry?"

"No, but I would like another cup of coffee." She motioned him back into his chair when he started to get up. "I will prepare it."

While she reheated the water and put coffee granules into their mugs, she hummed softly to herself. He did not recognize the tune. At times, it was a plaintive melody, like the mournful sighing of the earth itself, while at times it trilled with the joy of dreaming hearts. It sounded like a song from a faraway land, a song old and rarely sung.

Sam began to realize how complicated a woman Lily was, a woman of indeterminate capabilities whose personality could be at the same time discordant and hypnotic. He sensed a complexity to her, as if a black, featureless silhouette of a woman was superimposed over a lit figure. Both figures were Lily, and Sam wondered how separate and distinct the two images were. She was a mature woman, but sitting opposite him, balancing her chin on the back of her hand, she was a young girl.

Outside the rain continued to fall, providing a soft background noise, as if the storm-darkened night was murmuring to them with a pleasingly mournful voice. As they sat without speaking, Sam saw Lily listening to the rain, to its whispers, its tales of erotic passions, of night-scented blossoms and springtimes without end. The dim light of the ceiling fixture turned her tanned skin into a sheath of gold, her eyes into enigmatic pools in which reality drowned. The robe slipped part way down her arms, and the bareness of her shoulders and the supple column of her neck hinted at a never-ending beauty. When she finally spoke, her voice was a golden web spinning words which might have come from antiquity.

"Tell me about yourself, Sam. Obviously you are successful in business, because in my house-hunting I've learned what a beachfront townhouse like this costs. But I want to truly know you. I want to know the man who offered me help, the man who thinks and aspires." She leaned slightly forward, her eyes holding his. "Do you, like everybody, have secret chambers in your mind where you hide confidential thoughts and desires you want no one to have access to? I would like very much to meet the substance of Sam Young."

For a moment or two, he felt on guard, but then relaxed. She was, he decided, attempting to create a rapport with him other than that of the flesh.

"I've a feeling," he said, "that in comparison with what little you've told me, my life's a rather mundane affair. I'm thirty-five years old. I was born in Ohio, went to school there, then came to the University of Florida to study communications. I never went back north. I worked for advertising agencies in Miami and Orlando, then four years ago opened my own public-relations office in Indialantic. The business is small, but moderately successful, allowing me to lease, but not own, this townhouse."

Her eyes held steadily on his, and behind their surfaces he thought he detected shadows moving. Her mouth carried a trace of a smile. "I think, Sam, you are abbreviating your accomplishments. I sense an inquisitiveness in you, with which you evade the mundane life you say you lead." She looked toward the rain-washed door, stared at it for a short while, then swung her eyes back to him. "I have met many men who complained of the sameness of life, the day-after-day routine, and some of them I have found intriguing, because they were the ones who sought unknown things beyond the horizon. I feel you are such a man, Sam."

He shrugged. "Perhaps. But maybe my horizons are limited."

"No, I cannot believe that," she said softly, staring out at the downpour.

"You like the rain, don't you?" he asked.

"It gives life, and it denies life," she said. "It is beautiful and it is hideous. But tonight it whispers of promises of well-being."

Sam could think of nothing to say.

Lily sat looking up at him, smiling. "Maybe at a more appropriate time I can prepare a meal for you. I think I would like that, Sam. I would like it very much."

He nodded, then pulled his eyes away from hers. He knew he wanted that to happen. He also knew he had no right to want it to happen. A tingling burned along his arms and across his shoulders until he felt himself becoming warm to the very center of his being.

He stepped back from the table, then walked to the sliding door. The rain showed no indication of slowing. Through the mist and water on the glass, he stared out at the patio, seeing nothing but oblongs of shadows and dull sheens of wet foliage on the hanging plants. He knew he would not be phoning Susan tonight. No curiosity remained concerning the strange bird.

He heard movement behind him, a chair pushing back from the table, a soft sound of cloth sliding down taut flesh, and finally slow-paced footsteps.

"Sam . . ." Lily was standing at his side, a firm softness pressing against his upper right arm.

He stood for another moment staring out the door. Except for the whispering of the rain, the night was silent, but he knew that out in that silence and darkness something was moving closer and closer to him, something over which there was no control, over which there had been no control since the dawn of man. As he felt the pressure on his arm, his senses sharpened suddenly to respond to the subtle messages sent out by the body of the woman, and the flowing within him erupted into a passion he did not try to restrain.

He turned to face her.

"I think you are much man, Sam Young." Her voice was low, touched with a guttural quality unheard before. "Show me I am right."

Moving on their own, his hands slipped up and down her back; then he asserted mastery over them to turn the stroking into caresses. Lily moaned and pushed her body to his with a rippling motion.

"Prove to me, Sam, you are much man."

He said nothing, not only because he could not find the words, but because he knew none were needed.

His lips found hers, covered them, then forced them apart, and while their tongues dueled violently within the warmness of their mouths, he led her, cautious step by cautious step, up the stairs to the bedroom.

2

THE FIRST THING HE WAS AWARE OF THE FOLLOWING MORNING was the sunlight slanting in a brilliant shaft through the bedroom window. The next was the ache in his stomach that bordered on pain. It pulled his mind from the thinning cocoon of sleep into a world of consuming hunger. He grunted. He couldn't remember when he last awoke hungry.

Lying there, in the sunlight, he heard sounds of cooking from the kitchen. A strange mixture of excitement and expectancy moved through him as he savored the swelling promise of the morning. He thought of the previous night, the green eyes and enigmatic smile turned in his direction from across the table. The gently accented words spoken by the throaty voice were faint echoes in his ears. Listening to the clatter from the kitchen, he couldn't help but feel how in place it all seemed. For a brief moment, he wondered who Lily was, and from where she came, then gave a mental shrug. In time the answers would be given him. Whoever she was, she had brought with her an uninhibited companionship that, he realized, had reached his deeper wells of consciousness.

He knew there wasn't enough food in the refrigerator for Lily to prepare a lavish breakfast, but toast and coffee would suffice. In spite of the noises coming from his stomach, her company was enough.

Finally he drew a deep breath and, holding it, sat up on the edge of the bed.

"Oh, Sam, you're up. How wonderful."

He looked over his right shoulder to see Lily standing in the doorway, smiling at him. He nodded. "Barely."

"I've fixed breakfast," she said.

"I could hear you—but you shouldn't have done that. I don't usually eat breakfast. A cup of coffee is plenty." He stood up and immediately felt the stiffness flow from him. "My system could go into shock. It's not accustomed to being pampered like this."

"I think you are a man I would like to pamper, Sam."

He didn't say anything, still clearing sleep from his mind, studying the woman in the doorway. Dressed again in the dark slacks and turtleneck blouse, she blended into the shadowy darkness of the hallway behind her. She had returned her hair to the glossy cascades falling on either side of her face, probably by using his brush and comb. From what he could see, her features held none of the sharpness that had occassionally hardened them the evening before, making it obvious that, if not actually beautiful, hers was an enchanting face. For an instant, Sam vividly recalled the strength and ripeness of her body, the imaginative, erotic ways she had used it during the night. He looked away, touched with embarrassment.

"How long will it be before you're ready to eat, Sam?"

"Ten—no, make it fifteen minutes."

She nodded, smiling faintly as if she could see the images passing through his mind, then turned and slowly moved down the hallway until she was swallowed in its lingering nighttime darkness.

After showering, he rubbed a place clear on the steam-fogged mirror. While he combed his hair, he gave some attention to his face, an act in which he seldom indulged. What he saw did not particularly move him one way or the other. He wasn't handsome, but neither was he nondescript. His hair was brown, his eyes were blue, and his skin was a healthy tan. He did not look either older or younger than his thirty-five years, and he did not try, as did some of his acquaintances, to assume the characteristics and mannerisms of an older or a younger age group. He felt that he was not a yuppy, though this townhouse he rented and the BMW he drove were trademarks of that breed.

It was closer to twenty minutes before he walked into the kitchen, dressed in a three-piece brown suit, to find Lily spooning scrambled eggs onto plates already containing two slices of toast. Mugs of coffee steamed on the table.

"My God, Lily, to me that's a harvester's breakfast."

She looked at him over her shoulder as she set the plates on the table. "I like preparing food for you, Sam. I wish you had more in the refrigerator so I could prepare more."

"I could get used to this kind of treatment, you know."

"Could you, Sam?"

"Oh, yes. I'm very susceptible to the good life, and love to be pampered."

Her laugh was a mystical whisper. "You are kind and sweet."

With the ghost of the laugh still sounding in the rooms, she looked at him, sidelong, improbable glints of green light sparkling beneath her lashes, and as had happened at the beginning of the previous evening, he could not think of anything inventive or lighthearted with which to respond. Once again he felt doltish and inadequate in the face of this woman's powerful drives and enigmatic personality.

Lily made them each a second cup of instant coffee. When she returned to her chair, Sam offered her a cigarette, but she declined. "No, Sam, I don't smoke. You shouldn't either."

"I know."

She balanced her chin on the back of her right hand, her almond-shaped eyes fastened intently on him. "Do you know, Sam, I am glad I became stuck in the sand last evening."

He watched a spiral of gossamer cigarette smoke climb ceilingward between them. It reminded him of the previous night, real, yet existing on the borderline between illusion and reality. He looked through it at her and smiled. "I am too."

A sudden brilliance of sunlight slanted across her features, tinting her face with a golden hue and giving it a regal splendor. Lily blew gently into her coffee, watching the steam rise from the hot liquid as he had watched the rising cigarette smoke. "Last night," she said, "I definitely made up my mind to stay in this area, Sam. I like it here. There are so many things here that intrigue me." She looked up at him, studied him, then dropped her gaze back down to her coffee. "I'm going to transfer funds from one of my overseas investment accounts to a local bank and begin a determined search for a dwelling." Again she looked up at him. "What is the use of making profitable investments, if one doesn't enjoy those profits? Is that not true, Sam?"

"It sounds logical. I've never had to think about it."

He crushed out his cigarette, then stood. Lily also stood, and began clearing the table.

"What time do you have to be to work, Sam?"

"Nine o'clock, give or take ten minutes."

"Then we must hurry. You will drop me off at my motel, won't you?"

"Of course."

In spite of Lily insisting that he not wait at the motel while she phoned for a tow truck, he did, and was twenty minutes late starting for his office in the beachside town of Indialantic.

When he was alone in the car, a kaleidoscope revolved slowly in his mind, superimposing one memory of the night before upon another. In the changing patterns, he once more saw devouring lips, heavy breasts, and powerful thighs; interwoven with the images he heard soft murmurings and breathless laughter that spun into a silver thread of sound. Yet behind the kaleidoscopic patterns were questions to which he could supply no answers. When a vagrant cloud crossed the morning sun to lay a momentary gloom on the land, he was certain that a voice called out to him in terrible grief. Involuntarily he looked around. To his right, between the highway and the ocean, was the skeletal framework of a condominium under construction. Silhouetted against the luminescent water, the naked girders stretched like fingers stripped bare of flesh, reaching desperately toward the warmth of the sun. His hands clenched on the steering wheel.

The first phone call from a client drew the morning into perspective. Sam was once again on familiar ground. He was trained to do a certain job, and now he was performing it. By midmorning, after arranging for a photographer to cover a luncheon and cajoling a newspaper friend to interview a client's new store manager, all uneasiness had drained from him. The night before was a digression, a pleasant memory. If Lily stayed, if he ever saw her again, their relationship would develop normally.

At twelve-thirty he phoned Susan Rutledge at her apartment, hoping she would be there during her lunch hour. She was.

Her voice was warm, even across the dehumanizing lines of Southern Bell. Her voice was one of the things he liked about her. He had never heard it be other than warm and cordial and sparkling. Now, while they talked, he pictured his friend, mentally constructing an imaginary video screen on which to display her image.

Not as tall or statuesque as Lily, Susan was, nevertheless, above average height for a woman, with a figure not intended to fit elegantly into the boyish, straight-lined designs flaunted by runway mannequins. Her rich auburn hair was worn in a casual cut that complimented the perky arrangement of her facial features. To Sam, her amber eyes, which always focused directly on the person to whom she spoke, reflected the stability of her personality.

In a matter of a few minutes, listening to her animated voice, Sam felt what was left of the ambiguity of his thinking vanish. Staring at the make-believe video screen on the corner of his desk, he saw a wholesome woman, a good friend, and companion. He asked her to dinner, naming a long-established seafood restuarant built on stilts over the Indian River, suggesting he pick her up early so they might have cocktails.

The remainder of the afternoon slipped by comfortably.

They were seated at a table on the deck of the restaurant. Sunlight still quivered on the flat surface of the river, decorating the water with scallops of pink in an ill-defined shaft that eventually disappeared in the shadows of the trees on the western bank. Reflections from the water pulsed on the underside of the blue and yellow striped awning stretched over the deck. Sam watched the lights play hide-and-seek in Susan's hair, thinking they resembled muted fairy lights deep in the auburn curls. Watching them, he realized what a sleek, good-looking, completely alive woman she was.

"Okay," she said, "tell me what you're staring at. I'm beginning to feel as if I'm wearing a wig that's on crooked."

"The reflections from the water," he answered sheepishly. "They're making your hair shimmer. It's really quite attractive."

"Maybe we should bottle them. They'd be a hot seller in the cosmetic market." She very lightly touched her fingertips to her hair. "Shimmering, dancing hair. What a great idea. I know a dozen women who'd give a week's salary to have blinking coiffures."

"How could you catch them? Not with nets like butterflies."

She creased her forehead with an elaborate frown in a parody of concentration, then looked at him seriously and said, "With magic, of course."

"Of course." He shook his head in mock disgust. "Why didn't I think of it? But, hell, I can't even spell abracadabra, much less pronounce it with the correct inflection."

Susan held up her drink. "Daiquiris contain more enchantment than vodka-and-tonic; therefore the mind lubricated with them is much more adroit at bewitching."

"I see—I think."

"Well, besides the daiquiri I have another advantage. I work in a place filled with esoteric knowledge."

"Speaking of fantasies, I saw a living one last evening and was going to phone you." Suddenly his muscles cramped and as he prepared to say more, he grew certain that someone was listening to the conversation. He could not help but glance around the restaurant to see if they were being watched, but no one was paying them attention. "Last evening I jogged, and while I was on the beach I saw a huge bird. Its wingspan must have been at least eight or nine feet. It was black, a deep, shiny black. It came along just as the storm was about to break, riding the air currents like a ballet dancer. I was going to phone you to give you a description of it, but I watched it for too long and got drenched before I made it home." A rapid sequence of memories of what had occurred then flashed through his mind. He wasn't ready yet to tell Susan about Lily, he decided, and said, "By the time I'd dried out I'd forgotten most of the details."

"That's not much of a description."

"I know."

"I wish you'd phoned when it was still fresh in your mind."

"So do I." Suddenly he wanted to say more, but whatever was there among the diners was still listening, still alert.

Susan looked out at the sun-painted river. Its pulsing reflections played across her features like the trembling light of a bonfire. Looking at her profile, Sam suddenly had the odd suspicion that Lily herself was fiction, and a shiver ran across his shoulders. Close to the deck, a fish jumped, and the slap it made returning to the water was like a muffled echo of a sound from far away.

"You know, Sam, we're friends. Anytime you want to talk, I'm here to listen."

"I know." Still, he could not find it in himself to tell her of Lily.

"You're a great person, Susan Rutledge."

"You're pretty fine yourself, Sam."

It was nearing eight o'clock when they left the restuarant. They drove south along A1A, Sam holding the BMW to the forty-five-mile-per-hour speed limit between Cocoa Beach and Indialantic. On the ocean side of the highway, new condominiums, too young to show the signs of weathering, pushed their piles of concrete upward from skimpy plots of landscaped land which once had been undulating dunes matted with graceful sea oats and dune grass. Sam wondered how much time remained before the earth-gobbling machines of out-of-state developers tore his jogging beach apart.

"What are you thinking about?" Susan's question made him realize he had been silent for too long.

He gestured, waving his hand in the direction of the condominiums. "The rape of the land."

"I guess most of us have bitter thoughts on that."

"It's inevitable, I guess."

"I suppose so, but it's difficult to lay back and enjoy it."

He grinned.

When the traffic lights at the intersection of the Eau Gallie Causeway came into view, Sam eased his foot off the accelerator. "It's still early, and we'll have light for another half an hour. Why don't you come down to my place for a while? It's a great time of day to walk barefoot on the beach."

"Oh, Sam, I'd love to, but I've got a staff meeting tomorrow morning at the ungodly hour of seven-thirty, and I haven't even begun to put together my report." She looked sideways at him. "I shifted my priorities and went to dinner with a friend instead of working."

At Susan's apartment complex, he parked beside her Escort. Impulsively, she leaned toward him and kissed him on the cheek. It was quick, but he had the feeling it was a little more than platonic.

"Don't wait until you see a big black bird before you phone again," she said.

"Not even a little one," he answered.

Dusk was well settled when he eased the BMW into the townhouse's garage. A gentle breeze drifted in from the ocean, bringing a saline dampness that laid a sticky patina on his face and arms.

As if it had been waiting for him to arrive, a restlessness joined him on the threshold and stayed with him through his shower, persisted even as he dressed in a pair of tennis shorts and T-shirt.

He tuned the stereo to Orlando's easy-listening station, but the music merely seemed to overlay the odd silence that permeated the rooms. He looked around. Something was missing, distorting the pleasantries he should be feeling after the dinner with Susan. Finally, lighting a cigarette, he went out the sliding door to the small patio, leaving the glass panel open several inches so he could hear the music. He shifted position several times before settling comfortably on a chaise and staring upward at the virgin darkness of the young night.

He heard voices laughing beside the swimming pool beyond the fence. They sounded fragile and far away, the texture of another world. He looked up at the stars, realizing how few he could identify and locate.

The knocking on the fence gate came shortly after he had ground out his cigarette. Within the isolation of his thinking, the rapping boomed. Sam stared, uncomprehending, at the gate for several seconds before calling out, "Yeah, I'm here. Who is it?"

"Lily, Sam."

"Lily?" Suddenly he felt the brooding trap that had been ensnaring him open. "Lily, come in."

She came slowly through the gate, closing it softly after her, to stand leaning against it, hands behind her, eyes half closed, looking at him from under their shadowing lashes. What might have been a comfortable smile by another woman curved her mouth, but on her lips it was delicate sensuality.

"Hello, Sam."

"Hi."

"I'm going to be your neighbor, Sam. In the empty townhouse at the end of this building."

He pushed himself to his feet. She moved away from the gate and took a slow step toward him, then another, until she stood only inches from him, so close that when she spoke the warmth of her breath touched his face.

He had known of the empty unit at the end of the building, and now he wondered why he hadn't mentioned it to her this morning. Had he become so goddamned obsessed with physical adventure that all else had fled his mind, or had he unconsciously locked that knowledge away? He blocked the question, wondering if that sensation of being watched at the restaurant and the eerie impressions in the townhouse on his return from dinner had twisted his senses.

"I should have told you this morning that it was empty, but . . . well, I forgot." He knew it sounded weak, like the impromptu excuse it was, and made himself smile. "I think my mind was occupied with other things. I'm sorry."

"Don't be, Sam, not if they were good things on your mind."

"They were, but still—"

"No, Sam. No self-blame."

"How did you find out about it?"

She smiled. "That was not difficult, Sam. With the condominiums and apartments in the area only thirty-percent occupied, everybody with a realtor's license is representing all of them."

"I know. The developers have overbuilt."

She nodded. "Today I visited a realtor who I had spoken with before and told him I would like a place as close as possible to this complex."

"And he told you of the vacancy."

"Yes."

There was no responsiveness in him. His senses were dulling. He felt himself drifting away from the little corner of reality in which the patio existed.

"You're pleased, aren't you, Sam?"

He felt his head nodding. "Yes, Lily, I'm glad."

She laughed, then took his hand. "Come, Sam, let us walk together. I want the freedom of the night around me."

Below them, the ocean was darkly still. Where water met sand, tiny wavelets whispered as they attempted to crawl up the gentle incline of the beach. The evening breeze had long since disappeared, so the air was heavily-laden with the eternal dampness of the sea. Overhead, the stars, which had been hidden the previous night behind the boiling clouds, tonight sparkled with a sharp brilliance as though the storm had washed and polished them with its driving rain and buffeting winds.

Holding hands, they had been standing silently by the brick safety wall for several minutes when Lily said, "This is the real world, Sam, this world of the night. All the teachings of mankind have little meaning during the hours of darkness. Night is the voice, in the dialogue of the day, for those things scorned and suspected during the daylight hours. This is the world where the dawn of time still exists and where all its secrets still reside." Her hand tightened in his, her fingers curling around it until their tips dug into the flesh behind his knuckles. "When I move into the townhouse, we will spend many nights together, and I am going to teach you all the tenderness and the tempestuousness that exist in the hours of darkness. There is much for you to learn, Sam."

Somewhere in the back of his mind an ill-defined uneasiness stirred, whispering that events were accelerating too fast.

"Do you like the night, Sam?"

"I've never analyzed it. I've always considered it only a time period when everything slows down and the world rests between the hours of sunlight."

"Where is that inquisitiveness I felt in you?"

"Maybe it shuts down like everything else at night."

She said nothing, but lifted her face until it pointed at the black sky, and Sam received the impression she was thinking of things removed from the conversation while her eyes wandered from star to star. When she spoke, her voice was low, touched with a throaty guttural quality he had heard in it before, and he didn't know if she spoke to him or to the night surrounding them when she said, "I am at home here."

A wavelet slapped loudly on the sand.

Lily slowly lowered her face to stare at him, and in the star glow he saw sharp angles and taut planes soften into femininely handsome features, but even as they did, he glimpsed behind them a fleeting expression he thought could be either wanton lust or passionate hate.

"Perhaps we should go in, Sam."

He nodded. What he had seen in that brief instant lingered in his memory, but he began to convince himself it had been no more than a night-born fantasy. To relieve the silence, he asked, "When are you going to move in?"

"In about three days, I think. Tomorrow I will contact Damascus, where one of my investment accounts is located, and have funds sent to me. Then I must shop for odds and ends of furniture and make arrangements for my personal goods to be flown here from where they now are in storage."

"Where's that?"

She hesitated, then said, "San Juan."

"San Juan!"

She laughed her throaty laugh. "I told you, Sam, I am a vagabond."

"You were in Puerto Rico before you came here?"

"Some of the time, Sam. I was actually wandering among the Caribbean islands. I am partial to the tropics. Hot days and sultry nights to me are beautiful in promise. I stored my possessions in San Juan because I did not know how long it would be before I found a place I would want to settle in."

"How much time did you spend in the Caribbean?"

"A few months. But there, like so many of the lands where the sun bleeds the earth dry, beneath the gaiety of the people there is an eternal sadness. I do not like the feel of it. Here, I think, it will be different."

She turned and walked away. She preceded him into the patio. Halfway across it, though, she stopped, waiting for him to close and lock the redwood gate. When he turned to face her, she moved lithely to him, pressing herself against him.

"Are you going to invite me to spend the night, Sam?"

He ran a hand down the long sweep of her back, then slowly led her through the sliding door.

3

IT SEEMED MORE LIKE MONDAY MORNING THAN TUESDAY morning. A lethargic silence filled the library. The reference room was empty, its high-ceilinged vault a patchwork of shadows in the brilliant sunlight streaming through the arched windows that formed the eastern wall. Subtle and artificial, the scent of pine floated in the machine-cooled air.

Susan Rutledge sat behind her desk, idly leafing through a copy of *Smithsonian* magazine, now and then giving perfunctory glances in the direction of the eight people huddled at reading tables. Most of the student body was gone for the summer, leaving her too little to do. Boredom was approaching the brink of lassitude. She flipped a page, pushed the large circles of her glasses up her nose, and attempted to interest herself in an article on Patagonia.

So far the day was an absolute replay of previous mornings, a long line of hours frozen in the precise mold of all the mornings which had preceded it this month.

Even the seven-thirty staff meeting had been a preordained frustration. With her face set in a mask of concentration, Susan had sat through the inevitable discussion on conducting business in the simplest, most economical fashion. Then, actually interested, she'd listened very attentively while a suggestion was offered to minimize the complexities of bureaucratic overlap, only to become dumbfounded as administrators rejected the proposal by employing the exact tribal-habit philosophy it recommended eliminating. She had left the meeting feeling irked, discouraged, and helpless.

Certain that she would find nothing by using Sam's description as a working basis, Susan had nevertheless spent the better part of an hour in the stacks, pulling out one book after another as she sought the identity of the jet-black bird. Only the condor, which definitely did not inhabit the Florida coast, came close, with its nine-foot wingspan, but North American condors were grayish black with white wing markings. Sam had made no mention of white spots, and had not spoken of a flabby condor-like neck, which Susan was certain would be distinctive enough to stick in the mind. She left the stacks dissatisfied because she had not found what she sought, and irritable because the search had proven ineffective in relieving her accumulated boredom. She'd phone Sam during her lunch hour to tell him of her failure.

She looked out at the semi-vacant room again and scowled, then decided it wasn't all that bad. Sixteen months had drifted away since that blustery March evening in Chicago when Larry had spoken ramblingly of "needing more space in my personal life." As she listened to him say those words, the world had faded away. She kept remembering their time together, while

Larry's words hammered at her with lopsided phrases. Now she understood that Larry had been a frightened man who found adulthood too much with which to cope, a man unable to understand why a lucrative career had not simply been handed to him.

Susan knew that she herself had not been emotionally mature at the time, because, like a little girl, she'd run away. She'd known it was an act of weakness, but she'd also known that she needed a new environment. So she had come south, all the way to Florida, where so many came to seek so many things.

There had been no great hurry to find a job, for she had been conservative with her secretary's salary in Chicago and she did not want to work in another office. That particular routine was a portion of the scar tissue covering her old life's wounds.

When the employment service mentioned the library opening, she had applied. Despite her lack of experience, she had been accepted—because there were no other applicants. Soon she discovered that within the quiet atmosphere of the library the haunting eventually went away.

She never volunteered the story to Sam, and, out of respect for her privacy, he did not press, being satisfied with what she told him of her past. Likewise, he'd told her little of his engagement to a woman named Janet, which had gone awry.

"Time for lunch, Susan."

She looked up to see a portly woman smiling down at her over an ample bosom, then glanced at her watch, which read ten minutes after twelve.

"Busy this morning?"

Susan shook her head. "Dullsville."

The heavy woman eased her bulk around the desk. "Summers are like that. I wonder why we stay open."

Susan took her purse from the bottom drawer of the

desk and stood up. "The thought has crossed my mind several times too. I'll be back at one, Marge."

"You're getting a late start. Make it one-fifteen."

The school cafeteria was closed for the summer, but her apartment was less than half a mile from the library, so when she was hungry, she walked home to prepare herself a light lunch. Today she wasn't hungry, she just wished to walk. From the first, she'd found pleasure in strolling across the landscaped campus. The mowed lawns, the shade trees, a few of them bearded with Spanish moss, the arranged beds of blooming plants, all welcomed her.

A radio was playing beside her apartment complex's swimming pool. It had been casually tuned without regard to tone, so the music erupting from the small speaker was hollow, with overriding treble notes giving the top-forty selections a tinny sound. Huddled around the instrument, half a dozen women and two men, all in their mid-twenties, all in skimpy swimsuits, were engaged in intent conversation. Each of them was copper-toned and taut-fleshed. The entire group exuded health, that socially demanded look of health acquired at Nautilus machines and aerobic classes. They were people who had molded themselves to fit a molded society.

"Susan, over here!"

She glanced over to see a young woman sitting in a lounge chair on the cement slab which acted as a patio for a ground-floor apartment. Beside her was an infant stroller that she rhythmically pushed forward and backward with a hand that seemed to move automatically. In the stroller a diapered baby slept, head lolled on its right shoulder.

"Maureen, hi!" Susan's thoughts veered abruptly from the group at poolside to Maureen Neilson. "Are you trying to turn Bridget into a suntanned beauty at the ripe old age of eight months?"

"No. Mostly it's Mommy who's trying to brown."
Maureen laughed. Her petite body was clothed in a
conservative one-piece swimsuit. "You home for
lunch?"

"Only iced tea. I ate a big meal last night and haven't
done more than sit on my you-know-what all morning."

Maureen glanced at the group beside the pool. "You
mean you haven't jogged five miles and swum ten laps
of the pool this morning? Shame. You're going to
become gross with sedentary flab."

Susan smiled. She liked Maureen and her gawky
husband Niles, an intent man employed at one of the
local high-tech firms. They were a rarity in the Village
Green Apartments, a couple in their late twenties who
were willing to put up with a crying baby and drive a
five-year-old Dodge, and call it happiness.

"Well, unless you have something special to do at
your place, why don't I fix a pitcher of tea and we can
have lunch together?"

A crack opened in her boredom, and Susan nodded.
"Sounds good to me, but don't you dare do anything
but make iced tea."

"Don't even think I'll do it." Maureen laughed,
getting up. "Niles says I've become a lazy biscuit-eater
since Bridget came along. Could you watch her while I
fix the tea? We'll bring her in then, and sit in the
air-conditioning."

Susan looked down at Bridget. Oblivious to the
sunlight falling directly on her, the baby slept unmoving, smooth and plumply rounded. Susan watched a
tiny bubble ooze from between the infant's lips. It grew
bigger, caught the light to glint like a miniature Christmas tree ornament. Susan continued to watch it, waiting for it to burst, aware that her back and shoulders

were braced as though she were being threatened with a
severe blow. She felt the skin of her arms and shoulders
crawling. Suddenly, she had the sensation of being
watched, of eyes focused solidly on her and a mind
studying her. She looked away from Bridget and gazed
around the pool area. At the far end of the adjoining
building she thought she detected movement, a blur, as
of someone or something quickly stepping back around
the building's corner. She continued to look, but saw
nothing else, then swung her gaze to the poolside group.
All of them were still there, still paying no attention to
her. An almost imperceptible shiver ran through her.
She knew *something* had been examining her.

Maureen rapped on the glass panel of the sliding
door and motioned for Susan to come in. Pulling the
stroller, she slowly backed through the door. Bridget
made a whispered cooing and the bubble on her lips
burst.

"She's making up for the sleep she misses at night,
I'm afraid."

Susan sat in a chair at the dining table. "Is she having
problems?"

"Only one—me."

"Oh?"

Maureen sat with her back to the noontime light
flaring through the glass door. Her face was in shadow,
its features blurry and indistinct like a photograph
printed from an underexposed negative. She looked
down at her glass, watching her fingers turn it in sharply
erratic movements.

Finally, in a low voice, she said, "I've become
paranoid, I think."

"Oh, Maureen, what a thing to say! I can't believe
that. You're one of the most well-adjusted people I've
met here."

"Until recently." Maureen raised her head to look

across the table at Susan. "Have you been reading about the strange deaths of babies in the area over the past month? Five of them."

"Yes. It's being attributed to Sudden Infant Death Syndrome, isn't it?"

"Yes, but for some damn reason, Susan, it's scared hell out of me. I can't explain it, I can't even try, and Niles thinks I've gone bonkers. Maybe he's right, maybe I've heard the music of a looney tune and am dancing to it, I don't know. But last night, and the night before, I've taken Bridget to bed with us. That means none of us sleep well, but I feel safer with her there." She shrugged her shoulders in a slow hunching movement. "I guess I'm carrying this motherhood thing a bit too far."

"Oh, Maureen, I don't think so."

Maureen gave an exaggerated sigh and pushed back her brown hair. "I'm sorry. I didn't ask you in to listen to the ramblings of a neurotic woman."

They finished the tea with nothing more said on the subject, but Susan's mind filled with a vague anxiety she could not define.

Back at the library, she realized she had not phoned Sam. Sitting at her desk, she wished she had not gone home for lunch, because the uneasiness she'd experienced at Maureen's table stayed with her.

In the middle of the long, empty afternoon, Susan went to the newspaper files and reread the articles concerning the deaths of the five babies, trying to understand what was causing Maureen's anxiety over Bridget. Finding nothing to warrant Maureen's behavior, she hung the papers back on their racks feeling no better than she had before. Today had not been a day for researching, she decided. Today had not been much of a day for anything.

A late afternoon storm was building when Susan left the library. She stood at the library entrance for a moment, looking at the line of clouds creeping in from the west, thinking that a drenching would be a fitting end to this off-key day.

She gave a final look at the sky, then hurried across the driveway which circled in front of the building, counting her steps. If she could walk 130 paces a minute, she might cover most of the distance to the apartment before the rain came.

She had taken only a few steps along the cross-campus path when an automobile horn blared behind her. For an instant, in the deepening gloom and rising breeze, the sound had no identity. When it repeated, she recognized it for what it was and looked over her shoulder. A man waved from the driver's window of a familiar blue Toyota stopped in the center of the driveway. The car belonged to Kellen Atwood, an English and Literature instructor who occasionally sought Susan's assistance with reference material.

"Susan!" Kellen leaned his head out of the window. "I don't think you can make it home before the rain. Let me give you a lift."

She looked at the clouds that now claimed more than a third of the sky and were gaining weight as they grew blacker. She waved back to him. "I'll take you up on that."

When she was in the car and he had started down the driveway, Kellen said, "I assume your day was as jammed with action as mine."

"If you spent all day watching the paint flake from the administration building, it was turmoil in comparison to mine."

"Yeah, we're in high-tension professions, aren't we? Tonight should also be a whirlwind of activity. I've got an adult-education class, for which I'll guess nine of the sixteen people enrolled will make an appearance." He looked up at the sky. "Make that six, if it rains."

She canted her head and looked sideways at him, for

the first time examining him with an objective interest. She saw a man just beyond his middle thirties, whose rather regular features reflected a boy's wonder and intensity without succumbing to innocence. Blond hair was trimmed in a modish style, but gave the impression of being recently ruffled by a passing breeze, a lock of it tumbling down a high forehead to partially hide his left eye. His eyes were an ordinary brown, but she instinctively knew they were sensitive eyes which could express great emotion. The chin was strong, with no aggressive jutting. All in all, she decided, Kellen's was a nice face, an easy face to like.

"Why did you become a teacher?" she asked.

He looked at her and grinned. "Did I sound cynical?"

"Or discouraged."

"To tell you the truth, I'm not much of either. You know, I honestly can't give you a definite reason, other than I thought it might be fulfilling. Not the guiding of young minds; I wasn't that idealistic, God knows. It was mainly for my own personal satisfaction, I think. Selfishness, maybe. Perhaps even escape, now that I'm thinking about it. I would be miserable in an industrial atmosphere, because I've no interest in anything technical. In fact, I'm inept around mechanical things. But I'm happy living a life cluttered with old books and theories and toying with ideas that may never bear fruit. The halls of academia, even in a community college, permit exploration without impossible deadlines."

"I'm glad you've been able to do what you like best," she said.

"I've been lucky, mostly."

They could smell the coming rain and hear the thunder rolling toward them when Kellen pulled the car into Susan's apartment complex's parking lot.

"Thanks, Kellen." She opened the door and swung her legs out. "I appreciate this."

"All my pleasure. Maybe someday there'll be another storm and we can do it again."

"This is the season for them."

"I'll keep my fingers crossed."

She laughed and closed the car door. A raindrop brushed her bare arm, and she gave Kellen a quick wave, then hurried toward her apartment.

The storm arrived shortly after she closed the front door, its preceding wind howling between the buildings. Rain rattled against the windows, shaking them in their casements, at the same time transforming them into blank rectangles through which gray light seeped like the deadened illumination in the center of a fog.

Susan listened to the booming thunder as she went down the hallway to her bedroom to change the dress she wore for shorts and blouse. Inside the corridor's close confines, the thunder's reverberations seemed to squeeze her, and she found herself straining, as if she were climbing a hill. As she stepped through the bedroom door, a greenish flare of lightning exploded outside, its reflections filling the room. In the glare images danced back and forth in a madman's dance through the flaming light. She gasped, eyes shut tight, hands groping for the door jamb. Unaccountably terrified, Susan fled back down the hallway, trying desperately to escape her sudden fear. The living-room couch became her sanctuary.

In another twenty minutes the storm was gone, rumbling eastward, leaving behind it a landscape cluttered with dark puddles in which johnny-jump-ups erupted like little fractures on the water's surface. Susan stood at the living room window, breathing hard, terror still clinging to her thinking. Outside the twilight was uneasy. The gloom seemed to be hiding something.

Deep inside its growing darkness, she could sense a tremulous movement, as if unholy things were tiptoeing stealthily through it, seeking a gateway to reality. Susan shivered, then turned from the window. Uneasiness crossed the room at her side.

She didn't think of Sam and the bird and her unplaced phone call.

4

THE RECEPTION ROOM TELEPHONE WAS RINGING WHEN SAM entered his office Wednesday morning at eight forty-five. In the silence of the morning, its clamor plucked at his nerves. He felt trapped in a cube of sound. Hurrying to the reception desk, he punched the lighted button on the phone, and drew an exasperated breath as he lifted the receiver.

"Platinum Coast Public Relations, Young speaking." His voice was hoarse and lacked solidity.

"Jesus, you sound like a terminal case of the morning-afters."

An overwhelming weight suddenly straddled his shoulders as he recognized the voice. Far too buoyant for this time of morning, it belonged to Willy Kavanaugh. Willy was the local advertising manager for Versailles Garden, a combination health spa and social club. Sam edged around the desk to pull out the chair behind it, then sat down and leaned forward, planting his elbows on the desktop. Willy was an inexhaustible talker.

"Miami approved my budget, Sam."

The brevity of the statement caught Sam unaware. He groped for something to say before Willy's pause of expectation could stretch into an awkward silence. Squeezing his eyes shut, Sam forced his attention to focus on the Versailles Garden account, mentally stumbling through it, damning Cindy Chambers for being late to work, then said simply, "That's great news, Willy. They approve everything?"

"Everything, Sam, right through the bottom paragraph giving me personal authority to develop and manage the advertising with the assistance of Platinum Coast Public Relations. They're impressed down there with the work you've done so far, Sam, and told me I could add another nine percent to your fee. How's that sound, old buddy? That means another seven thousand in your coffers."

"You're not going to hear a complaint from me. When do we begin?"

"ASAP, Sam. That's why I phoned early. If your case of the wobblies isn't too debilitating, I'd like to meet for lunch today and shape up the details. Your agenda clear?"

"It is now, Willy. And I don't have the wobblies."

"Then meet me at the Steak House at twelve-thirty. I think we owe ourselves a little celebration. What say you?"

"I agree. I'll be there at twelve-thirty."

After hanging up, he pulled the Versailles Garden folder from a filing cabinet and flipped through it. He had remembered all the salient points of the proposal Willy had submitted to Miami.

Another ten minutes passed before a harried Cindy Chambers arrived.

"I'm sorry, Sam. Lucy was sick all night, and Carl

and I didn't get a bit of sleep." She dropped her purse into a desk drawer. "Took her to my mother's this morning instead of the day-care center, that's why I'm late. I know I should have called, but I was a bit rattled."

Cindy looked exhausted; the expression she wore and the slump of her shoulders combined to seemingly melt away some of the baby fat she would never outgrow. During the first weeks of her employment, Sam had thought of her as a cuddly-type woman, five feet five, 125 pounds, with little-girl blue eyes and corn-silk hair. Wonder and innocence looked out of those eyes as if seeing their own version of reality. Yet he quickly became aware that behind that teenage face was a very competent woman who was not all bemused by life, and who accepted challenge with unflinching confidence. She adroitly maintained a balancing act between motherhood, job responsibilities, and caring wife. He had long since removed her from his "cuddly" category.

"What was her trouble?"

Cindy frowned. "We don't know. Just a baby disorder, I guess. Maybe bad dreams, if a six-month-old dreams, maybe a stomach ache. She's too young to talk and give us symptoms, but she did fight for breath a couple of times—and that was frightening."

"Are you sure she's okay now?"

"Oh, yes. Babies are resilient, Sam. And besides, Mom will so outrageously spoil her today, her little memory won't even recall being sick when I pick her up this evening." She looked around the reception room. "What's planned for today?"

"Kavanaugh phoned. Versailles Garden has approved his budget request and our participation. I'm having lunch with him at twelve-thirty, and have no idea how long that will take. Are you going to be able to handle the office alone?"

"I'm just fine, Sam. Honestly. No problem."

"Okay. I'd like you to phone Murray Straus and tell him to hold himself ready for the photography. Tell him he might have to furnish one or two models." He started into his office, then stopped. "Better phone the papers to remind them that Congressman Davis is holding a press conference tomorrow afternoon."

If there was an Olympus in the area, it was the Steak House. Casual Florida life-style was not welcome inside its cut-glass doors. In its two dining rooms and bar, people spoke in muted tones. Soft, simulated-Tiffany lighting spread a veneer of tan on even the most newly arrived northern visitors. Silverware and goblets sparkled. Personal maneuvering across the heavy linen tablecloths was a daily occurrence, with developers closing land deals, coiffered young professionals earnestly talking with the perfect confidence only they possessed. At corner tables, over-garbed dowagers discussed the identical subjects they had worn out during previous luncheons at the same table.

Sam laid his memo pad on one of the unoccupied chairs. He downed the first vodka and tonic in pace with Kavanaugh, then sipped sparingly at the second one set before him by a stately, red-haired waitress. With his third martini only an olive in the bottom of its glass, Willy allowed the fourth to sit untouched at his elbow. It was the indication the pudgy man had shifted gears. During the remainder of the lunch, Kavanaugh would function not as an expense-account freeloader, but as the grudging executive who approved the bills.

"The home office didn't make one change, only suggestions on media involvement and the Versailles Woman." Kavanaugh pulled a notebook from his coat pocket and began to read directly from its pages.

"More TV spots. Orlando channels cover this area very adequately. The Versailles Woman should be older than we discussed. Early thirties. Sophisticated.

Worldly-looking. A healthy, sensuous capacity that will come through on film." He looked at Sam. "Know anyone like that?"

"Not offhand. Murray Straus might have one in his model stable."

"Okay." Kavanaugh returned to his notebook. "Balls out to get the campaign together and start a blitz in mid-September. People in the demographic group we're after begin to think of fall and winter activities then. Send TV tapes and print layouts to Miami for approval before release."

"How long will they keep them? We'll be fighting deadlines."

"Two days at the most, they promise. I'll drive them down and back myself."

Sam placed his memo pad beside his plate. When he left the Steak House at fifteen minutes to two, scratched notes filled three of its pages, and his mental list included items to be discussed with Murray Straus, a printer, and a media sales representative.

At the office he gave the scribblings to Cindy. Looking dubious, she promised to decipher and type them, then told him there were three messages waiting on his desk, that she had phoned reminders of Congressman Davis's press conference to the media, and called her mother, who said Lucy was crawling through the house with impossible energy.

Two of the waiting messages were from clients wanting him to contact them. Neither was urgent. The third was from Lily. It asked him to phone as soon as possible at the number given. The number given was his. He sat staring at the pink slip of paper with the orange lettering, wanting to ask Cindy if the number was correct, but knowing it was, and knowing that Cindy was aware it was his home phone number. Remotely, he watched his fingers tighten around the paper and crumple it into a tiny, uneven ball. He saw his knuckle rise into white knobs on the back of his squeezing hand, felt the beat of his heart increase its cadence. With a flip of his hand, he tossed the crumpled note in the direction of the wastebasket. It struck the rim, teetered reluctantly on it, then dropped in.

Slowly he dialed his number.

"Yes?"

It was her voice, touched with breathlessness, yet rippling with electric tension.

"Lily, it's Sam."

"Are you wondering what I'm doing in your townhouse?"

"Well . . . yes, I am."

"I hope it doesn't annoy you."

"No. I'm just wondering how you got in."

"That nice Mr. Acaley, the maintenance man, let me in."

"Oh?"

"My new furniture won't be delivered until at least tomorrow, and I convinced him you would not be upset if I waited in your place until you arrived home. I told him we were having dinner together tonight."

He suddenly knew what was happening, and he felt himself helpless to prevent it. "Are we?"

"Of course, Sam. I promised to prepare you a fine meal."

Abruptly she hung up.

Holding the dead receiver against his ear, he sat immobilized, staring at the splash of sunlight outside the office window, feeling his mind struggling to retain a sense of direction. A parade of ill-defined shapes filled his concentration, some slithering, some prancing, some drab, others exploding with prismatic illumination. He held the handpiece in front of him, staring at it with squinted eyes, then placed it in its cradle.

For no definable reason, he suddenly wanted to know what Susan had found out concerning the bird. Immediately he picked up the phone and dialed her number at the library. The evenly spaced ringing at the far end of the connection was slow-paced, as if the mechanisms along the line were weary of that special combination of numbers.

"Good afternoon, Sloan Community College Library. May I help you?" It wasn't Susan's voice.

"Miss Rutledge, please."

"I'm sorry, sir, she's in the stacks, assisting one of our instructors with a reference problem. May I help you, or have her phone you?"

Two bodiless, electronic voices speaking scripted words by rote.

"No," he said. "I'll try later. Thank you."

He didn't give his name, and as he hung up wondered why.

Cindy was at the copy machine, producing copies of a profile of a local politician to be included in a mailing kit seeking donations to inaugurate a new campaign fund. Boredom slackened her features.

"When you finish that, call it a day," he said. "Go see how Lucy is."

"Oh, Sam, I couldn't. I was late coming in."

"Go! We've had our major coup for the day."

She looked at him with her wide eyes sparkling in all their pre-teen innocence, and he thought what a lucky man Carl Chambers was.

An unnatural stillness filled the office suite after Cindy left. It was ponderous, out of proportion to the size of the three rooms. Beneath its surface the noises normally heard at this time of day lay in restless disorder. Sam stood in the middle of the reception room, looking at familiar furnishings, seeing in them the organization and formality that was his life. But he only partially understood their meaning. He was like a man trying to comprehend what he saw with a sleep-smudged mind.

At twenty minutes after four, he locked the outer office door behind him.

Lily waited for him, standing deep in grotto-like shadows at the living-room entrance beyond the oblong of sunlight that had spilled into the foyer of the townhouse when he opened the front door. Still somewhat blinded by the sunlight, he would not have seen her had she not shifted position. Light splintered on a jeweled pendant resting on her chest, for she wore her usual black slacks and dark turtleneck blouse. His first startled impression was of something malignant lurking in the gloom. Just as the office had been, the townhouse was infected with a strange silence.

"Sam, how nice. I didn't think you would be home so soon."

The brooding hush retreated immediately as Lily's voice reached for him. Outside noises and the steady murmur of the air conditioner assumed their rightful places. He closed the door and stepped into the foyer.

"I'm early."

"I hope because of me."

She took him by the hand and lead him to the patio, where on a serving table a vodka bottle was surrounded by three smaller ones of tonic. He saw the gold seal and the blue lettering on the vodka bottle, and knew it was Absolut, one of the finer vodkas.

He nodded at the chaise. "Am I supposed to make myself comfortable?"

"Of course. You are the man, Sam, and I am the woman."

"I've noticed that."

"No, it is not a witticism. From where I come, it is the obligation of the woman to see to the comfort of her man."

"You've still not told me where you're from, but it sounds like a male chauvinist's dream."

Her face tightened into those taut planes which

added to her age, and he noticed her fingers toyed with the vodka cap. Then she shrugged. "The Middle East. I am from one of those countries which are forever in turmoil." Her bleak expression vanished. A smile curved her lips and reached up to touch her eyes. "But it is of no importance, because I have become a citizen of the world."

It would be futile, he sensed, to question her more; for he was convinced that she was prepared to give only so much of herself to him. A very personal part of her was not for sharing. Yet, while he watched her pour the vodka, then the tonic, into a glass, he wanted to make one more query, certain that an answer to it would at least reduce the enigma. He tried to keep it casual.

"You know, counting today, we've known each other three days, and you've never told me your last name, Lily. You do have one, don't you?"

Briefly, so swiftly that he nearly missed it, a coldness darted through her eyes, then was gone. For that one fleeting second, something dark had looked out at him, something turbulent and filled with fury.

But suddenly, she was laughing, a merry laugh that brought into the cramped patio a spontaneous happiness. "Oh, Sam, you're so serious this evening. Does my using one name instead of two make me only half a woman?" Her laughter drifted into a throaty chuckle. "You, of all people, should know that I am a very whole and healthy woman." She ran a fingertip around the sides of the metal ice bowl, studying with averted eyes the streak she made. "Remember, Sam, I told you I am divorced. When that occurred, there was a . . . a decree forbidding me to mention my husband's name or his homeplace. I must obey it strictly. It was a small commitment to make in return for the special freedom I enjoy. As for my family name, I do not think you could twist your western tongue enough to pronounce it. So, I am Lily. A complete woman with only half a name. You do accept me that way, don't you?"

He nodded as she handed him a drink. "Of course, Lily. And no more questions."

"You promise, Sam?"

"Well, at least for a while."

"Then it is time for me to see to the comfort of my man." She gave him a quick kiss on his cheek and went to the sliding door. "Tonight I am going to serve you a thank-you meal to show my appreciation for all you have done for me."

"No, Lily, that's not necessary."

"Yes, Sam, it is very necessary. Now enjoy your drink while I am in the kitchen."

He settled on the chaise. Lily had closed the door to keep the cool air from escaping the townhouse, so he could not hear her in the kitchen as he leaned back against the chaise, closing his eyes. There was so much he wanted to know about this woman who had entered his life, because in only three days she was dominating it, changing its course. Perhaps it would be like examining a gift too closely, but he felt that he was on the verge of making an all-out commitment, and there were shadows obscuring much of what he needed to think about.

From the far side of the redwood fence he heard a conversation being held in muted tones beside the pool, and beyond the voices the heavy, endless metronome of the sea swishing its eternal count of the passing hours.

He stood at the top of the wooden steps that descended to the beach, looking first north, then south, along the narrow sand strip. While they ate, the ocean had swollen with a high tide. At places, the foam line looped like a gray coronet within a few feet of the bank, leaving its collection of spinach-like seaweed and ragged scraps of flotsam stranded in the shadow of the dunes.

Uncomfortable, Sam drew a deep breath, then tried to suck his stomach away from the cutting bind of his belt. He was overloaded, bloated. Staring at the refuse in the foam, he pressed his lips together. There was more to give thought to than overeating. He could feel his emotions stirring. For a moment, with his hands grasping the stair railing, he felt he was standing on a jerry-rigged scaffolding surrounded by a humid heat not born of the sea.

While she served the meal, Lily's movements had been luxurious, with her entire being faintly swathed in the elusive scents of musk and roses. She hummed nearly soundlessly as she moved about the townhouse.

She had proven herself a magnificent cook. Tossed salad, baked halibut with delicate garnishments, wild rice and buttered peas, accompanied by a white wine with a sturdy bouquet. All had been prepared and served in grand style, the meal capped by strawberries in heavy cream, the fruit lightly dusted with powdered sugar. Though Sam already felt stuffed, he'd been unable to resist the dessert. When he'd finished eating and had smoked a cigarette, Lily had chased him from the townhouse, refusing to accept his offer of help with the dishes.

Twilight came without warning, dissolving the sea and beach like a dreamscape, leaving nothing but a disarrayed memory of apricot-stained sand and indigo-tinted water. On a damp breeze Sam detected the smell of things too long out of the water and rotting on the beach. He turned to go back to the townhouse and saw Lily approaching. She was walking slowly, in her black attire an indistinct form little darker than the increasing darkness through which she moved. He watched her, squinting to pull her into detail, appreciating with

ever greater fascination her sensual elegance. Each
muscle in her tall body seemed activated by some erotic
stimulus.

At first she said nothing, just stood at his side with
her head tilted back, looking at the darkening sky. Her
thin nostrils quivered as though testing the scents
drifting through the humid air, and her lips were
narrowly parted in a thin reflection of a smile. For
perhaps half a dozen seconds, as when he first saw her
standing on the sand dune, he received the curious
impression of other-worldliness, of a person separated
from reality. To have something to do, he took his
cigarette package from his shirt pocket, carefully shook
one free, and deliberately lit it. Her nose wrinkled
when the smoke he exhaled curled between them.

"It was a damn good meal, Lily." He had already
told her that in the dining room, but now he repeated
it, wanting the sound of his voice to break this moment
of unreality. "You certainly showed your appreciation."

She turned her head in his direction, eyes studying
him speculatively. Unblinking, beneath half-lowered
lids, she appeared to be absorbing individual details of
his features as if she were seeing him for the first time,
recording each curve and plane for future identifica-
tion. He felt a rising embarrassment touched with
irritation, compulsively tightening his facial muscles to
erect a barrier should those eyes attempt to probe
behind the surface. Then suddenly she blinked, her
breath made a soft hissing in her nostrils, and the
remoteness was gone. She put her hand on his arm.

"Can you feel the vibrations in the air?" she asked.
"They're like little fingers running up and down your
body tickling your skin. Do you feel them, Sam?"

"No. All I feel are the trickles of sweat running down
my back."

"Concentrate, Sam. Try. Little electric shocks coming from the sky."

He tried, but felt nothing. Only the dew of perspiration and the dampness of the ocean. He shook his head. "No, nothing."

"Ah, Sam, you are so modern. You have lost your unity with nature. Right now nature is speaking, but you cannot communicate with it."

"I'm deaf as a dodo, Lily. What's it saying?"

"That a storm is on the way."

"Another one? Christ, we've had enough of those for a while. We don't need any more. Maybe it can send something else." He put an arm around her waist. "Ask nature to send us a full moon."

Lily laughed as she pressed the length of her body to his. "We've proven we do not need a full moon, so nature is sending us a storm." She pushed harder against him, fitting her flesh to his. "A storm will be more exciting than a full moon, much more exciting. I promise, Sam."

"Where did you learn to be attuned to nature? It's not something they taught when I was in school."

"You're forgetting I've no permanent home, Sam, that I've wandered in many lands. In secluded corners of the world, there are people who communicate with nature more frequently than with their neighbors. They possess an awareness long forgotten by the modern world."

"Oh?"

"Yes, Sam. Once mankind knew it was a part of nature, that life's rhythms flow with the rhythms of nature. To exist, people read the pulsations of nature and coordinated their existence with nature's flow. They listened, they watched, they felt. All the textures of nature were theirs to heed and study and interpret, but over the years they discarded that knowledge, they stifled their senses. Now mankind is a helpless play-thing, a blind creature not knowing what forces are ranged against and beside it."

He couldn't picture her sitting at the feet of a guru. "In what corners of the world are these remote segments of civilization?"

"Questions, Sam. You promised there would be no more."

"About you personally, Lily. It seems to me what I'm asking for now is a lesson in sociology, or maybe geography."

"But then you will want to know more."

"Why is that so bad?" He took a long draw on the cigarette, then flipped it out into the darkness. "I think, Lily, that I've the right to know more about you. You're causing changes in my life, and I'll be better prepared for them if I knew more about their cause."

"You will not accept me otherwise?"

"I didn't say that. But I am saying that my acceptance could be stronger and deeper if I knew at least a few of your background details. Not about your divorce, or even your last name, but about you, Lily. Lily, the woman. The traveler. An enigma is fine, sometimes fun, but it can also be frustrating."

She looked along the beach, her eyes narrow and unblinking. The absolute stillness of her body reminded him of an ancient statue. He said nothing, but waited to hear her decision.

Finally, without looking at him, she said, "Sam, you must try to understand me. This is my first visit to America for a long, long time, and I had forgotten the openess of your society and your people. I have been traveling in lands where, for their own protection, people jealously guard all things personal. I fear I have picked up that trait."

Again, as when she spoke of her divorce, Sam felt as if she spoke of a world younger in its history. But how long could it have been since a woman in her late thirties had visited the U.S.?

She turned to him, an odd expression of shielded concern on her features. "You will try to understand, won't you, Sam?"

He nodded, but he wasn't certain he would ever completely comprehend. "It looks like I'll have to keep being intrigued with a mystery."

"Many times one finds more beauty in a mystery impossible to attain than in that which is not concealed."

At first Cindy Chambers didn't know what awakened her. She lay in a dark netherworld between sleep and wakefulness, staring up at a ceiling that had disappeared behind black shadows. She worked to push the confusion away, trying to make her mind grasp something to pull herself out of limbo. Finally she focussed on the office, and ran down the various accounts, seeking one to which she could give her full attention.

The Versailles Garden account. Slowly she began placing its details into an orderly arrangement. She was perhaps halfway through her organizing when the explosion came.

Blue-green flame seared the room around her, blinding her, driving sharp bits of brilliance along her optic nerves to momentarily fry her brain. Simultaneously, a hissing roar of thunder shook the house, rattling windows and sending shock waves through the walls. A rush of wind circled the house, wailing, rapping at the windows, rasping against the ersatz fieldstone of the outer walls. Then rain poured down, hammering on the roof. Cindy huddled in the bed, dry and comfortable, feeling the rain's coldness seep into her, turning her blood into sludge that reluctantly circulated through her veins. She pushed her knuckles into her eyes, rubbed them hard.

When she opened her eyes again she felt the heaviness in the air. The darkness of the room had assumed a physical weight, bulky, expanding, centering directly over Cathy. She found herself struggling to breathe, as her chest and stomach muscles fought pressure. With a little whimper, she turned her head toward Carl.

He was on his left side, his back to her. The undisturbed rhythm of his breathing was a soft, easy cadence, a very faint chuffing from his mouth, which Cindy knew would be open. She envied his ability to slip so deeply and easily into the tranquility of sleep. He insisted that he never dreamed, while on the other hand, her sleeping hours were filled with fantasies, sometimes good, sometimes bad.

She was wide awake now with no hope of quickly returning to sleep. She drew a deep breath, and the ease with which she did it made her realize that the room's atmosphere had lightened to normal. For a few moments longer, she stared up into the shadows, feeling sleep drift farther and farther out of reach, then, with a defeated sigh, threw aside the sheet and sat up on the edge of the bed. With a final glance at Carl, she stood, then walked slowly to the window to stand looking out at the rain.

At first she thought what she saw was an illusion, a kind of nighttime mirage caused by the distortion of the rain which had turned the glass into a sheet of crinkled plastic wrap. Even as she tried to focus, she realized that she was sensing more than seeing the thing beside the low, skimpy fence of hedge between their house and the one next door.

Whatever it was, it was undefined. Briefly she thought she could make out the shape of wings, but they vanished and, for a fleeting instant, she was certain a snarling animal snout was pointed in her direction before it too melted away. Her heart began to thump. The thing rocked back and forth as though riding currents in the storm. It drifted toward the front of the house, then hesitated. Now Cindy was certain it was staring at her, almost mocking her. Slowly it moved away, blending with the rain, slowly being absorbed into the night. She was unable to check the tiny shudder that ran down her spine.

With a final long look out into the rain, she turned from the window. Apprehension and disbelief battled in her mind. Her sudden awakening had startled her, but the thing in the yard had frightened her.

There was no sound from the nursery across the hall from their bedroom, but Lucy was a quiet baby. If the storm had disturbed her, she might well be staring at the silhouettes of the plastic mobile hanging above her crib.

Cindy's bare feet padded across the hardwood floor as she made her way through the still unfamiliar arrangement of furniture in the new bedroom. She glanced at Carl. He had turned on his back, which meant that in a very short time he would be snoring. She smiled, feeling a great affection beyond love for the less-than-perfect man who was her husband.

Lucy was laying on her side, curled tight, as if an instinct which had accompanied her from the womb had directed her to assume the fetal position for protection. Cindy tiptoed to the side of the crib. As she bent over her daughter, she sensed a terrible wrongness in the child's stillness and ashen color.

She reached down and touched Lucy's left shoulder. The small body rolled onto its back, its right arm and hand bouncing flaccidly on the mattress. The jaw fell open, and what was usually Lucy's laughing mouth gaped wide with a hideous, loose-lipped slackness. A whisper of breath fluttered from the misshapen oval, the last workings of her tiny set of lungs.

Cindy screamed. She screamed again and again and again, until the curdling sound saturated the house and reached into the rain-chilled night.

He didn't know what time it was when the thunder awakened him. Quite suddenly he was laying on his back in a chaos of booming echoes and meteoric streaks of light that spattered the bedroom with flashes of blue and green. Then he heard the tidal surge of rain hissing in wave after wave across the roof, battering at the windows with a determination to splinter the glass and send an avalanche of water cascading into the room.

On the bedside table the red numerals of the digital alarm clock blinked on and off, notifying him that at some time the power had cut off. He turned his head to the right, wondering if the storm had disturbed Lily, and saw only an empty half of the bed. Without reasoning his action, he reached out to run his hand over her pillow. It was cool, the unnatural coolness of cloth long exposed to air-conditioning.

Time drowned in the rain while he lay staring at the walls and ceiling, watching the splashing blue and green designs painted by the lightning. There was a grotesqueness in the fleeting patterns of chiaroscuro, like malignant growths squirming on the cream-colored plaster. He shut his eyes to await Lily's return.

There were no noises in the townhouse other than the growling of the thunder, no hesitant sounds of a person groping their way through unfamiliar rooms in night-time darkness. He didn't know how long it was, as his mind slowly absorbing the household stillness beneath the storm's buffeting, before he began to suspect that he was alone in the townhouse.

He swung out of bed, groped with his feet until he found his slippers, stood up and drew the drawstring of his pajamas tight, then shuffled to the bedroom door. In an attempt to compensate for the time it had been off during the power outage, the air conditioner was whirring demonically, shoving a steady shaft of cold air throughout the rooms. He shivered, wishing he had put on his pajama top. The bathroom door was open; beyond it the room was empty. At the head of the stairs he stopped, listening for the sounds of movement, looking down the stairwell, hoping to see a lamp reflection from below, but the first floor was a silent, black abyss.

Knowing he was moving to keep from thinking, he wandered from room to room. Twice he stubbed his big toe, once on the leg of the dining-room table, again on a magazine rack beside a living-room chair. Every room was empty.

Finally he took a cigarette from a pack lying on an end table, lit it, then went to watch the rain dash itself into a dark sheen on the patio flagstones and bow the soggy foliage of the hanging plants with its relentless beating.

He was alone. Lily was gone.

5

GRUMBLING, THE STORM LOITERED OVER THE BEACH AREA, then edged eastward, giving the impression it was uneasy about leaving behind the land it had so thoroughly drenched. Its lightning jabs blazed a crisscrossing filigree on the dark water, cresting the waves with ghostly flecks and turning the troughs between them into bottomless chasms from which the ocean rumbled its protest at being disturbed. Slowly the rain moved out to sea. Only a pattering of drops remained.

Sam half sprawled, half sat in a recliner lounge chair, his feet up, his head laid back on the cushiony headrest. According to the wood-framed clock hanging on the dining room's wall, it was twenty minutes after three, an hour and a quarter since he had discovered Lily's disappearance. The cigarette burning in the ashtray on the table beside the chair was his sixth, and his tongue and the roof of his mouth were fuzzy and dry.

He closed his eyes, then squeezed them tight. Though

he had been blindsided, he wasn't out for the count, he told himself, but it would take some time, he knew, to recuperate from the shock and puzzlement he was experiencing. He crushed out the cigarette, grinding it into the tray with more force than was necessary, and made ready to heave himself from the chair.

At that instant, he heard the patio door softly open, then later gently close. A shadow moved through the darkness. With a grating of aluminum against aluminum, the glass door slid open.

Lily stepped into the dining room.

Dressed in her tight black slacks and blouse, she stood on spread feet, water dripping from her forming irregular stains on the carpeting around her sandals. She did not seem surprised to find him awake. Strands of soggy hair fell across her face, and through them her green eyes stared at him. She was breathing hard, sucking in lungsful of air through flared nostrils. From where he sat across the room, Sam could smell the storm scents clinging to her, salt and wet vegetation and the rankness of things washed up from the bottom of the sea. Not moving her eyes away from him, she slid the door shut behind her.

"Where the hell have you been?" Sam stood up.

She pushed the weighty strands of hair from her face. "I was walking."

"Walking? In the goddamn storm?"

"It is exhilarating. Unless you know all the beauties and mysteries of nature, there is no way I can explain it, no way to even describe to you the excitement of storm walking." Still keeping her eyes fixed on him, she arched the long length of her body, then, like a strip-tease dancer in an outdated burlesque show, her hands drifted up her thrusting curves. "It makes the blood sing inside you, Sam. It sets free the spirit to soar."

"It gets you soaking wet too."

Her laughter trilled, spiraling through the rooms like

a perfect-pitched aria, then, still looking straight at him, she grinned a broad, delighted grin. "I adore you! Do you know that, Sam? I adore you for all your prosaic nature."

He remained immobile, his breathing beginning to create tiny chuffing noises as he sucked in air suddenly turned hot. Lily was on a high, and he speculated on its origin: the storm, or drugs?

"Maybe I'm prosaic, but, damnit, I wouldn't wander around in a drenching rain with lightning blasting on all sides of me. It's dangerous as hell on the beach during an electrical storm."

A slight tightness hardened around the edges of her voice. "Are you criticizing me?"

"Yes, I guess I am, for being so careless."

She stared directly at him. "I will not take offense this time, Sam, because I believe you are thinking of my well-being, but your concern is misplaced."

"Why? Do you think you're immune to a lightning strike?"

"It would seem so."

"Well, tell that to the teenager who was fried to death last month up on New Smyrna Beach."

She held her smoldering gaze on him. "I told you, Sam, that I love the night. Now I tell you, I also have a great affection for storms, and, in turn, they both hold great tenderness for me. We are friends, storms and the night and I, all companion dwellers of the universe, and none of us would allow harm to befall our friends while we are in each other's company." A tint of green began to seep back into the darkness of her eyes. "Trust me, Sam. I am part of both of them. So worry, if you must, but do not issue ultimatums, because for years I have, as you say, 'wandered around in drenching rains,' and I do not intend to cease. I will not."

He wanted to shrug, but there was a sudden stiffness in his shoulders, so instead he reached down to pick up the full ashtray. "Okay, but if your friends decide to turn against you, your butt can be badly burned."

While he was still bent over the table, she crossed the dining room and living room in long-legged strides and flung herself on him. Caught off balance, he stumbled back a step, felt his knees caving in, the lusty weight of her driving into him.

A continuous, guttural growling, disconcertingly similar to that of a hungry animal on attack, erupted from deep in her throat. Her teeth pulled and nibbled at the flesh of his neck. He was still disoriented with surprise and shock, but he felt her hands greedily stripping off his pajama bottoms, became aware of his own hands working frantically at her wet blouse and slacks. From somewhere, he heard crackling noises as though electrical charges were filling the townhouse. For one abbreviated moment, he fought to regain control, a detached part of him knowing that to allow what was happening to continue would not be sexual gratification, but bestial rutting. Then he felt his own nakedness, and whatever remained of his resistence exploded in a furious surge of overpowering lust. Each and every one of his body tissues drove him with a frantic need to satiate himself. His growling matched hers, the sounds coming from his mouth in husky, hoarse monosyllables generated by a brain drained of every emotion but desire.

Then suddenly it was over. Whatever it had been was consumed. A margin of reality returned. Panting, their bodies still quivering with residual violence, they lay on the living-room floor interlocked in arms reluctant to release their holds, neither feeling the chill as the air conditioner relentlessly pumped out its artificial coolness.

"Sam, kiss me . . . gently." All the coarse texture was gone from Lily's voice. What might have been a childish longing underlay the whispered words.

After he did, then pulled his head back, he saw the most beautiful face he had ever looked upon. Thin wisps of black hair straggled across it, but following the exquisite molding of her features they created a strange sexual allure which touched some dark yearning deep inside him. He continued to stare, trying to superimpose over this magnificent face the sharp angles and taut planes he had previously glimpsed. It was impossible. In no way could the two faces be correlated. He removed his right arm from around her and gently laid his hand on the firmness of her left breast, knowing that he had entered some hitherto unknown territory of the senses where passion and love were synonymous and worshipped with erotic abandon.

Thursday arrived with a brilliant morning. As if the storm had washed away its coloring, the sky was a pale blue tinted with wispy streamers of pink. The rain had driven the mist back into the ocean so the air was pristine, reflecting the new light of the sun like the inside of a prism.

The ringing of the telephone was an intruding harshness. It ricocheted through the rooms without pity. Sam had no idea how many times its ring had violated the townhouse's silence before it penetrated his conscious mind, but when he became aware of it, he lay for a long time with Lily's nakedness sprawled beside him. He counted four rings before he decided to answer it.

He couldn't quite understand why he'd awakened on the living-room floor, Lily's naked voluptuousness at his side. He discovered his own nakedness, and when he was on his feet, moving toward the ringing telephone, the stiffness in his muscles. All of it lead to a sizable disorientation as he picked up the receiver and placed it to his left ear.

His voice was fuzzy when he said, "Hello."

"Sam . . . this is Carl Chambers . . . Cindy's husband."

"Yes, Carl." His eyes sought the clock on the dining-room wall. It said six thirty-five. "Is there something wrong?"

"Lucy . . . oh my God, Sam . . . Lucy's dead!"

"What?" A physical pain struck the muscles at the back of his neck and across his shoulders. "My God, Carl—what—how—?"

"We don't know for sure, but it looks like Sudden Infant Death Syndrome."

"Oh, Christ Almighty! Carl, listen . . . tell me what I can do. Is there anything . . . anything at all?"

"No, there's nothing. Cindy wanted me to tell you."

"Carl, I'm so sorry. Anyway I can help—you know I'm here. Do you understand?"

"Yes . . . yes, Sam. Thanks."

The line went dead.

Nausea churned his stomach, bile began to rise in his throat, and he quickly swallowed, making a sour face at the rancid taste.

He looked unseeing around the room, realizing he was in a mild state of shock, vaguely wondering what his reactions should be. This was the first time he had recieved catastrophic news, and he wasn't at all sure what one did to regain mental balance. His wandering eyes saw Lily quietly sprawled on the floor, still apparently asleep, lingered an instant, then moved on without sending a message to his brain. Finally, he realized he was still holding the phone's handpiece and hung it up.

A draft of cold air from a ceiling vent over his head made him abruptly aware of his own nakedness. Slowly, as if attempting to walk for the first time, he went to where his pajama bottoms lay on the living-room floor, put them on, then took a cigarette from the package lying on the table beside the recliner and, after lighting it, went to the sliding door to stand looking out at the patio.

The initial shock retreated, and a deep sorrow for Cindy replaced it. He wondered if, the next time he looked into her eyes, all her marvelous innocence would be gone.

"Sam?"

He turned. Lily had rolled onto her stomach, propped herself up on her elbows, and was looking at him through a dark filigree of hair.

"Why are you so dejected-looking?"

"You didn't hear the phone?"

An infinitesimal hesitation. "No."

"Cindy's baby died last night."

"Cindy?"

"The young woman who works with me. That was her husband. They think it was Sudden Infant Death Syndrome."

"That's too bad." Lily got to her feet and, still facing him, stretched, arching her lushness toward him. Then, with a little sigh, she dropped her arms. "I'm going to shower. Do you want to join me?"

"No, I don't think so."

"It could be fun."

"Not this morning, Lily. I'm not in a fun mood. Sorry."

She shrugged, picked up her blouse and slacks, and walked toward the stairs. He watched the swaying of breasts accompanied by the stately clenching of hips, and felt no response. For the moment, there was nothing in him but numbness and a sense of dismal emptiness.

He went upstairs to wait in the bedroom until he heard Lily go back downstairs after her shower, then went into the bathroom to take his own.

When he entered the kitchen, he discovered her preparing coffee and toast.

"I wanted to fix more," she said, "but I remembered you don't eat large breakfasts."

He nodded. "Just give me coffee, please."

She poured boiling water from the teakettle into a mug, stirred it, then set it on the table. As she passed him on her return to the stove, her hip brushed his. Though it might have been an accident, he suspected the act was very intentional. Self-disgust welled in him as he felt a tingling race through him.

Lily ate two slices of toast with the enthusiasm of one who was famished. He was a third of the way through his second mug of coffee before he felt the emotion-blotting haze which had curled around his mind lift. Holding the mug to his lips, taking a deep swallow of the cooling coffee, he saw Lily staring toward the patio door. And he saw, for several fleeting seconds, the face of that other woman, the flesh stretched tight over the bone, delineating sharp angles with accentuated planes, and behind it dark tensions boiling. Then it was gone, even, he knew, before she sensed his scrutiny. Lily of the classic features turned to smile at him.

"You are good for me, Sam." The words were a whisper. There was the softness of remembering in her eyes. She reached across the table to lay a hand on his. "When I am your neighbor, all our times together will be good. I promise you."

He nodded, then looked at his watch. It was ten minutes after nine. "I've got to go. Will you need any help with your furniture?"

"No, only a few pieces are due today, the bed and a table and some chairs. The delivery men were told to go to the manager's office. I have made arrangements with him to set up the bed and place the other pieces. For a few dollars, the maintenance men will do the work."

He hoped his curiosity wasn't too blatant. "Did you contact Damascus for funds?"

She nodded. "What I requested will be here tomorrow."

"Is Syria your home, Lily?"

Very briefly her expression became opaque, then slowly she smiled like someone who held a secret but was not on the verge of disclosing it. "No, Sam. The money is in Damascus because Syria has one of the more stable governments in that region." She paused, as though choosing what more to say and with what words to say it. "The money comes from Iran. Long before the current problems there, I made investments in the country's oil. There are those living there yet who make certain that royalties are paid into the Damascus account."

"And Swiss numbered accounts?"

A shadow drifted across her face. The fullness left her lips.

"Sorry." He wondered why he apologized.

Driving along A1A, Sam didn't want to go to the office. The news of Lucy's death had turned the day stale. What had occurred on the living-room floor was assuming the proportions of a fantasy performed in a dream, while the death of Cindy's baby was a stark reality which could not be exorcised from the mind. As he turned onto Fifth Avenue in Indialantic, he suddenly knew that what he wanted to do more than anything else was talk with Susan, spend an hour or two with her.

To ease the aloneness he felt in the office, he busied himself stuffing mailing kits with the political profile Cindy had copied the day before. He read over the typed notes from his lunch at the Steak House, jotted down several additions. Finally, at ten o'clock, when he was certain the studio would be open, he phoned Murray Straus.

Murray, who was too professional and too innovative

for this area, which did not require a great deal of commercial photography and did not pay well for what it used, immediately made two suggestions which Sam considered damn good and incorporated in his outline. Reluctantly, seeing a model fee disappearing, Murray admitted that he knew of no models to fill the role of the Versailles Woman. He promised to look and put out the word, but held out little hope, because there were not over ten or twelve professional models within a sixty-mile radius. Sam made a note to have Kavanaugh ask the Versailles Garden home office to contact an agency in Miami. He promised to meet with Murray the following afternoon for a detailed review of the campaign.

He was considering phoning Susan, wanting to ask her to steal an extra half an hour of lunch time so that he might take her to a popular garden-style restaurant, when Willy Kavanaugh walked in.

"Sam, I heard about Cindy's kid on the radio. Christ, I'm sorry. Is there anything I can do?"

"No, thanks, Willy. Carl phoned me early this morning. He sounded damn upset, naturally, but I got the feeling he and Cindy just want to be alone right now."

"Yeah, I guess that's the best." He took the chair across the desk from Sam. "I came by because Miami phoned late yesterday afternoon. They're sending a video crew up in four days to start taping the TV commercials. They wanted to send a still man too, but I told them we had one of the best in the state hiding out here."

"We've got a problem."

"What, for Christ's sake?"

"The Versailles Woman. Murray doesn't have one, nor does he know a model in the area who can fill the requirements. I talked to him about a half an hour ago, and he suggested that you have the people down there contact a Miami agency."

"Shit! I wanted us to be self-reliant all the way. The video crew, okay—we don't have the facilities here —but I sure as hell thought we could handle everything else. Are there any other possible glitches?"

Sam shook his head. As he did so, something brushed his senses, something invisible but real, and he knew that whatever had been listening to him at the seafood restaurant was eavesdropping on the current conversation with Kavanaugh. For a moment, a strange charge filled the office. Maybe he shivered, maybe he didn't. But when he spoke to Kavanaugh, he was very much aware of the presence in the office with them. "Everything else is under control."

"Okay." Will was looking at Sam from beneath a small scowl. "You feel okay?"

"Yeah. I didn't get enough sleep last night, and Carl's call this morning, I guess, disturbed me more than I thought. I'm worried about Cindy."

"Well, knowing her even as little as I do, I've got a feeling she'll come through." He stood up. "I guess that's it. I've got nothing else right now. I'll phone Miami."

Sam stayed behind the desk after Kavanaugh's abrupt departure. Throughout the office the atmosphere lost a bit of its oppressiveness, but whatever it was that was watching and listening still loitered, as if reluctant to leave him with his privacy.

It was too late to phone Susan about lunch, too late, in fact, to go to lunch. When he finally heaved himself out of the chair, he felt as if he were performing a strenuous athletic feat. He walked slowly into the reception room, stood looking at Cindy's vacant desk, then settled behind it and leafed through her "things to do" book. There were three items which required photocopying, plus reminders to herself to update certain file folders. All of this he could do, but nothing required immediate attention. He decided to put it all off. He was nose-diving into a funk.

The phone rang. It startled him, causing him to knock over the pencil holder beside his right hand. He answered, using the company name.

"Sam?"

It was Susan.

The depression that was coiling about him unfolded, but he immediately felt the movement again, forbiddingly heavy, circling closer and closer to him. For the first time, he truly felt that whatever was in the office was not benign.

"Sam? Are you there?"

Susan's voice was like a sanctuary, and he hurried to respond. "Yeah, sorry. I knocked over the pencil holder on the desk. You know, I was going to phone you." He liked the naturalness of his voice. "Honest. I was going to ask if you'd have dinner or lunch with me."

"I'd like that." Her rich, unaffected laugh crackled in his ear. Then her voice sobered, an overcast replacing the sunshine. "I really phoned about Cindy. I only heard of her tragedy a few minutes ago. How's she doing, do you know?"

"Not for sure. Carl phoned this morning, early. He was pretty incoherent. But I haven't talked with Cindy."

"God, that must be a horrible thing for a woman to go through."

"It has to be, but she's strong. Given time, I'm sure she'll pull through okay."

"Oh, I hope so, Sam. When you see her, give her my condolences, please."

"I will. She'll appreciate your calling." He paused, hesitant about returning too abruptly to the dinner invitation after talk of Lucy's death, but wanting to hear again the upbeat pulsation in Susan's voice.

"You're on then, for dinner when we can arrange it? There's something I want to discuss with you when we're together."

"All right. Give me a call."

"Wait. Let's make it definite. How about tomorrow night?"

"Well, yes."

"Okay. See you about seven."

He leaned back in the chair, smiling. With Susan's phone call, the meandering day had dramatically found a course to follow. As he extracted a cigarette from the pack in his shirt pocket, he hummed a few incoherent notes in salute to the approaching hours.

He felt so good he took no heed of a sudden weightiness of the atmosphere that forced him to expand extra energy to draw in his breath, and ignored the shifting movement as if an immense force had taken a new position from which to watch him better.

There was a heavy rapping on the glass of the sliding door. Zipping up the fly of the shorts he had changed into when arriving home, Sam impatiently descended the stairs. He was in no mood to be confronted with another problem. Like a gathering of creditors demanding instant payment, the incidents of the day had surrounded him all at once, draining him of his emotional reserve. The death of Cindy's baby, the difficulty of obtaining a model to become the Versailles Woman, the strange, unseen thing he'd felt watching him at odd times, and, not the least, the fundamental desires pulling him toward Lily. What he required was time alone to sort and catalogue the tumble of things all piled helter-skelter in his mind.

When he crossed the living room toward the dining room, he saw Glenn Ashley standing at the door, his right hand raised to knock on the glass, his left folded around a drink.

Glenn saw him, raised his glass, and shouted, "Party time."

Sam knew his smile was sluggish and awkward as he undid the lock and slid the door open.

"Bring your booze out to the pool, Sam. We've got ourselves a party ready to shift into high gear to welcome our new neighbor in Number Four."

He knew that was Lily. "Is she out there?"

"Oh, yeah. She's suffering from a big case of surprise and a little one of standoffishness, but she'll warm up when we get going. Jetta and Holly are already giving her the scoop about the area." He took a gulping swallow of his drink. "She says she's a friend of yours. That's a hell of a lot of friend, Sammy lad. How'd you manage to keep her a secret for so long?"

"She just arrived in the area, and I just met her."

"Man, she can stay and stay and stay." Ashley again took a large swallow of his drink, this time emptying the glass. "Holly's going to have trouble staying the sex object of our little community with your friend Lily around."

"I suppose so." Why did he feel that suddenly he was staring at a big black question mark painted directly in the center of his field of vision?

"Well, get your bottles and haul your ass out to the pool."

When he arrived, Lily was the immediate focus of his attention. Tall, abundant, and unflawed, dressed in a lavender, off-shoulder dress, she reduced the two women with whom she was talking to lesser females. Sam knew they instinctively realized it, and he had a premonition that Lily might be more tolerated than welcomed in the townhouse comples. He placed the bottles on a wooden table, then studied the two women with Lily.

In an abstract way, he felt sorry for Jetta Ashley. A pretty, dark-haired woman in her late twenties, she was nearing the end of what had been a troubled pregnancy, both physically and matrimonially. Her vivacious face was drawn, the muscles abnormally taut, and if one looked directly into her eyes a blunt collection of deadened emotions could be seen. Sam sensed a sad desperation in her. She had discovered that her husband was neither mentally nor emotionally equipped for adulthood. Desperately not wanting to assume the responsibilities of fatherhood, having failed to coerce Jetta into submitting to an abortion, Glenn was in the process of giving birth to his own personal demons, assisted by drinking a bottle of whiskey a day.

Sam looked at Holly Langston. A chemical and sun-bleached blonde, Holly, at the age of twenty-five, had refused to advance beyond the years when she had been a cheerleader at Auburn University. A devotee of health fads, she attended aerobic classes twice a week, jogged each morning, and could bore all who listened with rambling discussions on health foods. She would have been the perfect wife for Glenn instead of Todd Langston, who was fashioning a career in the local office of a national brokerage firm. Because of Holly, Sam suspected every credit card they possessed was at the limit of its approved charges.

The charcoal grill belonged to Todd and Holly, so Todd prepared the evening's hamburgers. Sam grimaced when he saw Todd's apron with "Come And Get It" scripted across the front, faded from several seasons of washing and partially obliterated with bleached red and blue and brown stains. Not a fancier of cookouts, and in a dark mood, Sam thought the apron was an inane affectation. Glenn Ashley, in total reversal, wore the tackiest clothes in his wardrobe, which Sam supposed was fitting, because since Jetta had become pregnant Glenn had ended all poolside get-togethers mumbling drunk. Sam's mood deepened.

He mixed himself a vodka and tonic, then sat at the

table, on which sat a bowl of potato salad, a relish dish, and assorted vegetables. In spite of willing his eyes to stay fixed on Todd at the grill, his gaze continually drifted to Lily.

This was the first time he had seen her in association with other people. In none of her mannerisms did he detect the standoffishness indicated by Glenn; yet there was an aloneness about her, and he found himself trying to decide if it was her incredible sensuality or the remote majesty with which she carried herself that set her apart from the others. Whichever it was, he came to the conclusion that she used her beauty to isolate herself. Within a few minutes after his arrival, she disengaged herself from Jetta and Holly to come sit beside him.

"Are all your friends as disturbed as these four, Sam?"

"No, thank God." He nodded toward the end unit. "I take it your furniture arrived and you're moved in."

"Yes. I was here only an hour when they knocked on the door, insisting that I come out here."

"That sounds like them, particularly Glenn."

Lily looked at the two couples. "I think Jetta and her husband would be happier without a baby."

"You're right. No one expects the marriage to survive the birth."

Some emotion moved behind her face, but it was too deep for him to recognize. She looked at Glenn and Jetta. Jetta's swollen body was braced, tense, and rigid, her head thrust toward her husband while she talked animatedly to him. A very faint smile touched Lily's lips.

For the remainder of the evening, Sam was unable to do more than sit on the periphery of the cookout. His senses were dry and brittle. He joined in conversations, but initiated none. He realized his mood had been spawned by the day's events. His muscles had begun to cramp and ache from tension. For a short time, he exchanged bantering remarks with Holly, but became aware of Lily watching him with a look he could only think of as smoldering. It didn't help his disposition.

At last, just before eight o'clock, Glenn Ashley wobbled unsteadily toward the gate to his patio, and Sam, saying he had work to do, gathered his bottles, two of which were now empty, and walked slowly across the recreational area. At the patio gate, he looked back to see Lily in close conversation with Jetta.

While he was replacing the partially filled bottles in their cabinet he felt the heaviness in the air around him, just as he had at the office, and once more he had the outlandish suspicion he was not alone, that something was sharing the townhouse with him.

Then Lily came through the door, and the feeling slowly retreated into the darkness beyond the light from the dining room's fixture.

Lily stood just inside the door, studying him with the same smokey gaze as before. Finally she said, "You are in a bad mood tonight, Sam. Why?"

He shrugged. "Just call it a leftover from a bad day."

The smoke left her eyes. They danced in the soft light. He watched the undulating movements of her body beneath the sheathing of the lavender dress as she walked slowly across the dining room to stand before him.

"Then I must change your mood, Sam. Let me chase away the moody man I do not care to know."

6

SAM AWOKE TEN MINUTES BEFORE THE ALARM, WHICH WAS SET to go off at seven o'clock. He was alone in the bed. Lily was gone and her pillow was cold. Instinct told him she was not in the townhouse. Minutes dragged by while he lay staring out a window. He felt abused, and embarrassed. He tried to remember if he had somehow bungled his responses to her aggresiveness after the bedlamp had been turned off, but didn't think he had. He looked at the indentation in her pillow, the faint impression of her body on the sheet, and suddenly felt that he was sharing his nights with a phantom. It was five nights since she had become a portion of his life, and still there were moments like this when he wasn't certain she really existed.

He showered, shaved, then dressed in an open-necked sports shirt and casual slacks. When he went downstairs, the *Orlando Sentinel* and *Florida Today* were laid on the breakfast bar awaiting his morning skim for items which might engender business contacts. An empty mug, the jar of Nescafé instant coffee and a spoon were beside them. Lily the ghost had struck again.

It was a gray morning. A milky scrim of thin clouds hugged the blue dome of the sky, which could be seen here and there through ragged holes in the creamy overcast. There was a chance, Sam felt as he stepped out the front door, that the overcast would thicken into rain clouds as the day progressed, possibly leading to a thunderstorm during the evening.

After closing the door, he stood on the front stoop looking down the length of the building. Todd Langston had left their garage door open for Holly to close when she returned from jogging. The Ashleys' garage was still closed, probably indicating Glenn was hung over and not planning to go to work until the world righted itself. Feeling ashamed of himself for thinking this, Sam stepped out into the driveway curving along the front of the building and looked at the end unit. Number 4. Lily's. The garage door was open, the car gone. He tried to look at the vacant space with open-mindedness, but felt a rush of consternation that pulled his mind farther out of shape. As he drove down the driveway, he wasn't certain if he was suffering from jealousy or inadequacy. During the drive up A1A to Indialantic, his disposition harmonized with the drabness of the morning.

Small pneumatic instruments, drills and jacks and hammers, were at work in the base of her skull, and the muscles in her neck were stiff, feeling encrusted with sharp granules that gouged at the inside of her skin. Her stomach rumbled and gurgled. Down her left side she could feel a fluttering of her muscles. She was, she knew, very close to being sick.

Susan Rutledge let out a long breath as she leaned back in her desk chair, reviewing the previous afternoon and evening's incidents which might have left her feeling as she did. Nothing surfaced in her thoughts. She had not eaten anything out of the ordinary, and, other than water, the only liquid she had drunk was iced tea from the pitcher in her refrigerator. There wasn't even the possibility of blaming it on tension, because that was a non-existent factor in her life, unless boredom could be considered tension. She looked out across the formation of empty reference tables.

The woman came through the archway between the reading lounge and the reference room, halting a step or two inside the room to survey the emptiness with a deliberate turning of her head. She was a tall, stately woman with blue-black hair falling in raven wings down either side of a starkly chiseled, but handsome, face. Though she was dressed in plain black slacks and a turtlenecked blouse, there was an elegance to her that Susan found intimidating.

Finally the woman's gaze found Susan. From under dark lashes, she looked unblinking at the librarian, the green hue of her eyes seeming to increase in intensity, as some inner fire kindled behind their almond shape. Susan felt them roaming over her like tiny laser beams, following the curves of her body beneath her summer frock, meeting her own inquisitive gaze and pushing it aside to see into her mind and evaluate her thought patterns. The pain in the base of her skull began to expand, and she had the terrible sensation that her brain tissue was swelling and would soon come squeezing out through the orifices in her skull. She closed her eyes, shook her head.

"May I help you?" she asked, not wholly recognizing her voice.

The woman disengaged her stare, then shook her head. "No. I am new to the area and am familiarizing myself with what it has to offer."

Without another word, she turned and went back

through the archway. Curiosity pulled Susan to her feet and drew her to the archway. The black-clad woman was nowhere to be seen. Susan went into the lounge, but found only a young man sitting in a rattan chair idly leafing through a magazine.

"The tall, black-haired woman, did you see where she went?" Susan asked.

The young man looked at her as if seeing her from another dimension and shook his head. "No one passed here."

Susan stood for another moment or two, feeling that something very strange had just happened, then turned to go back to her desk. Apprehension prickled at her as she walked through the vaulted silence. For an instant, under the arch, the air was suddenly cold. She shivered and remembered once hearing how the air chilled when a ghost passed by.

She had almost reached her desk when the throbbing in the back of her head exploded into a rush of pain that shot lightning bolts through her skull and down her back. She sucked in her breath. For the space of several gulping breaths, it seemed her heart was absolutely motionless. Her stomach churned, warning her she was going to vomit, and she hurried to the restroom.

When she returned, Marge Anderson, her bulk looking uncomfortable in the small chair, was seated at her desk. She looked up at Susan's approach. "You okay?"

"Yes."

"Donna heard someone being sick in the ladies' room, and you were the only one missing."

"I'm okay now. Something I ate, I guess."

"Go home. No one's going to miss you today." Marge swung a thick arm in an arc indicating the empty reference room. "This tomb doesn't need a baby-sitter."

After the one onslaught, the pain in her head subsided, and after the vomiting her stomach no longer gurgled, but Susan felt bruised and disoriented. She ran her tongue around her lips, tasting bile. She nodded, and said, "I guess I will. I do feel kind of squeamish."

"Take the time while you can. Come fall, you'll be begging for a day off."

By three-thirty Susan knew she would be unable to have dinner with Sam. While the pains in her head and stomach had not worsened, they continued to nag at her, discomfort running through her entire body. And for some reason she could not forget the incident of the silent, handsome woman, and the sudden explosion of pain after she had disappeared.

Reluctantly, she dialed the agency number. The phone rang five times, there was a click, and Sam's recorded voice came on the line. "This is Sam Young. I'm sorry, but at the present time the office is unstaffed. Please leave your name and number, and I will return your call as soon as I get back."

She detested talking into answering machines. Invariably she lost the first ten seconds of the alloted thirty sorting out the words which would consciously express her thoughts. "Sam, this is Susan. I'm not feeling well, some kind of bug lodged in my stomach, I think, and I'm afraid I can't keep our dinner date tonight. I'm sorry. Please phone me at home."

She hung up, then, feeling mentally disjointed, stood staring at the ivory-colored instrument hanging on the kitchen wall, wondering how orphaned her voice would sound among the others on the answering machine's tape.

She was quite disappointed. She'd been looking forward to talking with Sam, as her curiousity had been aroused by their phone call the previous day. Sam's voice had carried an undertone of bewilderment that Susan doubted he was aware of. Something was troubling him that he was having difficulty defining. If that was so, she wanted to help. But she would be of no assistance this evening.

Around her a silence crept into the apartment. At first it was the normal stillness of the afternoon, then it began piling upon itself, stuffing the rooms with a great downy mass. She felt it squeezing her, compressing her lungs to squash the air from them.

"Damn it!" She said it out loud, wanting to hear her voice in the crushing silence.

She continued to stand motionless, like a wild creature trying to elude an undefined danger, with her senses darting probes through the layers of stuffiness surrounding her. At the base of her skull the pain began to nip again and from her stomach came a faint rumble. With a little moan, she headed for the bedroom and the waiting softness of her bed.

From the crescent top of the high-rise bridge arching the Indian River between Melbourne and Indialantic, Sam stared glumly through the windshield of the BMW. It was a new bridge, the cement still bone-colored, the traffic lanes not yet blackened with oil drippings, a huge multimillion-dollar monument to the progress that was relentlessly erasing the poetry of small-town charm. Due east, along the beach line, new condominiums shouldered their geometric slabs up into the sea-mist haze; sharp, blunt forms in cruel contrast to the rolling canopy of treetops on the barrier island. He sighed and shook his head. This progress which he hated so was the sustenance on which his business fed.

Three messages awaited him on the answering machine's tape. Willy Kavanaugh wanted a meeting the following morning—Saturday. DJR Industries, a computer software company, asked for an appointment to discuss a direct-mail campaign. Then, sounding very much like a disappointed little girl, Susan told him she was not feeling well and would be unable to have dinner. Sam felt all pleasure flood out of the day.

He dialed Susan's home number. The ringing at the other end of the line began persistently, but after the sixth buzz an emptiness crept into the sound. He hung up. As he recradled the handpiece, a coldness, thin and sharp as a piano wire, eeled down his spine. His hand trembled violently. Grunting, he jerked it back from the instrument, certain, for that one instant, that the telephone contained a vileness that would corrode his skin.

When the feeling passed, he phoned Kavanaugh to set up an appointment for the following morning at ten o'clock, then DJR Industries to tell them he could meet with them Monday morning.

Sam lit a cigarette, drew the smoke deep into his lungs, and leaned back in his chair. It was time to tell Susan about Lily. He needed her evaluation of the relationship, because he knew he had passed the point where he could trust his own objectivity. Maybe she could help untangle him from the patchwork of congested emotions his life had become.

"Shit!"

He crushed out the cigarette, pushed back his chair, and was ready to stand up when the telephone rang. His initial inclination was to let it ring, to let the answering machine pick up. Then, sighing, he lifted the receiver.

"Sam? Are you mad at me?"

It was Lily.

He settled in the chair. "No, not mad. Mystified, I guess. Where did you go this morning?"

"Oh, Sam, I could not sleep, so I took an early morning drive. I should have left you a note. I'm sorry. Did it upset you terribly?"

"It gave me one hell of a jolt. I felt like I was a one-night stand."

"Oh, Sam, no! Never!"

"Okay, I'm sorry. It was just a new experience. Where are you?"

"My funds arrived, and I went shopping. I need a Florida wardrobe, and there are sales in the mall." He could hear the happiness creep into her voice. "I think you will be pleased with my purchases—especially one. We are going to be together tonight, aren't we, Sam?"

He hesitated. He should drive by Susan's apartment to check on her.

"Sam?"

"Yes?"

"We are going to be with each other, is that not so?"

"I-I suppose so, Lily." He felt no stirrings.

"I tried to call you several times, but only your machine answered, and I do not talk into them. You should hire someone until your assistant returns."

"I know."

"We can talk about that tonight."

"All right, Lily."

"Then I will be with you in a little while. This is such a marvelous place to spend money I can hardly pull myself away."

"Do your best, and I'll be home waiting for you."

When the connection was broken, he sat staring at the desktop. Everything had slipped back into abstraction again.

The overcast had thickened during the afternoon, so by ten minutes after five, when Sam left the office, the sky was dark. An early twilight laid a gray wash over the landscape. He smelled distant rain on the westerly breeze.

While he was changing clothes the storm broke. Fast-moving, it rolled in swiftly from the west, sweeping waves of black clouds across the heavens. Lightning tore holes in the boiling mass. Thunder smashed. Gray shrouds of rain blurred visibility outside the windows, obliterating everything more than a hundred feet from the water-smeared panes. Sam watched the brilliant fretwork of lightning over the ocean, feeling small and insignificant. Behind him, the lamp hanging above the recliner flickered, went out, then blossomed again.

Carrie Wadsworth leaned forward over the steering wheel of the van, squinting through the opaque cascade of water that covered the windshield. In spite of their determined, clicking efforts, the wipers were merely skeletal fingers flipping back and forth in useless arcs. Several minutes before, she had turned the headlights on; however, their beams were no more than a diffused patch of pale illumination reflecting off the darkly shimmering mirror of rain.

Common sense dictated that she pull to the side of the road, stop, and wait for the storm to slacken. Not only was it dumb, she told herself, it was dangerous to continue driving through the gray tidal waves of water rushing at the van from the deepening dusk. She was too tense to continue but too afraid to stop. Her imagination clearly visualized a crying seven-year-old Dena bravely trying to watch over her five-month-old brother. Carrie's plump hands clenched tighter on the steering wheel.

This return trip to the mall had not actually been a necessity. It had been generated soley by a pride which stated that she could and would accomplish everything she had set out to do. Forty-five minutes before, when she and Dena and baby Ricky had arrived home from spending the afternoon in the mall, Carrie had discovered that she'd forgotten to pick up Harry's watch at the jewelers. She had promised Harry she would get it, and the trip back to the mall would be less aggravating to spending an evening listening to his complaints.

She remembered looking at their purchases spread on the dining-room table, and saying, "Oh, damn it!"

Dena asked, "What's wrong, Mommy?"

"I forgot to pick up Daddy's watch at the repair place."

"Oh. Does he need it real bad?"

"Yes. Anyway, he says he does. I'm going to have to go back to the mall and get it."

"But it's going to rain, Mommy."

"I know, Dena, but the mall's only four miles away and the jeweler's just inside the entrance. I can get there and back before the rain comes. Honest." She had turned to look at the baby asleep in the blue bassinet on the living-room couch, then turned back to her daughter. "Dena, honey, can you watch your brother while I go back to the mall? I'll only be gone about a half an hour, and he's asleep, so he won't make any trouble. You'd be helping Mommy a lot."

"Okay." Dena looked at her baby brother. "Can I turn on the TV soft?"

"Sure." She headed for the door. "Now you watch Ricky good."

"I will, Mommy. I promise."

Now she looked at the slat-like curtain of water ahead of the van. It looked impenetrable, and Carrie was almost convinced nothing existed on the other side of it. Resembling a huge flashing strobe light, lightning backlit the gray curtain. Thunder sounded somewhere in the non-existent world beyond the gray.

"No, damn it! I'm going through." She came close to screaming the words. "Just a few minutes more, Dena, and I'll be there. Be brave, honey."

Five minutes later, she was at the corner of Lee Street. Water was swirling across the road but she inched the van through and around the corner. Another block, and she'd be home.

Thirty yards in front of the van, the world exploded, then disintegrated, in a roaring boom and holocaust of red, blue, and green fire. She screamed, blindly stomping her foot on the brake pedal, while reflex jerked her arms, twisting the steering wheel to the right. The van shuddered and bucked as it lunged up over the curbing before coming to a rocking stop.

She had no idea how long she sat, listening to the demon cries of the wind howling around the van and the hammering of the rain on its metal sides, before her eyes again began to register images. With hands and feet trembling just short of uncontrollably, she backed the van into the street, then slowly inched it forward.

The house sat somber, its windows dark. The power must be off, she realized as she turned into the driveway, because Dena, leery of the dark, would have the lights blazing. The headlight beams, fragile and jaundiced-looking, swung across the front of the house, then pointed along the rain-scattered gravel of the driveway, barely reaching far enough forward to touch the closed door of the garage.

She was maneuvering the van as close as she could to the side door of the house when she saw it. Like a shadow, it moved out of the rain from behind the house into the feeble illumination of the headlights, hesitated, then drifted backward until it reached the far end of the fan of light. Slowly bobbing up and down, as though riding the erratic winds swirling in front of the garage, it remained there, becoming darker, but remaining shapeless, no more than a blackness in the suddenly descending twilight.

Even as she saw what might have been a form taking shape in the blackness, she knew it was an illusion, a trick of the rain-soaked light, maybe something temporarily out of kilter in her optic nerves because of the lightning strike; but as she continued to look at it, the

sensation came to her that the thing was watching her
with great intensity, studying her, and with that realization came the first touch of apprehension. Next came
the chill, spreading a membrane of cold around her
heart and lungs, and then her stomach. It seeped out
through her skin to lay a rim of frost on her arms and
across her shoulders.

She couldn't help herself: she whimpered.

The black thing moved then. Almost casually, it
drifted to her right, becoming darker and losing what
identity it possessed as it glided away from the background of the garage door, gradually blending into the
darkness beyond the edge of the headlights' halo.
Suddenly it was gone. Vanished. But Carrie was aware
of something remaining in the turbulent air, something
she could think of as only the residue of an intense
hate.

She clawed at the door handle. Unable to stop the
continuous whimpering now coming from her fear-
twisted mouth, she wriggled her overweight body out of
the van. The rain slapped her face, its coldness adding
to the chill already in her, leeching away her strength.
She tried to open the house door. It was locked. One of
the escaping whimpers became a moan, threatening to
explode into a scream, as she remembered the keys,
still dangling in the van's ignition.

"Mommy, is that you?" There was a rattling on the
other side of the door.

"Yes! Yes, Dena, it's Mommy. Let me in. Open the
door, sweetheart."

The door swung open. Crying, laughing, Dena was in
her arms.

"Oh, Mommy, Mommy." The little arms tightened
around her neck. "I was so frightened. The lights went
out and the TV went off, and it was so dark and noisy."

"I know, baby. I'm so sorry this happened. But

everything's all right now. I'll make it up to you. I promise." She pushed Dena back to arm's length. "Did you watch Ricky?"

Dena's eyes wavered. "Y-Yes . . . but when the storm got too bad, I-I hid in my bedroom." Then she smiled. "But it's okay, because he slept all the time. He's still sleeping."

Carrie took her daughter's hand. "Well, let's go see how he is."

The living room was dark, darker than she'd ever seen it, and its whole atmosphere felt strange, as if it were a room she had never before entered. She stopped in the archway leading to it from the dining room and stood rigidly still, her hand closing tightly around Dena's.

"Mommy, what's wrong?" Dena's voice was thin, trembling.

"I-I don't know."

"Is—is Ricky all right?"

She didn't answer. Releasing Dena's hand, she hurried across the room. Ricky was laying on his back with his arms straight along his sides. Because of the darkness, she was forced to bend low over the bassinet to see his face. His eyes were closed, as they would be if he were sleeping, but there was a terrible, unnatural blankness laying on his tiny features, a nothingness, which even in the relaxation of sleep should not be present. His skin was chalk-hued, all the color drained from his rosy cheeks.

"Ricky!" She reached out to cup his chin in her hand. Under her fingers, the skin was cold, the flesh of his cheeks flaccid. "Ricky!"

"Mommy?"

"No, Ricky! No!"

"Mommy, what's wrong with Ricky?"

Carrie slowly sank to her knees beside the couch and

bent forward, resting her forehead on the bassinet. Her plump body began to quiver with great, raking sobs from the core of her being.

"He's dead, Dena. Ricky's dead."

As suddenly as it had struck, the storm was gone, swirling eastward to lash the tossing waters of the ocean with its fury. Within minutes, only the steady rhythmic patter of rain remained.

Most of the restlessness had left Sam, sucked away by the tide of the storm. Suddenly aware of his isolation in the townhouse, he felt as if he was alone on a darkened stage, watched by a distant audience.

The knocking at the door came just before eight-thirty.

Lily, her arms burdened with packages, pushed into the small foyer before he pulled the door completely open. He could feel the excitement coming through the door with her. She dropped the boxes and plastic bags in the center of the floor and whirled, laughing, to face him, executing an amazing pirouette on the toes of her left foot.

"Oh, Sam, what a glorious evening!"

With one long stride she was on him. Remembering the previous time she threw herself against him, Sam braced himself. As before, she was voracious in her wants, hands clutching and stroking him, mouth sucking the breath from his lungs, while all the time the long, solid length of her body ground into him.

Finally, she drew back. Her nostrils flared. Her mouth hung open. Her eyes were wet chips of crystal penetrating to the very corners of his being. Bones of cheeks and jaw were sharp-edged beneath the stretched skin. The face of a hunting predator filling his vision, only inches from him, the hot breath from its curled mouth burning on his cheeks. Before he could react, the face was gone, and he was staring into the passion-hazed features of an extremely beautiful woman, adoration replacing lust on the handsome features, leaving him feeling his mind was playing tricks on him, or that he was standing on the edge of a dark fantasy.

He knew that this was going to be a sleepless night.

The report of another infant dying during the previous night's storm was broadcast on the morning news while Sam was having his first mug of coffee. The baby had apparently died of Sudden Infant Death Syndrome.

He gave the announcement little attention, because his thoughts were occupied with the proposition made by Lily in the early hours of the morning when the fury of her needs had finally subsided. She had lain quietly at his side, staring at the ceiling. He was not surprised when she turned on her left side and looked seriously at him.

"Sam, I want to work at your office until your assistant returns. It will occupy my time until my things arrive and I can pursue my own work."

"Work for me? Are you serious?"

"Yes, Sam, very serious." Nothing in her face reflected anything but the confidence of a poised woman. "I'm not a neophyte in office rituals. I know the procedures. I can type and file and answer the telephone. And I learn quickly. Any situations unique to your business, I could master with one showing."

Automatically, he wanted to inquire where she had obtained her experience, but just as instinctively knew it would be another question she would avoid answering. "I can't think of you as a person to tie herself to a routine."

"I'm adaptable, Sam."

There were no shadows in her eyes, but he was

cognizant of complicated movements of color within their green depths. He looked away.

"Oh, Sam, don't look like that. There are many things we do not know about each other, are there not? Our pasts are inconsequential to our present."

He could only agree, if he didn't want to lose her. In the silence of the townhouse he could hear the murmuring of the air conditioner like a deeply buried engine. "You said working would occupy your time until your things arrive. What sort of work will you do then?"

"Mostly I sculpt, Sam, but I fear that many of my pieces do not get beyond a clay model."

"You're a surprising woman, Lily. Office worker. Sculptress. Are there any other secrets you'd like to confess?"

The shadows in the back of her eyes surfaced, became tiny glints, then rapidly receded. A muscle along her jaw quivered, then quieted. "I do not confess, Sam. Those who disclose their secrets to a listener, even one sitting in a booth behind a fretwork of wood, are fools and cowards."

He lay motionless, listening to the air conditioner. Something dark moved into the room, lingered, then went away. He made himself ignore it.

"Do you sell your work?" he asked. "Or is it just a pastime, a hobby?"

The severity was gone from her eyes. He was aware of her body relaxing and the warmth from it creeping over him. She ran her fingertips softly along his cheek. "It is both, Sam. Primarily it is done to occupy my time, but occasionally I will sell a piece to supplement my income. Mostly it is a solitary venture . . . a fulfillment of memories and wishes."

Her fingers moved from his cheek down the side of his neck to his chest, where she spread her hand and began a slow caressing.

"You will allow me to work in your office, at least for a time, Sam?"

"Hmmm—mmm—"

She smiled then, a slow, moist smile, while the green in her eyes became fathomless.

Shortly after that, she was gone to her own place, saying she would commence work Monday.

7

MOST OF SUNDAY AFTERNOON THE BIG, NOISY SOUND OF
hard-rock music, too full of twanging guitars, came
from the stereo which had been set up beside the pool.
It was all momentum, a raging beat that bounced back
and forth between the walls of the apartment units
surrounding the pool area like physical waves. Around
the stereo gathered the aerobic dancers and joggers in
their string bikinis and abbreviated swim trunks, some
squirming to the rhythm, others shouting to each other
over the clamoring guitars, giving no thought to the
discomfort of their fellow residents, aware only of their
own self-gratification.

Usually Susan was able to turn down the audio
switches in her mind, dulling the noise into a thudding
background irritation, but this evening she could not
concentrate. Pulsing vibrations streaked through her.
She shifted uncomfortably on the bench before the
vanity's mirror, feeling the tension in her hand as she

began to apply the lipstick. She worked her lips together to even the color, and the image in the mirror appeared to grimace at her, tendons swelling in its neck while tiny muscles corded along the sweep of her jaw. She drew a sharp breath and quickly looked away.

She stood up, hesitated, fearful of another illusion in the glass, then slowly pivoted before the mirror, running her eyes up and down the yellow and brown dress she was wearing for the first time, deciding it blended well with her auburn hair and the amber of her eyes. She smiled, then turned off the overhead light with a flip motion of her finger on the switch.

It was a week since her illness had forced her to break the dinner date with Sam, over a week since she had last seen him. He had phoned twice, inquiring about her health, inviting her out to dinner again. She drew in her breath and chuckled to herself because, whatever Sam wanted to talk about, she also had something very important to discuss with him.

Twice this past week, Kellen Atwood had driven her home from work, even though there had been no rain, and last night they had had their first date. They went to a movie and for sandwiches afterwards, but some of her self-installed emotional insulation had been stripped away. Kellen was attractive and companionable. She wanted to tell Sam, because she knew, although he never mentioned it, that he was concerned about her social life. Once again she thought that in some ways it was too bad she and Sam were just friends. Yet they both knew that sex might teeter and unbalance that which was between them, and neither wanted to chance losing the very special and beautiful friendship they shared.

Ten minutes later, when she opened the front door in answer to the chimes, Sam was standing on the threshold with a smile on his lips. His eyes, though, were empty of pleasure. It was as if they were looking at her through mist. She looked away, down to the white cardboard box he carried.

He held it out to her. "I'm sorry."

She took the box, opening it to reveal an orchid, white with a yellow throat. Smiling, she asked, "What about?"

"Not rescheduling before now. I've been ungodly busy." He looked back over his shoulder at the group bunched around the stereo. "Does that take place every night?"

"No, only when they have something to celebrate, like swimming an extra lap or jogging an extra kilometer. About three nights a week." She stepped back. "Come in. The walls give some protection."

She closed the door, slightly muffling the racket, then picked up the orchid. "How did you know I'd be wearing yellow?"

"I didn't. I was thinking of your eyes."

She looked at him again. His eyes had cleared and were watching her with a little boy's eagerness to please. She held out the blossom. "Would you pin it on?"

When he was finished, he placed both hands on her shoulders, and she felt a pressure in his fingers as though he was trying to hold her from slipping away.

"I've missed you, Susan." He squeezed her shoulders, then dropped his hands.

He had reservations at a small, stylish restaurant that had opened recently, hoping to cater to the expanding cosmopolitan area. A pianist played inoffensive selections, waiters tiptoed between the tables, the entrees struggled to be seen among the garnishes on the plate. Without changes, the establishment would not survive.

Halfway through the meal, Sam looked around the shadow-haunted room, then shook his head. "Well, coming here wasn't my first mistake this week."

Little lines she didn't remember traced the outline of

his mouth, and between his brows the beginning of a furrow shadowed the bridge of his nose.

"Are you feeling all right, Sam?"

"Yes. Why?"

"You look tired."

"No, just busy." Once more he scanned the shadows. "There're times when I wonder if events haven't gotten beyond my control. More than once, I've thought I can't keep the pace up much longer. Events to be rescheduled. Meetings to attend. Clients to be soothed."

"Has Cindy come back to work yet?"

For the moment he looked at her before answering, the haze that hung before his eyes at the apartment's door moved across them again. Then he shifted his stare to gaze over her shoulder.

"No, not yet. A woman living in my townhouse complex is filling in for her. She's very competent and is doing an excellent job. But I wish Cindy would come back. I've phoned several times, and she seems to be recovering, but more slowly than I'd have thought."

He seemed to be reciting the words from memory, revealing only an abridged version of what he truly thought. Susan could not look at him and allowed her gaze to wander the room. She immediately became aware of a stirring around the edges of her vision, of shadows moving, and a vague silhouette formed in the darkness at the back of the restaurant. It seemed to have a woman's shape, seemed to be studying the couple. Quickly Susan took a long swallow of her wine. Its tartness counteracted her goose pimples.

"Have you been to see Cindy?" she asked, finally, striving to turn her mind away from what it was imagining.

"No, I'm sorry to say. I've phoned and sent flowers."

"I think you should go, though. You know she'd appreciate it."

"I know I should. But it's this damn tight situation I'm in, Susan. The Versailles Garden account, in all honesty, is more than I'm equipped to handle. It's the type of campaign to be handled by a big-city advertising agency, not a backwater PR firm specializing in four-bit accounts. Thank God, Lily is so goddamn exceptional . . . so competent."

"Lily?"

"The woman filling in for Cindy."

While he spoke the restaurant continued to darken, transformed into a cavern filled with creatures that never saw the light of the sun. She knew this was all in her mind, but nevertheless was powerless to ward off the piercing intensity of the effect.

"You said you had something important you wanted to talk to me about. What is it?"

He did not answer, but continued to study the shadows somewhere beyond her. The subdued clattered of silverware combined delicately with discreet voices and the bland piano music. Susan was certain she saw the indistinct form move, drifting closer.

Finally, he said, "The woman who's taking Cindy's place. Lily."

"Well, it sounds to me as if you were lucky to find someone like her, if she's so good in the office."

"Actually, she found me." He spoke so low she was forced to lean toward him. "It was the night I saw the strange bird I told you about. Not too long after the bird disappeared, she called to me from the top of a dune. Her car was stuck in loose sand at that beach access south of my place."

"Oh?"

He began to talk. The words came slowly, establishing their own cadence, some of his sentences short, others rambling and awkward. He was like a man attempting to cleanse his being of thoughts and memo-

ries which had become too great a burden for him to
carry alone.

He told her the woman was from someplace in the
Middle East. Lily, he said, was the only name she had
given him because her surname was difficult to pronounce. She was a divorcée, apparently receiving a
substantial monthly allowance from oil and other investments. She had traveled throughout the world, and
in her wanderings, he'd gathered, she had studied both
Nature and Self. Now she had rented a townhouse in
his complex—in his building, in fact.

The inflections of his voice carried a suggestion of
disbelief, as if what he was saying challenged credibil-
ity.

Before she asked the question, Susan knew what the
answer would be, but she asked it anyway. "Is she
beautiful, Sam?"

"Very." The answer came immediately, without fore-
thought.

"But you're troubled, aren't you?"

"Yes."

"Why, Sam? From what you've told me, she seems
like quite a woman. Beautiful, competent, and apparently good company."

He ran his tongue around his lips and hunched
toward her across the table. "I know, that's all true,
but—well, there's something undefinable about her,
something that borders on the eerie. Sometimes I've
received the impression there's another person living
inside her—and when that woman looks out through
Lily's eyes, all I see is seething hate."

"A dual personality?"

"I don't know."

"Sam, if that's so, and if that inner person is filled
with hate, there could be danger there."

"I know."

"Then why take the chance?"

He shook his head and leaned back in his chair. She watched the weariness descend on his face again. Then a thin smile touched his lips. "Well, she's very physical."

"You mean she's good in bed?"

"And about any other place when the mood hits her. Particularly after she's been walking through a storm."

"She goes out in storms?"

He nodded, then told her what Lily had said about her affinity with the night and with storms.

He was looking down at his empty wine glass while he talked, and Susan studied his face. Beneath the surface, she detected frustration, and strain. Whether he realized it or not, something more than the flesh of her body was binding him to Lily, something, Susan felt, that was intricate and committed. She wondered if a mild shock treatment would help.

"Sam, you look like hell. I mean it. I can understand a man working himself to a frazzle, but I can't understand a man fucking himself to death."

He looked at her sharply. "Susan—"

"I got your attention, didn't I?" She reached across the table to take one of his hands in hers. "Sam, I don't think you've told me everything about this Lily. I don't think you can, because I don't think you know everything. Be careful. Maybe she is just a weird nympho, Sam, but don't let your libido overpower your mind."

"That's what I've been doing, isn't it?"

"I don't know. This is the first you've told me about her, and there might be more to it than what you've said . . . but it sounds like it, yes."

For a long moment, he stared through her, and she had the feeling he was searching for an identity that had become lost. Then he squeezed her hand. "Thanks. You're a hell of a person, Susan Rutledge."

"You're something yourself, Sam Young."

He laughed. "Okay, okay. Enough of the mutual-admiration society. Between you and me, I've had enough of this place. What say we go?"

She nodded, then remembered she hadn't told him about Kellen.

Walking to his car, they saw the fan-shaped reflections of lightning below the western horizon and, barely audible over the engine noises and swishing tires of passing traffic, heard the distant thunder's rumble.

When they were in the car with the engine running, Sam said, "Let's take a ride."

On Highway A1A, he drove south. Susan looked out the window at her side, watched lights blurring past in subdued streaks of amber, white, and yellow. He passed the entrance gates to his townhouse complex, continuing south on A1A through an area only recently discovered by the developers and therefore still virgin. To the right, night-hidden fields stretched to the Indian River; on the left, sand dunes rose in dark humps against the still-unclouded eastern sky. Eighteen miles ahead lay Sebastian Inlet, where the waters of the Atlantic and the river battled one another in a narrow channel between the dunes. To the west, the storm had shoved its way over the horizon. The lightning was defined veins of greenish-white scampering across the sky. With the windows up and the air conditioner running, the thunder was muted.

"Sam, I've got something to tell you too." The words came hesitantly. "I've met a man who I'm beginning to like in a very special way."

"Hey, that's great! That's just great." He was genuinely pleased. "What's his name and what does he do?"

"His name's Kellen Atwood, and he's an English and Literature instructor at the college."

"Tell me about him. You've been listening to my teenage outpourings all evening; now it's your turn to talk."

She discovered it wasn't difficult to speak of Kellen, and she told him of Kellen's outward bashfulness, his rather low-key life-style, even the wayward lock of hair that continually fell over his left eye.

"Of course," she finished, "we've only had one real date, but, well—"

"The chemistry's there?"

"Yes, I think it is."

He took his eyes off the road to look at her. "There've been times I wished our chemistry, as great as it is, was that kind."

"Me too, Sam, but what we have is very, very special, very enduring and true."

"I know. We're lucky, Susan. We're so damn fortunate."

They rode in silence, while to the west, the first storm in a week moved toward the coast. Sam's fingers began to flex on the steering wheel. Susan knew his problems were still prying at his mind.

"You're still tense, aren't you, Sam?"

"I'm in over my head with the Versailles Garden people," he said. "Oh, I can give them one hell of a job for their money, but I'm straining my ability and my facilities to do it, and I keep wondering if I could do it without Lily. I don't know where she obtained her experience, but, my God, she's an exceptional woman." He stopped abruptly and shook his head. "If only there wasn't all this mystery surrounding her."

"Sam, it sounds as if you're trying to justify the relationship." She reached over and gently laid her left hand on his thigh. "Are you comfortable with her? Like I am with Kellen?"

"Damn it, Susan, I just don't know. There's this unreality about her I can't comprehend, an ethereal quality that just doesn't belong, if you know what I mean. Yet, God knows, I'm attracted to her."

"More than biologically, Sam?"

He stared ahead into the night for a moment. "I'd
like to think so, but I can't really get a fix on her values,
so I can't say." He sighed. "I guess I'm caught in an
erotic web that I helped to weave. Christ, I envy what
you and Kellen have."

The rain came all at once, in a roaring, curling wave.
Somewhere above them, hidden behind the black
clouds, a cosmic dam had collapsed and a hurtling
avalanche of water battered the car.

Sam let up on the accelerator. Buffeted by a swirling
wind and rocked with the solid hammering of the rain,
the BMW lost speed immediately. Susan pressed her
arms across her stomach, digging suddenly nervous
fingers into her upper arms. Something about this
storm wracked her nerves. The automobile seemed to
be the focal point of its fury, the sole intent of its winds
being to blow the car out into the dark waters of the
Atlantic. She looked at Sam. His hands were tightly
curled on the steering wheel. His eyes were narrowed,
peering through the nearly opaque waterfall which had
filled the windshield. In spite of the air-conditioning, a
sheen of perspiration on his face reflected the instrument lights to give his features a green-tinted, waxwork
appearance.

"This is a bummer," he muttered. "I think we'd
better turn around and go back."

"I agree. This is worse than usual."

"If it's still coming down like this when we reach the
complex, we'll pull into my place."

"I think that's a good idea." Her voice was calm, but
her entire body, every muscle and fiber and tendon,
ached with tension. Deep inside her something stirred
from its coils in a remote area of her consciousness. She
felt herself growing more alert, stretching her senses.
Ancient memories were subtly adjusting her muscles
and tendons to a defensive attitude.

Gradually the rain slackened, the wind lost its banshee wail. Its strength faded as well, and Susan imagined that the great set of lungs from which the wind had come must surely now need refilling. But the lightning continued its jagged slashing of the heavens, and the thunder prowled along the coastline.

Sam gave her a quick look. "It's easing a little. Maybe we'd better keep going. We'll probably be out of the worst of it after we cross the causeway."

She only nodded.

More like will-o'-the-wisps than lightning fixtures, the amber lamps at the entrance to the townhouse complex glowed faintly.

The black car emerged from the driveway to the accompaniement of a brilliant flash of lightning. Like a shiny, nocturnal beast spawned by the hissing explosion of light, the automobile lunged from the driveway and turned north on A1A, its speed increasing as though it wanted to lose itself once more in the darkness from which it sprang.

Before her eyes snapped shut against the brain-gouging light, Susan glimpsed a woman behind the wheel of the car, a black-haired woman who cast a hurried glance in their direction as she steered the car through its turn. Susan had the distinct impression the driver of the car was not a stranger to her.

When she opened her eyes, they were past the complex entrance. Sam was slowly feeding gas to the BMW. Beneath a scowl, his eyes peered straight ahead to where the taillights of the black car disappeared behind a curtain of rain. Susan was certain that if she had not been with him, he would be pursuing the black machine at top speed.

"Do you know the woman driving that car?" she asked.

He gave a stiff-necked nod. "It was Lily."

"Oh."

"Like I told you, she likes storms."

She made no comment. Inside her confusion and astonishment mixed with a cold splash of remaining apprehension.

Despite her protests, when they arrived at her apartment, he walked her through the rain to her door. When they reached the stoop, she dug into her purse for her keys. Before she put them in the lock, she turned toward Sam. Very deliberately, he slowly raised his arms and put them around her waist.

He brushed her lips with his. "Thanks for listening, and good luck with Kellen."

"Thanks, Sam. And remember I'm always here to help, if you need me."

He nodded.

Out in the rain something moved, sending sluggish ripples through the rain. They both felt its presence and stepped apart, looking out into the blurred night. Other than the steady patter of the rain, there was no sound. A chill, not from her rain-wet clothing, crossed her shoulders and streamed through her.

Then Sam pulled her closer. She felt protected.

"There's something out there," he said.

"I know."

"Maybe it's a security guard, trying to be discreet."

"There's no security patrol here."

"A Peeping Tom, then?"

"It could be." But she didn't think so, and knew that Sam didn't either. Whatever was watching them could not be explained by quick rationalizations. If there was a living thing prowling about in the darkness, the ancient memories which had started to awaken in Susan told her it was nothing human.

Then it was gone. The night was empty. Sam's arms loosened around her. She shivered, her mind immediately erasing the half-images it had begun to form.

Sam dropped his arms. "It must have been some kind of atmospheric depression caused by the air currents among the buildings."

She knew he didn't believe that any more than the Peeping Tom suggestion, but nodded in agreement, wanting to believe it herself.

He gave her a quick kiss on the forehead. "Get inside and lock your doors."

She gazed at him, trying to see his thoughts in his eyes. "Do you want to come in until the rain lets up?"

He shook his head. "Thanks, but I think I'll head back home."

"Sam, be careful, please."

"I will, and you lock your doors and throw your bolts."

He stepped out into the rain.

For some reason, she felt a terrible cold loneliness as he disappeared into the darkness.

Inside the apartment, she immediately went to the bedroom, where she struggled out of her clothing, the wet dress material clinging to her, heavy and cloying. Free of it, she hung the garment to drip into the bathtub, worrying if it would ever recover from tonight's soaking, then vigorously toweled her hair.

Slipping into a short nightgown, she sat at the vanity to brush her hair. She made faces at the mirror, contorting her features as far out of form as her muscles would permit, but not once did the grotesque reflection that had glared at her from the glass reappear.

After sixty strokes, she became bored with the task and laid the brush down, then switched off the blue-shaded vanity light. Darkness tumbled into the room, black darkness in which there was no center, no end. When it had filled the room it tried to pry into her mind. She fought it off, erecting a wall around her mind.

She went to the window to see if the rain was

slackening. It still etched the night with flutes and veins, drawing squiggly designs on the windowpane. The shower was abnormally long for a summer thunderstorm, and she hoped Sam had gotten home with no difficulties.

She was turning from the window when she glimpsed movement. She blinked rapidly, causing the outside scene to flicker as if strobe-lighted. At first she saw nothing, then an undefined blackness moved swiftly from around the corner of the neighboring apartment building, heading for the parking lot. She thought she saw shoulders and haunches, and four moving legs, but the black thing seemed to be part of the rain itself, wafting through the night as if propelled by the air currents circling the buildings. Then, as she focused on it, what could have been a head turned red eyes on her just before it vanished, leaving the rain and the night undisturbed.

8

SAM STOOD AT THE KITCHEN SINK, ALLOWING HOT WATER TO run into the empty coffee mug, watching the rising steam. Outside the townhouse, the morning was sullen. A high haze filtered the sunlight into a murky gray. When he had stepped out onto the patio half an hour earlier, the air was oppressive, damp enough to be wrung out. Like the sky, the ocean was dingy and depleted. The stench of things spewed onto the beach by the night's storm was musty and overrich, the smell of decomposition, the stink of death.

He turned off the faucet, shook the mug, then placed it in the wire basket on the drainboard. He looked around the kitchen, then the portion of the dining room he could see from where he stood. Both rooms were drab. His mood was not any better. The day, he decided, was commencing with a dull monotony.

For the second time since her arrival, Lily had not

spent the night with him. He wondered when she had returned to her apartment from the drive in the storm he and Susan had seen her starting the night before.

He lit a cigarette and looked at the clock on the dining-room wall. Ten after eight. In an hour and twenty minutes, the final meeting with the Versailles Garden people was due to begin. It would be the wrap-up to the fuss of the last ten days. He was sorry that it was ending, because in spite of the gulped meals and endless meetings, the project had been fun. Soon he would once again be just a small-town public-relations firm with too few clients in an area with too small a population.

The telephone rang. In the gloomy stillness, the sound was shrill, shattering the quiet.

"Sam? Oh God, I'm glad I got you before you left for your office." It was Susan. Her voice was piping and scratched. "I saw something out in the dark last night, from my bedroom window."

"What was it?"

"Sam, I don't know—a black blob of an animal of some kind. I-I think I saw four legs and—and red gleaming eyes looking at me."

"What?"

"Oh, Sam, I know it sounds crazy. It is crazy. But I saw it! I saw it, and I know it was real. I almost called the police, but how do you report a black blob?"

"Not very easily, I guess."

"Sam, have you heard the news this morning?"

"No."

"Another baby died last night, shortly after I saw that thing. It lived only a short distance from here."

The back of his neck prickled. His fingers tightened around the telephone.

"You think whatever it was you saw is connected with that death?"

"Yes. No. Oh, I don't know, Sam. But there's a very sweet baby living in the building next to me. Bridget Neilson."

"So?"

"Maybe our standing out there prevented it from getting Bridget."

"Jesus!"

There was a long pause as though she was examining thoughts before putting them into words. Then she said, "I didn't say anything because I thought it was my imagination, but last night in the restaurant I kept seeing something in the shadows, a blurry form that looked like a woman watching us. Now that I think more about it, it was as if whatever it was was jealous we were together. Oh, Sam, I don't know . . . I'm having crazy thoughts this morning."

He remembered the sensation of being watched at the seafood restaurant when he and Susan were there. "No, no, maybe you're not. But why does that make you think the baby in your apartment was in danger from whatever you saw?"

"I told you, these are crazy thoughts, but—but, damn it, what if we were being watched, what if it was jealous of me being with you and wanted to punish me by killing a baby I know and like? If something can make itself practically invisible and hide in shadows, it certainly could learn how I feel about Bridget." She drew a deep breath. "There—I said it all."

For a moment, he thought he again smelled the putrid stench of the things the sea had vomited up during the storm. He wondered if this was what evil smelled like.

"Maybe you'd better phone the police."

"They wouldn't believe me, you know that."

"I know, but it might free your conscience, and, though I doubt it, they might conduct some sort of half-assed investigation. If there was something there, it's possible it left a trail of droppings, some kind of spoor."

"Well . . . you might be right." She tried to give a self-deprecatory laugh. It was a hoarse rasp in his ear. "I guess I'm overreacting, aren't I?"

"No, I don't think so. We did feel something, and you saw something. I'm glad you phoned."

"Well, I appreciate your listening, Sam, and putting up with my wild theories so early in the morning, but I've got to scoot. I've only twenty minutes to get to the library. Phone me when you can, will you?"

"Believe it."

When he hung up, he drew a long breath. The expansion of his chest and lungs hurt. Other than Cindy's baby, he hadn't paid that much attention to the baby deaths occurring in the area. He didn't know how many there had been, but guessed at least six or seven over the last month or so. All diagnosed as Sudden Infant Death Syndrome. On a depressing morning such as this, one might question if it was coincidence. He tried to remember more of what he had heard or read, but couldn't.

A semi partially blocked the entrance to the driveway when he went out to his garage. Two men balanced a massive, ornately carved wooden chest on a four-wheel dolly they were pushing along the edge of the driveway's asphalt. Both men were big, their slabbed muscles bulging T-shirts stained with sweat. Sam watched them manipulate their load around the driveway's curve. The oversized chest, Sam thought, was designed as a piece of furniture, not a shipping crate.

The chest was intricately carved. Intertwining vines were covered with delicately detailed leaves, and behind the vines, as if growing deeper in a shadowy garden, flower blossoms extended long, curling petals. Though he wasn't sure, as the chest moved past him, he thought he saw shadow-hidden animals peering out

from secret haunts in the vegetation. Age had darkened
the wood and laid a patina on its tight, smooth grain.

"Good morning, Sam."

Startled, he swung to his right. Lily, dressed for the
office, was striding toward him and the men. She
stopped at Sam's side, but spoke to the men.

"You are early. I was told you would not arrive until
later today."

The older of the men stopped pushing. He ran a hand
across his forehead, then snapped the sweat accumulated in it to the ground. "That's the way it was
planned, but somehow this got loaded last, so we have
to get it out to reach the other stuff." He pulled a sheath
of papers folded lengthwise from his hip pocket,
"You're gonna have to sign for this, lady, if you're
Lily."

"I'm Lily."

The man looked perplexed. "You don't have a last
name?"

Her laugh came quickly. "Yes, but it is so difficult to
spell and pronounce in your language, I seldom use it."
She moved closer to Sam, very nearly touching him.
"My friend here will tell you that by not using a last
name I am not an incomplete woman."

The man looked at Sam, studied him speculatively
for a moment, then shook his head and turned away.
"Anything you say, lady. Come on, Ted, let's get this to
Number Four."

"Jesus Christ, Lily, what was that all about?"

"Did I embarrass you, Sam?" She closed completely
the narrow distance between them, pressing her left
breast into his right arm, canting her left hip against
him. "You are so full of morals, my sweet and innocent
Sam."

She had embarrassed him, and he didn't try to deny
it. Even her pneumatic softness against his arm he felt
with a clinical awareness. She looked at him, first

questioningly, then amused, then with annoyance. Scowling, she backed away from him.

"What's wrong with you, Sam? Did you arise from the wrong side of the bed this morning?"

He turned to face her directly. "No."

"Then what is it?"

"I had a phone call."

"So?" She was standing very still, her almond eyes watching him intently.

"So?" He shrugged. "I have a good friend who saw something strange last night, and shortly after she saw it, not too far away a baby died."

"And you are permitting that to upset your day?"

"I guess I am."

"That's foolish. A friend has an hallucination, and a baby dies. They are both common occurrences, happening all the time."

"So I let it get to me." He looked at the two men who were almost to her front door. "What's in that thing?"

"Me, Sam." Her voice was suddenly warm. "It contains all the things that make my life. Bric-a-brac. Memories. Bindings to my past. It has been in my family since the family began."

"An heirloom? What you sent to San Juan for?"

"Yes."

He watched her face draw taut. It was not the rigid sharpness he'd witnessed before, but rather the bleakness of features when a person is experiencing deep emotions and withholding them from others. Whatever was in the chest, he realized, was very precious to Lily. He looked at the two men again. They were at the front door of her townhouse, impatiently awaiting her.

"I've got to go," he said. "The Versailles people are due at nine-thirty."

"Yes, I know."

He nodded in the direction of the chest. "Are you going to be able to come?"

"Yes."

He watched her stride along the driveway in the direction of the waiting men, seeing the firm hip and thigh flesh rippling over long, flexing muscles. He sensed, at that moment, the powers in her, a force beyond comprehension.

Jackson Cotter leaned back in his chair, crossing his hands behind his neck. Everything about the man was an advertisement for Versailles Garden Spas, appropriate, since Cotter was corporate vice-president. Well over six feet tall, his heavy frame carried accentuated muscles, all neatly packaged by a skin tanned one shade lighter than walnut. Thick, modishly cut hair, blond with the cooperation of nature and ointments contained in various bottles, gave the impression of a mane. Sam liked the man. During the past ten days, Cotter had made four trips from Miami, watching, suggesting, but never intruding.

"It's been fun," Cotter said. "You know, I wish it wasn't over, but I think we've put together a campaign the health-freaks won't be able to resist." All of the man's masculinity was jeopardized by his voice. It was thin, dangerously close to tenor.

"It turned out better than even Sam or I envisioned," Willy Kavanaugh said. "It's a slick package. Everything is a ninety-percent improvement over what we've been using: brochures, TV commercials, and radio spots —everything."

"Make that one hundred and ten percent." Sam laughed.

Murray Straus said, "Let's give a lot of credit to Sam's new secretary. That woman has a computer brain in her skull."

"Yeah, and what a skull! What an everything. God, I wish we'd been able to talk her into being the Versailles Woman. She makes the model we used look washed out." With his hands still clasped behind his neck, Cotter shook his head. "I can't believe a person refusing compensation either. Who the hell does anything for free these days? She wouldn't refuse if we made her guest of honor at a small wrap-up party, would she, Sam?"

"I shouldn't think so. We can ask her when she gets here."

The talk drifted back to business, but Sam felt an expectancy in the office, as if each man was merely marking time, waiting for Lily, dreaming of her.

When she arrived, Lily paused immediately inside the door, tall, assured, and poised. Very slowly, holding their attention, she surveyed them gathering. There was no smile on her full lips. But her mouth was softly set, full and broad. Sam thought he detected a humming in the room as the bodies of the three men responded.

Then she laughed her most throaty laugh, and said, "I feel I am trespassing."

Willy Kavanaugh pushed himself to his feet. "God, no, Lily. The fact is, we were waiting for you."

She smiled prettily. "Should I be honored or worried?"

"Honored, my dear." Jackson Cotter dropped his hands from behind his neck and sat up straight in his chair. "Since you refused to accept any pay for all the work you did on this job, we want you as guest of honor at a small party. What do you say?"

"I say yes, Jackson Cotter, and I thank all of you."

"I'll make reservations at the Hilton," Wally said.

"No, hold on." Murray Straus's amiable smile crumbled his broad face into a patchwork of creases. "These kinds of parties are to make noise at, to relax at, you know what I mean? So, what's wrong with an old-fashioned beach party? Willy, you could bring your kids. That way we can have a real shindig without bankrupting Versailles Garden."

"Fires aren't permitted on the beach anymore, Murray," Willy said.

Murray looked at Sam. "What about your place? We can use the beach and do the cooking by the pool. That allowed?"

"It is my place too," Lily said, "and I think it is a wonderful idea, Murray."

Sam glanced at her, taken aback. This was the first time she'd been interested in social activities. He saw nothing on her face, but in her eyes something was forming, some mixture of feelings he could not define. Then, suddenly, the green was as clear as the purest Columbian emerald.

Cotter stood up. "How about tomorrow evening? I've got to get back south as soon as possible."

There was unanimous agreement. Willy Kavanaugh said he would be responsible for obtaining the food and drink, and the meeting broke up. Watching Willy, the last to go out the door, Sam realized how close these men had been drawn together during the hectic ten days just past.

"I think I'll go over to the post office." He wanted a physical action to offset the melancholy he was once again feeling.

"What is wrong, Sam?"

"It's just the natural letdown after an emotional high."

She walked slowly toward him. Just before she put her arms around him, he realized to what extent he had come to accept her influence.

She kissed him. He felt an overpowering lust invade him, driven into him by her probing tongue. When she finally pulled her mouth away, only her green eyes occupied his field of vision. Even as he tried to look away, his senses started to funnel into them as if a maelstrom was sucking him into a place from which there might be no escape.

Then he heard her whispering softly. "Tomorrow night, after the party, my Sam, I will take you far away from depression, so far you will never return to it." There was no way to extract himself from the emotional whirlpool. "My home is ready for you to visit."

He thought of the chest that had arrived that morning, and what she had said about it. "Oh?"

"Do not sound so skeptical, Sam. I promise you a wonderous night beyond all dimensions. Time will be a meaningless thing to us."

He shook his head. "That's a big promise."

She smiled gently. "It is one I will keep."

After a moment, he nodded.

"You astonished me when you said holding the party at our place was a good idea."

Her mouth curved in a generous smile, and her eyes widened. "It will be more interesting there, Sam."

"Maybe we should ask the Ashleys and Langstroms if they would mind. Their places face the pool too."

"Oh, Sam, you know they will love it."

He nodded. Glenn Ashley would love anything with which alcohol was connected. Holly and Todd were infatuated with whatever promised a good time. And Jetta, even knowing her husband would become the party drunk, might experience some escape from her fears.

"Go to the post office, Sam," she said, "and let me get acquainted with our other accounts. We have ignored them this past week."

The morning haze was gone, melted in the sun's determined heat. In its place, oversized, puffy clouds elaborately decorated the aquamarine sky. Sam turned on the BMW's air conditioner. He seldom used it on the trip across the causeway, but pulling out of the parking lot he'd impulsively decided to visit Cindy. Susan had clearly disapproved of his lack of attention to his assistant and friend, and he was feeling guilty.

With the mail from the post office box on the seat beside him, Sam drove south on Babcock Street to Palm Bay.

Cindy's house was in a new development, so recently completed that it still looked untenanted. The entire neighborhood still looked sterile. The lawns were manicured, the concrete of the streets still retained its bleached whiteness. In time, Sam supposed, it would become likeable, much the same as a bland young face matures with character lines and individuality.

Cindy's house was L-shaped, constructed of imitation fieldstone. It looked naked and exposed behind a scrubby growth of young plantings. The grass of the front lawn was in the first stages of becoming unkept.

After parking in the driveway, he walked along a concrete path that curved to the front door. Perhaps half a minute passed after he pressed the door bell before Cindy opened the door the six inches permitted by a safety chain and peered out at him.

"Sam! Oh, Sam, come in. Just a second while I undo this contraption."

The door closed, then opened again, revealing Cindy of the golden hair, the perennial teenage face, and the vital body. She was a different woman. Much of the creaminess was gone from her complexion, replaced by a chilled pallor. Her eyes remained petal blue, but the vivid sparkle, as he had feared, had been washed away by tears. Her grief was apparent, but she managed to smile.

"Come in, Sam, please. It's good to see you."

Behind closed drapes, the inside of the house was gloomy, the silence cloying, giving him the feeling of wading through strands of a huge, invisible web. Anger at such a capricious fate surged through him.

When they were seated, she asked if he would like something to drink. He declined, then asked how she was doing. She answered, "Just fine, Sam."

"I should have come before now," he said. He heard a wisp of shame in his voice. "I'm sorry, Cindy."

"You shouldn't be. You were thinking of us. The lovely flowers you sent and your encouraging phone calls prove that. Besides, you've been busy with the Versailles Garden account."

"Yes. It was bigger than we bargained for. The damn thing kept growing and growing until we had ourselves involved in a first-line advertising campaign. Platinum Coast was suddenly playing with the big boys, and there were times I felt like a Little Leaguer standing in the middle of Yankee Stadium."

"I wish I could have been there to help, Sam. Were you able to find someone to take my place?"

He nodded. "A woman who lives in my building."

"I'm glad. I thought about it often, and I felt so guilty."

"Good God! How could you feel that way when you were going through what you were? Hey, look—if there's any guilt to be handed out, I'm the one to receive it. There were things I could have done for you and Carl, and I didn't. I'm not proud of that, Cindy."

"There's nothing anyone can do at a time like that. There really isn't, you know." She looked down at her hands.

He was becoming uneasy in the company of this meek woman whom he remembered as vivacious and driving. He leaned forward with his elbows on his knees. "Are you planning to come back to work?"

"I'd like to."

"Well, I want you to. We make a hell of a team, Cindy Chambers, you and I."

"Thanks, Sam." She looked up, and far in the back of her eyes, a sparkle was trying to ignite. "If you want me to, I can start next Monday, a week from today."

"I'd like that." He stood up. Suddenly it was imperative for him to escape the gloom. "Nine o'clock next Monday morning. Okay?"

"Okay, Sam." She rose too, and walked toward the front door with Sam. "Thanks again for coming—and for the flowers."

He opened the door, then hesitated before stepping out into the flare of sunlight. "You're sure, now, that you're feeling good enough to come back?"

"I'm sure. I'm positive." She looked past him to the uncut lawn. "The worst is over. I'm in control again, and so is Carl. It was bad at first, so terribly bad, as if everything inside me just went away, leaving me with nothing, no emotions at all, only a cold emptiness. But I'm filling up again, Sam, and everything is starting to balance out." She looked at him, and he saw a pink flush on her face that he knew was not sunlight reflection. "We're going to start a family again. Carl and I are going to give Lucy a brother or sister."

He felt a sudden affection toward this young woman. Impulsively, he leaned forward and kissed her on her forehead. "Give her twins, Cindy."

On the causeway to Indialantic, he was pleased with himself for the impulse which had caused him to ask Cindy to return to work. Cindy was part of his life, his business. Lily, even with her amazing competence in the office, belonged to the private compartments, away from the public.

He wondered what Lily had planned for tomorrow night. Suddenly he felt young and naive and full of erotic expectations, anticipating the visit to her townhouse more than the big party. If she promised something special, then special it would be, beyond anything he could imagine. His hands clenched on the steering wheel.

Lily was at the receptionist's desk when he entered the office, leafing through a stack of manila client folders she had taken from the filing cabinets in the work room.

She smiled. "You have some interesting clients."

"Some dingbats, too."

She laughed and stood up, pushing the desk chair away with the backs of her knees, at the same time restacking the folders into a neat pile.

"I went to see Cindy. She must have gone through unadulterated hell, but she seems to have recovered nicely." He hurried through the next statement. "She's coming back to work a week from today."

"She is that well?"

"Yes. She's still rocky, but being here will be a therapy for her, I'm sure."

Lily said nothing as she picked up the file folders to return them to the cabinets. Sam watched her, then went into his office. He was still opening the first envelope in the stack of mail he'd brought in with him when she came to his office door.

"Sam, business is slow, and the day is all but over. Would you mind if I left?"

"No. Go ahead."

He stood at the office window and watched her leave the parking lot in her rented, black Oldsmobile. He wondered where she was going, and it was only then he remembered that neither of them, at any time during the day, had spoken of her drive into the storm the night before.

The recreational area was empty. Glenn Ashley sat on the retaining wall, his back to the pool, his sandaled feet dangling outside the wall. Sometime after three o'clock, his mind muddied around the edges, he had left the store, telling the assistant manager he had to take Jetta to a doctor's appointment. He knew the man hadn't believed him, knew the man was certain he was leaving to get a drink, and wondered how much longer he could use that damn baby in Jetta's belly as an excuse. Perhaps another week, maybe two. But no longer. He shrugged. What the hell. This job, like all the others he had ever held, was becoming too much to tolerate. Shit. All the demands made on him, plus the ones to come when the kid was born, had destroyed his whole perspective of life. Freedom—that's what it was all about, the right to choose one's destiny and follow it. Those people back in the sixties had the right idea. And now, he was going to have to drag along a squalling baby while he tried to reach his goals. To hell with it.

He didn't know where Jetta was, probably visiting somebody in the complex, and that was just fine. If she had been home when he arrived, there would have been a battle. Probably his first mistake had been to marry her, even though he loved her. Shit, he still did. But she'd been careless and got herself pregnant, then, for Christ's sake, become bull-headed and refused to have an abortion. That meant his plans went blooey—no string of shops along the coast renting recreational equipment. Damn it to hell, why did everybody think he could be a father and still follow his plans, do what he wanted? Because they didn't understand freedom, that was why. Every frigging one of them was a robot mechanically moving through a programmed life cycle. All of them were spiritually bankrupt. He looked at the half-full glass of bourbon sitting on the wall beside him, liking the way it glowed in the late afternoon sunlight. It was beautiful. In its amber hue, he found the freedom denied him everywhere else.

He lifted the drink. While it was at his lips and his head was tilted back, he saw the bird, high in the sky, a black silhouette against the empty blue, moving up leisurely from the south. Great wings occasionally stroked lazily, but mostly they remained quietly extended, forming a dark triangle that absorbed the sunlight in their blue-toned blackness. There was a stateliness about the creature, yet Glenn sensed a malignancy, a foulness that his dulled senses associated with things that lived by scavenging.

He closed his eyes, certain that when he opened them the bird would be gone, like other creatures he now and then saw after an afternoon of bourbon, especially that damned black thing that floated outside their bedroom window some nights. But the bird was still there when he looked again. He glanced around. There was no one else around to see it and verify its existence.

Opposite the townhouse complex, the bird ceased its northward flight, hovered, then circled, dropping lower to the water. Glenn's fingers tightened around his glass. A thin mesh of coldness settled on his shoulders. That damn thing was watching him.

It swooped lower. Its neck stretched, triangular head swinging back and forth. Its red eyes scanned the beach and surrounding area, glinting in the sun like hard marbles of cut glass. The bourbon turned sour in his stomach.

"What the hell are you?" he mumbled.

The bird hovered, looking directly at him, its red eyes boring right into his mind. After a long moment it rose a few feet in the calm air, slowly beating its wings, and slid south, toward a vacant area of land, disappearing behind a row of pine trees.

Glenn sat unmoving, afraid that if he even twitched, he'd tumble ten feet to the beach below. A thought tried to weave through the alcohol in his brain, but it became lost in the fog of bourbon and he sat staring down at the drink in his hand, wondering what next it would spawn.

"Are you as lonely as you look, Glenn?"

The woman's voice was low and well behind him, but he swung around startled just the same, grabbing the wall to steady himself. Standing beside the pool was the handsome woman who had just moved into Unit 4. She was dressed in black slacks and a black blouse.

He sucked in a breath and tried to smile, but knew what appeared on his lips was a lopsided grimace.

"Maybe. I don't know how I look."

"Dejected," she said in the same low voice. "Like a person alone in a great and terrible vastness."

He sat staring at her, seeing her through a multicolored mist which suddenly seemed to curl between them, diffusing her, causing her to appear to waver as though he were looking at her through a sheet of restless sun-dappled water.

"Yeah, that's me. All by myself in a frigging wasteland."

"Why, Glenn? Why are you so lost?"

She came toward him, slowly, in an almost choreographed series of movements, and even through the dullness saturating him he felt a stirring as he watched the shiftings of her strong body under the dark material of her clothing.

He forced himself to shrug. "Who knows?"

She was standing beside him now, and he could feel a warmth radiating from her and smell a faint scent that reminded him of summer gardens.

"Why, Glenn?" she asked again.

"Lots of reasons," he mumbled.

She turned her green eyes away from him to look out at the ocean. "Is one of them the pregnancy of your wife? I have received the impression you do not want a baby."

Glenn nodded. "That's part of it. I can't care for a kid and do what I want to do—at least not now. Maybe in another year or two, but not now."

"And your wife does not understand?"

"No one understands."

"There are those who do."

"Yeah? Well, not around here."

"You are not alone, Glenn. You are not the first to not want children, not the only one to know that having a child destroys all personal liberty and brings subjugation."

"Tell that to Jetta."

"I feel that it would do no good. She is merely a thrall."

Taken aback by the words, he looked at her. Then squinted. Something had happened to her face. The handsomeness was gone from it, replaced with a sharpness made up of angles and planes and tight skin. He looked away quickly.

She stirred. "I must go, Glenn."

"Yeah, sure, ah—Lily."

He remained in a huddled sitting position, staring down at the glass in his hand, as she stepped back from the wall, then moved out of his peripheral vision. He felt no desire to turn and watch the sensual swaying of her hips as he'd done on other occasions. What he had seen on her face for that brief time a moment before had drained from him all feeling of having met a kindred soul.

He lifted the glass and drank the remaining bourbon in one swallow.

9

IT WAS A BRIGHT, CLEAR NIGHT, WARM, BUT WITH AN OCEAN
breeze that reduced the humidity to a bearable sogginess. Tumbling surf provided a continuous background
murmur to talking and laughing voices. Cold and
forlorn, halfway up the eastern sky, a scimitar moon
spangled sand ridges on the beach with a lackluster
gloss. Holly Langston's stereo did its electronic best to
override the voices and the murmur of the sea with
adult contemporary music. By all criteria it had been a
successful party. Why, then, did he feel so odd, Sam
wondered. Maybe because it was Tuesday, and parties
were weekend functions.

He sat on the low wall that followed what once had
been the top of the dune line, a vodka and tonic in one
hand, a roast chicken drumstick in the other, studying
the small crowd wandering around the pool area. What
had begun as a party for eleven people had swollen into
an assembly of thirty or more. The occupants of

neighboring apartments had been drawn toward the lodestone of music, laughter, free drinks, and the possibility of puffing some Columbian Gold. Sam took a bite from the drumstick and scanned across the heads, looking for Lily. He located her on the far side of the pool, standing beside the diving board. Three unfamiliar men, probably from one of the condominiums down the beach, formed a semicircle around her. She saw him and waved. He waggled the drumstick in answer.

"She's got everything, doesn't she?"

He hadn't heard anyone approach. The woman's voice, not too far from his left ear, caused him to start. Some of his drink spilled over his fingers.

"I'm sorry. I didn't mean to startle you."

"I was daydreaming, I guess."

"Like half the other males here, about the woman in the dark blue slacks and blouse?"

"No."

He turned then, to see who he was talking to. It was the model from Miami who had posed as the Versailles Woman. A tall, darkly blonde woman in her late twenties, with a hint of muscular voluptuousness in her five feet ten inches. Hers was the modern woman's body, bursting with Nautilus machine health and potency, the body that could be obtained by any woman with the assistance, of course, of the Versailles Garden Spa. Her name was Amati Blythe. Sam suspected it wasn't the name on her birth certificate.

"She's got everything you people wanted for the Versailles Woman, plus, I understand, she works for free. Why didn't you use her instead of me?"

"We thought about it, but she indicated that she'd rather not."

"Shit, that broad doesn't kncw what she's got going for her." She turned and left.

Sam watched Amati Blythe walk toward the drinks

table. He wondered if her thought processes reached beyond the physical.

He gnawed the last of the meat off the leg bone and carried it to the garbage pail beside the food table, shouldering his way between people he had never seen before. Except for the Ashleys and Langstons and Lily, it was a gathering of strangers. The Versailles Garden people, not counting the model, were gone. Willy Kavanaugh had taken his wife and three kids home an hour before. Not much later, saying he had a job the next morning, Murray Straus and his wife had left. Not too long after that, the outsiders had begun to drift in from out of the darkness, and Sam had watched Jackson Cotter slip into the night with one arm about the waist of a platinium blonde from a neighboring condominium. No food remained, and the bottles on the drinks table were mostly empty. The freeloaders had enjoyed themselves.

"You look so alone, Sam." Lily was at his side. She looked startlingly alive. "Are you having a good time?"

He swept his arm in an arc, indicating those people who still lingered. "I feel like a stranger in my own yard."

"Ah, Sam, then I must remedy that, mustn't I? Another hour. In my home."

She turned and walked away. Maybe it was the vodka playing with his senses, but her hips seemed to sway with an uncompromising invitation.

Now he had to occupy himself for an hour. He looked at his watch. It was a few minutes after one. The party was dying. Lily was talking to two women and a man he didn't know. He thought about helping Todd and Holly gather their belongings together, but dismissed the idea. If he did that, he'd be overwhelmed by Holly's vitality. Todd flipped the off switch on the stereo. The music's abrupt ending left a hole in the air; then the silence of the night rolled in as if reclaiming a private sanctuary. Complacent in its ageless rhythm, the sea whispered.

He walked to the retaining wall and looked down at the beach. Standing at the waterline, a bulky figure was silhouetted against the moon-dabbled water. He watched it for a long time, feeling that never had he witnessed such a dreadful loneliness as that solitary figure represented.

The woman was staring out to sea, standing so rigidly she could have been mesmerized by the endless shifting of the black water. Sam suddenly recognized the brooding figure as Jetta Ashley.

He stepped back from the wall, hurried down the wooden steps to the beach, then almost jogged through the spongy softness of the sand. She heard him coming and turned to watch his last few steps.

"Jetta, what are you doing here alone?"

He was close enough to see a wan smile attempt to find life on her lips. "You mean, a woman in my condition, Sam?"

"Well, any woman, but mostly one in your condition, I guess."

He took two long breaths before she spoke. "I don't know why I'm here, not really. It seemed like a good idea to come and wade in the water, to get my feet wet."

He listened to his own still-hurried breathing, then, although he knew what the answer would be, asked, "Where's Glenn?"

"Where do you suppose? Jack Daniels got to him early tonight."

"I didn't see him leave."

"For once he was smart and just snuck away."

He reached out and took hold of her upper arm. Her skin was slippery and cold, making him think of pliant porcelain.

"Come on, let me help you back home."

She stared at him mutely, without moving. Sam knew she was desperately unhappy, though she rarely showed it, hiding her feelings behind a mask of enthusiasm for life. He dropped his eyes, unable any longer to return her stare.

"Sam, what do you know about Lily?"

"Lily?"

"Yes, the woman who moved into Number Four, the one we all know you're sleeping with."

Anger flared briefly at this unanticipated intrusion into his privacy. But it instantly died.

"Not too much, I guess. Why?"

Jetta made no answer at first, then said, in a quiet voice, "I just wondered. I think she's made you her private property. She's watching us now from up there."

He glanced up in time to see Lily turning away from the retaining wall. A wave broke on the sloping sand to send tendrils of foam around their ankles. From up on the roadway, a speeding automobile's engine snarled past. Sam was suddenly uncomfortable physically as well as mentally.

"Come on, let me help you home." He took her arm again, gave it a gentle pull. Life's warmth had returned to her skin.

She smiled. Unlike the first smile with which she greeted him, this one was healthy, almost contagious.

"Okay, let's go. Guide me and the little rascal inside safely to our door."

Neither spoke while they crossed the beach, then slowly climbed the stairs to the pool area. Sam heard only Jetta's heavy breathing. All the night sounds, all the perpetual murmurings heard only in the dark, were nonexistent, as if a great baffle had been erected between him and their source. He had the uncanny feeling of walking through a vacuum of timelessness.

Everyone was gone. Only their litter remained, spread around the pool area in desolate heaps of crumpled paper and soiled Styrofoam. When they stood before her patio door, Jetta turned to face him squarely.

"Thanks for coming down to the beach, Sam. I really appreciate it, in spite of my bad joke." She took a step toward him, stopped, and looked down at herself, then patted her stomach. "Oscar here won't permit me to thank you like I want to, but pretend I gave you a good-night kiss. Okay?"

"Okay."

She opened the gate, started through, then stopped. "Sam, you're a great guy. Be careful, please, and don't change."

She was through the gate before he could respond.

The blackness on the far side of the pool was moving, keeping pace with him as he walked along the fence to the gate leading into his patio. When he stepped through and shut the gate behind him, it hovered opposite the gate, shifting to the edge of the pool, hesitating, then slowly drifting back in the direction from which it had come. Abruptly it vanished. The darkness of the night and the humidity scurried to reclaim the place it had occupied.

She had been waiting for him, he was sure, though she behaved in the manner of a person interrupted while performing a task that required extreme concentration. He felt as if not all of her was responding when she opened the door after his second ring, because there was a distance in her eyes. They were focused on vistas where things roamed only in the mind of the watcher. Then she pulled herself back from that distant place and smiled at him.

"You came."

"Did you think I wouldn't?"

"No." The smile became knowing. "Come in, Sam . . . and welcome to my home."

But she took only a half step back, so he was forced to squeeze by her, brushing her, feeling her firmness against his chest as he did. She caught his hand and walked beside him into the small foyer.

He was surprised. Only two low-wattage bulbs burned, one in the living room atop the slender pole of a floor lamp, the other in the ceiling fixture of the dining area. What furniture he could distinguish was simple and austere, similar to Swedish Modern, mostly black and white. In the living room were three chairs, a glass-topped coffee table, and a sofa. On the floor was a white rug, on which a black design interlaced leaves with curling accentuated lines. He thought the lines and curlicues were vaguely familiar, but was unable to identify them. Beside the chairs, and at either end of the sofa, white pedestals held statuettes of the same stark hue. He was unable to define details of the carvings, but two or three he was certain had protuberances that could possibly be wings. There was a coldness in the room, which felt untouched by personality.

"Your work?" he asked, nodding at the sculptures.

"Yes. This is my own private gallery."

"Shouldn't you have the pieces spotlighted?"

She reached out and flicked on a light switch. A narrow shaft of illumination slanted down from a track light hidden in the ceiling to bathe one statue with light before vanishing as Lily again flipped the switch. Sam stood motionless, eyes still registering the image of a bird with outstretched wings swooping in a dive toward the pool of shadow that was the floor.

Lily tugged gently at his hand. "Come, Sam. This is not my home, and it is my home to which I invited you."

Still holding his hand, leading him by it as she might

a small child, she guided him up the stairs. His heart switched to a faster cadence; his breath caught in his throat. His hand within the grasp of hers began to tremble.

In the short upstairs hallway, his initial awareness was of a subtle scent filling the air. At first, he thought of cut flowers, then sachet, but there was a pungency to it too strong for either, and finally he realized the aroma was burning incense. He swallowed hard, feeling a thin sheen of perspiration dampen his skin.

Lily opened the door to one of the two bedrooms. They stood on the threshold looking into a room seen only by the pale illumination reflected from the night sky coming through the windows.

It was her studio, Sam decided. A number of pedestals held shrouded objects, ghostly looking, hovering motionless in the gloom. Another covered object sat on a table. A second table supported a mountainous gray lump of clay that occupied the center like a miniature mountain from a toy train set's landscape. On the same table lay chisels and mallets and objects he didn't recognize. Although the room was innocuous, Sam felt the first signals of tension moving through his neck and down his spine, warnings from a brain preparing its body for an unknown assault. The hand that Lily held began to sweat, and he was suddenly consumed with shame, wanting to draw it from her grasp.

He had to say something. With his free hand, he pointed at the covered object on the table in the center of the room. "Is that your present sculpture?"

"Yes."

"Can I see it?"

"Ah, Sam, I am sorry, but I never reveal my work until it is completed." The hand holding his tightened. "Besides, Sam, you did not come here to examine carvings, did you?"

She opened the door to the room across the hallway.

The perfume from the incense seeped into the hall. It eddied and curled, skimming lightly across his senses, beckoning him, luring him with wanton promises.

Looking into the room, Sam had the odd sensation that he had stepped across boundary lines into a surreal fantasy. While his beleaguered senses sought alignment, his entire awareness was of his own harsh breathing and the accompanying thump of his heart.

It was a dark room, a cube cut from the night. From pedestals draped in darkness, marble creatures of the wild examined him with blank eyes. He saw a hawk, a pelican, a kite, and an owl, their detailed stone heads craned in his direction. Snarling, with fangs exposed in mouths opened to bite, a wildcat and a jackal crouched atop their pedestals, muscles bulged before a spring.

The incense caressed him, stroking him ever so gently, slyly teasing him, building the anticipation in him with gentle expertise. He searched the room for the source of the fragrance, and found it in a bronze salamander setting on top of the wooden chest which had been delivered the other morning. A tiny flame glowed within it. Now that his eyes were acclimated, he began to pick out other details.

Thick brocades draped the walls concealing the windows so that even during the daylight hours, the room would remain dark. The bed was like nothing in his experience. Approximately king-size, it appeared to be a verdant plot lifted from a garden. Fresh flower petals were strewn across it. He recognized rose and violet and daisy among others he did not know. Weaving around the sides of the bed were lush vines and creepers in living duplication of the carved ones on the wooden chest. Fronds from potted palms arched gracefully down, creating the impression of a hidden grotto in which the bed nestled secretively. Looking at it, Sam felt a thickening in his loins. But somewhere within

him a suspicious instinct whispered that interwoven
with the vines and strewn petals, concealed with the
sweetness of the incense's headiness, there was a base-
ness and hostility. But at that moment, Lily's hand
closed tight around his and gave a little pull.

"Come, Sam. Join me in paradise."

He stepped into the room and walked by her side to
the bed of flower petals.

He had no idea what time it was. He couldn't tell if
minutes had passed, or hours, or a day. Perhaps a
lifetime. He didn't know. He didn't care.

He lay on his back on the rumpled bed among the
scattered and crushed flower petals, staring through the
canopy of arching fronds at the row of candle flames
twinkling like stars. Just before joining him on the bed,
Lily had lit the candles in their candelabras, murmuring words he did not understand. But, watching and
listening, he had known it was an oft-repeated ritual.
Along his entire length, though she was a dozen inches
away, he felt the heat of her body as if it was a crucible
in which all the wildfire of desire burned.

He squinted his eyes at the candles, diffusing their
flames even more until they became a rippling line of
amber froth. Watching them, he had the uncanny
sensation that he was seeing a serpent slithering
through the darkness, hurrying to disappear into the
eternal night. He widened his eyes, looked away from
the candles and around the darkness enfolding him,
then at Lily. While he gazed at her, he felt a strange
separation inside himself. His mind was dividing into
two antagonistic halves, one that tried to erase from its
memory banks the carnality which had occurred here
among the flower petals, while the other sought to hold
those same memories as images to recall on future
bidding.

His gaze roamed up and down the long, undulating length of Lily's sleeping nakedness, and knew that he was laying in a time and place that could not exist outside the realm of sensuality. Ever so slowly, he began stroking her.

She murmured to herself, a muzzy whisper of contentment, while he continued moving his hand over her warm, firm softness, watching her face, seeing the infinite flutter of her eyelids. He was uncertain, but he thought he sensed a movement someplace behind him in the room.

Lily's eyes slowly opened, the long black lashes dusting their green with shadow. Full and ripe, her lips parted in a slow smile.

"Have I pleased you?" Her voice was unusually small. "I want you to know that I am capable . . . that I could have."

He didn't understand what she meant, but he hunched himself forward, almost touching her, and kissed her on the tip of her nose. With a tiny sigh, she arched so their bodies touched.

"I belong to you." Her murmur was nearly inaudible. "I was meant to belong to you."

His caressing hand stopped on the fullness of her flank. She stared at him through her lashes a split second longer, then encircled his shoulders with her left arm, drawing herself tight to him, hungrily seeking his lips with her own, finding them and feasting on them.

He rolled onto his back, pulling her with him, so she sprawled on top of him and he felt the fires that burned within her searing him from his chest to his loins.

She took his face between her cupped hands. He felt her legs spreading, her thighs on either side of his hips.

After a while, she laid her cheek on his chest. A great shudder ran the length of her.

"Oh, Adam . . . Adam . . ."

When she spoke, a ripple ran through the darkness of the room. In their candelabra, the candles flickered as if a wind was hurrying through. And in the wavering light, he saw the marble fowl and animals staring at him.

10

KELLEN ATWOOD BRUSHED ASIDE THE WAYWARD LOCK OF blond hair hiding his left eye, in the process dropping the two books he carried under his left arm. While he picked them up, he looked quickly around to see if his clumsiness had been witnessed by anyone in the library and saw Susan Rutledge watching from behind her desk. An amused smile was on her lips. He grinned in return and walked across the reference room to stand in front of her.

"You should see me juggle three billiard balls," he said. "It's every man for himself, run for cover and pray."

"We all have our weaknesses." She removed her reading glasses and laid them beside the report she was preparing. "How are you?"

He laid the two books on the desk and tapped them. "These are for that long-winded article I told you I was writing on books and their history. I know that probably it will never reach the stage to be submitted for publication, but it's fascinating research." He laughed. "Just another one of the useless activities with which I clutter my life. Oh—I'm fine, thank you."

The smile grew broader on Susan's mouth. She found Kellen's circuitous speech pattern charming. Looking at the two books lying on the desk, she realized he must have gone deep into the stacks of historical and out-of-print material, because both volumes were old, the titles all but faded into obscurity. Running her fingers over the leather covers, she wondered if Kellen used his esoteric projects to escape from life. She decided not. Probably these difficult and quirky tasks were simply Kellen's way of relieving everyday tensions.

Kellen watched her fingers on the books, then looked at her face. "Susan, I had a fine time Saturday night. I hope you did."

"I had a good time too."

"I'd like to ask you out again."

"I'd like you to do that."

He looked at her for a short while, then his eyes began to crinkle around their corners, and the next instant he laughed. "You know, we're acting and sounding like a 1930's motion picture, all decorum and hesitation and goody-goody, as if the Hayes Office had a representative standing back there in the book stacks, scissors in hand, waiting to cut if we showed the tiniest hint of physical agressiveness."

She nodded, still smiling, still feeling good. "It's kind of pleasant, thought, isn't it?"

"It is. It really is." He picked up the books, swiped back the hair lock, and grinned. "I'll be parked in front at five o'clock."

She watched him walk through the archway leading to the lobby, and was surprised how big he was, with wide shoulders and an easy walking movement. For the first time, she was actually seeing Kellen Atwood. And she liked what she saw.

She put her glasses back on and looked down at the report. Thanks to the cranking up of her emotions during the conversation with Kellen, the report on the individual life spans of books, grouped by ethnic authors, seemed a greater example of bureaucratic overkill than before.

At five o'clock Kellen was waiting for her, his blue Toyota, engine running, in a No Parking area directly in front of the library entrance.

As they turned out of the library driveway onto the campus's main street, he asked, "Can I buy you a drink?"

Susan again realized, as she had on their first date, how wonderfully at ease she felt with this big, bashful man, and said, "I'd like that, Kellen."

Sam was breathing hard. Three weeks without jogging had allowed his body to lose tone. Now it was protesting this sudden exertion with twinges in his leg muscles, a heart he could feel hammering against the inside of his sweat suit, and lungs gasping for air, though he had stopped running. Frowning, he looked down at a bleached scallop shell half embedded in the sand, toed sand over it, then stared out across the evening sea. During the past two days, he had been set upon by disbelief, nervousness, and apprehension. What had happened Tuesday night in Lily's townhouse had left him ripe for these conflicting emotions.

He walked north along the beach, arms swinging idly at his sides, pulling from his memory the scene in Lily's bedroom. He could not consign the occurrence to fantasy or nightmare, but his entire being refused to accept it as reality. If he accepted it, he feared, much of life as he understood it would disintegrate.

He remembered the scene: on their pedestals the animals and the fowls waited, the blank tunnels that were their eyes fixed on him, their marbled muscles rigid and brittle.

He remembered . . .

. . . his hands dropped away from stroking Lily's back. "Who's Adam?"

She squirmed, but made no move to get off him, nor to answer.

"Who is he, Lily?"

She moaned into his chest.

On the other side of the palm fronds, the candle flames began to gutter, and in their waning, flickering light the creatures on their pedestals moved closer, empty eyes more intent, muscles flexing under ghostly skins. Around him on the bed, the crushed flower petals released their fragrances to mingle with the incense. And in the darkness, something unseen was twisting and writhing as though in the throes of dreadful emotion.

Lily shifted then, her weight on him lessening as she placed her hands on either side of him and lifted herself a few scant inches.

"Lily?" He laid his hands on her sides, feeling the sweaty wetness of her skin and the torrid heat seeping through her flesh. "Lily, say something. Tell me who Adam is."

She turned her head slowly, pointing her face directly at him.

Sam heard himself gasp, felt his muscles violently recoil in reflex action.

He was staring into the face of an incredible creature. Lily's honey-colored skin was drawn to a splitting tightness from cheek bones to jaw bones, looking like a sheath of wax. Her eyes, their almond-shape slanted more than he had ever seen them, burned in the shadow of her brows. Under flared nostrils, her mouth was stretched into a smile which held no pretense of invitation but was the blood-hungry grin of a conquering predator. For an instant, he tried to return the stare of those glaring eyes, but his gaze fell away before the power of those ovals of hellfire burning behind a mask never designed by a human mind. Desperately, in what he felt was a bid to save his sanity, Sam turned his head away.

He heard the palm fronds rustling above his head, dry and rattling, as they would if rain were falling lightly on them. The air calmed, and he sensed, somehow, that the animals and the birds were relaxing on their pedestals. Reality was returning, slowly but persistently reclaiming the room.

"Sam?"

The weight pressing on him lessened further, becoming a soft brushing of warmth on his chest and down his stomach. He turned his face to look upward, but did not open his eyes. If he looked again into the greenish-red glow coming from those almond slits, he knew he would go mad. He ground his teeth together and kept his eyes screwed tightly shut.

"Sam?" It was Lily's voice. *His* Lily's voice.

He opened his eyes slowly, ready to snap them shut if the two discs were still burning behind the terrible mask. But it was Lily's splendid face hovering above him, the enchanting face of the woman who had descended from the dune that stormy night. All the fire was gone from her green eyes. Where the searing flames had burned, a doe's pliant eyes now persuaded him to push from his mind the dark chaos through which he had just traveled.

He drew in just enough breath to speak one word, and asked, "Lily?"

"Of course, Sam. Who else would it be?"

"I don't know . . ."

A veil, like the shadow of a hurrying thought, passed across her face. While she continued to look down at him with a steady gaze, he thought he saw a furtive movement behind her irises, in the exact places where the fires had burned, as if another Lily were sharing the almond-shaped eyes to stare at him.

He wished she would move from her position straddling him on her knees and elbows. There was no response in him to the warmth cascading down on him from her naked body. Where her nipples brushed his chest, there was only a slight itching irritation.

"You are troubled, my Sam?" She quickly kissed the tip of his nose, then raised her head again. Her hair fell on both sides of their faces, tenting them in a fragrant darkness. "Have I displeased you that much?"

"No." Her obsession with pleasing him had at first been a bulwark to his ego, but now the original good feeling was changing and beginning to fade away, turning just a little rancid. "No . . . not displeased, Lily. Surprised, I guess, is the right description."

"My bedroom, is that it, Sam? Because it is so different, you are surprised. You think it is overdone, too bizarre."

He wondered if she knew about the transformation she had under gone. Fearful of saying something which would cause it again, he said, "Maybe it's because I don't understand."

"Sam, we all have memories, do we not? Some we put away in the mind's prison and never give parole, keep in isolation so they cannot interfere with the lives we lead today. But there are others, which we cherish and which we keep where they can forever be recalled, and some of these we incorporate into our living. This room is such a memory. The home I remember most was in a land that was lush with all the flowers and plants nature could provide. I liked little else there, Sam, but I enjoyed the greenery and the creatures that roamed through it, so wherever I have stayed for any length of time I have created that memory in my bedroom. It is unusual, I know, but, Sam, is it so bad?"

Deep in the core of his understanding, there was confusion. "Where was that, Lily? And who is Adam? I think I have a right to know."

"Why are you so forever curious, Sam? I have given myself wholly to you. Why not accept me as I am? What change would knowledge of my background make between us?"

"It would give you existence. Sometimes I can't help but think you're only a fantasy."

"Oh, Sam, what is the reality of existence? I am here. I am now." Her eyes gazed directly at him. "I am no disembodied entity. I bring no less meaning to our relationship because I bring no background to it."

As usual, she was responding with vagueness, but this time he would not give up. "Who was Adam, Lily? I think you were making love to him tonight instead of me. And, if that's so, it kind of makes me feel as if I participated in—well, an almost pornographic act."

"You are so rigid in your definitions. Pornography is merely an interpretation of the individual mind."

"Then tell me who Adam is."

For a brief instant, the red flared in her eyes, then as abruptly subsided. "He was my husband. Now ask me no more about him, Sam, for speaking of him is forbidden by the divorce decree. Telling you even that much is more than I am permitted."

They stared at one another for a tense moment, then, with a laugh, she swung out of her crouch and sat on the edge of the bed. "Come, Sam, let us shower, then I will prepare breakfast."

He glanced at his wristwatch. It told him the morn-

ing was gone, that already on the other side of the
window coverings the ocean was shimmering and the
land was wilting under a noontime sun. And the office
was unstaffed. Still, he was reluctant to leave the
gloomy room and shower away the smell of rose petals
clinging to his skin. Then he rolled over and sat up,
wondering where all the happiness and confidence that
once was his had gone.

He still did not know . . .

. . . and now it was Friday, and he had not seen Lily
since. Her garage had been empty the last three days, so
he knew she wasn't home, that she had gone somewhere without telling him.

He had been watching his feet while he walked,
watching the sand spurt from under the toes of his
jogging shoes. He kicked at the tide-smoothed remains
of what might have been a sand castle, then looked up.

A lone figure stood at the high-water line, looking out
at the darkening water. In their final moves, expiring
waves sent the last thrust of their water slithering up
the sand to curl around the figure's bare feet. It didn't
move, either not aware of the sucking water or ignoring
it. As Sam angled to the inland side of the beach to
avoid the person, he recognized Jetta, and a faint
apprehension cooled his skin under its sweaty dampness. He was within six or seven yards of her before she
heard his footsteps in the sand and turned to look at
him.

"Hi, Sam." She stared soberly at him. Her hair was
mussed, and he had the uneasy feeling that it had been
that way before she'd come down to the beach, that the
sea breeze had only ruffled it a little more.

"Jetta."

He waited for her to say something more, but she
dropped her gaze to her swollen stomach, then raised it

to continue her inspection of the blue and purple sea.

He dug a short furrow with the toe of his right shoe while he tried to decide what to do. Obviously Jetta had isolated herself in a very private world to which she would offer no invitations. The sensible, gracious, thing to do, he knew, was to back away and continue his walk to the complex, pretending that she wasn't there. But he noticed a tight trembling in her hands and a tiny knot of muscles quivering in her jaw.

"What's wrong?" he asked.

She shook her head, then, after drawing a deep breath, turned to face him. "Like they say: nothing, but everything."

"Do you want to talk?"

"Would it do any good?"

"I don't know." Out to sea, a stain of purple darkened and widened until all the blue was swallowed in it. "It might not hurt, though. If you want to take the chance, I'll listen. It seemed to help, Tuesday night."

A smile tried to find a place on her lips, couldn't, and faded away. She nodded. "I remember. All right, let's talk."

"Let's go sit on the steps. Nobody will be using them this time of day." He took her gently by the arm. "Come on. We'll walk slowly."

After she found a comfortable position on the wood planking, Jetta said, "I guess there's not really a whole lot to say, Sam. You know the foundations of our problems. God, everybody in the complex knows them: good old John Barleycorn. Glenn's getting worse, much worse. He's dependent on it now. It's food and air to him, a buttress to support his conviction that life shit on him. He's slipping so fast and so far, I'm afraid he's going to turn to the harder stuff, Sam, the real mindblowers that come in little plastic packages. He's already seeing things that go bump in the night, shadows in the dark, things that peek in the windows at us when the sun goes down." She looked sideways at him, then bent her head to look at her hands, clasped in her lap. "I'm frightened, Sam. I'm frightened of the future and want to hold it back, because I know there's trouble waiting, bad trouble."

"Glenn can get help, you know. There're places that specialize in his kind of problems."

She gave an almost imperceptible nod and her hands tightened their grasp on one another. "We each have small, separate incomes from trust funds, but they only supplement his earnings. We couldn't live on them . . . and he's been warned so many times at work . . . too many times. I know he's going to lose his job too."

Sam could think of nothing to say. All purpose had been taken from this miserable woman who sat at his side, clasping and unclasping her hands. He wished now that he hadn't asked her to confide in him, not because he didn't want to be involved, but because it saddened him that sensitivity and beauty could be so threatened with destruction. First Cindy, now Jetta. Suddenly Fate was playing a malicious game with two of the people close to him.

"Did you know that Lily is a sculptress?" Jetta asked.

The question caught him off guard. He looked sharply at her, but she was once more examining the murky sea.

"Yes. She's really very good, from what I've seen."

"I began posing for her today. She's doing a clay model of me, and intends to do a small marble piece." She turned to look directly at him. A look of defiance pinched her face. "She's paying me well."

He struggled to suppress the memory of blank-eyed creatures watching him from atop their white pedestals. After a long pause, he licked his lips and said, "I think she picked a good model. Your features are what artists and photographers look for, excellent bone structure and definition."

Jetta smiled briefly, then said, "She's doing a full figure study." She rested her elbows on her knees, then leaned forward to hold her head between her hands, her fingers digging into her hair. "God, I never felt so exposed in my life as I did standing there naked before her. Not nude, but naked."

Sam felt a chill—not connected with the evening dampness—not knowing what he should say to this woman who was sick with anxiety and deprived of hope. Groping, he reached over and laid a hand on Jetta's shoulder.

"Jetta, did Lily say why she wanted to sculpt you? I thought she only did wild life."

"Only something about me having an inner being that intrigued her. But she hasn't said much of anything, really, not even while she works." She shrugged. "I guess I can handle the embarrassment and the silence for the money she offered. She's paying me a hundred and fifty dollars an hour, Sam!" She gave a choked laugh. "Maybe I should feel like a prostitute."

"Absolutely not!" He squeezed her shoulder. "Where is she working, in the upstairs room she converted into a studio?"

"Yes."

An image of the terrible glaring eyes burning behind a ghoul's mask seared in his memory. "Did you go into her bedroom?"

"No." Jetta frowned. "The door to it was closed. Why do you ask?"

He didn't know how to answer, because he didn't know why he'd asked—perhaps some portion of his mind was seeking confirmation of that other world hidden behind the door.

He shrugged. "It's uniquely furnished. I thought

maybe she'd want to show it to you."

They sat silent for a while, then she said, "I think we'd better go in, Sam."

The first roll of thunder rumbled in the west as they passed the swimming pool.

Jetta shuddered. "I don't need a storm tonight."

"None of us do, but it's the season for them. Two or three a week."

"I know, but I don't like it."

"We might not get it." He looked up at the expressionless sky. "It's still far away."

At the patio gate, she smiled with real warmth. "This is, as they say, getting to be a habit, isn't it, you dragging me home from the beach?"

Her smile loosened one in him. "It's a pleasure, not a habit, for me. I'm sorry I couldn't be of any help. I guess I'll take down my psychiatrist's shingle."

She reached out and took his hand. "No, Sam. You cared enough to try. No one else has."

Back in his place, he wandered through the living room, turning on the light above the recliner and one on the end table beside the sofa, studying the shadows they created, as he might the ink blots used in psychological testing.

The storm began meekly, with erratic patters of rain, the isolated drops disappearing immediately in the sandy soil and drying instantly on pavement still radiating the day's heat. But the thunder rolled closer, with one peal instantly following its predecessor until a continuous booming domed the landscape. Then the tentative pattering of rain became a hammering. Like nighttime ghouls playing a screaming game of hide-and-seek among the trees and around the buildings, the wind howled and cried. Stray eddies rattled the windows, pounded at the front door. Sam went to the door to check if the rain had forced its way through the weather sealing. Twice before puddles had formed in the foyer during a heavy downpour.

For most of the evening, Sam paced through the empty rooms, seeking something, but unable to define what it was that eluded him. At times he thought he was walking among the fragments of every one of his emotions, that they lay scattered around him in the shadows, defying him to piece them together. Something was happening to him, but he could not determine what was changing, or how.

At ten-thirty he prepared for bed, very much aware that no sleep awaited him. There were too many vibrations pulsing through his mind, too many images and suppositions being accepted, then rejected. Lily. Susan. Cindy. Jetta. Marble animals perched on white pedestals around a petal-strewn bed. Invisible things that moved around the periphery of his office and among the tables in restaurants. Something black and formless that drifted through rain-drenched nights. All separate, all together. All jamming his brain, leaving no room for sleep.

The front door chimes echoed through the silent rooms. To the out-of-time pulsings in his brain, their harmony was a discordant jangling. He allowed their metallic summons to ring twice before he pushed himself from the bed, found his slippers, and shouldering into a robe, went down stairs.

Lily stood framed against the night when he pulled the door open.

Surprised, he stepped back. She followed him, closing the door behind her, eyes dancing, nostrils flared. He watched the strong muscles sleekly flexing under her black blouse and tight-fitted slacks as she advanced toward him. The sibilant whispering that had come from her mouth in the flowered bed spouted from her lips.

"Oh, you've decided to come home. Where have you been?"

"Exploring." She ran a hand through the thick mass of her hair. "I wanted to familiarize myself with my new homeland. I was in Miami for a while. It is interesting there, Sam."

He sensed she was on a high, much as she had been after the first time she'd disappeared. He felt the heat of her, as if the night's humidity had entered her and was boiling inside her body, and he remembered her predator's attack, which had ended with them sprawled on the living-room floor. But as strong as that memory was the recollection of red eyes glowing down on him in her bed.

"You could have told me you were going away." He wondered if he sounded petulant, but didn't care.

She tilted her head back. Something smoldered under her half-lowered lids. "Are you my jailer from whom I must seek permission to live my own life?"

"No, only someone who cares for you."

While the clock on the dining-room wall ticked away a dozen seconds, she gazed at him, and once more he had the feeling of being evaluated. Finally she gave a tiny nod. The hissing smoothed into even breathing. "That is good to know."

"You didn't before?"

A smile delicately brushed her lips as she closed the distance between them and took his hand. He felt her heat and excitement pulsing in her palm while she tightened her grasp and gave a little tug.

"In India, Sam, in the town of Puri, I have seen hawkers in front of the temples selling little soapstone statuettes depicting some of what is carved on friezes inside the temples." Her grip tightened, even as her smile broadened and her green eyes burned with such potent want he could all but feel the intensity singeing his face. "Come, Sam, let us go up to your bedroom, and I will show you what those little statuettes depict."

As he went up the stairs with her, he realized the fragments of his emotions still lay in the shadows on the living-room floor.

11

SAM LEANED FORWARD, CLASPING HIS HANDS TOGETHER ON HIS desk, trying to will his eyes away from Cindy, who was standing in the office doorway. An expression between horror and agony formed, then dissolved, then re-shaped itself on her face. A shiver ran down his back, and he quickly funneled his attention back to the woman sitting opposite him.

Her name was Anita Galloway. An executive secre-tary at one of the local electronic firms, in her mid-thirties, she was the mother of a six-year-old son. Sam had a great deal of respect for her. This morning she was acting in her capacity as president of the local chapter of the League of Concerned Professional Women, and there was a fissure in her armor of self-possession. She sat rigid in the chair, her hands picking at the clasp of the oversized purse in her lap. The toe of her right shoe tapped an erratic beat on the floor.

With Anita Galloway's first words, Sam had felt the day begin to crumble. For the first time he could remember, neither he nor Cindy had listened to the morning news; so when Anita rushed into the office with the information that a baby had died during the night at the League's charity project, Sunshine House, Sam felt rocked with sudden tremors. He had watched Cindy, with her face showing the first hints of horror, back away from Anita.

Sunshine House was a fifty-year-old residence that the League of Concerned Professional Women had purchased, renovated, and transformed into what they referred to as "an inn for unwanted and neglected babies." Under the direction of a full-time nurse, volunteers cared for nine or ten infants while appropriate government agencies sought foster homes and adoptive parents. Contributions and twice-yearly social functions provided operating funds. Sam's contribution was a low-key public-relations campaign.

Anita smiled bitterly. "I know I'm going to sound callous and emotionless and self-serving insofar as the League is concerned, Sam, but there is one thing we'd appreciate you handling in regards to this."

When she hesitated, Sam threw a quick glance at Cindy. She was leaning against the door frame. She had grown terribly pale. He wanted to go to her and comfort her with words or a hug, but his business sense kept him focused on Anita Galloway.

"What is it you want me to do?"

"I guess the best description is . . . suppress it. Something occurred last night at Sunshine House just before the child's body was discovered. According to Mrs. Doran, the live-in nurse, she saw something moving through a clump of trees not far from the window by which she was sitting. I say something because she says it had no absolute form. All she could see, she said, was a dark area, which she described as darker than the night." Anita tried to make a negative gesture, but her hand merely flopped in her lap. The movement reminded Sam of a dying bird. "That's what we'd like to keep out of the news, Sam. Alice Doran is a dedicated, level-headed woman, and the public would certainly misunderstand if we disclosed this. That kind of criticism could destroy Sunshine House and all the good it has done, and is doing. Do you see what I mean?"

"Does Alice Doran have a history of hallucinations?"

"No, of course not. If she says she saw something, there was something there to be seen."

He glimpsed movement from the corner of his eye, looked up to see the doorway was empty.

"I don't think we have a problem," he said. "Ask the nurse—no, tell her—not to mention it again, to anyone, and I'll get with my media contacts. You're right, something like that can be a hot item; however, if it's not out yet, we can probably keep a lid on it." He looked at the empty doorway again. "The baby that died. What have they diagnosed as the reason —Sudden Infant Death Syndrome?"

"Yes." Anita Galloway looked over her shoulder as if suddenly noticing Cindy's disappearance. A stricken look froze her face. "Oh, my God, Sam! I forgot. Your assistant's baby died recently of the same thing, isn't that right?"

"Yes."

"I'm sorry. I'm sorry for that, and I'm sorry for being so forgetful. I'll apologize on my way out."

Sam shook his head. "No, don't. Cindy's coming around, and she'll handle this okay."

Anita nodded, then stood up. "You'll do your best, won't you, Sam?"

"Yes, Anita, I will."

Cindy was in the work room, operating the copy

machine, when Anita Galloway hurried through the reception area. When the outside door shut, she turned off the machine, and turned fear-widened eyes on Sam.

"Sam—"

"Honey, try to ride it out. Anita was thoughtless."

"Sam, what she said about the nurse . . . about the nurse seeing something. Sam, the nurse wasn't hallucinating."

Sam pushed himself away from the door frame against which he was leaning. "What do you mean?"

"The thing in the night . . . just darkness on darkness. I—" She placed both hands flat along the sides of her face, pressing her cheeks. "Sam, I—I saw the same thing when Lucy died." At his disbelieving look, she said, "It's true, Sam! I swear it is." She dropped her hands to the desktop, curling her fingers into fists. "In the yard between our house and the next, there was something just like the nurse described. I thought it was my imagination—I wanted to think it was my imagination—but I knew all the time I was watching something . . . something terribly evil."

"Susan too!"

"What?"

He looked at her, startled. He hadn't meant to speak aloud.

"Cindy," he said, "if you don't feel like staying, go home. I wouldn't blame you."

She sat looking at him quizzically, her mouth sagging open just a little, then shook her head. "No, I'm going to stay, Sam. I'll be better here, where I have something to do."

He was already in his office and dialing the library number. "Okay."

A pleasant voice answered, then switched him to Susan's number. "Susan, this is Sam."

"Hi!"

"Did you hear the news this morning?"

"No, I didn't have the radio on. Why?"

"Another baby died during the night."

"And they're calling it Sudden Infant Death Syndrome?"

"Yes. It was one of the babies at Sunshine House."

Susan sucked in her breath. "Sam, what's going on?"

"I don't know, but the live-in nurse at Sunshine House says she saw something moving outside her window at approximately the same time it's believed the baby died. Something black and shapeless hovering in a clump of nearby trees."

Fear sounded in Susan's voice. "Sam . . . what we felt when we were on the stoop . . . what I saw from my window after you left!"

He drew a deep breath, forcing himself to speak slowly. "Susan, Cindy saw the same thing the night Lucy died."

"Oh, dear God!"

"Susan, there's something very wrong here."

She hesitated, then said, "Should we go to the police?"

"I think it's a good idea, but let's get some facts first. I don't want them telling us they don't investigate ghost stories. Sometime today, can you go through back issues of both local newspapers to find the exact number of recent cases of babies whose deaths have been diagnosed as Sudden Infant Death Syndrome? I haven't paid that much attention, I'm afraid."

"I can start right now."

"Good. And, Susan, try to discover if there's anything common to all the deaths. You know, what time of day, what the family was doing. That kind of stuff."

"Okay. I'll get back to you. Are you going to be in the office?"

"Yes."

"Then I'll phone you there."

* * *

Although it had long owned the equipment, the school library was dilatory in microfilming periodicals, performing the task on a when-there-is-time basis, usually using a student employee during the winter term. Therefore, Susan had come directly to the storage room, where the items to be filmed were bundled on rows of steel shelving along two walls and down the center of the room. Sometime after the spring term, one of the two long fluorescent tubes had burned out and not been replaced, allowing shadows to form deep pools on the floor between the rows of shelving and cling to the walls in non-geometric blotches.

This was her first visit to the room, and it took her a short time to determine the manner in which the bundles were stacked. Newspapers for the last month, she finally discovered, were in the rear of the room, on the bottom of the center shelving unit.

She soon found the four bundles she sought, two weeks of the *Florida Today* and *Orlando Sentinel* in each pile. She knelt before the two *Florida Today* bundles, and as she reached out to pull them to her, she saw two legs on the other side of the shelves. She had heard no one come into the room, but the black-clad legs, slightly spread, were directly opposite her.

"Hello," she said. "I didn't hear you come in."

There was no answer.

Still kneeling, Susan looked up. "I said, I didn't hear you come in. Can I help you find what you're looking for?"

Only the muffled sound of her voice, deadened by the rows of stacked paper, answered her.

Like a tickle at first, then a current, a coldness drove up her spine. Very suddenly, kneeling as she was, she felt vulnerable to whoever stood on the other side of the shelving. She started to push herself to an erect position, but from above her came a growl, deep-throated and rasping. She froze. Half crouched, unable to see past the bundles on the second shelf, she waited, helpless, for whatever was to occur.

Around her the shadows took on substance, night-darkened buttes and plateaus, serrated mountains and jagged ridges, as if the room had become a part of a desolate landscape on which she was a hunted prey.

Then, as quickly as it had descended on her, the sensation was gone. She looked toward the door, which stood open perhaps twenty feet away. All she had to do was make a run for it, or scream. In the silence of the library a scream would be as effective as the ringing of a Klaxon. But before she did either, she was going to face whatever was on the far side of the bundles.

She slowly sucked in a deep breath, at the same time bracing the muscles in her legs. Then, clenching her fists, she released all the tautness in her body at once, springing up to her full height. Through the narrow, shadow-clogged opening, she stared directly into a pair of glowing red eyes.

Susan stood rigid, her suddenly frozen muscles incapable of moving, while the unblinking eyes glared at her, burning through her irises like molten streams to stab into her brain. Time ceased to flow. Powerless to help herself, she felt everything substantial and important being sucked from her.

Abruptly the eyes vanished! Blackness filled the narrow opening.

While her senses scrambled to refocus, she heard, from what seemed a great distance, a padding noise that made her think of animal paws stalking toward the doorway.

She whirled and ran to the door. The short corridor outside was empty. Susan supported herself on the door jamb, drawing deep breaths in an attempt to slow the unsettling rhythm of her heart.

It must have just been the result of an overactive imagination. Even as she thought this, a coldness slithered through her, because her primitive instincts told her that something *had* been in the store room with her, and that whatever it was, it was completely evil.

With a final look up and down the hallway, she turned and re-entered the storeroom.

Jetta Ashley curled her fingers around the arms of the deck chair in which she sat, wanting to shift position but fearful the weight of her bulging stomach would pinch one of the nerves where her thighs met her torso and send a hot wire of pain through her.

Never in her life had she felt so awkward, never so helpless, so increasingly aware of lost hope. It was so easy to wonder whether it was she or Glenn who was to blame for destroying all their dreams and plans. What a bleak world the child within her would be born into. Jetta looked out at the black and silent ocean. She felt perspiration forming trickles on her cheeks and wriggling down her spine. From far out, where the darkness of the sea met the blackness of the sky, she thought she heard a murmur, but pulled her attention away, fearful that she was becoming like poor Glenn, who heard and saw things where nothing could possibly exist.

She thumped a fist on the arm of the chair, braced her legs, and carefully pushed herself to her feet. For a moment, she stood swaying, counterbalancing the weight of her uterus. She looked at the townhouse building. It appeared darker than normal, a great looming cliff towering over the pool area to block out the whole of the western night sky. Muted music came from Holly and Todd's place; a feeble light glowed in Sam's, indicating that he wasn't home. Her own home was illuminated like a carnival midway, but it too was empty. Although it was nearly ten-thirty, Glenn had not yet come home from work and neither had he phoned. Standing in the darkness, looking at the blazing windows, Jetta realized that he must have lost the job, that he would never find another. She swung her eyes to Lily's townhouse. As usual, it was no more than a blank, not a crack of light and absolute silence. She wondered if Lily was out with Sam, and felt a strange anxiety snip at her.

She gave a mental shrug, telling herself not to think ill of her benefactor. In an envelope in the bottom right-hand drawer of her vanity was twelve hundred dollars, in hundred-dollar bills, that Lily had paid her for two days of modeling. Jetta felt it was far too much money for two days' work, but if her intuitions were correct, every bit of the twelve hundred dollars would soon be needed.

The fetus kicked. Jetta jerked, more with surprise than discomfort. She turned from looking at the building to stare once more out at the ocean, so black and endless under the moonless sky. This time she was certain she heard a distant, sweet-sounding murmuring. While she listened, she thought she saw something move along the beach, but when she blinked and concentrated on the spot, there was nothing there. The fetus kicked again.

Slowly, holding tightly to the handrail, she went down the flight of wooden steps to the beach. Down here, the murmuring formed itself into words spoken by a voice as beautiful as any she had ever heard.

Come, Jetta. Come into the coolness of the sea. There is wondrous peace and no discomfort here. Come, Jetta. Come into the soothing darkness. You, and the little one within you, will know joy and love and security, for time unending. Out here, Jetta, out here . . . come. Only tranquility awaits you. Come into the dark and peaceful waters.

The sand was cool. She looked down at her feet, saw they were bare, that she had forgotten her sandals,

leaving them by the chair at the swimming pool. She
was almost to the water's edge. The murmuring swish
of the waves toyed with her consciousness. The rhythmic sound was soothing. Fingers of water caressed her
toes, then reached up to so very gently grasp her ankles.
Far out toward the horizon she could not see, the
whispering voice spoke with its unimaginable beauty.

A dozen yards or so down the beach, a small portion
of the night changed position. An area darker than that
surrounding it, it swayed slowly to and fro in rhythm
with the sea. Then, as if stalking the woman, the
blackness drifted slowly in her direction, along the
skein of froth left behind on the sand by the retreating
waves.

*Feel the water, Jetta. Feel its soothing caress. Let it
enfold you in its sweetness while it carries you to a realm
of ancient beauty far from the turmoil of the land. Do
not hesitate. Come, Jetta, come.*

The water was up to her thighs, creeping higher as
she waded eastward. The sea was helpful, taking some
of the weight of the baby from her, billowing the skirt
of her robe upward, so it did not hinder her by clinging
to her legs. Once she looked toward the brilliant
windows of her home, but turned again to face the
unseen horizon and continued moving in the direction
of the murmuring voice. Around her, the water twinkled with luminescent pinpoints. The world retreated,
becoming inconsequential. When finally the ocean
closed over her head, she could hear the whispering
with more definition. There was a singular beauty to it.
She felt herself becoming a portion of a great, inte-
grated system of sun rays and moonbeams and a
darkness that was almost sacred in its peacefulness. She
began to use her arms and hands to push against the
water, to hurry toward the voice.

On the beach, the small area of darkness lingered for

a time, swaying to the heartbeat of the sea, then dissolved slowly into the night. A moment after it disappeared, a lone pelican, which should have been nesting, swooped silently out of the night sky, circled lazily, then plunged into the ocean where Jetta had vanished.

12

IT HAD BEEN A LONG FRIDAY. FROM THE TIME SAM HAD entered the office in the morning until he locked the door after himself in the late afternoon, the day had fit snugly into the mold of near disaster, a perfect example of Murphy's Law: if anything can go wrong, it will. Two not completely satisfied clients, detailing their complaints, occupied the morning, interrupted, every fifteen minutes by a new account, calling to suggest changes to a developing campaign. A second visit from a Brevard County deputy with further inquiries into Jetta's personal problems followed lunch, and, finally, during a long run of form letters for a bank, the copy machine broke down with no hope of service until sometime Monday. At four-thirty, he told Cindy to pack it in, locked the door and stopped on the way home at a seaside bar for a beer.

The air was restless, and he thought it was bracing

itself for the onslaught of a storm. There had been none since the death of the baby at Sunshine House, and now, as the air currents began to change, Sam began to feel uneasy. Since Susan had told him that the only apparent common denominator in the baby deaths was a storm at the time of each death, something had been gnawing at him, but he was afraid to open his mind enough to receive the message. Susan had also told him of her "encounter" in the storeroom. He didn't want to think about glowing red eyes that stared with ungodly hate. Storms and red eyes . . .

There was a light tapping on the unlatched patio gate.

"Sam, are you in there?" A woman's voice.

"Yeah, come in."

Holly Langston pushed the gate wide and stepped into the miniscule patio. She was dressed in an extremely short-skirted tennis outfit. A long-visored sunshade held back her golden curls. Looking up at her from his lounge chair, Sam thought that no matter how mundane a woman's features might be, the popular golf and tennis visors transformed them handsomely. On Holly, the long beak only accentuated her good looks, and he was certain she was aware of it.

She carried a drink in her hand. He assumed it was a diet cola. Without waiting for an invitation, Holly sprawled into Sam's second patio chair. She laid her head back, gazing at the plants hanging above their heads before peering at Sam from the shadow of the sunshade. "Why in hell did she do it, Sam?"

"I hope that's a rhetorical question, because there's no way in God's world I can answer it. Probably nobody can, precisely."

"We all knew she was depressed—who wouldn't be, living with a slob like Glenn—but, my God, Sam, she not only took her own life, she murdered her baby."

He looked up at a long streamer of gray cloud thrusting across the lavender-washed sky, and knew there was another storm out there, heading in their direction.

"Holly, something inside Jetta gave way, but we'll never know what it was."

"She talked to you, Sam. Didn't she say anything?"

"Nothing definite."

Holly ran her fingertips up and down the condensation-dampened sides of her glass. "Did you know she was posing for Lily?"

"Yes."

"Don't you think that strange?"

"No, not particularly. Lily's a sculptress. I suppose she saw something of merit in Jetta. She was a good-looking woman."

"What did Lily see?"

Shock made him look sharply at Holly. "What do you mean?"

"I don't know, that's just it. I don't know why that question comes to mind. Like you say, she was a good-looking woman, but she wasn't classic, Sam. And she wasn't unusual or unique."

"There's a very special beauty about a woman when she's pregnant."

"Oh, I know, but still it doesn't sit right with me. I just have this feeling that Jetta's posing had nothing to do with her beauty . . . and something to do with her death." She took a quick sip from her glass. "It's a creepy feeling, Sam."

He didn't answer, though he knew what she meant.

Finally, Holly sighed, emptied her glass with one long swallow, and stood up, performing the movement with the special skill and tidiness of a woman who knows her figure is attractive in every detail.

"I've got to go. It's time for Todd to come home, and

we decided we'd try to get Glenn out of that pigsty of an apartment for a meal. I think the only solids he's put in his stomach the last two days are martini olives, and I'm sure he's run out of those by now. I don't imagine you'd want to come along."

"No." Other things had been gnawing at Jetta's mind but Glenn's behavior had been her primary concern, and Sam didn't want to face the man whom he could not help but hold more than partially responsible for her death. "Maybe next time."

"There's not going to be a next time, if I have my say." She went to the gate. "See you later, Sam."

He lay back in the chaise, wanting to find a comfortable position for his body and his mind, wanting to shut the world away while he attempted to sort out the conflicting emotions which had flooded him in the two days since Jetta's suicide.

The thunder was closer. Sam looked up at the sky and saw the edges of clouds creeping from behind the concealment of the roof's overhang.

"Sam?"

He looked to the gate. Lily was standing in its opening. She was dressed in her usual black blouse and tight slacks, her black hair brushed smooth and framing her face. Looking up at her, he received the impression of vertical darkness, like a tall, beautiful flower born of the storm and living in the night.

He smiled. "Hello."

She stepped into the patio, carefully, slowly, her body movements, unlike Holly's, unplanned, but emitting sensuality. Thunder rumbled overhead, and a breeze whirled around the patio fence. Sam straightened as much as he could in the chaise.

"You have been avoiding me for a week." Her voice was low, with no special articulation.

"No, of course, I haven't, Lily. It's just that so many

things have happened. Jetta's death, for one."

Lily shrugged. "She was a weak woman, otherwise she would not have done what she did."

"You actually feel that way?" There was a slight edge to his voice. "You have no other feeling about her death, only that she was an emotional cripple?"

She fell to her knees beside him. "Oh, Sam, you are too soft in your heart, too kindly in your thinking. I have seen times and lived in places where, if such a death occurred, the entire family would hang its head in shame."

"Well, this isn't one of those places, Lily, and Jetta had friends who'll miss her and feel sorry not only for her but for Glenn." Sam took a deep breath and forced the anger building in him to calm down. "I don't think you knew her well, Lily."

"Ah, Sam, I knew her better than you think." She leaned toward him, her lips parting. He felt the weight of her breasts on his right forearm. "I know all the secrets of all women, my Sam, and tonight I will divulge some of the more exciting ones to you."

"Lily, I—"

Her mouth opened, and her warm, clean-scented breath fanned his face. Then her lips were on his, devouring him as surely as if she were feasting on a rare delicacy.

Overhead a cannonade of thunder tore apart the heavens, rattling windows and trembling the earth with its percussion, growling as it lumbered away. Lily moaned. Heavy drops of rain spattered on the flagstones and hanging plants. Lily pulled away.

While the rain began to fall steadily on the leaves of the plants, the couple stared at one another for a moment. Lily's eyes radiated excitement blended with anticipation, but touched, Sam thought, with a suggestion of cruelty. He wanted to look away, but found his eyes were locked to hers, held tight by the dazzling green sparkling in their depths.

In one graceful motion she rose to stand on slightly spread legs, smiling down at him, eyes still glowing with their curious light. Against the gray of the lowering sky, with droplets of rain shining on her hair, there was something pagan about her, something ancient.

"Tonight, Sam," she said, then turned and with two powerful strides disappeared through the gate.

He didn't want to move. He wanted to stay sprawled on the chaise and turn over in his mind the words Lily had spoken concerning Jetta, to put them in perspective. But he heard the main body of rain hissing on the far side of the building, its advance streams washing across the roof, so he shoved himself to his feet. He had just entered the dining room and was sliding the door shut when the rain drew a gray curtain across the ocean.

He looked at the wall clock. It was twenty minutes to eight. He looked at the glass of the door, opaque with the rain water, and thought what a dumb way to spend TGIF. Alone, with probably nothing in the refrigerator.

The windshield wipers were working at top speed, but the rain could not be turned aside. It transformed the glass into a cloudy plate through which Susan squinted at diffused lights and wavering objects. It was impossible to continue driving and she slowed the car and steered it to the curb, applying the brakes gently. She turned off the wipers but left the engine and air conditioner running.

"So much for being home by seven-thirty," she said out loud.

She had told Kellen she would be ready by eight o'clock. They were having dinner at a new beachside restaurant, and she had decided to purchase a blouse she'd seen in a Jordan Marsh advertisement. That side trip seemed likely to be more trouble than it was worth.

Switching on the dome light, she looked at her watch. It was twenty minutes before eight.

"Damn it!"

She sat staring straight ahead while the rain rattled on the roof and hood like handsful of pebbles thrown from the dark. The windows started to steam up, giving her the uncomfortable feeling that a cocoon was encasing her. At the same time, a silence crowded into the car, causing her flesh to prickle as if sensing danger. Since the episode with the glowing eyes in the storeroom, there had been a twitchiness in her.

Ten minutes later the storm front passed and Susan turned on the windshield wipers. They swung back and forth in a clicking rhythm, clearing two arches on the glass. She pushed the gear shift into drive.

Within several miles, the rain ceased altogether and she traveled on a street already drying. Ahead a traffic light changed from green to amber, then to red. Susan raised her foot from the accelerator, allowing the car to slow, hoping to avoid a complete stop.

From behind, a car rushed up on her, its headlights splashing into her rearview mirror. The car did not slow in its approach, but suddenly swung to the left, into the passing lane.

The traffic light remained red, and Susan braked to a stop. On her left, tires shrieked as they gripped the damp pavement. Startled, she looked out her window. Drawn up beside her was a black car with a black-haired woman behind the steering wheel. The woman was holding her head pointed rigidly forward, staring into the darkness beyond the headlights' illumination, as though she was searching for objects untouched by the fans of light.

Something in the back of Susan's mind stirred, then

suddenly became a full-fledged realization. The woman and the car were the same as those that had swung out of Sam's townhouse complex the night they had driven in the storm. Lily. For some reason, alert bells tinkled in Susan's mind.

The traffic light changed to green. Instantly, the black car lunged across the intersection, gaining speed, its taillights dwindling to glowing sparks, then pinpoints.

Susan jammed her foot down on the Escort's accelerator. The little car sprang ahead, its engine whining in protest. She could still see the red dots that were the Oldsmobile's taillights, and pushed her foot down harder. Amber streetlights skimmed through her peripheral vision like frightened will-o'-the-wisps streaking through the darkness. Ahead, the taillights grew in size. She kept her foot pressed to the accelerator pedal, thankful traffic was still sparse because of the rain.

As she sped in the black car's wake Susan began to understand what the kernel in the back of her mind was trying to tell her: something about more than a coincidence of events. The old news stories, the accounts of storms in progress when babies died, and Sam's telling of Lily's disappearances during turbulent nights, of her returning filled with exuberance. Was there a pattern to which this all belonged?

The Oldsmobile's taillights were closer. A barely contained excitement gripped her, strumming her nerve ends, telling her that something was going to happen. Her heart began to accelerate to correspond to the speed of the car, pumping adrenaline through her in surging rushes. In spite of the tight grasp she took on the steering wheel, her hands trembled.

Suddenly the taillights ahead turned right, disappearing. Frantically Susan tried to fix in her mind the place in the darkness where they vanished, using a street light as a reference point. Approaching, she located a dark side street half a block before the light. She threw a hasty glance up it, and not too far into the darkness saw the taillights. They were moving slower, but gave no indication of stopping. Not bothering to check the rearview mirror for following cars, she tramped on the brake pedal with all the force she could put into the movement. The Escort's tires squealed as the little car tried to break into a fishtailing skid, but she fought the wheel, careening the car around the corner.

The Oldsmobile was rounding a shallow left curve, moving even slower now. With a start, Susan became aware of her surroundings. This street, on which as yet no houses had been constructed, was the back entrance to the Village Green Apartments' parking lot.

The Oldsmobile was moving at no more than a crawl as it entered the apartment area, as though Lily was looking for a spot in which to park. Susan allowed the distance between the cars to close. A jolt of anticipation slipped through her at the thought of meeting the strange woman face to face. She was somewhat surprised at the intensity of this desire.

Without warning, the brake lights ahead of her flared. The Oldsmobile stopped abruptly. With a gasp, Susan jammed on her own brakes. The Escort nosed down, but squealed to a stop with its front bumper very gently nudging the rear of the other car. Hands still clawed around the steering wheel, she sat rigid.

Finally, drawing a deep breath, she reached for the gear shift lever, to place it in reverse. As her hand closed around the lever's knob, she had the feeling that she was being studied. She glanced out the side windows, but no one was standing anywhere in the parking area. She felt a chill that quickly deepened into a coldness that numbed her, freezing her in place.

Suddenly she became aware that the stare was coming from the car in front, and she looked through the windshield at the rear window of the Oldsmobile. It was darkly blank, tinted an almost opaque black, but she could feel the impact of that look, the coldness of that stare.

She had no thought of passing time, aware only of a warping around the edges of her mind as the chill penetrated deeper and deeper, and then, unexpectedly reversing itself, the coldness swiftly melting to be replaced with a mind-filling heat. She sat helpless, her muscles flaccid and her flesh doughy, while the heat entwined itself around her. Then she felt it: Hate. Directed straight at her. Encompassing her. Raw hate. A hate so consuming that if not checked it would splinter her reason. She heard herself whimper, and was neither surprised nor ashamed. She wanted to scream, but the ability was denied her.

The Oldsmobile's brake lights went out. Its powerful engine roared. An instant later, the big black car was careening through the parking area, losing itself in the darkness, headed in the direction of the main entrance.

Susan sat trying to dislodge the cold that had settled on her chest, attempting to gather the strength leeched from her by the malignancy that had surrounded her. She didn't know how long it was, but slowly strength siphoned back into her body. She eased the car across the parking lot to her assigned space. Kellen's Toyota was in the space next to it, Kellen's familiar figure behind the wheel.

Susan watched Kellen take the last bite of his dessert, then looked around the restaurant and finally stared down at her own empty dessert plate. She had eaten too fast, the subtleties of the excellent food missed, and she felt ashamed because she knew Kellen was paying more for the meal than he could probably afford. Yet her mind had not been on food. During the meal, she had thought again and again of the black car and the black-haired woman in it.

"You're quiet tonight. Is anything wrong?" Kellen was looking at her around the lock of fallen hair. "Are you feeling okay? I hope you're not still upset about being late. That storm was a crusher."

"No, I'm all right." She didn't want to make excuses to this big, shy man, but she didn't know how to rationally explain the disquiet haunting her. With a limp smile, she said, "I guess I've got too many things on my mind."

"Your work?"

"No, there's nothing I can't leave there at five o'clock." Not really wanting to discuss her worries, she tried a frivolous remark. "Maybe I'm just being female. You know, just prickly and out of sorts."

"Oh." He fingered his fork, which had bits of cheese-cake still clinging to it. "Would you like to go home?"

"Oh, no, Kellen; although you'd have every right to take me there. I know I'm a bore tonight, and I'm sorry, but please believe me, what has me in a funk has nothing to do with this evening."

He stopped playing with the fork, then pushed the hair from his left eye. "I'd be glad to help, Susan, if you're having problems."

She looked straight at him, and behind the facade of his masculine innocence she saw strength, a virility that represented determination and understanding. She knew this man would be a loyal ally.

She pushed aside her dessert plate, spread the linen napkin on the table before her, smoothed it carefully, and then, choosing her words with care, told Kellen of the occurrences which had been taking place. She told him of the floating black thing she'd seen, of it being seen by Cindy Chambers just about the time her baby died, of the nurse at Sunshine House seeing it the night the baby there died. Then she confided in him her nagging wonder concerning Lily and her unexplainable fascination with storms, and how many of the babies had died while a storm was in progress. She finished by telling him of the episode in the apartment's parking lot.

Not once while she spoke had Kellen's eyes shifted from her face, and they still stared at her as he said in a hushed voice, "Jesus Christ, that is all pretty spooky. No wonder you've been inside yourself all evening."

She reached across the table to lay a hand on his. It took a great deal of effort, but she forced herself to smile. "I apologize, Kellen, for being in the mood I am, but I promise you, if you're willing to try again, it will be different." A surge of pleasurable feeling went through her. She squeezed the hand she held. "I'll make it up to you, I promise."

A faint flush touched his cheeks. "No bribes are required, Susan Rutledge."

The telephone rang. Its abruptness startled Sam, and he allowed it to ring two more times before getting out of the recliner to answer it.

"Sam, come visit me."

It was Lily.

He looked at the wall clock, saw it was ten-forty, and said, "It's rather late, isn't it?"

"Time has no meaning to us, does it, Sam? You and I, we are divorced from such contrivances." Her voice lowered, slipping down into her throat and coming along the telephone line like a whispered strain of music. "Come to your waiting Lily, Sam. I will be grateful, and you know the ways in which I can express my gratitude." Her voice became more melodious. "Did I not tell you I knew all the secrets of womankind, and did I not promise to share them with you? Come and learn, Sam."

He looked at the clock again, thought of the dreary evening he had spent so far, and mentally shrugged. "Give me a few minutes."

"Only a few, Sam." She hung up.

None of the mystique remained when she led him across the threshold into her bedroom. The curling, pungent incense smoke, the drooping palm fonds, the petal-strewn bed were the bizarre components of a stage or motion-picture set, too outlandish to touch even the deepest buried shamelessness in his being. The animals and fowls were exquisitely sculptured chunks of marble displayed on white-painted wooden columns. It was like trying to return to a dream from which you had been awakened. It could not be done. All the structures, excitement, and essence were gone, lost, never to be recaptured.

As after all her storm wanderings, Lily was voracious, pulling him with her as she ascended to the summits of dark, impossible pleasures. It was an on-going process, flesh gratifying flesh, beast and man blending to create carnality beyond sensuality. But this time only one of the creatures watched from its pedestal, a bird more symbolic than real.

A transparent dimness bordered the eastern horizon when Sam let himself out of Lily's townhouse to return to his own. The young morning's coolness, even laden as it was with humidity, felt fresh and untarnished. The thick vapors of incense and crushed flower petals, which had clogged his nostrils since his awakening beside Lily, were clearing from his nasal membranes, so he could smell the saline scent of the sea and the sweet dampness of the dew. He had the odd feeling that the short walk he was taking down the length of the still-sleeping building was an escape into the real world.

He showered, dressed in shorts and a knit polo shirt, and was heating water for instant coffee when the front door opened. Lily walked in.

Instead of her customary dark blouse and slacks, she wore a loose-fitting garment too elaborate to be considered a housecoat yet without the classical grace of a gown. Her hair was piled on the top of her head, reminding him of the beehive hairdos of twenty years ago. She walked slowly to the end of the serving bar, where she stood staring at him for a few seconds. Finally she spoke. "Why did you leave?"

There was a gutturalness in her voice that he heard again. Like a young boy, he responded by shrugging his shoulders.

"I was awake, and it seemed like the thing to do. You were sleeping so well I didn't want to disturb you with a lot of twisting and turning."

"That was considerate of you." Mixed with the guttural hoarseness, there was a sneer in her voice.

"I thought so." He felt the beginnings of an irritation. "I'm a considerate person."

"There is a thin dividing line between consideration and weakness."

"Then I'm weak too."

She continued to stare at him, the pupils of her eyes dilating ever so little. The air conditioner clicked on and the initial thrust of cold air struck Sam like a northern January breeze, causing him to shiver. A tight smile thinned Lily's lips.

He nodded at the jar of coffee and the mug setting on the serving bar. "Would you want some coffee?"

Her nod was as tight as her smile, but the gutturalness had smoothed some in her voice. "Thank you."

They sipped the coffee in silence, heads lowered with eyes downcast.

Finally she said, "You rejected me."

"Where did you get that dumb idea? Can't you accept what happened for what it was—a desire to let you rest?"

There was a tightening of her facial muscles. "Perhaps I will, perhaps I won't."

"Well, do what you want."

Exasperated, he reached out and turned on the portable radio he kept on the serving bar. The seven-thirty news was in progress, and a young voice was completing an item concerning traffic problems on Highway A1A. There was a pause, then the voice announced the death the previous evening of a second baby at the League of Concerned Professional Women's Sunshine House. Because there was no obvious cause, the death was being classified as the result of Sudden Infant Death Syndrome. This death brought the number of infant deaths to nine within recent weeks in the Melbourne area alone. It was believed, the voice concluded, that health officials, with the assistance of law enforcement personnel, were prepared to start an inquiry.

"Jesus Christ, another one!" Sam felt his body go limp. He turned off the radio.

"And what do they think they can do?" Lily chuckled.

"Who?"

"Those people who are going to investigate the deaths." She was sneering, her eyes opaque ovals of green. "They will only ask pointless questions and make meaningless statements."

"At least they're going to try."

"And while they do that, the babies will continue to die."

"Lily, that's a hell of a thing to say!"

She gave an eloquent shrug. Then, with a slow unfolding movement, she stood up. "Have it your way, Sam, but the brats will continue to die. When one is selected, nothing can interfere."

"What the hell do you mean by that?"

Without answering, she turned and walked swiftly to the door. It slammed behind her.

Sam sat staring after her. He felt adrift; his entire body was burning with fever. While he looked at the closed door, his mind was as blank as the door's paneling. But he did know one thing: his relationship with Lily was nearing its end.

The telephone rang sharply.

13

"SAM, I DIDN'T GET YOU UP, DID I?"

It was Susan. There was a tightness in her voice, all animation repressed under taut pronunciation, as if the words were being squeezed through vocal chords which had lost their flexibility.

"No. I've even had my coffee." He tried to make his own voice buoyant, but it was a hoarse monotone.

"Did you hear the news?"

"Yes." He looked out at the sunlight sprinkling the storm-washed leaves of the plants hanging in the patio. "Another baby died at Sunshine House."

"Sam, last night during the storm, was Lily in her apartment?"

"I don't know. She was definitely home later. Why?"

Susan ignored the question. "Sam, does she always drive that black Oldsmobile?"

"Yes. Now what's going on?"

"In a minute. Please tell me what she looks like."

He felt a rise of irritation, then suddenly an uneasiness. Gripping the handpiece tight, he described Lily. When he finished, there was a slight abrasiveness in his voice as he asked, "Now, will you tell me what this is all about?"

"One more question, then I will."

"Damn it, Susan, this isn't a quiz show!"

"I'm sorry, Sam. Here's my last question. Do you know if Lily has an outfit of dark blouse and slacks?"

"Yes, I know that. In fact, she has several. It seems to be her favorite attire. There, now that I've answered all your questions, will you please answer mine? Why do you want to know all this?"

She didn't answer immediately, and he received the impression she was thinking how to tell him what he wanted to know without compromising some kind of caution. "Last night I was at the mall. On the way home, I was caught in the storm, and when I stopped at a traffic light Lily pulled up beside me. I remembered you telling me about her storm travels, and—oh, I don't know, but something made me follow her. Curiosity, I guess. I did follow her, Sam, and she came here to Village Green."

"So?"

"So. She stopped suddenly, and I almost bumped into her, and, well . . . well neither of us got out of our cars, but I felt a sensation of terrible hate directed at me. It was almost as if I'd interrupted something she'd planned to do . . . something very important to her."

"Okay, but why the question about her blouse and slacks?"

"One day a woman answering the description you just gave me came into the library. She was dressed in a black blouse and slacks. For what seemed an awfully long time, she stood in the archway between the reference room and lobby, watching me, then turned and walked away. It affected me because it was more of an

examination than curiousity, so I followed her—and
she disappeared. A young man sitting a few feet from
the archway said no one had passed him. It was as if
she'd never existed, but I know she did. After she was
gone, I got terribly ill. That was the night when I had to
break our dinner date. Sam, I'm sure it was Lily."

Shadows from the plants hanging outside the sliding
door formed a fretwork across the dining room. They
trembled on the tabletop and appeared to crawl along
the floor. Staring at them, Sam had the absurd thought
they were moving with a life of their own, slithering
into the townhouse to take possession of it.

"Sam?"

"Yes, I'm here."

"Sam, are you deeply involved with her? Real deep?"

"Deeper than I want to be, I think."

"So deep that if I said something, you'd get mad?"

"No, but I know what you're going to say, and I'm
beginning to wonder too about some things. A woman
travels in storms, and babies die during storms."

"Sam, don't do anything rash, please. It's only a
thought, a speculation—a maybe."

"And pretty circumstantial."

"Be careful, Sam. I've got to run. I'm going to drive
Maureen and Bridget to Buttons and Bows. Maureen
wants to buy Bridget some new clothes. But, Sam,
please don't do anything until we compare notes.
Promise?"

"Promise." When he replaced the handpiece in its
cradle, he stood staring at nothing in particular, the
shadows no longer holding his interest. He knew he was
approaching a fork in the path of his life, and he had to
decide which branch to follow. To further complicate
things, he had the feeling that no matter what choice he
made, life would never be the same again.

Holly and Todd were standing at the low wall on the

far side of the pool talking to a middle-aged couple
from the complex's north building. Sam did not know
their names, having seen them only occasionally, here
in the pool area. He headed directly toward the beach
steps, not wanting to talk with anyone, but Holly saw
him and waved to him to join them.

Todd introduced him to the couple, John and Ethel
Stahlman. Sam hoped his handshake was firm and the
rigidness he felt in his facial muscles did not hold his
features in a disinterested mask.

Their conversation, he discovered, was centered on
Jetta's death. Her body had never been recovered,
which, even with the occasional erratic currents off-
shore, they all thought strange. Spooky, in a way,
according to Holly.

Sam listened, but said nothing, nor did he join in
when the conversation turned to the deaths of the
babies throughout the area. He did not want to be
asked about Cindy, and he definitely didn't want to be
asked for opinions or speculations. He felt like a secret
carrier of a disease about which everyone spoke with
awe and fear, and he just wanted to get away, to be
alone in an isolation ward and convalesce.

He heard Ethel Stahlman say she thought seven or
eight babies had died.

"Another one can be added to that," Holly said.
"Jetta's child. It was due in less than a month."

Sam looked sharply at her. She had mentioned it
before, but the fact had not registered with him. A
shadow moved across the pool area as an isolated cloud
wandered westward like a puffball rolling across the
sky. The momentary dimness hid nothing from sight,
yet Sam had a brief impression of unseen movement.
He looked at the blank windows of the Ashley townhouse, then watched the retreating shadow crawl up the
side of the building.

"Is Glenn home?" he asked.

The four looked at him, surprised. The question was at odds with the drift of the conversation; Todd shook his head, saying Glenn's car was gone.

"And I hope he stays away," Holly said, bitterly. "He was an embarrassment at dinner last night. Todd might feel differently, but insofar as I'm concerned Glenn Ashley is washed up. He's finished."

"Is he blaming himself for his wife's death?" John Stahlman asked.

"What do you mean?" Todd asked.

"Well, Jetta committed suicide. I was wondering if he thinks of himself as a contributing factor."

Holly shrugged. "If he doesn't, he should. But who knows? Frankly, who cares?"

Even considering Glenn's behavior, there was cruelty in the remark, and the others stood quiet, embarassed, looking out over the ocean or watching a couple seeking shells at the water line.

There was the sound of a car in the driveway, the protest of brakes applied too abruptly, followed by the slamming of a car door.

"That's him now," Todd said. "Maybe I should go see how he's doing."

"You stay right here, Todd Langston." Holly planted a theatrical expression of anger on her face. "He's a big boy now, and he'll have to take care of himself. We tried to help him, and fell flat. I don't think he wants help. He's found his place, groveling in the mud of self-pity."

"Holly!" Todd frowned at his wife. "You're being pretty damn unreasonable, you know that, don't you?"

Holly shrugged, drew a deep breath, then turned to concentrate on the couple below them on the beach.

"I'll go talk with him," Sam said.

He walked around the pool to the Ashley patio gate,

tried the latch, found it unlocked, and pushed his way in. It was dark inside the sliding door, and he watched his own reflection in the glass as he closed the gate. He took a half a dozen steps across the tiny patio, raised a hand to rap on the glass, then saw the door was not completely closed. A narrow opening ran between the frame and the casement. Undecided, he stood looking again at his reflection, then placed his fingers in the opening and slid the door along its track. He stepped into the dining area.

"Glenn! It's Sam. Are you here?"

There was a noise from the second floor, like the bumping of a body against furniture. Sam went to the bottom of the stairs, hesitated, then began to climb. From the rooms below, the rancid odor followed him.

A moan came from the bedroom overlooking the ocean. Sam stopped, sucked his lips between his teeth, then continued down the short hallway. He had another step or two to go before reaching the open door, when Glenn's voice shouted inside the room.

"Damn it, go away! Go away! I see you. You're in that corner. You can't hide in the daylight like you do at night. Now, damn it, go away!"

Sam stopped again, instinctively holding his breath while he listened for a response. None came. Cautiously he took another step toward the door, not at all certain he wanted to go into the room. A moan came from the bedroom, muffled, like a cry from a mouth pressed tightly into a pillow. Sam stepped into the doorway.

Glenn Ashley was sprawled on his stomach on the bed with his face pushed into a pillow. He was fully dressed, but his clothes bore the signs of not being changed for some time. His pants and shirt were a crisscross of wrinkles and creases, spotted with brown and ochre stains between smudges of dirt. From the doorway, Sam thought Glenn's yellow shirt and brown slacks resembled nothing less than a cleaning cloth used too long and hard without washing. He stepped into the room, glancing at all four corners. Nothing was to be seen.

He went to the bed. "Glenn, are you awake?"

"Go away."

"Glenn, this is Sam. I want to ask you a question, just one question. That's all. And then I'll leave. Will you answer it?"

Keeping his face pressed into the pillow, Glenn mumbled, "Maybe."

Looking down at the human wreckage spread on the soiled bed, Sam realized he had no idea how to ask the question which had brought him here, and he found himself fearful of the physical reaction which might follow. Gnawing his lower lip, he took a step back and ran fingers through his hair.

Finally, in as soft a voice as he could muster, he said, "Glenn, try to remember . . . before Jetta . . . before Jetta died . . . did you see anything outside your apartment or feel anything inside it?"

"Yes, goddamn you! Yes!" Glenn flopped over on his back. He glared up at Sam with swollen, red-rimmed eyes. Beneath a stubble of beard, his face was without pigmentation, absolutely white, so his eyes and nose and mouth appeared to have been drawn on white paper.

"Okay, go ahead and laugh. Have your fun, you son of a bitch, just like the bastards at Jimmy's Bar when I told them I saw a black thing floating outside the windows and the patio gate at night. Go on, Sam, laugh. That's what Holly did, that bitch." He tried to sit up, wobbled, and fell back with a sobbing grunt. "Laugh, Sam, laugh."

Sam shook his head. "I'm not going to laugh, Glenn.

I believe you." He reached down to lay a hand on a twisting shoulder. "Other people have seen it."

Again Glenn endeavored to sit up, and this time he succeeded, bracing himself with widespread arms, digging his hands into the mattress's edge. An expression Sam could not read slithered its way across the chalky features before the man bowed his head to look at the floor.

"Others?" His voice was as shallow as his complexion. "What others?"

Sam sat down beside him on the bed. He felt unexplainably weak, conscious that his heartbeat was quickening. "Cindy, my associate at the office. A nurse at Sunshine House. And a good friend of mine. They all saw it. I didn't see it, Glenn, but I felt it one night moving through the darkness." He hesitated, swung his eyes around the room. "Was it here a minute ago? I heard you talking to it, saying you could see it in one of the corners."

"I—I don't know." Glenn groaned and moved his head from side to side, attempting to loosen his neck muscles or clear his thinking. "I thought so, but I'm juiced to the eyeballs—so maybe I did, maybe I didn't —maybe it was my imagination. I don't know."

"Glenn, have you seen the thing since Jetta died?"

"Who the hell knows? If it was floating around in that corner over there, then I've seen it, yeah. Just like Jetta's body's floating around somewhere out there in the ocean." His hunched shoulders gave an abbreviated shrug. "Then maybe I never saw it at all, only think I did. Who the hell can say? A drunk seeing a black thing floating in the night. No wonder people laugh and shake their heads."

"The people I told you about weren't drunk when they saw it, and I wasn't drunk when I felt it moving by me."

Glenn braced his hands on his knees and turned his face straight at Sam. "And, by God, Sam, I wasn't drunk when I saw that frigging bird flapping around out over the ocean looking at me." He bobbed his head up and down. "Goddamn frigging right, I wasn't drunk, and I saw a bird like you wouldn't believe, circling around out there watching me with red eyes that were as mean as hell, then I watched it come into land behind those trees south of here."

Sam's hands dug into the mattress so hard his palms hurt. "Bird?"

"Yeah, a big one . . ."

"With red eyes?"

"That's right." Glenn's voice dropped to a mumble. "Eyes red as hell."

"Glenn, did anyone else see the bird?"

It was a long moment before the answer came. "No, but . . ."

Like his thoughts, Glenn's voice trailed away.

Sam waited, then, "But? But what, Glenn?"

"Lily . . ."

"What about Lily?"

"She came by a minute later . . . don't think she saw it, though. Nice woman . . . nice talking to her . . ." Glenn fell back across the bed, covering his eyes with a forearm. "Later, Sam . . . we'll talk later . . . okay?"

"Okay, Glenn."

Sam pushed himself to his feet to stand looking down at the rumpled, defeated figure sprawled on the wrinkled and dirty sheets. Inside his mind a small voice had begun repeating questions, the answers to which were beyond logical comprehension. He felt a trembling in the deeper layers of his body, and for the space of several breaths thought he could hear the erratic thumping of his heart in the fragile silence of the room. With a shake of his head, he whirled and hurried from the bedroom.

Outside, he looked toward Lily's garage. Her car was in.

He pressed the ornate doorbell button three times, listening to the chimes ringing inside the foyer, and was about to walk away when the door opened. Lily stood rigidly looking at him. A dusting of white powder covered her hands, and her left cheek carried a smear of it. Beneath the curve of her brows, there was no emotion in the unyielding stare of her eyes. No loathsome fires burned in their depths, but Sam had the disquieting sensation he was being studied by "the other Lily" along with the one who was framed in the doorway.

"May I come in?" he asked.

A tense moment passed before she shrugged and stepped back into the foyer.

He entered, then stood in the foyer. Her eyes never left him, and he found that he wanted to do something to break that stare, tap his feet, snap his fingers, anything to cause a ripple of expression on her blank, taut face and make those watching eyes reflect a glimmer of interest.

"Why are you here, Sam?" It was more a demand than a question.

"To talk."

"Oh?"

"There are some questions I want to ask, some things I want to say."

"I do not answer questions. You know that."

Sam stirred uncomfortably while Lily rubbed her hands down the sides of the blue smock she wore, leaving white streaks on the material.

"You're not making it easy, Lily. You're not trying to help."

She said nothing, only continued to stare at him.

From the surrounding rooms, the cold, impersonal atmosphere of the townhouse glided into the foyer to wrap around him, and, for a moment, he experienced the sensation of standing in a house whose tenants were away from home.

He shook his head. "I'm sorry, Lily, but I want to know some things."

"Sam, do not waste our time. You know everything I intend to tell you."

"Why? What are you hiding?"

"Many things. We all conceal certain portions of ourselves from others." Here and there tiny muscles twitched in her face. "Do not pry, Sam. Be content with me as I have presented myself to you."

"I cannot, Lily, not anymore."

"That is too bad, Sam; for I am what I am. I will not change. I like what I am."

Suddenly he felt determined. "Lily, that evening when we met, did you see a huge black bird flying out over the ocean? A bird that flew inland and landed behind the dunes?"

No expression shaded her face. Its symmetrical features remained impassive, but he felt the chill of the rooms become a degree or two colder. And back in the gloom among the white pillars with the white creatures perched on them, he sensed a shifting in the air as though unseen things were moving through it to take positions surrounding him and Lily.

"A bird?" she finally asked, and he heard the echo of his own voice asking Glenn the same question. "Just before I called to you?"

"Yes . . ." From the corner of his eye he was certain he saw things circling back there in the gloom. "Black with red eyes."

For a moment longer, she stared at him, then took a slow step toward him. He watched a smile being born on her lips. "I am being irrational, am I not, Sam? Forgive me. I was working in my studio when you came, and my thoughts were on the marble."

Through the smock he felt her radiating warmth driving away the chill of the townhouse's barrenness. He became aware that his body was responding, and, at that instant, he knew he must escape from these stark rooms. Away from here, from this contorted, hostile atmosphere, they might be able to talk rationally, to discover the roots of the blossoming discord between them and dig them out.

Impulsively, he said, "Let's go for a ride. Let's drive down the coast and stop someplace for a sandwich or a drink. What do you say? We've never done that. Let's just get away from this place for a few hours and try to find our perspective."

She reached out to take his hand. "Yes, perhaps it will do us good. Give me five minutes to get ready, will you, Sam?"

"Of course. I'll bring the car to your front door."

Dressed in her black slacks and blouse, Lily was closing her door when he braked to a stop in front of her place. The darkness of her hair and clothing and her honey-amber skin was a striking contrast to the flamboyant reds and yellows of the geraniums and sand-dune sunflowers bordering the entrance path. He watched her come down the path and walk in front of the car to the passenger's side, and wondered if he had adequate defenses to erect against her.

He drove south on A1A toward Sebastian Inlet and Vero Beach. Traffic was scarce on the two-lane road, but Sam kept the speedometer needle below the fifty-five-mile-per hour limit. He was in no hurry to pass through this region left over from the simple, languorous childhood of the state.

Lily turned her head from side to side, looking at the sun-splashed ocean on their left and the placcid blue-green of the Indian River on their right.

"Soon," she said, "this area will lose its freedom. It will be forced to submit to the desires of men. They will rape it, take from it what they want, then move on, leaving the land drained of beauty and vitality and burdened with the things it has been forced to spawn, like a woman burdened with children."

"Yeah, I guess so."

"The land is helpless. It cannot defend itself. Women can, but they deny themselves the excitement and joy of freedom by giving their bodies to men. They do not have to, and only the weak ones submit. Those women are like the machinery used to disembowel the land. They give birth to things that befoul the landscape."

He glanced at her. "If I didn't know better, I'd think you were either an activist feminist or a celibate."

She turned to look directly at him. A tiny movement, which might have been a sneer, played on her lips. "Poor man, you do not understand why I have proffered my body to you."

He didn't like what he heard in her voice. "Maybe not, but if you offer it, I'm going to accept it."

The atmosphere inside the car suddenly seemed emotionally charged. Sam kept his attention on the black asphalt ribbon stretching before them through the scrub vegetation.

They passed the ornate gates and featureless walls of high-priced housing projects on the north side of Vero Beach. Just ahead, Sam knew, was a city park. When they arrived at it, he would turn around and head back north. He no longer felt the desire to talk over their problems with her. Any attempt would only add new difficulties to the old ones, he knew.

The park was on their left. Cars were parked two deep around its fringes. In a gentle sea breeze, balloons floated and bobbed between the reaching branches of oak and peppertrees, while from the frameworks of swings and slides crepe-paper streamers rippled like garish tails. Scattered among the trees, booths of equally brilliant colors were identified by hand-lettered signs as places to purchase various items from fast food to trinkets, or to test one's luck and skill at games of chance. Bodiless bluegrass music blurted from the metal throat of cheap public-address speakers. Moving from booth to booth among the trees and around the playground equipment, a crowd of people gave the first impression of a single heaving mass drifting through the dappled light.

A car backed out in front of them, forcing Sam to step heavily on the brakes. On impulse, he turned the BMW into the space. He turned off the ignition, telling himself that if they walked through the festivities, ate a hamburger or hot dog, drank a cola, made some trivial purchases, goodness would come to the afternoon. He looked at Lily.

She was intently watching the activities, her entire concentration locked on the panorama of color and moving people.

"Want to walk through the place?" he asked. "It doesn't look like much, but it would be different."

She nodded. "Yes. It reminds me of a medieval carnival."

The trees and the press of bodies reduced the effectiveness of the sea breeze, and before long Sam's skin began to itch from the humid heat. Lily, despite her dark blouse and slacks, seemed to draw stamina from some secret source of power, and towed him from booth to booth, eating first a hot dog, then a hamburger, and finally a thick wedge of homemade fudge. She was suddenly a lighthearted child, furiously excited, making her way through a great adventure. Following her, caught in her enchantment, Sam felt the grotesque possibilities he had begun to envision in the car disappear. The strikingly beautiful woman holding his hand and laughing at his side was indeed the woman he had started to love.

Twice they wandered around the small circle of

booths, stopping at some two or three times for Lily to repeat performances with baseball or dart throwing. An hour passed before they began to make their way slowly toward the car, Lily licking the residue of her second piece of fudge from her fingers. They approached an animated group of middle-aged people who were excitedly discussing something. A man detached himself from the cluster and hurried in their direction.

"Are you leaving us?" he asked.

Surprised by the man's interest, Sam nodded. "Yes."

"Well, we're happy and pleased that you visited our little festival." From under curling white brows, the man looked around at the activities. "I'm surprised we had such a fine turn-out, especially among the young people. A get-together like ours must seem old-fashioned to them, but we had a goodly number come today."

As if following the man's example, Lily looked around, her eyes scanning the park with slow deliberateness, then nodded and smiled at him. "Yes, you have a fine number of young people here. May I ask who you are?"

The man stared at her with a stricken expression. His round face slowly fumed a vivid red beneath his sunburn. He made no attempt to hide his embarrassment.

"Oh, my," he said, "I am sorry for failing to introduce myself. I suppose I'm just so elated over the crowd that I forgot the amenities. I'm Reverend Henry Allison, pastor of the Church of the Watchful Shepherd. Do you live in Vero Beach?"

"No," Sam smiled. "We're from farther up the coast, in the Melbourne Beach, Indialantic area."

"Oh, yes, that's nice up there too." He pulled a thin packet of folders from the hip pocket of his rumpled seersucker slacks. The folders were creased and their brown paper appeared sweat-dampened, but he separated two from the pile to hand one to Sam and another to Lily. "Let me give you these. It's a history of our church. If ever you're down here on Sunday mornings or Wednesday evenings, you're always welcome to visit us. I think you would enjoy our approach to the Testaments."

The cover of the folder was a surprisingly delicate pen-and-ink rendering of a large building nestled in a grove of palms and other trees. Sam assumed it was the Church of the Watchful Shepherd. He was preparing to open the folder when he heard the minister gasp, "Madam!"

He glanced up. The Rev. Allison's round face was an illustration of horror. A few feet away, Lily was grinding the folder she had been given into the dirt with the toe of her right shoe. With a final twist of her foot, she stepped back from the torn brown pulp.

"There is the history of your church, dirtied and worthless as it actually is!" She stared directly at the Rev. Allison. "You speak of Testaments, old man, but what are they? Can you, in your blind faith, tell me?"

"Madam, I'm sorry. We each—"

"You are sorry! Oh, you puny little man, your whole sanctimonious life has been built on half truths! Hearsay compiled from hearsay collected from legends. Half tales. Falsehoods. And you call them Testaments. You pitiful fool—you, and all those who accept and live by those Testaments, have been deluded."

"Lily!" Sam took a step toward her, a hand raised to lay on her shoulder. "What the devil are you—"

She whirled on him, a sharp, hissing coming from her mouth. "Stay back, Sam; you are no better. You are as weak and deluded as they."

Burning eyes glared at him from the chiseled face of the "other" Lily.

Rev. Allison had fallen back several steps, and now he too looked at Sam. "Is she ill?"

Lily gave a discordant laugh. "Can you seek no better explanation than that? Is your thinking so narrow that you cannot conceive of ideas that exceed your miserable little contemplation?" She laughed again. "Give unanswering belief to half-told stories, pitiful little man, and your life becomes a fantasy. You are an unimportant spector. You believe in a fiction written by hucksters. That is what your Testaments are, Little Reverend, writings marketed with great fanfare and unfulfillable promises."

"Lily! Goddamn it, that's enough!" Sam felt rage building in him. "Let's go. Now, Lily! Come on, get to the car."

A number of people had gathered in a tight knot around their pastor, their faces disfigured with frowns, horror and anger tightening their muscles. They were hearing their lifelong rituals and ceremonies being blasphemed, their beliefs crucified.

Sam started walking in the direction of the car. "I'm leaving. If you're coming with me, Lily, now's the time to do it."

From behind the mask of sharp-edged planes covering her face, the searing eyes focused on him. Slowly she began to follow him.

Rev. Allison raised a hand. "May God have mercy on you."

Lily froze, only her fingers opening and closing, reminding Sam of the talons of the creatures in her townhouse, perched on their white pedestals. Very slowly she turned her head to direct the flames sizzling in her eyes toward the minister. Before the force of her stare, he backed a step, bumping into those grouped around him.

"Mercy? From Him?" Lily's voice was guttural. "He has no mercy. I can speak firsthand of His vengeance, little man. I can take you back through the millennia, back to before your myths were created, recounting

time upon time when His rage and fury were unleashed. Little Reverend, you, and those who follow
you, seek forgiveness from a wrathful God who has no
mercy. You are fools!"

At no time that he could remember had Sam been so
nauseated with anger. His mouth was dry, and when he
turned the key in the ignition his hand shook with such
force that it nearly dropped from his fingers. The
engine was running and the car was in gear, with his
foot trembling on the clutch pedal, when Lily got into
the seat beside him, slamming the door after her.

Without a word, he backed out of the parking space,
turned the car north, then jammed his foot down on
the accelerator. Though he couldn't see them in the
rearview mirror, he knew Rev. Allison and his group
were watching.

"What kind of behavior was that back there?" His
voice filled his mouth like a physical entity. "I'm not a
bible-slapping believer, and I'm not a churchgoer, but,
by God, I can't accept what you did back there. I
cannot, will not, be a party to that kind of vicious
attack on any man's religious beliefs, no matter what
teachings he follows."

"Should I care?" Her voice was still uneven, rough.

"If you have any feelings toward our relationship,
then, yes, you should care."

Her head was pointed straight forward so the heavy
fallings of her hair blocked his view of her face when he
glanced at her, but he knew he did not want to see her
features, because she would be wearing that horrible
mask of otherness.

"Our relationship? Is that what you call it?"

"What would you name it?"

"Sam, you innocent fool, it has been no more than a
dalliance. Surely you could not have placed great hopes
in it, unless you are a greater idiot than I pictured you."
The throaty laugh she emitted was more of a snarl.

"You have been a needed outlet, that is all, Sam."

He was certain the steering wheel rim was going to snap in his hands as anger raced in waves through him, tensing his muscles.

"Do you know what you are, Lily?"

"I know what you are going to say I am, but I have been called bitch and slut and whore before, many times in many places; so try to be more inventive."

It was a challenge which he refused to accept. He watched the road, desperately attempting to hold at bay the uncontrolled thoughts searching for an entrance to his mind.

The Sebastian Inlet came and went, followed by the gaunt, high concrete piles of isolated condominiums looking like advanced scouts for an approaching horde of square-shouldered structures. The sun was still well up in the western sky, but an amber haze was settling on the land as the slanting light tinted a mist slowly advancing inland from the sea.

They reached the complex, and he turned into the driveway. Lily remained rigid. He hesitated mentally, then decided not to drive her to her front door, instead turning into his own garage.

"End of the line, Lily."

The words hung inside the car with a terrible ring of finality. In spite of the air-conditioning, the interior was hot and airless, unnaturally so, as though the heat surrounding them came from a place immune to the technical devices of man. Finally, for the first time since leaving Vero Beach, she turned to face him. Her features had recomposed themselves, but the face he looked at was withdrawn and stern, void of living warmth. The handsomeness was still there, but filtered through a dimness which he could not help but feel was a patina of age, as if her face belonged to a long-forgotten time.

Then he saw the flames, deep behind the green pupils

of her eyes, flickering at first, then thickening until they glittered and gleamed in a continuous flare of crimson. The hellfires that had seared at his brain the night in her bed now reached for him again, seeking entrance into his mind to consume its contents. He knew if they found their way in, his mind would become an empty chamber, that there would be no comprehension remaining, no reasoning, nothing with which to understand and feel. As he had done that night, he closed his eyes and turned his face away.

"I think you'd better leave, Lily." It wasn't his voice he heard. The cadence was wrong, the tone was wrong. It was an abstract sound coming from somewhere beyond reality. "Now!"

She made a hissing, guttural noise that might have been that of a predator cornering a fleeing prey and toying with it for a moment of evil pleasure before pouncing.

"You are weak, Sam." There was something less than human in her voice, something crude and violent as if her larynx was not nimble enough to reproduce complicated utterances.

"Lily, don't talk. Just get out and go home." He spoke into the darkness behind his closed eyelids. "Just go away. Okay?"

What might have been another snarl came from the passenger seat. But there was no movement. He received the impression that she was intensely staring straight ahead into the dark interior of the garage. He squeezed his eyes tight, resisting the growing impulse to look at her.

There were so many important things to say, but right now he did not feel the need to say them.

There was movement, then, a shifting of body weight on the seat, followed by the sound of the latch handle being pulled and finally the door opening.

"You are expelling me."

"You've forced me to."

"You are a fool!"

"Perhaps."

A long, deep breath was drawn in. He heard it hiss passed bared teeth and through flared nostrils, and he instinctively hunched his shoulders and tightened his hands on the steering wheel.

The car door slammed.

He knew he was being a coward, but he sat with his eyes tightly closed while long minutes dragged past, knowing that if he opened them and found her standing beside the door, he would be lost forever in darkness. Eventually the awareness of being alone transcended his feelings of pain and humiliation and anger, and he opened his eyes. While he closed the garage door and walked to the townhouse's front entrance, he didn't glance in the direction of Lily's place.

Twilight was spreading along the beach. Already it had found its way into the townhouse, filling the corners of the rooms with shadows which in a short time would be a black drapery hiding the ceiling. The silence was a thick pressure relentlessly pushing at the walls.

Sam turned down the air conditioner's thermostat, then lit a cigarette. He turned on the stereo. A contemporary hit blasted out of the speakers, not heavy rock, but discordant to his senses, so he pushed one of the set's memory switches and changed to an easy-listening station. For a long time, he stood in the middle of the living room, looking through the dining area and out the sliding door at the patio, from which detail was already erased by the settling twilight. His mind was in neutral.

He thought of mixing himself a drink, but knew that the vodka would taste bitter and when it reached his stomach it would burn, and so dismissed the idea. He was in limbo. For the past weeks, his emotions had exploded time and time again as he'd plunged deeper and deeper into a void of carnal saturation, never giving thought to the consequences.

But now, somewhat slowly, his mind was tentatively throwing off its lethargy. The memory banks kicked in. Rationalization and intuition reformed. He stared at nothing while his thought processes slipped into gear and a pattern took shape.

"Christ on a crutch!"

He looked at the wall clock. It was ten minutes after eight. He went to the telephone and dialed Susan's number. At the far end of the line, the evenly spaced signal sounded six times, and he was about to hang up when she answered.

"Yes?" She was breathless.

"Susan, this is Sam."

"Oh, Sam, hello. Kellen and I were just on our way out. In fact, I heard the phone ringing through the closed door."

"Susan, I've got to talk to you. Can I pick you up in the morning around ten o'clock? We can have brunch."

"Oh, Sam, Kellen and I are going to do just that ourselves. Why don't you join us?"

"Thanks, but what I want to talk about is for your ears only. Maybe we can ask Kellen for help, if we think there's anything to help with."

"It sounds important. Is it what we've talked about? The babies?"

"Yes."

"Can you give me a small hint?"

He felt his heart pounding in his chest and became acutely aware that the hand holding the telephone was sweating, making the instrument slippery. At the same time, he became conscious of the other presence, somewhere in the darkness on the far side of the living room. Like the times before, it was heavy, displacing the air as it shifted its position, watching him and, he knew, listening to what he was saying on the telephone.

"Sam?" Susan's voice came from far away.

His concentration was slipping from him. If he didn't pull it back, it would become like a power failure, turning off all the little circuits in his mind. He turned his back on whatever it was lingering in the shadows.

"I'm having completely unbelievable thoughts about that thing seen in the night," he said softly. "I think there's a relationship between it, and the babies dying . . . and someone."

"Sam! Who?"

He shook his head and saw the motion duplicated in the glass of the sliding door. "I can't say now. Anyway, it's mostly conjecture. But that's why I want to talk with you—you'll either straighten me out, or confirm what I suspect."

"All right, Sam, I'll be here. Come over at nine o'clock, and we can take as much time as we need. I know Kellen will understand."

"Good. Thanks, Susan."

"See you then. I'll have a pot of coffee ready."

None of the heaviness inside him was alleviated when he hung up the phone. The pattern he was weaving with his thoughts was quite intricate. Spoken out loud, he was certain his conjectures would sound like the blundering concoctions of a bruised mind. But he was determined to tell them to Susan.

He stood unmoving for a long time, waiting for the thing in the darkness to move again. But if it was still in the townhouse, it had either retreated to a place where his senses could not detect it, or become too small to disturb the atmosphere. After a while, he sat in the recliner, not turning on any lights, wrapping himself in the blanket of darkness inside the townhouse.

It was almost ten o'clock when he got out of the chair. The artificial coolness inside the dark rooms was close and clammy, the silence too weighty, the aloneness an unbearable companion. Without turning on a light, he went through the sliding door, across the patio and pool area, and down the steps to the beach. He was certain that on the beach his feeling and understanding would expand.

The tide was low, and under the hazy starlight the beach was a dismal gray. Sam walked south, kicking at the sand, conscious of little more than the darkness shrouding the coast. He felt a vague resentment, but he wasn't certain at who or what it was directed, himself or Lily or life in general. Here, with only the company of the restless sea, he knew there had never been anything authentic in his relationship with Lily. In some ways she was no more than a shadow fallen across his life. He shoved his hands into his pockets and continued walking.

Along the crest of a dune, a darkness, only slightly blacker than the night behind it, moved lightly through the sea oats and around the frayed silhouette of a sea grape bush. It drifted, matching Sam's slow, meandering pace, neither moving ahead of him nor falling behind him, making no attempt to descend from the dune top.

An empty bottle, to which a Sun Country Wine Cooler label still clung, lay partially buried in the sand before him, part of the refuse left behind by the Saturday afternoon crowd. Instead of the disgust he normally felt, he experienced a kind of sadness at the mistreatment of the beach. He gave the bottle a little kick, then moved on. Memories filled him, memories of storms during which Lily drove at breakneck speeds and babies died, of Jetta Ashley deliberately drowning herself and her unborn baby after modeling for Lily. Where was the clay statuette now? And what was to become of Glenn Ashley? He shook his head. He thought of Lily's emotional highs when she returned from her storm travels, the overpowering sexual stimu-

lation she brought home with her and his succumbing
to it. He didn't struggle to keep the thoughts away,
because he wanted to put them in a logical sequence for
the morning's meeting with Susan.

A few moments he felt a touch of heat on his nerve
ends, the pressure of the darkness against his skin. He
stopped and looked around. The sky and the sea were
like great opposing mirrors of darkness, each reflecting
the emptiness of the other. He was by himself, his eyes
seeing nothing but shadows within shadows and his
ears hearing only the swishing metronome of the waves,
but in the deepest core of his mind, instinct whispered
that he was not alone. And at that instant, he knew the
thing which had been watching him in his office and in
the restaurant had just been in the townhouse and was
with him now.

Twice he turned in a circle where he stood, his eyes
carefully searching the blurred pools of starlight and
the depthless caverns of shadows spotting the faces of
the dunes. There was nothing, only horizon-to-horizon
emptiness, but the primeval stirrings within him would
not permit his brain to accept the messages sent it by
his eyes and ears. Somewhere close by in the night,
something was watching him.

He stood very still. Above him, the sky seemed to
lower itself. To his right the sea became restless, waves
slapping the sand, their rhythm suddenly erratic. The
air grew heavy and laden with the smell of salt, coating
his arms and face with a damp stickiness. He had the
odd sensation nature was realigning itself into a pattern
from which everything now associated with it would be
dissolved and replaced with things always considered
unnatural.

He drew a deep breath, feeling a muscle tighten
across his shoulders, then, shaking his head, began
walking back in the direction of his home.

The transparent darkness lingered a moment longer

on the dune tip, expanding slowly while it rocked gently back and forth and its shape began to alter. Then, very slowly, disentangling itself from the sea oats and grass, it floated from sight down the inland slope of the dune.

On the way home, Sam felt the eeriness of the beach receding. At the base of his skull, a small round spot of pain began to throb, then almost immediately sent streamers down his neck and up into his skull. Tension, he told himself, and walked faster.

A thick, opaque darkness soared between the stars and the earth, casting a shadow along the gray-white ribbon of sand. Over the slapping of the waves, another sound came from above him, like the powerful workings of great wings stroking the heavy, saline air. Instinctively, Sam looked up.

Out over the water, spiraling higher and higher, a huge, solid-black creature soared upward in what appeared to be the direction of a distant star cluster. Sam stopped and watched. Like something stirring at the far end of a labyrinth, a memory sought entrance to his mind, but could not find its way through the maze of passageways. He saw huge wings tilt, their great sail-like surfaces blotting out a third of the stars, as the creature ceased its upward spiraling, hovered momentarily, then plunged beachward in a plummeting dive.

Memory rushed through his mind like a cold draft of arctic wind, carrying with it the picture of the strange, outsized bird riding the storm winds, so many weeks before.

It was gathering speed, diving directly at him. Suddenly he could see red glaring eyes focused tightly on him, a triangular head thrust forward on a straining neck. Very distinctly, as if filmed in slow motion, he watched the opening of a curved beak and the extending of spread talons.

The goddamn thing was attacking him!

Without thinking, he began to run, but the soft sand

slithered beneath his feet, rolling out from under his shoes. He staggered, advancing only a few steps before he heard the rushing of air across the surfaces of the great wings. With a cry, he threw himself to his right, diving for the packed sand above the water's edge. All sound was concentrated in the hammering of his heart and the gulping gasps of his indrawn breath.

A half dozen red-hot branding irons streaked along his back, searing molten pain from his shoulders to his hips. Through the initial agony, he felt the warmth of spurting blood soaking the shreds of his tattered shirt.

He heard a piercing, high-pitched sound, but he didn't know if it was a scream from his own gaping mouth or a cry from the curving beak of the giant bird. Ignoring the protests of his shock-numbed muscles, he pushed himself to his hands and knees, swaying drunkenly, his fingers clawing into the sand beneath them. Painfully raising his head, he looked over his left shoulder. The bird was circling low above a dune top, almost stationary in the air currents, the almond-shaped slits of its eyes burning with solid flames.

He knew he must get to the water. The salt would make the pain in his back all but unbearable, but the bird would be helpless to reach him beneath the surface of the waves. Everything inside him cried out in protest as he tensed himself to make the lunge for the ocean, and when he finally shoved himself to his feet, he was dismayed at how much energy the movement drained from him.

He had managed two or three steps when he heard a high-pitched keening. Somewhere a woman, erupting with rage, was screaming her fury into the night. Then came the beating of wings and the screaming was directly behind him, filling his ears with its rage. A terrible force slammed into his back, wrenching his spine and pitching him forward, feet stumbling in the sand, arms flailing in front of him. He hit the damp,

hard-packed sand with a sliding fall that drove his face
into the abrasive wetness and sledgehammered the air
from his lungs. Pain squeezed in on him from all sides,
jabbing and gouging at his flesh and muscles until his
entire awareness was of throbbing agony that threatened to explode his being into tiny, blood-drenched
bits.

The bird's wings beat the sand with a furious thudding as it danced around his torn body. Like an
attacking snake, its beak darted forth to clutch flesh
and clothing already shredded by its curved talons. Its
slanted red eyes glowed brighter and brighter as though
within the triangular head its brain was a mass of
flaming hate being stoked by the sight of blood.

Blood from the lacerations crisscrossing his skull
mixed with the sand clinging to his face to form a
mixture that pasted shut his eyes. But he pried them
open to see a taloned claw, red with his blood, working
convulsively in the sand only inches from his face.
Inside his head, he felt his brain being reduced to a
cinder from the pain searing through it. His arms and
legs were no longer controlable, just appendages somewhere below his line of vision, each individually
jammed with anguish. Yet beneath the layers of pain,
there was still a remnant of strength. Without even
crying out in response to the pain slicing and hacking
through his torn muscles, he threw himself to his left,
both hands groping for the clawed foot beside his face.

The bird hissed as his hands closed around its foot,
its wings beating the air and slapping the sand. It lifted
a little way into the air, pulling him with it so his
shoulders raised from the sand. Desperately, he twisted
at the foot, hoping to unbalance the bird, but feeling
the surge of strength which had gone through him
rapidly ebbing away. The bird's other foot was clawing
at his stomach, shredding the front of his shirt and
peeling the flesh away in long, bloody ribbons. He

screamed. His hands lost their now-useless hold on the writhing foot. With a cry as much of frustration as of pain, he fell back to the sand.

Groaning, he stared up into the triangular face hovering over him, into the slanted eyes burning with their special hellfires.

Then, suddenly, the bird twisted and turned in a flurry of movement. He caught a glimpse of hooked talons slashing at him, felt an abrupt pain across his throat followed by a warm bubbling of blood. Almost immediately the darkness of the night thickened while the red eyes staring down at him expanded and expanded until all the universe was a burning red, fringed with black . . . and then that too began to fade, and he felt himself slipping sideways toward a great nothingness.

At the instant the void closed around him, he saw the bird glide across the beach to disappear behind a sand dune, and a moment later he saw Lily standing atop the dune, her black hair blowing in the storm winds.

14

Susan Rutledge poured her second cup of coffee of the morning and carried it to the dinette table, where she set it down among the scattering of papers fanned haphazardly on the maple surface. She looked out the jalousie window at the sun-drenched small lawn sloping down to the parking area thirty yards away. Sunlight flared off the cars. Nothing had changed, but everything was different.

It was Saturday. A week ago tomorrow, at just about this time, Sam's mutilated body had been found on the beach by a group of surfers. When he hadn't appeared for their nine o'clock meeting that Sunday morning, she'd waited until nine-thirty, then phoned his home and after that his office. As she'd hung up the phone after receiving no answer at the office, she had had a premonition that something was very much wrong. Half an hour later, when Maureen Neilson had banged on the door saying the radio had just announced that Sam's body had been discovered on the beach, Susan was not surprised.

That was almost a week ago, and still the authorities professed to have no clues. Inevitably there were the usual whispered speculations that Sam's death was drug-related, that while walking the beach he had come on a transaction in progress and been killed to hide the identity of those involved. It had happened before, not too far from that very spot. But Susan knew that Sam would never have approached strangers on a nighttime beach. No, Sam had died because he had patched together a theory concerning the baby deaths. Of that, she was frighteningly certain.

Yesterday had been the memorial service for him at a local mortuary. She had assisted Cindy Chambers in arranging it. Though he had lived in the area ten years, Sam, like many residents, had not sunk deep roots into the sandy soil. At the request of his parents, his remains had been sent north to Columbus, Ohio, where the funeral would be held.

Although she shouldn't have been, Susan was surprised at the number of people who had attended the service. Some had come from Orlando and Miami. But she was genuinely astonished that the woman named Lily had not made an appearance. Why did the person who had had such a dynamic effect on Sam's life ignore his death?

She took a sip of the cooling coffee and looked at the papers spread before her. They were covered with a hodgepodge of notes, compiled from the news stories concerning Sam's death, the sudden upswing in baby deaths, random jottings of random thoughts, and bits and pieces of information she had gathered from the library's material. Now she looked at them, preparing to shuffle through them one last time on the off chance one little item had gone undetected.

First, there was the information she had obtained concerning Sudden Infant Death Syndrome. It was very skimpy. SIDS, as it was referred to by doctors and researchers, was a medical mystery. In Landover, Maryland, there was a national foundation attempting to find the cause of SIDS, and in Atlanta an institute conducted research, but insofar as she could determine no breakthroughs had been accomplished. SIDS cannot be predicted or prevented, her information indicated. An apparently normal baby can die suddenly and unexpectedly, with the death remaining unexplained even after an autopsy. That was all, except that Florida rated eighth in the nation in SIDS tragedies.

Next were the notes she had made from the information in the library's newspaper files and from her own memory. These contained more hard facts with which to work, although, she was forced to admit, some of the information was circumstantial and possibly could not be directly associated with the local deaths. But there was one item that was fairly consistent with the area deaths: the majority of the babies had died during fierce electrical storms. She couldn't help but feel the storms were a fact which could not be ignored.

The third pile consisted of what she thought of as "unreal reality." It was the description of the thing seen in the night by Cindy, the nurse at Sunshine House, and Susan herself. For some reason she had the terrible certainty the true reason for Sam's death could be found in this set of notes. His phone call to her the night of his death, she thought, verified that.

There was one final item. It was short, with no speculative notations. Only a question mark. Lily and her drives through nighttime storms.

She laid the notes aside and shook her head. Nothing new there. She emptied the cup with one long swallow, making a face because the air conditioner had cooled the coffee and made it bitter. Hating to do it, as if by putting them out of sight she would remove their contents from her thoughts, she gathered the notes into a neat stack and placed them in a drawer of the small writing desk in the living room.

On the desk was a cream-colored envelope with her name handwritten on it. Someone had dropped it at the library's main desk on Wednesday. She picked it up. In brown letters, "Civic Art Center" was scripted in the upper left-hand corner. Inside was a one-fold pamphlet of semi-glossy stock. Once more she pulled it out to look at it.

The front was a well-lit photograph of a sculpture of a hawk. It appeared to be alabaster or marble, she couldn't determine which from the picture. Beneath the illustration were the words: *A one-time showing of selected works of wildlife sculpture.* Beneath that, she read: *You are invited to attend this exclusive exhibit of samples of the nation's finest sculpture. No admission charge. 7:00 PM to 10:00 PM Monday, August Third.*

The inside pages bore three more photos: an owl, what appeared to be a jackal, and a bird which bore no resemblance to any Susan had ever seen. As she had before, she looked long at the photographs. Although she could not identify it, there was something about the spread-winged bird that was vaguely familiar, as if at some time, some place, a bird like that had touched her life in some way. The longer she looked, the stronger became the impression that she should recognize the bird.

She continued to study the photograph for a short time longer, aware of the coolness of the apartment's air-conditioning, conscious of the troublesome half-thoughts playing with her mind, then, scowling, put the invitation back in its envelope and laid it on the desk.

She took the coffee cup to the kitchen, and had just rinsed it out when the telephone rang.

It was Kellen. "Are you hungry?"

She hadn't thought about food. The coffee had taken the edge from her hunger, and scanning her notes had kept her from thinking of it.

"I don't know," she said.

"Well, why don't you think about it for the next forty-five minutes, and by that time I'll be there to pick you up and take you to brunch at Jamie's Inn."

Although she wasn't in any particular mood, the idea of becoming a portion of a crowd trailing around a buffet table, heaping her plate with food, did not set well.

"I'm not all that hungry, Kellen," she said, "but why don't you come by and I'll put together something for us. I've got eggs, bacon, fruit, and a package of instant grits. It won't be posh and it won't be lush, but it won't be crowded."

"I think you talked me into it. Still forty-five minutes?"

"That sounds just about right to me. Oh, why don't you pick up a carton of orange juice? I'm not sure I have enough."

"Will do."

She was dressed in an old blouse and faded jeans, her hair clipped into a pony tail. Her first inclination was to change into a dress, but that would be contrary to the idea of staying home; however, she did go into the bathroom and apply a thin coating of lipstick.

When brunch was finished, they sat at the dinette table sipping coffee. It was Susan's third cup, two more than she usually allowed herself in the morning, and she had lost her taste for it. During the meal, the conversation had been light and general; Susan felt Kellen was being careful to choose neutral subjects and equally judicious with the words he employed. She appreciated his concern; however, there were moments when she felt he was close to patronizing her.

"You know," he said at last, "the contracts for next

term are going to be handed out in two weeks. Are you going to reenlist?"

She stared at him and blinked. She had completely forgotten that it was contract time.

Kellen misread her silence. "You aren't thinking of leaving, are you?"

"No." She shook her head. "I—well, I forgot it was that time. If they give me a contract, I'll sign it, so I won't be forced to job hunt while I . . ."

Kellen pushed back the shock of hair over his left eye and looked down at the half-empty coffee cup before him. "While you satisfy yourself about Sam Young's death?"

"That, along with other things."

"Susan, I know you and Sam were friends, and I understand your feelings, but isn't it possible that, well . . . maybe you're chasing a will-o'-the-wisp?"

Though she might have felt resentment at the question, she did not. It was understandable that what to her was definite purpose might to others appear as an obsession.

"It's possible," she said, "but it's something I've got to do, Kellen, and not only for Sam. There are a lot of dead babies out there, and there are a lot more who could die. I'm just not convinced Sudden Infant Death Syndrome is the cause."

"What do you plan to do? Everything you've told me, Susan, is pretty spooky. You know that."

"I know. But I have this very positive feeling that something horrible is taking place around here."

He reached across the table to take both her hands in his. "I'm in your corner, Susan, you know that, and I'll do everything I can to help you. I promise."

She was forced to blink away a sudden burning in the corners of her eyes. "Thank you, Kellen."

It was approaching one o'clock when they finished

washing, drying, and putting away the dishes. As she took a damp dish towel from Kellen and hung it over a cabinet door to dry, Susan knew this was going to be a deliciously lazy day. Quite unexpectedly she felt relaxed and did not want to burden her mind with anything more than enjoying the company of this big, bashful man who had touched her senses so keenly at the table. The feeling of emptiness which had separated her from her surroundings the past week was beginning to fill. Emotions were restoring the dimensions of her life.

"Do you have anything planned for today?" Kellen asked from where he stood looking out the dining-area window.

"No."

"Would you like to plan something?"

"No. I'd like a spontaneous day. Just let things happen. Nothing planned, nothing mapped out, nothing set in concrete."

"That's the best kind of day."

"I think so."

"Well, how do we start?"

She laughed. "I don't know. I guess we do have to plan the first move, don't we?"

"Unless we want to stand around like this all day, I guess so."

"We could just get in the car and start driving. An idea will surely come to us."

He grinned. "That somehow reminds me of my life, aimlessly wandering toward no destination."

Outside the apartment the heat was a physical mass, inert and weighted with humidity. It rebounded upward from the wilted earth in shimmering sheets that seemed to suck the oxygen from the air. Susan regretted her suggestion to take a drive.

"Susan! Kellen!"

She recognized Maureen's voice even though the heat seemed to give it a fluting, unnatural quality. They stopped to turn and watch Maureen coming toward them.

"Do you two have any big plans for tonight?" she asked when she reached them.

Susan looked at Kellen. "I don't think so."

"Oh, good. We have four steaks in the freezer which really should be eaten, so Niles and I were wondering if you two would like to help do it."

After they agreed, Susan said to Maureen, "There's one stipulation, though. You've got to let Kellen and me buy some of the goodies that go with steaks."

It was decided they would pick up some fruit and vegetables for a salad. They'd be back at the apartment by six o'clock, when Niles had one of the complex's portable grills reserved.

Although they had been together no more than three or four times, Kellen and Niles had developed a comfortable acquaintance, due, Susan deduced, to the unassuming characters of both men. It was possible, in fact, that tall, lanky Niles, with a pipe usually clamped in his wide mouth, was even more constrained than Kellen. She knew they'd have a pleasant evening.

In spite of the heat, and the Saturday traffic and crowds, Susan felt the pleasure of being with Kellen soak her through and through. Her internal senses also told her that Sam would be happy for her, that he would approve of this man. It saddened her that Kellen and Sam had never met.

It was a gentle afternoon; some of the tensions clutching her lessened their hold, some of the obscenities that had wedged themselves into her life retreated a little way.

They stayed away from the congested beach, wandering west along back roads until they found a small stream. They sat on the banks with their bare feet immersed in the shallow water, smelling the phantom scent of mint.

At a little after five o'clock they went into a Publix Supermarket, bought provisions, and were at the apartment by five forty-five.

Later, while chopping up a head of lettuce, Maureen looked over at Susan, and asked, "Have you noticed that I'm over my case of paranoia?"

"Yes. But I knew you'd recover."

Maureen laughed. "I think the best thing is that Bridget doesn't sleep with us anymore."

"Where is she? Napping?"

"Yes." Maureen placed the bowl of lettuce in the refrigerator, then wiped her hands on a towel. "Let's go out and see how the guys are doing with the steaks. We might end up with Big Macs, you know."

"Oh. You're a member of the Friends of Art, aren't you?"

"Yes."

"What's the exhibit that is being presented at the Art Center Monday night? I received an invitation to it."

"I didn't know of one. There's been no announcement."

"Well, come over to my place, and I'll show you the invitation I received. If it interests you, maybe you and Niles would like to go with me. Kellen has an adult-education class to instruct."

"Niles isn't all that interested in art. He can baby-sit."

In her apartment, Susan showed the folder to Maureen, who studied it, shaking her head. "I haven't heard a thing about this."

"And I've no idea why I got it, or why it was dropped off at the library and not mailed to me. Would you like to go?"

"Yes, but this folder certainly doesn't say much, does it? I wonder whose work it is."

Susan took the folder, but before replacing it in its envelope looked again at the strange bird on page three. It continued to nag at her.

"Is there something wrong, Susan?" Maureen asked.

"This bird. I feel I should recognize it, but I'm certain I've never seen one like it, and I know I've never seen the sculpture."

"That's odd."

Susan shrugged and put down the flyer.

The steaks were delicious, the Burgundy chilled and full-bodied, and the salad crisp and cool. Bridget woke, but contented herself with a variety of colorful play things. The evening drifted. As they were finished eating, the physical-fitness group in their string bikinis gathered at the end of the pool. Turning their radio to a hard-rock station, they surrounded themselves with a clamorous barricade, through which they defied the world to seek entrance.

The storm moved in swiftly and without warning from the southwest. It was double-layered, an upper strata of white clouds giving the impression of snowy crests atop the darker, lower ones. Thunder rumbled in short, immature growls. Very rapidly the clouds built mountains above the buildings' roofs, and the oppressive air began to stir between the apartment buildings, to fan out and swirl around the pool area. A hint of the chill advancing across the land with the approaching rain rode the air.

Susan watched the steady advance of the clouds. As they covered more and more of the sky, she felt a tingling across her shoulders and down the backs of her arms. The fine hairs on the back of her neck stirred. Why? she wondered. What about this storm sent little shock waves through her? Her body was reacting to it beyond all normal responses, as if within the clouds' interiors something seething with hate was centering its attention on her.

She quickly looked at the other three. Kellen and Niles were talking in low voices. As she turned toward Maureen, the other woman shot a glance in her direction. Whatever was in the black clouds, Maureen was also aware of it.

For a while longer, as the stirring air became a breeze, they sat on the cement slab enjoying the coolness. After the first sensations, Susan felt no more sickle-swipes at her nervous system, and wondered if her imagination might not have played an elaborate trick on her, even in her interpretation of Maureen's expression.

The rain came slowly, not in oversized drops but in a fine spray blown in the rising breeze. The radio beside the pool abruptly ceased its blaring. Laughs and suppressed squeals accompanied the nearly naked bodies as they ran toward an apartment on the far side of the pool. Moments later, the main body of the rain thundered in with tidal-wave ferocity.

Inside the apartment, Niles said, "The wine's gone, and we don't have much to offer, but does anyone want a brandy? And I think we have a bottle of Bailey's Irish Cream."

Susan took a small brandy, as did Kellen.

Whatever they had been discussing outside still held Kellen's and Niles' interest. They sat at the dinette table to continue their conversation. Maureen watched them for a short while, then left her chair to cross the room and sit beside Susan on the sofa. Bridget watched her mother from a playpen in the middle of the room.

"You felt it, too, didn't you, when the storm first came up?" she asked. "Like a shock."

Susan ran her tongue around her lips, licking the taste of brandy from them. There was no need to deny the sensation she had experienced, yet when it came to speaking of it she was reluctant, fearing that even with a sympathetic person like Maureen the acknowledgment would sound crack-brained. Finally she nodded, saying, "Yes, I felt something."

"I knew when I saw how you were watching the clouds build up—you realized something wasn't right." She nervously turned a cordial glass in her fingers. "What do you suppose it was?"

"I'm not certain it was anything, Maureen."

"We wouldn't have felt it if there was nothing there."

"It's possible." What was she doing? Trying to deny her own reactions? "Maybe we both are becoming obsessed with storms."

"I don't believe that, Susan. Not at all. And neither do you." She looked squarely at Susan, her dark eyes narrowing. "If you're trying to make yourself believe that, then you're turning your back on yourself . . . and Sam."

Susan returned her friend's stare as long as she could, then moved her gaze to the two men at the table. Maureen spoke the turth. Why was she denying her beliefs? She pulled her attention back to Maureen. "You're right. It's just that the whole situation is so weird that I'm afraid to hear it put into words."

"Don't be. At least not with me." Maureen glanced at the men, then leaned toward her. "Let me help, Susan. Between us, maybe we can discover answers. I want to be a part of what you and Sam began. Please . . . for Bridget. I'm over my paranoia, but babies are still dying."

Susan nodded, but before she could answer, Niles asked, "What dark secrets are you conspiring over?"

"Nothing special," she said, suddenly finding it easy to smile. "Female mysteries which can never be told to any male."

"And about which no man should ask," Maureen added.

Kellen laughed. "I think, Niles, you've been told to mind your own business."

Around nine o'clock, after shifting through a variety of subjects, the conversation began to dwindle. The rain was still falling in a gentle, steady shower. From somewhere far away, the muted rumble of thunder sent continuous reverberations through the night, taunting reminders that the heavens were still in turmoil and had every intention of again battering the helpless earth beneath them.

After the reflection in the windows of a close lightning flare, followed instantly by an angry crash of thunder, Susan and Kellen made a hasty exit.

Inside her apartment, Susan went into the living room to turn on a table lamp while Kellen stood just inside the front door. Susan looked back at him, suddenly feeling the delicate balance of their relationship. She stood for a moment, seeing him first as a friend, but then as something more. For the first time in a long, long while, she felt stirrings inside her, became acutely aware of the way the wet blouse was plastered to her and how the damp jeans molded her hips and thighs.

Kellen stepped slowly, hesitantly toward her, and she realized that what was happening inside her was duplicated in him.

Then his arms were around her, pulling her tight to him, and she remembered how good it felt to have her softness pressed against the firmness of a man's chest.

15

SUSAN SAT AT HER DESK, SURVEYING THE EMPTY TABLES IN THE reference room, vaguely wondering why the school went to the expense of opening the library in August, particularly on a Monday morning. The acquisition of knowledge was far down the list of requirements to minds slowly shedding the weekend's lethargy.

For that matter, her own mind wasn't well focused, but for her it was more than Monday morning "blahs." The disorder and abstract confusion of the day before still filled her senses like a pungent vapor.

Yesterday morning another baby was reported to have died during Saturday's evening storm. She and Kellen had listened to the news while they drank their morning coffee, and both had known that the day, which should have been as warm and tender as a summer dawn after the magic they had experienced the night before, was destined to be a precariously balanced procession of hours strewn with emotional ob-

234

stacles. All day yesterday, she had had the terrible
feeling of having failed at something, but could not
define what it was.

She floated through the remainder of Monday, which
became one series of abstractions following another.
She skipped lunch, ate a small salad for dinner, then at
six forty-five went to Maureen's apartment.

Now it was twenty after seven and she stood beside
Maureen in the main gallery of the Civic Art Center, an
old building renovated with the contribution of funds
collected by the Friends of Art.

She couldn't remember experiencing such a saturated quiet. No one else was in the building, and to all
appearances no one had been for several days. When
they entered, no hostess had greeted them at the door.
A long table which normally held a guest registration
book and literature describing the current show was
empty, pushed against the wall, looking derelict and
shabby. Not one other viewer wandered through the
room, studying the display. There was only the subterranean silence and emptiness, along with the sublimi-
nal smell of new paint and a fainter one of disinfectant.
When first they had entered, they had waited for a
receptionist, but none made an appearance.

"You know, this is weird as hell," Maureen said. "It's
as if there wasn't a showing at all."

Susan nodded, but said nothing, then looked around
the room once more, feeling her perplexity growing,
aware that under it an uneasiness was also stirring.

"I guess," Maureen said, "as long as we're here, we
might as well see what there is to see."

Susan didn't know if it was the room itself that was
so stark, or if the cold, unwelcoming atmosphere was a
product of the eight white pedestals randomly placed
throughout it. On top of each pedestal, individually lit
with ceiling spots, was a marble sculpture. Six were
animals and fowls, two were human figures. All eight

were rendered with exquisite detail, so precise that if it were not for the colorless stone out of which they were shaped, they might have been taken for breathing creatures, each filled with the throbbings of life.

It was then, as they stood in what might be considered the center of the erratic pedestal arrangement, that Susan felt a heavy pulsing in her left temple, a rapid throbbing of the artery at her hairline. For a fleeting instant, she imagined the six wild creatures turning their heads to stare at her with eyes no longer smooth blanks of stone but tinted with colors and glinting with intelligence.

"What do you think?" Maureen asked.

Susan shook her head. "It's disturbing."

"It's more than that. Have you noticed that of the six animal and fowl statues, four represent scavengers? There's the owl, the pelican, the jackal, and the wild cat. I don't know if a snake is or not. And there's that bird that gave you the creeps when you saw it in the folder. I don't recognize it either; maybe it's an imaginary creature."

Susan studied the sculptures more closely. She hadn't realized it, but what Maureen said was correct, all the creatures were scavengers. She looked at the two human figures, wondering why they were included in the collection, then walked slowly toward them. One was a tastefully done nude of a pregnant woman, the other an infant on its hands and knees.

She stood staring at them while the pounding in her head increased until it filled her skull, then found the nerve centers in her neck and blossomed into a repeat of the pain she had experienced in the library.

The infant's head was raised, its face pointing directly up at her. The mouth was open. At first she thought the baby was cooing, but while she studied the softly carved features she saw the mouth begin to tremble, then stretch wider and wider until the sculptured marble formed into a taut oval. At the same time she watched the eyes widen in what at first appeared to be surprise but immediately turned into terror. Their blank circles stared past her into darkness, and suddenly Susan had the horrible, unexplainable sensation that the infant was watching something in that darkness, something which even so young a mind would recognize as impossibly hideous.

And at that very moment she recognized the subject of the statue, despite the distorted features. The terrified infant before her was Bridget Neilson.

Instinctively, Susan squeezed her eyes shut, then, after taking a deep breath, cautiously opened them. The baby was looking up at her as it had at first, cooing.

Now, as though she had wandered into a catacomb of horrors, she saw details she had not noticed before. The figure of the woman was only three quarters completed. The side nearest the wall was rough-hewn, with distressing, painful chisel marks gouged deeply into the stone. She wanted to move on, but something would not allow her to turn away, and soon she began to see form in the chisel marks. Suddenly she clearly saw a woman who had been brutally mutilated. She stared in horror at the woman's screaming face and the gaping wound in her side. Sickened, she turned away. The pain in her head slithered around her brain, ensnaring it in a net that squeezed tighter and tighter.

She backed away, shaking her head. Her senses were crumbling, her blood racing through her veins like streams of fire. Concentration was no longer possible. She looked around. All the creatures were watching her. The unknown bird had shifted its position and was preparing to dive straight at her in a deadly attack.

She threw a hasty look in the direction of the baby. Its mouth was open again, silently screaming.

Susan turned and began walking swiftly to the gallery's entrance. Part of her insisted that she was retreating from hallucinations, from a waking nightmare unfolding inside her mind. But she knew that if she did not get outside, away from the evil she felt, her sanity would completely shatter. Behind her, Maureen's voice was only a faraway sound to which she paid no heed.

Then she was through the door and the night wrapped its soggy darkness about her. She felt exhausted. She felt as if under her fevered flesh her entire skeleton was constructed of twigs which would snap if she forced it to move. Inside her chest, her heart was hammering savagely, threatening to tear itself loose and jam into her throat. Shuddering, she leaned against the building's wall, bracing herself on trembling legs, squeezing her eyes as tightly closed as they would go. Opening her mouth, she began sucking in huge gulps of the wet night air, filling her lungs to their capacity, clenching her fists while frantically trying to steer her mind in the direction of normal thinking.

"Susan! Thank God, there you are." Maureen was at her side. "What happened?"

She pulled in another breath, then opened her eyes. Looking into Maureen's face, she saw only concern and knew her friend had not seen Bridget's face on the sculptured infant. She tried to smile, but knew a grimace formed on her lips. She shook her head. "I'm not sure," she lied.

The drive to the apartment was almost silent. Maureen spoke little, allowing Susan to think about what she'd seen and gain control over her fear. Still, she shivered as she parked the car.

"Do you have anything stronger than wine at your place?" Maureen asked.

"There's some vodka. Sam brought a bottle once."

"Then I'm going to mix you a strong vodka and orange juice. And while you're downing it, I'm going to make a telephone call."

The drink that Maureen prepared was far too strong,

but, sprawled on the sofa, Susan found that the warmth it generated throughout her body immediately jolted her back into the real world.

Maureen was leafing through the telephone book, muttering to herself.

Careful to sound neutral, Susan asked, "What are you looking for?"

"Not what, who." She ran her finger down a column. "Here it is."

"Who?"

"Irma Hutton. She's an officer in the Art League, and I want to ask her about that so-called show tonight."

Susan watched her dial, aware how rigid and still her muscles had become in her reclining body. What explanation, she wondered, could describe tonight's exhibition.

"Mrs Hutton?" Maureen was speaking into the telephone. "This is Maureen Neilson. Oh, everything is fine, thank you. Mrs. Hutton, I wanted to inquire about the exhibit tonight at the gallery, the wildlife sculptures. Yes, tonight. But we were there, Mrs. Hutton. A friend and I—we just got home. Well, no. No one else was there, absolutely no one, and that's why I called you. Oh, yes, there was an invitation sent out. My friend received one. None? Nothing at all mailed? I don't understand. The work? Well, it was exquisite, but the subject matter was depressing. Yes, yes . . . Oh, I certainly will, and I'd appreciate it if you phoned me about what you discover. Yes, thank you. Good-bye."

Susan felt her fingers tightening around the highball glass. Some of her reclaimed mental confidence slipped away.

"There was no show scheduled, was there?" she asked.

"No." Maureen stood staring at the telephone as if she had just caught the instrument in some kind of a lie. "She said there was no show tonight, that there was

no function at all planned. In fact, she said, the
building should have been locked up."

Susan looked at what remained of her drink, and
knew she wanted no more of it. She set the glass on a
table at the end of the sofa, overly careful to place it on
a coaster.

"I don't understand what's going on," Maureen said.
She sat in a chair, her hands clasped together in her lap.
"I just can't believe this."

"There has to be an explanation."

"I know, but what?"

"Maybe tomorrow, when we're calmed down, we can
come up with one."

Maureen got up. "You're probably right. I think we
both need some calming."

As Susan stood at her front door watching her friend
walk slowly toward her apartment, she had the uncomfortable feeling that calamity and horror had taken up
positions in the darkness.

The telephone rang. Its sharp jangle shrilled into her
with such force that she took an involuntary step out
into the night, feeling her heart begin to race as it had
outside the gallery.

Kellen was calling. His evening class was finished,
and he wondered if he would be welcome if he dropped
by her apartment.

"More than welcome," she told him.

She poured what remained of her drink into the sink
and rinsed out the glass, then went to the bedroom to
study her reflection in the full-length mirror. She gave
her hair a halfhearted push and, leaning close, tried to
find any residue of her emotional turmoil on her face.
There was a hollowness in her eyes, and her cheekbones
thrust out prominently under tautened skin. However,
she told herself, on the whole she didn't look bad for a
person who had seen a mutilated woman and a terrified
baby, and almost been attacked by a stone bird.

Forty minutes later, she and Kellen were seated side by side on the sofa. She had told him of the show which did not exist, describing the strange sculptures, the intricacy of their detail, and finally the way in which they shifted and changed, terrifying her. He sat frowning, staring at nothing, while he attempted to rationalize the story she told.

Finally, he shook his head. "I believe you, Susan, but I don't understand. An unknown person sets up a sculpture show in a locked building, apparently without the knowledge of the owners, then sends invitations which nobody responds to but you."

"If it hadn't happened to me, I wouldn't believe it. But it scared the hell out of me, and spooked Maureen too. And, Kellen, the face on that infant statue was the face of Bridget Neilson. Thank God, Maureen didn't see it like I did. And my head hurt—the same way it did one day at the library when Lily came to look at me."

He thumped his fist on his knee. "Goddamn it!"

"Kellen! What's wrong?"

"I feel so damn inadequate. I want to help you. I want to be the big, strong man who you can come to and lean on, but instead I sit here with my mind in a vacuum.

"Kellen, don't think that way, please. You've done so much more for me than you realize, more than I can tell you. Please don't try to set yourself up as a super-macho hero." She took his hand. "I find you attractive the way you are."

He looked at her with his right eye, his left one hidden behind the fallen lock of hair, and she watched a blush creep across his features. She became aware of a tingling running through every fiber of her body. Kellen as yet might not realize it, but he had become her anchor to reality.

* * *

The following day was routine, almost boring. Susan assisted nearly a dozen students and two faculty members with reference problems. Only at lunch time, when she sat on a pined-shaded bench, did her thoughts try to wander back to the evening before, but in the brilliant sunshine they lost their way. Her emotional equilibrium had almost returned to its natural balance. She suspected Kellen had much to do with this comfortable feeling.

When she left the library at ten after five, she hoped to see Kellen's blue Toyota waiting for her, but it was nowhere in sight. She didn't try to ignore her disappointment.

She was nearly across the campus. The path along which she strolled was bordered on its right by a row of hibiscus bushes that formed a hedge between it and the campus road that also curved in the direction of the main gate.

At first it was no more than a sensation, an awareness so small as to be nearly non-existent. Then it took on substance. The skin of her arms prickled. She had taken no more than a dozen steps after that first awareness, when she suddenly knew she was being watched. She looked around. There was no one there. Slanting sunlight painted elongated shadows of trees in blue and gray filigrees across the grass, but nowhere was there anybody displaying the least bit of interest in her. Yet the feeling was definite.

It was more a stirring of her consciousness than an actual sighting, but she became aware of a dark form on the far side of the hibiscus bushes. Through the mass of twigs and foliage there was no definition to it, but there was solidity. She frowned, took a step or two toward the bushes, then tried to open a small viewing tunnel through them with her hand. A motor immediately speeded up and the dark form moved away in the direction of the gates. But she caught a glimpse of a black Oldsmobile, and a briefer glimpse of a black-haired woman in the driver's seat. Lily.

Apparently Maureen had been waiting for her. Susan was still unlocking her door when she came hurrying from her apartment.

When they were inside, Maureen said, "Irma Hutton phoned. No one knows anything about last night. They notified the police, who looked the building over and said there was no sign of a break-in. Whoever used the building must have used a key to gain entrance." She dropped her voice. "I don't think they believe we were there last night, Susan."

Susan stared out the window. From far, far away it seemed she heard the sound of delicate and beautiful things smashing, and she knew it was the lovely day, tumbling down around her.

"What are we going to do?" Maureen asked.

"Is there anything we can do? We know we were there. We know what we saw."

"Why us?"

"Not 'us,' Maureen. Me. I'm the one who received the invitation. You went as my guest."

"You're probably right, but why was it done, and by whom? Whoever set it up went to a lot of trouble for some reason."

"I'm going to find out."

"And I'm going to help."

After Maureen left, Susan opened a can of tuna and added Miracle Whip, some celery, and a hard-boiled egg to make a simple tuna salad, half of which she ate on a lettuce leaf with several Ritz crackers and a glass of ice tea. While she ate, she called from her memory the events of the previous evening, studied them one by one, then mentally worked her way down the list of items she had put together in her notes, trying to find an explanation for them, reasonable or otherwise. Only one terrible answer came to her: Lily had challenged her by using Bridget Neilson as a pawn in some horrible match of wills.

Kellen phoned around eight o'clock, apologizing for not picking her up at the library, saying he'd lost track of time working on his history of bookbinding project. She didn't tell him about Lily watching her.

When she went to bed, her mind refused to accept sleep, holding it at bay but incapable of coherent thought.

Maybe she should tell Maureen of seeing Bridget's face on the marble statue, even if Maureen's paranoia would return with a rush. But she could take Bridget away until these terrible deaths ceased. Speak with Niles? Maybe. And why did Lily dislike her—hate her? What twisted thoughts were going through that strange woman's mind?

Bridget and Lily . . .

In a place in her mind she couldn't quite reach, she sensed a correlation.

16

THAT MAUREEN BROUGHT GOOD NEWS WITH HER WAS EVIDENT
the moment she walked into the library's reference
room Friday morning. Dressed in a lavender and blue
summer dress, the woman who came through the
archway was a poised, self-possessed woman whose
resilience was evident in the direct look of her dark
eyes and the firmness of her stride. Susan watched her
approach her desk, realizing that the tumult that had
been in her friend was gone.

Susan glanced at her watch. It read ten minutes until
twelve.

"I was wondering if you'd care for some company at
lunch." Maureen smiled at her from beneath the neat
coiffure into which she'd arranged the dark brunette
mass of her hair.

"I'd love it." Susan took her purse out of the desk
drawer. "Do you have any place in mind?"

"No, no place in particular." Maureen shook her

head. "It's not really food I'm interested in, but rather a friend with whom to share some good news."

"Well, the school cafeteria is closed for the summer, but we could—"

"I saw a sandwich truck parked in front of the administration building. Maybe we could get something from it."

"Well, okay. I don't know really what they have."

"They must have soft drinks or juice and cottage cheese or yogurt."

"We can certainly find out."

At the vending truck, Susan bought a pineapple yogurt and Maureen a diet Pepsi, then repaired to a nearby bench beneath the shading canopy of three old pine trees. Susan stirred her yogurt while Maureen sipped her Pepsi. The sounds of the heat-hardened campus were so muffled that she was aware of them only as background noise. Beneath the trees there was an ever so faint movement of air, just enough to dry the perspiration sheening their foreheads and arms, creating an illusion of coolness.

Susan could feel Maureen's excitement and was eager to hear her news, but it was obvious that the other woman would speak only when she was ready.

After a while, Maureen set the empty can on the bench beside her, smiled, and spoke. "I think I'm pregnant. No, damn it, I'm sure I am. I've had this strange, wonderful feeling that I was; you know, all warm and glowing, so last night I gave myself a home pregnancy test—and it came up positive."

Susan felt her friend's joy sweep over her. She threw her arms around Maureen to pull her close in a tight hug.

Maureen laughed. "My God, Susan, it's only a home test."

"I've always thought that a woman could somehow tell when she became pregnant."

"Me too. I remember how I felt when I was pregnant with Bridget. Niles wants me to double-check by going to a doctor, which I will, but I'm certain last night's test was accurate."

"Oh, I am too, Maureen." The conversation turned to other subjects.

Ten minutes remained of Susan's lunch break when Maureen turned full face to her. Susan saw the sudden seriousness in her friend's eyes, the slight tightning of her jaw muscles, the way her lips parted to draw in a lung-filling breath.

"There's something, Susan, I want you to understand," she said without preamble. "The results of that test makes me all the more determined to become involved with investigating the deaths of the babies. I might become the mother of two. I want protection for them. I know you and Sam were working on a theory, and I'm sure you still are. I said before I wanted to help you, and I meant it then, but I mean it more now—and I can be a lot of help. It's Bridget's due. If life starts to form in me, it's that baby's due. And, Susan, it's Sam's due."

Susan squinted her eyes to look across the light-drenched campus. In the sheets of noontime heat, the buildings and vegetation were indistinct, rippling like objects underwater.

"I haven't a real theory, Maureen. All I have are thoughts and assumptions, but with no definite way of putting them together. Sam had something, I'm positive. But I don't know what it was. He was to meet with me to tell me what it was the morning he was found dead."

"You're not going to shove it all aside, are you?"

"No. Like you said, I owe it to Sam."

"Then let me help you, Susan, because of Bridget, and her possible brother or sister. I want to find out about last Monday night too."

"I can't see how it's related to the deaths."

"Nor can I, but I was involved in it, and I want to discover what it was."

Quite unexpectedly, Susan felt a surge of relief racing through her, followed by a newborn hope. This determined, Maureen would be ideal to work with. She was intelligent and predictable with no pretentious affectations, but what could be even more helpful was that she was inclined to believe an answer other than four could be obtained when two and two were added together.

"I'd like you to help, Maureen."

"Just tell me what I can do."

"Tomorrow night I'll show you what I've put together and tell you my thoughts."

"I'll be at your place at eight o'clock."

Kellen handed her a rose when she got into the car that evening in front of the library. Susan was touched and leaned over to give him a kiss on his cheek.

"Is there any place special you'd like to go?" he asked.

She held up the rose. "You're filled with excellent ideas this evening. You make the choice."

He chose a small, rustic restaurant, specializing in local seafood, on the banks of the river south of town. They were early for the dinner hour, so they had their pick of tables and selected one beside a picture window overlooking the water. The still river reflected the first flush of the evening, its wide breadth transforming into a plain of color which eventually disappeared to the north and south in the misted vista of the ending day. A feeling of being a portion of a rising flood of beauty and tranquility settled on Susan, and she found herself wishing all the clocks everywhere be stopped so time would linger in the lushness of these moments.

Both ordered a combination shrimp-and-scallop platter, and Kellen requested a bottle of chilled white wine. Halfway through the meal, Susan realized she was attacking the food with a concentrated ferocity, having eaten only the yogurt all day. While she tried to apologize, Kellen laughed, saying that was what good food was meant for.

When they were finished eating, enough of the wine remained for Kellen to refill their glasses. He told her more about his history of bookbinding project, and she told him of Maureen's exaltation accompanying her feeling of being pregnant.

After a while, the conversation began to drift. The wine slowly disappeared, and their hands found excuses, then reasons, to reach across the table to stroke or hold the ones opposite them. Susan felt something compelling and sensuous join them at the table. Kellen, she saw, was aware of it too.

His voice was husky, and he made no attempt to push away the lock of hair falling over his left eye, when he said, "Maybe it's time to go."

She could only nod and whisper, "Maybe it is."

The square LED numerals of the bedside clock read 11:52, their red lines glowing dispassionately in the shallow darkness of the bedroom. From the living room, little more than an undertone to the endless whirring of the air conditioner, came the soft sounds of an easy-listening station on the stereo. Not too far away, imitating thunder, a determined jetliner climbed into the night sky.

Susan lay on her back; the dampness of the rumpled sheet beneath her was sticky and warm along the naked flesh of her back and legs while, at the same time, her breasts and belly tingled in the draft of cold air from a ceiling vent. At her left, Kellen stirred, turned on his right side, then reached out to gently undo the web of damp hair weaving itself across her forehead and down her cheeks.

"Tell me," he said, his eyes roaming over her face, "Have you done anymore research about the baby deaths?"

"No."

"If you do, I still want to help you."

"I know. Maureen is going to help too." Using her right hand and foot for leverage, she rolled onto her left side, then, not feeling in the least wanton, arched herself to thrust the length of her naked body against his. "I'm going to like your help more, though."

He kissed the tip of her nose. "I'm sorry, but I still have misgivings about you getting involved. I believe enough of what you've told me to think that something very unnatural is happening, and I don't want you to be hurt."

Looking into his troubled eyes, she said, "I won't be."

"I wish I could be sure."

"Be sure."

"That means I'm going to be tagging along at your side all the time."

"I want you at my side."

He moved his lips to hers and kissed her.

An hour later he was gone, and she lay in bed staring up into darkness. She dug her fingers into the mattress on either side of her, wondering how far this compulsion was going to lead her. And if Kellen would walk with her all the way.

17

THE FOLLOWING MORNING, SUSAN EASED THE ESCORT INTO ITS
parking place. A bag of groceries lay half-spilled on the
seat beside her, a carton of orange juice, a can of tuna,
and a head of lettuce tumbled like the contents from a
frayed cornucopia.

Though it was only nine-thirty, the heat swelled
around her, reflecting from the automobile's metal and
the asphalt of the parking lot. The high temperatures
were continuing, with the heat index, because of the
humidity, predicted to reach 107 degrees before the
day was finished.

She balanced the bag in her left arm and was starting
for the walkway leading to her apartment building
when she became aware of an almost indefinable tingling on the back of her neck and across her shoulders. It
wasn't a physical irritation, but more of a subtle touch
on her subconscious.

She turned to look behind her but saw only the flat

empty expanse of black asphalt bordered on the far side with ixora, hibiscus, and twisted peppertrees. For a moment, she squinted at the caves and wells of shadow pockmarking the line of vegetation, but saw only the glint of sunlight on the leaves. There was nothing there that did not belong there, but the feeling had been one of being watched, of eyes probing at her, intent and searching. And she remembered the red eyes staring at her in the library's storage room.

She shook her head, turned, then went slowly up the walkway.

Already there was a gathering of sun- and exercise-worshippers forming at the edge of the pool, their bronze bodies shining under the coatings of oil and sun screens lavishly applied.

Although the thermostat was set at seventy-two degrees, her apartment felt cold and dry. The perspiration on her arms and face dried to a short-lived clamminess as she carried the groceries to the kitchen.

She had not made many purchases at the supermarket, mostly fruits and vegetables, and it took her only a few moments to transfer the food from the bag to the refrigerator and cupboard shelves. She concentrated on the movements, deliberately focusing her thoughts on each individual flexing of her muscles, so there would be no space in her mind for recollections and theories.

She was folding the bag to store it for future use as a wastebasket liner when she became aware of the wrongness in the apartment's atmosphere. It was subtle, very, very faint and delicate, yet something was not as it should be in the cool, filtered air, in the overall feel of the empty rooms. She turned her head slowly, studying the furniture, the shadows, nostrils flaring as she drew in short, tense breaths.

Nothing.

She went into the living room, then down the hallway

to the bedroom. Everything was as it should be, yet the feeling persisted that her privacy had been violated.

In the narrow confines of the hallway, returning to the living room, she smelled the fleeting odor. For one indrawn breath it was there, the next it was gone, the air odorless and unsoiled. She tried to recapture it, drawing in several long breaths, but it no longer existed.

It had been a putrid smell, a stench of carrion decomposing in suffocating heat. Unable to relocate the scent, Susan went back to the living room and looked out into the parking area.

The space where the Neilsons' Dodge should have been was empty, meaning Maureen was still out visiting the parents of babies who had died, trying to confirm that the deaths had occurred during a thunderstorm, and if, perhaps, any parent had noticed a nebulous black thing floating around the house at the time of death. Rather than wait until this evening, Maureen had knocked on Susan's front door at eight o'clock this morning, wanting something to do. Susan had given her a list of the families who had lost their babies. Now she rubbed a hand across her forehead, wanting to slow down the thoughts flowing too quickly through her mind.

Thirty minutes later Maureen arrived. She was smiling when, without waiting for her to knock, Susan opened the door.

"I talked to six families," Maureen said, holding out a sheet of tablet paper to Susan. "In every instance, there was a storm in progress when the babies died, or there'd been one just prior to the discovery of the death. Every time, Susan. And three couples—the Stuarts, the Fraziers, and the Rubins—saw the thing through a window. Then there's Carrie Wadsworth. She not only saw it, she swears it looked at her, studied her."

An irrepressible rush of excitement raced through Susan. Suddenly her suspicions were not nearly as nonsensical as she'd feared.

"Those storms seem to make Lily's involvement more emphatic," Maureen said.

"Evidence does seem to be mounting. But damn it, there's no explanation for that black thing."

"And it's all still circumstantial, isn't it? All the evidence we have means nothing to anyone but us—and not too much to us when you think of that black thing."

Susan considered that for a moment or two before nodding agreement.

There was a touch of helplessness in Maureen's voice, when she asked, "What else can we do?"

"I'm not sure, for now."

Maureen glanced at her wristwatch. "I've got to get home and take my turn at baby-sitting. If you need help, or think of something, phone me."

"Have you told Niles what we're doing?"

Maureen made a gesture with her right hand. "No, not yet."

Susan said nothing as she watched her friend walk to the front door. Inside her head there was a vibration, as if something in her subconscious was trying desperately to hammer its way into her conscious thinking.

She poured herself a Pepsi. She didn't really want it; the action was a response to the currents flowing through her. The information Maureen had gathered had left her thoughts jumbled. More out of habit than hope of discovering any new slivers of information, she went to the desk to once again bring out her notes. The pamphlet announcing the sculpture exhibition lay beside them in the bottom of the drawer. She hesitated, then took it from the drawer also.

At the dinette table she sipped the soft drink while she scanned the notes, but she could make no sense of them and pushed the papers away. Reluctantly, her hand hovered over, then seized, the pamphlet.

Once again her attention was drawn to the strange bird on page three. She stared at it, and saw the bird slowly swell and fill out until it assumed a third dimension. Just as it had Monday night, the bird stared directly at her. Under its feathers muscles tensed as if it were making ready to lift itself off the paper and swoop up at her. She wanted to look away, but found it impossible to move her eyes, the force of the bird's stare too strong for her. Sweat broke out on her forehead as a sudden heat wrapped around her. From the photograph, the bird continued to stare up at her.

Unable to move, she felt as helpless and vulnerable as she had that day in the library storeroom, incapable of doing anything other than wait for whatever was occurring to reach its climax. Just as in the storeroom, though there was no form to be seen, she knew she was not alone, that something was in the room with her, watching her, examining her. And she had no way to protect herself from it. She was sure now that there had been something in the shrubbery watching her. She was certain something had been in the apartment while she was gone.

Then, as suddenly as it had come, whatever it was was gone. Immediately everything was normal.

She looked at the photograph. It was simply a striking picture of a striking piece of sculpture. But she knew that an instant before the photograph had been a channel through which something very dark and evil had reached for her.

She remembered Sam telling her of the strange bird which he had seen the evening that Lily had first appeared, the bird he had described to her that evening at the seafood restaurant. She looked at the photo again, and a quiver ran across her shoulders and down her arms. Suddenly there was so much to remember.

The irrefutable sensation of being watched while she and Sam discussed his affair with Lily over dinner. The storeroom incident. Lily watching her through the hibiscus bushes on the campus. Now this. Did they form a pattern?

And then she knew!

She pushed herself away from the table, got up, and hurried to the telephone, glancing at the kitchen clock on the way. It was one forty-five. Not knowing if he'd be home, she dialed Kellen's number. When he answered on the third ring, she didn't wait for amenities.

"Kellen, you said anytime I needed help, you'd be there. This is one of the times."

"Oh?" He sounded like he was trying to detach himself from a problem he was already working on. "Of course. What do you need?"

"I want to go out to the townhouse complex where Sam lived, and well . . . I'd feel better if you were with me."

"Are you sure you want to do that?"

"Yes, Kellen, I'm very sure."

"You've a good reason, I suppose."

"Yes."

"Can I be told?"

"Of course, but may I do it on the way out there?"

"Well, I can't think why not. I'll pick you up in about twenty minutes. That okay?"

"Kellen, I'll drive. Your place is on the way and it will save time." She heard the crispness in her voice, and tried to bring softness back into it. "Besides, I think it should be my turn to play taxi driver. You've been ferrying me around for weeks."

"I love understanding, sharing women."

"Any of them in particular?"

He chuckled. "I'll tell you on the way to the complex."

"I'll be there in fifteen minutes."

Kellen's apartment was in a small complex of only six units. The architect had attempted to duplicate a Spanish hacienda, but had somewhere completely lost the design, so the final, single-storied structure was a hybrid in which touches of art-deco styling had slipped in to make the building a structure alien to any style. Kellen said he lived there because, for the rent he paid, he received a lot of room, and besides, it was the inside, not the outside, where he spent his time.

He was standing in the small parking area when she pulled in.

After he was in the car and had closed the door, he leaned toward her and gave her a quick kiss on her cheek. He smelled of shaving lotion and sweat, and her responding smile was more than mere greeting.

When they were out of the parking lot, he asked, "Now are you going to tell me why we're making this trip?"

She nodded. "Yes, but you've got to keep an open mind, because some of what I'm going to say is based on speculation, some on circumstantial evidence, and some on female intuition."

"Sounds like an open-and-shut case."

"I admit it all fits together tighter when I push it around in my mind. It doesn't play too well out loud, I'm afraid. That's why, well—try to be understanding."

"Okay. I promise."

As before, in the restaurant, when she'd told him her speculations concerning the baby deaths, he once again did not interrupt while she told him of Lily watching her on campus, the information that Maureen had gathered that morning, and the episode with the photograph of the bird sculpture.

When she finished, he remained quiet for a short time, then finally said, "You know what you're saying borders on the supernatural, and at the same time you're pointing a finger in the general direction of this woman named Lily, almost accusing her of all the deaths."

She wanted to look at him to see the expression on his face, but instead kept her eyes pointed straight ahead. "Yes, I guess you're right, on both accounts."

"Are we on our way to confront this woman?"

"No." She shook her head. "No, I just want to meet her, or, if she's not there, ask her neighbors some questions. I want her to be a person, not just a name. Maureen already blames her, but I want to know more about her before I reach any kind of conclusion."

"Susan, I'm with you all the way. You know that —but isn't it possible that, at least on this one occasion, you might be shooting from the hip with a half-cocked pistol? If this woman is even a little bit as strange as you think she is, she could be dangerous, and I'm not sure the neighbors are going to answer questions from an unknown outsider."

She remembered telling Sam that Lily might be dangerous, but asked, "Are you suggesting we turn around and go back?"

"No, but maybe we should think of some kind of approach to use."

For a brief moment, she felt very young and naive. On impulse, disregarding foreordained consequences, she had rushed headlong toward a situation about which she knew close to nothing, which, in all truth, might exist only in her imagination. A touch of embarrassment tinted her cheeks when she turned her face to him and smiled. "You're a good man to have around, Kellen Atwood."

He gave her right thigh a more than friendly pat. "You're learning, love."

"I know."

Kellen gave her thigh a gentle squeeze. "There's one game we can play."

"What?"

In a move uncharacteristic of him, he ran his hand up and down the inner curve of her leg. "Well, we could pretend to be a couple planning to marry soon and spending the afternoon looking at possible places to live."

The sound of his words and the feel of his hand on her thigh sent a surprising desire through her. Without looking at him, she shifted her leg under his hand, and said, "That's a fine idea."

When she turned into the entrance, he asked, "You know which building, don't you?"

"Yes, that one." She pointed at the unit in which Sam had lived. "The apartment on the south end was Sam's. The one on the north end has to be Lily's."

She parked the Escort in a visitor's space. When she turned off the engine, she became immediately aware that the area surrounding the three buildings was unusually quiet, and, a moment later, as they stood beside the car, she felt the stillness closing in. She looked at Kellen. He had just pushed aside his lock of hair and was frowning.

She ran her tongue around her lips, which had unexplicably gone dry, then nodded at the building in front of them. "It's the people who live there I'd like to talk to, if we can't meet Lily."

Kellen swung his eyes along the closed garage doors. "There might not be anyone here."

"The pool's on the ocean side of the building. Maybe someone's out there."

"Yeah, maybe."

A gravel and shell path wound around the south end of the building, and they followed it, neither speaking, dominated by the oppressive silence. Although the shadow of the building had started creeping across the recreational area, it had not yet reached the pool. Tiny sun stars twinkled on the shimmering blue water. Around the concrete deck, canvas chairs and two white, umbrella-shaded metal tables sat empty. Desolation pervaded the area.

"I wonder where everyone is?" Kellen shoved back the lock of hair from his left eye. "You'd think on a Saturday things would be jumping."

"You'd think so."

Leaving him standing at the corner of the building, she walked slowly toward the pool, keeping her eyes averted from the closed patio gate of the townhouse where Sam had lived. Although she had been here no more than a half a dozen times, she had the peculiar sensation of walking through an oft-traversed dream-hazed area. When she stepped out of the shadow of the building, the sun struck her full in the face, blinding her, sending dazzling darts of light into her brain. Suddenly she existed in a world of exploding brilliance, then immediately was plunged into a void of unending darkness. But coming through the blackness she heard a high-pitched screeching, a raucous cry that her bedazzled senses recognized as the call of a great fowl. And from somewhere else, she heard the padding of animal paws on a hard surface.

"Hello. Can I help you?" It was a woman's voice.

"Possibly. We're apartment hunting," Kellen said. "We understand there's a vacancy or two here."

Susan turned and saw a man and woman standing at the top of the wooden steps leading down to the beach. Vaguely she remembered the man, being introduced to him by Sam one evening when they walked the beach, but she couldn't recall his name, and his face was somewhat different, more gaunt and hollow, than what her memory recalled.

"I'm Ann Davis," the woman said, "and this is my brother, Glenn. Glenn Ashley. He lives in this building."

Susan suddenly remembered the name and the man, and what Sam had told her of his drinking problem. Most of all, she remembered that his pregnant wife had drowned herself in the ocean right off this beach. She looked away from him, not knowing whether or not to admit to her recognition.

"I'm not certain about any vacancies," the woman said. "I'm down from Virginia visiting my brother, but I think I've heard there are two or three unoccupied apartments."

Kellen moved to Susan's side. "That's encouraging. Almost all the places we've looked at do have vacancies, but we have a certain feeling for this particular one."

"I've only been here three weeks, but I find the place lovely. I'm sure you'd like it here." The woman turned to Glenn. "There's a vacancy in this building, isn't there, Glenn?"

Glenn frowned, darted his eyes to the closed patio gate at the southern end of the building, then looked directly at Susan. "I remember you. I can't remember your name, but you were a friend of Sam's, weren't you?"

She forced herself not to hesitate, not to glance at either Kellen or Glenn's sister. "Yes. Yes, I was. A very close friend. I'm Susan Rutledge, and this is Kellen Atwood."

Glenn's eyes swiveled around in their sockets with a loosely fluid movement. "He always said you were a fine person."

"So was he, Mr. Ashley."

Beside him, Glenn's sister stirred, taking a protective step closer to him. "I assume, then, Miss Rutledge, that you're aware Glenn was suffering with a rather special problem, one he's recovering from slowly."

"I know he lost his wife."

"Lost her?" Glenn's eyes focused momentarily. "I killed her."

"Glenn!" His sister clamped her right hand on his left shoulder. "Don't you dare say that! Don't you dare think that."

"I did," he mumbled. "Everybody but you, sis, knows me and my bottle of booze drove her into the ocean."

"That's enough of that! We're going in the house."

Glenn pulled free of his sister's hand and took a sideways step away from her. Then once again his eyes aimed at Susan, and she thought she could all but see ragged thoughts and memories falling into place behind them, and if what she thought she saw was correct, they made up a bleak and desolate pattern.

"You know, Sam and I talked," he said. "We had a long talk before he was killed. Yeah, we did, and you know what he told me? He told me a good friend of his saw a black thing floating in the night—just like the black thing I saw before Jetta died. That's what he told me . . . a good friend of his saw it, and that friend hadn't been drinking."

Deep inside her a quiet voice cried out.

"I'm that friend, Glenn. I saw the floating black thing too."

At her brother's side, Ann Davis was frowning, her attention shifting from Glenn to Susan, once turning in Kellen's direction as though seeking his assistance.

"Ann," she said slowly, "please don't be upset. Kellen and I are here, we think, to help. I don't know the extent of Glenn's problem, Sam only mentioned it to me in passing, but I can assure you that if your brother saw an object floating through the night, he was not suffering from the D.T.'s. There are others, besides myself, who have seen it."

"That's right," Glenn said. "I was crocked when we talked, but Sam told me about other people seeing it."

"Yes, Glenn. And since Sam's death, still more people have said that they saw it . . . all of them at the time of the death of a baby." She hesitated, glanced sideways at both Ann and Kellen. "Your wife was pregnant, wasn't she?"

"Miss Rutledge, please!" Anger sparkled in Ann Davis's eyes. "This is getting out of hand."

"Mrs. Davis." It was Kellen. He reached out to take Susan's right hand. "Please listen. I'm going to tell you the truth. I've been a skeptic about what Susan is trying to do investigating this black floating object, and I've offered to help her only because, well—because I think a great deal of her. From what she tells me, there've been incredibly bizarre things occurring, and now, I must admit, my skepticism is wearing very thin. I think Susan might be about to discover something very important concerning the recent deaths of so many babies in this area—and maybe Jetta's death. So please, bear with her for just a few minutes more. Okay?"

"You hear that, sis?" Glenn looked at his sister.

"Yes, Glenn, but—"

"No, Ann, no buts . . . no buts." Susan saw him desperately attempting to hold his eyes on his sister's face and wondered at his force of will. How sad that he had not been able to find that strength before his wife's death.

"Glenn—" Ann was frowning.

"Look," he said. "I appreciate you and the family pulling me out of the stink hole I was wallowing in, you know that, but—but . . ." He stopped speaking. It was as though his sequence of thoughts had suddenly run their course, and his eyes shifted away from his sister to stare out across the blue plain of the ocean. Susan knew he wasn't all the way out of the "stink hole." He blinked, then without looking at any of them, said in a hollow voice, "I killed Jetta and the baby she was carrying. I drove her into the ocean, because I was a goddamn selfish and spoiled brat. Do you understand, sis? Do you?"

Ann Davis nodded and dropped her eyes.

The building's shadow had now moved partially across the pool, staining the west side of it purple, making the water appear dark with the depthlessness of oblivion. One of the table umbrellas, stirred by the sea breeze, rattled with a hollow sound.

"Glenn," Susan said slowly, "maybe you're taking too much blame for Jetta's death. Where was the black thing when you saw it?"

From wherever he was, Glenn pulled himself back. "Always outside the bedroom window or the patio gate."

"How far into her pregnancy was Jetta?"

"Over eight months."

"Did you see the black thing the night Jetta died?"

"I—I wasn't home."

Ann Davis took a breath as though about to speak, but let it out slowly, without uttering a sound.

With a little nod of her head in the direction of the last apartment in the building, Susan asked, "Is that where the woman named Lily lives?"

Glenn nodded.

"Do you know her?"

"I don't think anybody knows her. We hardly see her. I think she travels a lot."

"I wonder where."

Glenn shrugged. "Maybe on field trips, looking for things to sculpt."

"Sculpt?" Susan felt her eyes widen. "She's a sculptress?"

"Yeah. And you know something else? I found twelve hundred dollars in a dresser drawer. I didn't know where it came from, and when I mentioned it to Todd and Holly, Holly told me Jetta had been posing for Lily." Pinpoints of moisture glinted in the corners of his staring eyes. "She was trying to save herself and the baby—and maybe even me—by modeling. She wanted the money to keep our family together."

"That's enough!" Ann Davis put her arm around her brother's shoulder. "That *is* enough, Miss Rutledge."

"Yes," Kellen said. "I think it is."

"I'm sorry," Susan murmured.

"You should be." Placing both of her hands on her brother's shoulders, the woman turned Glenn away and started to lead him around the pool. "You've nearly destroyed what we've all worked so hard to achieve, Miss Rutledge. There are other people in this complex who love to talk. Find them and listen to their gossip."

Susan watched the couple until they disappeared through the patio gate next to the one that was Lily's. She was trembling. Her nerves were tingling in tiny jabs that sent goose pimples over her entire body. Yet, for all that, she knew the image of the tears in Glenn Ashley's eyes would remain a haunting memory of a misery revisited.

Without looking at Kellen, she walked slowly to the waist-high retaining wall and stood staring out at the ocean, watching its gentle undulations while she allowed the circuits in her mind to sort out the information she had just received.

Behind her, she heard Kellen's footsteps approaching, slowly, as though he felt he might be intruding.

"I think I know what's going through your mind," he said. "You're thinking about that sculpture show you and Maureen went to, aren't you? You're thinking Lily was behind it."

"Yes."

"I think I agree, but how did she do it?"

"I don't know." She dropped her hand from his arm. "I don't know how, and I don't know why."

"Maybe I know why." Kellen shoved his hands in the pockets of his slacks and walked to the retaining wall, where he stood looking out at the ocean. "Glenn Ashley said something else, while you were thinking."

"What?" Susan went to stand beside him.

"He said Sam was having a hot affair with Lily."

"Yes, he was, but he told me he was thinking of backing away from it, because he felt it was consuming him. I agreed with him. In fact, I used a harsh word or two to get my point across."

Kellen nodded. "If this Lily found out about that, she could be jealous. And you know about hell's fury and a woman scorned—or something."

"Dear God! In the restaurant that night with Sam, when he and I were talking about his relationship with her."

"Restaurant? What about the restaurant?"

A wisp of hair blew across her forehead and she brushed it away as she searched for the words to tell him about what she'd thought was an hallucination of a female figure watching and listening to them while they talked. Finally she very deliberately and precisely told him, and when she was finished they both stood looking out to where the purple and lavender were commencing to saturate the blue of the ocean.

It was Kellen who spoke first. "I wouldn't have believed that a month ago, but now it doesn't seem right not to believe it."

"Believe it, Kellen. Like everything else, it happened, but I'm not certain Lily is jealous. If she possessed the ability to eavesdrop on that conversation, she knows there was nothing sexual in my relationship with Sam, that I was no threat to her that way."

"Not that way, no. But you weren't in favor of her affair with him, and she might look on that the same way."

"Maybe, but what I really think has her interested in me is that I suspect her of being connected with the baby deaths in this area."

"Maybe we should go to the police."

"With what? Like Sam said, a ghost story?"

"Oh shit, I don't know. We're involved in something that can't be happening, but is."

Neither moved, both abstractly studying the darkening sea, while conducting individual studies of their respective thoughts, realigning their beliefs.

Two laughing couples came up the steps from the beach, followed shortly by another. They looked inquiringly at Susan and Kellen, but said nothing, moving past to cross the recreational area.

Susan saw another group ambling along the beach in their direction, watched them for a short period, then said, "Let's go. I think we've learned everything we can for now."

Kellen nodded agreement. "Sounds good. I'll make a deal with you."

"Oh? Somehow you're making that sound suspicious."

"It should. It's filled with ulterior motives."

"Now it sounds interesting."

"I'll buy the steaks and trimmings, if you take charge of preparing them."

"That's a good deal. But what about the other part, the ulterior part of it?"

Kellen brushed aside his lock of hair. "Well, I guess that will be up to nature."

She laughed and took his hand. "That sounds even better."

She lay on her back, staring with half-closed eyes at a spray-like splash of morning sunlight sending gossamer tendrils across the ceiling. By opening her eyes slightly, or squinting them tighter, she was able to change the flimsy design of clear light from a sparkling radiation to a subdued pulsing blurr, and she played this visual game for several minutes, feeling comfortable and safe in Kellen's bed, a rumpled sheet half covering her nakedness.

Kellen was still sleeping, lying on his right side with his back to her, breathing with the slow shallowness of slumber. She pulled her attention away from the sun, opened her eyes wide, and turned her head on the pillow to look at his bare shoulders and tousled hair. His shoulders were broad and muscular, and from the angle at which she was now looking at them they appeared herculean. She felt a tremor ripple through her body as an unbidden memory recalled the explosive alchemy their flesh had created during the night.

Never, she thought, had her body responded with such joy and eagerness as it had last night under Kellen's gentle, but determined and knowing, caresses. For truly the first time in her life, she had experienced the physical ecstasy of love, and now, lying here at his side, she wasn't ashamed to admit that she was hungry for it to occur again.

Kellen's breath caught, then made a sighing sound. She waited expectantly, every fiber in her body wanting it to be an indication he was awakening and that in a moment he would turn onto his back, see her, and, smiling, gather her into his arms. An erotic sensation passed through her; from her abundant breasts to her strong loins, she pressed tightly against his body, her flesh sending him invitations to once again enter her. But he remained still, his breathing regained its even-spaced rhythm. She gave a silent sigh, feeling restless. She knew sleep would not return. Carefully, she pushed the sheet from her, and just as deliberately swung her legs off the bed and slowly stood up.

She carried her clothes to the bathroom, thought about showering, then discarded the idea, fearful it would wash away the delicious euphoria still clinging to her. She dressed quickly, used Kellen's brush on the auburn tangle of her hair, then tiptoed from the bathroom down the hallway and into the kitchen.

The first ripplings of hunger quivered in her stomach, and she knew Kellen would want breakfast when he got up. She looked in the refrigerator. It was sparsely filled, but she saw half a dozen eggs, an unopened package of bacon, a carton of orange juice, and a partial loaf of bread. In a cupboard, she found a jar of Taster's Choice coffee. Altogether, there were enough ingredients to prepare a decent breakfast.

Satisfied, she wandered out of the kitchen, looked toward the living room, then saw that the door from the hallway to the apartment's second bedroom was open. Kellen had furnished it as a workroom. Undecided, she stood looking at it, knowing that he wouldn't mind her going into it, but fearful that she would feel like a prowler if she entered.

She looked in at him once more. He was on his back with his arms spread out, the lock of hair hiding his left eye, still sleeping soundly. Resisting the impulse to enter the room and crawl into the bed beside him, she turned abruptly and hurried into the workroom.

At first glance, there was disorder in the books and papers laying on two tables, as though they had been tossed down nonchalantly, ruffled through in search of reference material and never rearranged. But closer inspection showed that each pile consisted of related subjects or was indexed with a handwritten note clipped to its top sheet.

Out of curiosity she wanted to leaf through some of the books or shuffle through the papers, but the sense of invading Kellen's privacy still remained strong within her, so she turned her back to them and began examining the books filling the homemade shelving along one wall.

The volumes were both old and new, bookstore clean or tattered. Unlike the material lying on the tabletops, no attempt had been made to index them or arrange them in order of subject, and she received the impression they had been shelved merely to keep them out of the way.

She didn't have her reading glasses, so a few of the titles on the older, more scuffed books were too blurred for her to decipher, but she quickly discovered that the books' subject matter was as diverse as their condition: novels, non-fiction, how-to reference volumes. She smiled. Kellen, it was obvious, was not addicted to one particular field of interest. A cheery feeling of gratification settled on her.

Without her glasses, reading was going to be limited to scanning illustrations or skimming through short passages. She ran a forefinger along the books on one shelf, seeing nothing of sufficient interest to remove, and couldn't help but wonder why Kellen had them. *Worlds of Science. Household Medical Dictionary. Mastering the Social Graces. All about Winemaking. Magic Made Easy.*

With a sigh, she was about to turn away when she saw, on the upper shelf, a thin volume lying down instead of standing vertical like the others. For some reason, her first impression was how forlorn and alone the slender book looked among its bigger, thicker neighbors.

No words on its spine identified it. More out of a feeling of sadness for the disconsolate-looking little volume than a sense of curiosity, she pulled it from the shelf. On the dusty cover in faded blue letters was an odd title: *The Unexplainable Unexplained*. It was written by someone with the single name of Valdis, and published by Limetree House in London, England. The date of publication was 1911. Its rough-edged pages were turning a sepia brown and felt brittle.

The table of contents listed seven phenomena which had, at least until the publication date, never been solved or explained by science or exploration.

Squinting, she moved her eyes down the column of subjects: Discovery of a Cadmium Battery in Mesopotamian Tomb, Engineering Feat of Stonehenge, Lost City of the Incas, Disappearance of Population of Jamestown, Darting Lights in the Night Skies, Unexplainable Deaths of Infants.

Her eyes stopped their slow scan of the page. She blinked and reread the listing. As if something cold had come into the room, she shivered and felt the chill seep into her skull to pry at her brain. She opened the book to the appropriate page.

The print was too small. It fuzzed against the sepia background.

"Damn it!"

Helpless, she looked around the room, feeling inadequate. A tiny light reflection, like a spark of colorless flame, from the far end of one of the tables caught her eyes. There was a magnifying glass laying there, partially hidden under the corner of a loose sheet of paper. In three long strides, she was across the room and had snatched up the glass. Without looking for a chair, Susan held the open book in her left hand and, with the glass in her right, began to read.

Only two and a half pages were devoted to the subject, and, because the writing was embroidered with

stilted words, the information they imparted was difficult to extract.

"At irregular intervals throughout history," she read,
"a strangely selective plague visits an area of the world,
during the visitation of which, no newborn infant is
safe, but is, in fact, a probable victim of an
undiagnosable death." Although Valdis admitted written records were scarce, some few were available, and
in more primitive areas storytellers told about "the
time the babies died." It was apparent, he wrote, that
"no part of the world is immune. This abominable
bane visits all lands, from Asia through the Middle East
to Europe, Africa, and South America." Though only
one episode, in the late 1800's, was reported in North
America, and that in Mexico, "it can be assumed that
the United States has, at one time or another, experienced it." The medical profession possessed no answers, the story said. Deaths came fast, unexpectedly,
and with no prior indications of illness. In ancient
times, and up through the Middle Ages, many people in
an affected village or town believed that a demon or
evil spirit had settled among them to exact vengeance
for a wrong committed by the populace. The account
ended with the statement that "the medical authorities
profess bafflement, and many feel that, until greater
advances are made in their profession, these strange
and terrible deaths will continue; although there are
those who state emphatically they are not dealing with
a medical problem, so it is possible a way will never be
found to stop them."

After the second reading, even with the magnifying
glass her eyes starting to ache, Susan felt herself trembling, as she would if she were standing on the edge of a
great, dark abyss with someone or something unseen
making ready to push her over the brink into the
darkness yawning below. She was breathing heavily,

noisily. Here was proof. Proof, but no help. She set down the magnifying glass and left the room, the book still in her hand.

Kellen was up, dressed in jeans, and slipping a yellow T-shirt over his head when she walked into the bedroom.

"Glad to see you," he smiled. "The place was so quiet that I was starting to wonder what had happened to you."

She held out the book. "Where did you get this?"

"Not much of a greeting from the woman with whom I just spent one of the nicest nights of my life." He looked at the book. "I don't know. Let me see it."

She handed it to him. "Page fifty-seven. Read the story that starts there."

Kellen read swiftly through the account, and Susan watched a frown form beneath the fallen lock of hair. He turned the page back and reread the two and a half pages again. The skepticism on his face slowly transformed into unconcealed interest.

When he finished with the second reading, he closed the book and looked at the title, then shook his head. "This is from the workroom shelves, isn't it?"

"Yes."

"I only vaguely remember it. It came in a carton of books I bought for a couple of dollars at a garage sale several months ago. The title intrigued me and I thought I'd read it someday." He shrugged. "But I never got around to it."

"Well, what do you think?" She was surprised how clear her thinking had suddenly become. "Do you see the similarity between what's described in the book and what's happening here?"

He slapped the little volume against his thigh. "Yes —but it still could be coincidence."

He was striving not to allow it to surface, but Susan

knew his entire attitude was altering, and she was unable to prevent the flutter of excitement she felt from hurrying across her face.

He saw it, and laughed. "Okay, you've got me hooked good and proper."

With a little trilling sound that was dangerously close to a giggle, she threw her arms around him. "God, I'm glad I found the right bait."

Tossing the book to the bed, he pulled her close, and while his lips pressed tight to hers, his hands moved gently up and down her back, finally coming to a stop on the curve of her tightly jeaned hips. When he pulled his mouth away, he said, "The book is only a teeny-weeny portion of the bait."

"When did you get home? Niles and I were watching for you." Maureen stood at the apartment's front door. "We didn't know you were back until we saw your living-room light come on."

"Oh, I don't know. About six-thirty, I guess." Susan turned. "Come on in and sit a while. I've got something to tell you."

Inside the apartment, Maureen ostentatiously looked around. "Where's Kellen?"

"He had a meeting with a friend. They're trying to work out a new course for the Lit Department."

"On a Saturday night? That's not very romantic, is it?"

Susan smiled. "Well, truthfully, I think romance is something new to him, and besides, schedules don't mean much to him."

"That's kind of sweetly naive."

"I guess so. You look like you've something to tell me."

"Just an update on what I told you the other day. I've made an appointment with Dr. Markham for Tuesday, to double-check my pregnancy test."

"I think that's a good idea."

Maureen nodded. "They say the home tests are accurate, but Niles and I want to make certain."

"Oh, I'm sure you're pregnant. And it's going to be the luckiest kid there is, because you and Niles are such terrific parents."

Maureen smiled. "Thanks, Susan. Now, what is it you have to tell me?"

When Susan finished telling her that Lily was a sculptress, Maureen stared at her, her face reflecting the mixed association of thoughts taking place in her mind. Then she told Maureen of the account in the little book she'd discovered. While she spoke, the deepening twilight filled the apartment with darkness.

In a surprisingly emotionless voice, Maureen said, "She's a demon."

Susan frowned, surprised at the words.

"Lily is an evil spirit, Susan."

Susan shook her head absently. Events were evolving rapidly into matters that could not longer be considered merely a fanciful brainchild of an overactive, dogmatic mind. Even Kellen was now a believer. But a demon in their midst? An evil spirit dwelling among them? No, it was impossible for her to accept that. She wasn't ready to add that to her notes.

"I—I just can't believe that," she said. "What's occurring with the babies has to be rationally, naturally explained. I'm not exonerating Lily but, Maureen, demonology passed into history with the Middle Ages."

Maureen scowled. "Then how do you explain the black thing that's been sighted whenever a baby dies? Lily likes to travel in storms. And how do you explain the sculpture show in a closed-up gallery? I'm sure it was her work, Susan."

For a moment, she felt bereft of her instincts and common sense as she sought a rational answer to the questions. None emerged from the building confusion in her mind. Finally, she was forced to shrug her shoulders and shake her head. "I can't."

Maureen stood up. "Don't shut your mind, Susan. It's possible there are other dimensions beyond what we see, beyond the three our minds accept. Today there are so many gadgets and manufactured pleasures to guide our thinking that maybe much of the ancient knowledge our forebears possessed has been taken from us, or, at least, hidden in some portion of our minds."

"Do you believe that?"

"I don't completely disbelieve it." Maureen started walking toward the door. "Think about it."

"I will."

When Maureen was gone, Susan stood looking at the closed desk drawer which contained her notes and descriptive pamphlet of the sculpture show. They were all part of her jumble of bewildering, impossible theories. She went to the desk, pulled open the drawer, and on the sheet devoted to Lily wrote "demon." She followed the word with a half a dozen question marks.

Mondays were unpredictable in the library. Either the reference tables were circled with students seeking information that should have been gathered over the weekend, or the entire building echoed with a ghostly emptiness due to Monday lethargy.

To Susan's relief, today was one of the latter Mondays. Only two young people huddled over separate tables in the reference room for the first half hour of the day. Susan prepared her first-of-the-week reports, all the time holding in check the impatience that threatened to jumble her thoughts into little curlicues. When the reports were finished and given to Marge Anderson, a man required help to find biographical material on Thomas Sheraton, the English furniture designer, and then there was nothing more to occupy her. With a quick look around the room, she pushed away from her desk and hurried to the card file, and as she did her impatience gave way to excitement. Without an exact idea of where to begin, she decided on the categories of myths and legends and unexplained phenomena. The library contained next to nothing on medical reference.

Twice while fingering through the cards she stopped to mentally steady herself, but in the end she pulled three titles from the files. Two books, once she removed them from the stacks and read the forewords, she replaced. But the third, a small, inconsequential-looking volume, like the one she had found on Kellen's shelf, was entitled *Dictionary of Nocturnal Demons*. It gave a listing in its index of twenty-two mythical entities.

It wasn't what she was primarily looking for, but thanks to the seed planted in her mind Saturday evening by Maureen, she was curious enough to check it out. She took the book to her desk. But still, she wasn't ready to accept wholly, or even in part, the demon theory, in spite of the terrible strangeness that surrounded Lily.

She laid the book aside and took from the lower drawer of her desk a copy of the campus telephone directory. There was no pre-med study offered at Sloan, which was only a two year college but a phone call to the Biology Department might direct her to some agency that could answer her questions concerning the baby deaths. Another call to the History Department, might get her more information on the recurring phenomenon of infants dying unexplicably.

The head of the Biology Department was gone for the summer, but his assistant was in charge. A Mrs. Edith Shofner.

Susan discovered she suddenly felt embarrassed, like

a person seeking thrills from a catastrophic situation, when she talked to Mrs. Shofner. But the biologist apparently sensed nothing of the sort and was gracious with her explanation that there was very little known about Sudden Infant Death Syndrome. Unless some virus could be isolated, the deaths would continue. No, she didn't know about it being an historically recorded phenomenon, but suggested Susan phone the County Health Department. They would, she was certain, be cooperative with a school librarian seeking reference material.

Susan thanked her and hung up.

It was now noon, and only a dozen people had used the reference facilities all morning. Susan sat staring into space, trying to tell herself she was devoting time and energy to what was no more than an obsession born in her imagination. She came very close to succeeding, but was forced to admit that the physical evidence that the deaths were not entirely natural was too overpowering to be brushed away without substantial facts to the contrary.

When Marge Anderson relieved her for lunch, Susan hurried to her apartment. Without thinking of eating, she looked up the number of the County Health Department, fearing that at this time of day there'd be no one there to help her—if, indeed, they would be willing to give her information anyway.

However, once again she was pleasantly surprised. A Tod Logan answered the phone and, when she identified herself as the reference librarian at the Sloan College library, became as helpful as it was possible to be on the subject of SIDS. No, he said, there was no known reason for the sudden upward swing in infant deaths. They had investigated every death, as required by county law, and were unable to discover a cause other than a form of asphyxiation. One of the puzzling elements, he said, was the rise in SIDS was not confined to the local area. Miami, Jacksonville, and Orlando were reporting an uncommon number of infant deaths in recent weeks. The State Department of Health had sent a team, but they too were baffled.

Susan's heart raised its beat. "Do you know if this sort of thing has occurred before?" she asked. "You know, an upswing in infant deaths in a localized area."

"That's being looked into," Logan said. "There have been sensationalized reports, yes, but our investigators are contacting medical organizations in other states for hard facts. So far, we've received responses from four, and two were affirmative. Puerto Rico says Jamaica and the Leeward Islands were recently struck. Texas says nothing in recent years, but there are confirmed reports of an occurrence in Mexico some years back. Our state organization is trying to make contact with the World Health Organization, but I personally hold little hope there. I'm afraid they consider it low-priority, what with all their other projects."

Susan thanked the man and left both her personal and the library's phone numbers, asking him to call her if any new information was received.

Back at the library, she tried to reach the History Department, but no one answered the phone. As she sat at her desk, looking at the still-deserted reference room, she had the odd sensation of feeling both drained and exhilarated at the same time. There were so many pieces of the puzzle to put together, so many pieces obviously missing, that the final picture it would reveal was as hazy as it had been when she'd first begun to assemble it; yet some of the existing pieces were interlocking and a hint of the finished illustration was slowly emerging.

She picked up the thin little book, *Dictionary of Nocturnal Demons*.

With a forefinger that was surprisingly steady, she ran down the demon names listed in the index. She'd heard of none of them, which meant there was but one way to discover if the book contained anything fitting the situation. Go through it demon by demon.

She found it on page 37.

At first she scanned the page as she had the preceding ones, picking out words and phrases to obtain the gist of what was written, preparing to leaf on to the next one, aware of approaching disappointment. Then, all of a sudden, the words were telling her what was happening here and now. Her first reaction was how strong the parallel was, then realization brushed aside the laxity which had crept into her attention. She stared without reading at the words before her, watching them blur into a rectangle of gray on the page, feeling a pulse starting to throb in her throat. Everything around her came to a standstill.

Slowly she began to read again, unconsciously gnawing at her lower lip, at the same time holding her breath. She read deliberately, cautiously, one word at a time, sometimes not certain of the relationship of one word to another.

Halfway down the page her confusion went away, the words were clear and sharp, the sentences driving their message into her mind with precise detail. And as she began to comprehend, fear found its way into her like ice water rushing through her veins.

In the Garden of Eden, before Eve, Adam had the company of a wife, created like him from the clay of the earth. A beautiful woman, she was also willful, eventually refusing to accept the order of life as lived in the Garden.

When the time came when she and Adam were told to procreate, the woman refused, quarreling viciously with Adam, refusing to accept the discomfort of carry-

ing their offspring, finally denouncing him along with
the One who had created the Garden. She was expelled
from the Garden but, filled with insatiable fury,
screamed her damnation of babies because they were
the indirect reason for her expulsion, vowing to avenge
herself. Once, she returned in an unsuccessful attempt
to ensnare the children of Eve, whom she now hated for
taking her place in Adam's affections.

Consumed more and more with her rage and hate,
she made her home in the black world of the night. She
used the winds of the night storms to wander the world,
carrying her vengence from land to land. As the eons
passed, she directed her fury not only at the newly
born, but at the women who carried within them the
embryos of life, for in her rage-darkened eyes they were
the women who had replaced her at Adam's side.

Today she remained as beautiful as the day she had
left the Garden, and through the millennia she had
used her beauty to conduct schemes and strategies, but
mostly to lure men. It was possible that she still loved
Adam as she had once in the Garden, and now replaced
him in her mind with the lovers she took. However,
eventually she would turn her back on each man, as she
had on Adam, and search out a new one to entrap in
her demi-paradise.

Through the ages, she learned and adapted to her
uses the powers from certain creatures that were ancient enemies of mankind and the One who had
created her. To these powers she added the black magic
of the Babylonian and Persian wizards. She could send
herself forth as a spirit with no bodily substance, could
transform herself into a creature of the wild. Kites,
pelicans, owls, wildcats, and jackals were her favorites.
Sometimes, though, she chose the form of a beast or
fowl no longer associated with the modern earth.

Her name was Lilith.

Susan sat staring at the name. She repeated it to herself. Slowly, letting its flow guide her, feeling its rhythms, listening to its intonation.

Lilith—Lilith—Lilith . . . Lily . . . Lily . . .

Lily!

18

THE EVENING AIR WAS SOGGY, UNNATURALLY QUIET. A HIGH
vault of finely spun clouds diffused the sun, draining
from the ixora and hibiscus blossoms the brilliant reds
with which they sparkled all day, laying a gray undertone beneath the blue-green shimmer of the grass.
From the highway a mile away, the rumble of rush-hour
traffic was muted under the over-heavy burden of
humidity.

Kellen had not been waiting for her, and Susan
hurried along the campus path in the direction of her
apartment. It had taken her most of the afternoon to
gather her thoughts into a semblance of cohesiveness
after reading the page-and-a-half description of the
night demon Lilith. She had struggled to sustain her
mental balance while she read, intensely aware of great
shadows looming at the edges of her consciousness,
threatening to creep closer, to reach out dark tentacles
to wrap around her and draw her into their mass.

283

Throughout the afternoon, she read and reread the story of Lilith. It was another person she watched, as from a great distance, who assisted six people needing reference help during the remainder of the afternoon, and a stranger who said good night to Marge Anderson. Now, walking across the campus, she knew that she was not the Susan Rutledge who had walked this same path this morning. This one hurrying to her apartment had endured a bizarre kaleidoscope of emotions leaving a new perspective on all things, both good and evil.

The apartment's atmosphere was out of balance. A silence too large for it to contain was squeezed into the small rooms, and she felt the weight of it lean on her nerves to make them tingle.

She stood undecided beside the writing desk, on which she had laid the *Dictionary of Nocturnal Demons*, wondering if she should phone Maureen. She looked around the apartment, noting that everything seemed normal. No shadows surrounded her as they had in the library, yet the tingling from the out-of-balance silence was taking on the prevailing feeling of uneasiness.

She finally turned her back on the book and went to the bedroom, where she undressed, then to the bathroom, where she showered, endeavoring to make her movements deliberate and mind-occupying. Dressing in a blouse, shorts, and sandals, she went to the kitchen to pour herself a glass of orange juice from a carton in the refrigerator. She knew that what she was doing was a weak attempt at ignoring her growing uneasiness, and she felt ashamed, for she'd thought she was more civilized than a primitive child to whom ghost stories were tales of life's realities.

The door chimes rang, trying to send their harmony through the rooms, but in the burdened atmosphere the notes were dull and discordant.

When she opened the door, Maureen was standing on the stoop, holding Bridget in her arms.

"Kellen not here?"

"No, he has a class tonight."

"Niles is working late too."

Just inside the door, Maureen hesitated, scanning the gloomy dimness of the apartment with widened eyes before looking at Susan with a frown. Slowly she ran the tip of her tongue around her lips, then surveyed once more the gathering shadows in the living room, her arms tightening around Bridget.

"What's wrong?" Susan asked.

"Don't you feel it?"

Susan had no need to answer. As Maureen asked her question, something passed between the two women, like a sudden blending of warm air currents. Bridget whimpered.

"What's going on?" Maureen asked.

Susan went to her desk, picked up the book, and held it in both hands for a long moment before offering it to Maureen.

"Page thirty-seven. Read it."

Maureen put Bridget, who was restless, on the sofa. "Hush, honey, for just a minute or so."

How many times Maureen read the page and a half, Susan didn't know, but when she closed the book Maureen's face wore an expression Susan made no attempt to define. Her mouth was a rigid straight line, as if behind her lips her teeth were grinding harshly together, her nostrils were pinched and her eyes reflected a conflict of certainty and uncertainty waging in her mind. The hand holding the book trembled.

While they stood silently looking at each other, the late afternoon light abruptly disappeared, as it might if a great shade had been drawn across the westward-moving sun with a furious yank. Darkness, as thick and heavy as the already existing silence, cascaded into the apartment, cramming itself into every corner and oozing like thick oil to fill the spaces beneath the furniture.

Maureen placed the book on the desk, carefully picked her way to a floor lamp, and turned it on. The illumination from the 150-watt bulb was a peculiar jaundiced hue, only managing to create a small fan-like glow in the darkness. The darkness became heavier, more solid. It seemed to squeeze the air out of the apartment, turning the atmosphere stifling in spite of the air conditioner.

Susan felt a pulsing in her temple and wondered if this was a nervous tick or if she was becoming starved for oxygen. Maureen exhaled a deep breath with a whooshing sound.

At first it was subtle, lightly caressing the senses like a faded memory, but as the temperature in the apartment continued its slow rise the aroma became as evident as the darkness and the silence. Sharp and sweet at the same time, it was the decaying stench of a once-verdant garden grown rank after years of neglect.

"What's happening?" Maureen's voice gave the impression that it was wedged in her throat.

On the sofa, Bridget made a whimpering sound, then was quiet.

Susan could only shake her head. Her own vocal cords were contracted. Opening her eyes wide in an effort to take advantage of what little ambient light existed, she looked around, struggling to pick out details in the darkness of the living room. She saw nothing strange. She tried to assure herself that they were alone in the room, yet she had a dreadful certainty that something evil was either with them or watching them from the other side of the blackness, something that took careful note of their reactions.

That was when they heard the noise. At first, it was

muffled, as though its vibrations were coming to them from some place not too distant. While they listened it came steadily closer in a relentless approach along the short hallway that lead to the bedroom, and as it drew nearer it took on substance, becoming distinct and recognizable: the cushiony thudding of paws being carefully placed. It was the sound of stalking, of primal stealth, the guarded movements of a predator making its final adjustments before attacking. Mixed with the smell of decayed vegetation, the odor of dirt-matted fur now spread through the heat, turning the air foul and heavy.

Then, just before reaching the end of the hallway, the movement stopped.

Susan felt sweat beading on her forehead and starting to trickle in hot rivulets down her spine. She stared at the entrance to the hallway, and knew that something was watching her, studying her, with a brooding anger. She couldn't help herself: she cringed. Around her the fragile wall between self-control and fear was cracking. Time stretched into an eternity while she struggled to keep her attention fixed on that place in the darkness. Finally she felt its interest turn away from her. In the next instant, Bridget gave a tiny whimper, followed by a sigh.

"No!" Susan wasn't aware she had cried out, was only partially cognizant of rushing to the sofa and scooping the baby up in her arms.

"Susan! What—?" Maureen, as if breaking free of an overpowering grasp which had held her helpless, whirled from the rigid position in which she had been standing.

Susan shook her head. Speech was impossible. Her actions had been automatic, but, through the numbness deadening her nerves, she could feel Bridget trembling against her breast.

Like a person struggling through a clinging morass, Maureen stumbled to her side and, with shaking hands, took Bridget into her own arms. Neither of the women spoke, their attention and fears concentrated on the infant.

At some point Susan's mind began functioning again and she realized the animal smell was gone. A moment later the sweetly rank scent began to fade. She could feel the temperature dropping steadily down to the seventy-two-degree setting on the air conditioner's thermostat, and at the same time watched the output of the lamp grow steadily until the darkness was pushed back to the edges of the room and they stood facing one another in an oasis of clear illumination.

"It was her, wasn't it?" Maureen asked. "It had to be. It was Lily."

"I don't know."

"What else could it have been? Didn't you smell that stench? It's like the book said, Susan, that—that bitch can turn herself into wild creatures. It was her, Susan. It was!"

"Maureen!"

"I—" Maureen shook her head in such a way Susan was reminded of a person coming out of a trance. "I'm sorry." She hugged Bridget tighter to her, then looked straight at Susan. Tears sparkled on her lashes. "I think you saved Bridget's life."

"Oh, Maureen."

"Yes, Susan, you did. I heard her whimper and then make that awful sigh, but you got between her and —and that thing that was in the hallway, protecting her from whatever it was going to do to her. I—I just stood there." She blinked. "Thank you."

"Hey, come on! Let's have some coffee. I think we need it."

"All right." Maureen sat on the sofa with a smiling Bridget on her lap.

"I want you and Bridget to stay here until Niles gets home. No arguments."

Maureen shook her head. "No arguments."

She parked in a space designated by a sign, white letters on a blue background: Reserved For Guests. Standing beside the car, feeling the heat radiate up from the asphalt and reflecting from the glinting metal of the automobile, for the first time since leaving her apartment Susan wondered if she was on the verge of a massive mistake. She looked at the gracefully designed wood-and-fieldstone building with the neatly tended beds of flowers following its contours. Instead of the agreeable response the architecture deserved, beneath her already sun-warmed skin she felt a chill; for to her this building housed sorrow, dark memories, and evil.

The decision to come had been spontaneous, made over her morning coffee while she toyed with the temptation to eat another half a danish. She had phoned Marge, blatantly lying to her, telling her she was suffering with a sinus headache, but, because of the reason for the untruth, she felt no shame.

She drove past the townhouse complex once, continuing south on A1A, reconsidering her actions while pulling together her composure. If Lily was an enemy, she must be met face to face, for only during a personal encounter could she be evaluated. Yet, as Susan swung her Escort in a U-turn, she almost wished that she'd asked Kellen to take off work this morning and accompany her.

Now she stood looking at the building in which Sam had lived and in which Lily resided. Thoughts raced through her mind, each one endeavoring to cancel out the others. She wondered if she should talk again with the sorrowful Glenn Ashley and his sister Ann Davis, then immediately decided she didn't want them to see her here. It might have been the unrelenting heat, but she felt queasy, with a passing touch of vertigo, as she approached Lily's door.

There was no answer the first time she pushed the doorbell button, though from inside the townhouse she heard chimes like a distant carillon. She pushed the button a second time. Nearly half a minute passed, then abruptly the skin on her neck prickled. Invisible things crawled down her arms. She knew she was being closely watched. Someone was not just looking at her, but studying her with intense interest, through the tiny peephole in the door's panel. She made herself smile and stared directly at the small, round cyclopean eye. For half a dozen heart beats, she returned the scrutiny coming from the little hole, then drew an exaggerated breath as if with boredom, shrugged her shoulders, and commenced to turn away.

She heard the sounds of a lock being undone and a bolt slipping. With a slow, almost deliberate motion, the door swung inward.

Framed in the doorway, black-haired, black-clothed, the woman who had appeared in the archway at the library now stood against a black background. Behind her the darkness was unmeasurable, a brimming blackness from which all color had hemorrhaged, receding on and on, it appeared, to the final fringes of eternity.

She did not speak. Unblinking, her green eyes stared at Susan, slowly immersing her in their depthlessness. Susan felt those eyes probing into the most private chambers of her mind. She suppressed a shudder, feeling the chill within her becoming colder and colder.

"I'm Susan Rutledge."

The woman dipped her head in a slow, shallow nod. "I am aware of that."

Susan felt no surprise at the statement. "If you have a moment or two of free time, I'd like to talk with you."

A dark brow arched. "Why would you want to do that, Miss Rutledge? We have nothing to discuss."

Returning the woman's stare, Susan was certain she saw the irises grow larger in the center of the green pupils, becoming touched with flecks of red. A throbbing pulsed in her right temple. Like a double-exposed image in a photograph, super-imposed over the eyes, she saw red eyes staring at her from between the bundles of old newspapers in the library storeroom.

"I think we do," she said. "I think we have very much to discuss, Lily."

"You are bordering on being presumptuous."

The aloof remoteness of the black-clad woman, for a brief instant, made Susan feel as if she were an adolescent standing before an autocratic adult, but the a rush of adrenaline that surged through her carryed the initial traces of a developing anger.

"And you, Lily, are stepping over the borderline of decency."

The red speckles in the centers of the green eyes flared momentarily as the eyes themselves narrowed, and Susan felt an anger to match her own pulsing from the statuesque body. Inside the townhouse, the darkness seemed to stir with a sudden restlessness.

Then, without a word, Lily stepped back.

Caught unawares, Susan hesitated, not certain, for a moment, if this was an invitation to enter or a prelude to the door being shut in her face. When Lily made no further move, Susan stepped into the darkness, telling herself she might have won a small battle.

When the door closed behind her, she discovered the darkness wasn't as complete as it appeared from the outside. Drawn drapes created a twilight, a grayness that diminished perspective, giving the impression of unending distance. Her first awareness was of austerity, of straight lines and cubes and a lack of gentle curves.

As her eyes accustomed themselves to the gloom, Susan saw that the furniture was cleanly modern, upholstered in black and white, expensive-looking but not inviting. Then she saw the pedestals, shafts of cold, white light drilling tunnels through the gray.

At that instant, a series of small ceiling lamps came on. The isolated lights sent their separate narrow beams downward to illuminate the sculptures perched atop the white pedestals, duplicating the scene she had seen at the Art Center.

She stared at them. As at the Art Center, one slanted column of light bathed a ghostly bird of white alabaster swooping out of the twilight. The blank ovals of its eyes were focused tightly on her, continuing the attack it had begun that night in the gallery. But this time Susan solidly returned the fowl's stare, asking, "This is your favorite piece, isn't it, Lily?"

"Yes." Lily gave an amused chuckle. "You recognize it."

"Yes."

The bird appeared to relax onto its pedestal. Susan pulled her eyes away from it and looked around the room. The second survey made her realize once again that there was nothing warm about the room, that it was like a sample room in a furniture store, not a home. She wondered if the apartment had looked like this to Sam.

"Miss Rutledge, tell me what it is you want to talk about."

To her surprise, Susan found it took all the energy her muscles and sinews could generate for her to slowly pivot to face the other woman. In spite of the air-conditioned coolness, she felt sweat run down her face and arms. Her heart thudded. She clenched her hands at her sides.

Lily was standing not half a dozen paces away. Her face was closed, but her green eyes pulsed and the corners of her mouth curved in a mocking evaluation.

"Do my sculptures intrigue you, Miss Rutledge?"

Behind the mocking in the other woman's eyes,

Susan was certain that Lily was taking careful note of her responses. She willed her face to remain void of expression, her tension-tautened muscles to refrain from trembling.

"They're as interesting here as they were at the Art Center," she said slowly. "But the pregnant woman and the child are missing."

"Yes. Essentially the woman was finished when you saw her that night. Now she is gone. But the infant yet remains—for a while."

"I recognized the baby, Lily."

"I thought you would."

"The pregnant woman, who was she?"

"Just that, Miss Rutledge; a pregnant woman."

"Glenn Ashley's wife. The woman who was modeling for you and who drowned herself."

"Your inquisitiveness is not only morbid, Miss Rutledge, it is being carried too far. The two human figures were incidental to the show. Look at the other pieces. They are my favorites, my friends, each one a very precious portion of my spirit. Do you have that feeling about anything, Miss Rutledge?"

Susan's heart still thundered in her chest, but she thought the facade of her artifical calmness was thick enough to hide her trembling. "No, I'm afraid there's too much pragmatism in my make-up."

"Your life must be a dreamless sleep."

"Oh, I have dreams. Recently I've had nightmares."

Lily turned to face her. Susan saw something move in the woman's eyes, something basic and primitive that did not belong in human eyes. Lily took a step toward her. It was a languid movement, and Susan was aware of the flexing of strong muscles beneath the black blouse and snug slacks. It was the coordinated movement of a sleek animal.

"What is it you are here for, Miss Rutledge? I believe it is time you tell me."

Susan swallowed hard.

Lily advanced another slow step. She was so close now that Susan could feel the woman's extraordinary body heat. "Tell me, Miss Rutledge."

Susan felt a rivulet of sweat run down her left cheek, but made no move to wipe it away. Instead she clenched her hands tighter until she could feel her nails dig into her palms. She would not speak.

A hint of savagery appeared on the tawny face before her.

"Why are you here?" Lily's voice was low, powerful.

"The sculptures," she heard herself say. "I wanted to see them again." Susan wasn't planning the words, only listening to them. "I was very impressed with them at the showing."

"You are lying, Miss Rutledge, but I do not care. I know why you are here. However, tell me, was your friend also impressed?"

"Yes." Instinct told her not to challenge Lily's disbelief in her story. "She was."

"That show was very special, very important, because it was a lesson in the abstraction of reality. What exists often cannot exist, and what cannot exist very often does exist. Do you understand, Miss Rutledge, or is this too esoteric for your pragmatic mind?"

"I know the show existed, even though the facts indicate it didn't."

"Then put that knowledge to use, Miss Rutledge. Remember, reality is no more than a vague conception." She smiled stiffly. "There are dominions that human senses cannot record. It would be well for you and your friends to cease seeking entrance to them. Particularly your pregnant friend. She is very vulnerable."

Susan couldn't pull her attention away from the eyes that seemed to be reflecting the heat of the other woman's body as their green became swallowed by red.

Susan took a step back, then froze in place.

The twilight deepened into total darkness and ever so slowly began to swirl. Susan was aware of Lily leaving her side to disappear into the darkness. She shook her head as instinct took command, sending a warning through her.

In the narrow beams of light slanting down from the ceiling, the alabaster creatures stared at her. Inside their stone bodies, muscles, accentuated by the harsh cross-lighting, seemed to be trembling and tautening as if preparing for movement.

There was suddenly a red-hot vehemence in the darkness throughout the townhouse. Susan stood rigid, her arms hanging at her sides, staring at the creatures, knowing that the animals and fowls were more than stone carvings, that they were living inhabitants of the dark world surrounding her.

"Miss Rutledge." Arms folded across her chest, Lily was standing in front of her, her red-tinted eyes focused directly on Susan's. "Go now. There is nothing more for us to discuss. You are seeking answers to questions which throughout the infinity of time have been unanswerable. You are wasting your energies."

Behind Lily, the strange bird with its outstretched wings stirred on its pedestal, turning more directly toward Susan. The alien heat became more stifling.

Whatever was happening, hallucination or reality, she knew she must escape it. This was an occurrence beyond all her beliefs, and to protect all the things she had accepted all her life as believable, she had to get out into the authentic warmth and brilliance of the sunshine. She willed herself to take a step in what she thought was the direction of the door.

Lily moved away, receding into the darkness.

The doorknob was cold in Susan's hand. She turned it and pulled. A luminous wedge of sunlight sliced into the townhouse. Immediately, she felt a rightening of her senses, and a flow of strength and energy throughout her body. Not hesitating, she pulled the door wide and, without looking back, hurried out into the brilliance and heat of the real world.

She drove by habit. North along Highway A1A, then across the arching causeway to Melbourne, response mechanisms reacting to instinct to guide the car through the traffic to its space in the apartment's parking lot.

She was more than halfway along the path to her apartment when she heard the distant thunder. Startled, she looked skyward. A blanched cobalt dome arched unbroken from horizon to horizon, unmarked by even the most wispy of clouds. Yet while she continued to stare upward, another rumble came from along the western horizon. She listened to it until it became lost in traffic sounds and laughter from the pool area, and knew that the distant rumbling was not her imagination, but a reminder that this morning she had entered a distant world. She wondered if she would ever return from it.

19

REMNANTS OF SUSAN'S EMOTIONAL STORM LINGERED. LIKE reflections of distant lightning, wavering flashes of what had taken place played around the corners of her mind. She spent hours pacing slowly around the pool area and standing at the apartment's rear window, staring out at a day that appeared so normal.

For a while the sight of the familiar, cozy shapes of her own furniture and the rectangles of sunlight spreading over them and across the floor from the uncovered windows had pulled her back toward rationality.

But now she felt fear. It was newly spawned, a piercing invasion of her senses, generated by Lily's statement that Maureen was vulnerable because of her pregnancy. She kept thinking of Jetta Ashley. The *Dictionary of Nocturnal Demons* said that Lilith directed her fury at women who carried within them the embryos of life. Twice she'd gone over to the Neilsons' apartment, but Maureen had not returned from the doctor. Susan found herself praying the test would turn out negative.

The telephone rang at a few minutes after three o'clock. The harsh sound pummeled at her like invisible fists.

"Marge said you're sick. What's wrong?" Kellen's voice was warm and concerned.

She looked out the window at the sloping lawn and the cars in the parking area, wondering how to tell him that she had been pyschologically raped, that her mind, perhaps even her soul, had been beaten beyond endurance.

"Hey! Are you still there?" He sounded worried.

"Yes." But she wasn't certain which part of her was leaning against the wall, looking out the window, and which part of her was talking to Kellen. "Can you come over after your last class? I need to talk to you."

"Susan, are you sure you're all right? You're giving a damn good impression of a sick person."

"No, I'm okay physically. I lied to Marge."

"Oh." He was silent a moment. "Look, I've got a Lit class from three-thirty to four-fifteen. There're only six in it. Maybe I can give them something to read and get out half an hour early. If not, I'll be there no later than four-thirty."

"Fine. And, Kellen—thanks for phoning."

She felt better, and her thinking began to wind its way back into rationality.

She showered and dressed in a pair of shorts and a blouse. Both garments were snug, she knew, but this afternoon she wanted to signal a sexually receptive mood to a man. As she turned slowly in front of the bedroom's full-length mirror, she wondered if what she was feeling was an example of danger and violence stimulating the sex drive.

*   *   *

Kellen sat at the dinette table, turning in his fingers the glass of Pepsi Susan had poured him. The movements of his fingers were deliberate; he seemed to be attempting to create a design on the plastic place mat with the condensation on the bottom of the glass. Susan knew what she had told him was moving through his mind with the same unhurried motion.

She said nothing, waiting for him to assimilate the bizarre story of her morning.

Finally, he raised his head, brushed aside the lock of hair, and said, "One of the great things about you is your keen mind. You might not know it, but you're perceptive and more than usually analytical. You're not the type to hallucinate; so, I guess, what we're faced with here is something far beyond the fundamental elements of reality."

"But you believe me?"

"Yes. I'm just having a hell of a time correlating it with everything I know to be factual."

"I am too."

"What do you think is happening?"

Susan sighed. What she thought seemed fantastic. "I have a theory, but . . ."

Kellen looked out the window. "I agree. It can't be."

"What can't be?" Susan joined him at the window.

"What you're refusing to believe."

"They say most legends and many myths have their beginnings in actuality."

"That's what *they* say, yes."

She pulled her eyes away from the creeping darkness out on the lawn and looked at him. "I'm going to try to find out more about Lilith."

"And I'll look through more of my books and some we have cached in the department's mini-library."

She reached across the table to take his hand. "Thanks."

For a while they sat looking at one another, silently,

Susan fearful of speaking, lest the sound of a human voice shatter the spell which was enmeshing her and Kellen.

The knocking at the door came as a sharp intrusion. A long moment passed before they walked to the door, holding hands. Looking into Kellen's eyes, Susan knew, however, the interruption had not destroyed what had been building in each of them.

Maureen stood smiling on the threshold. "Oh, Kellen's here. Wonderful! Now this can really be a celebration."

Susan stepped back. "Come in and tell us what's to celebrate."

Maureen came into the tiny foyer. "I'm going to be a mother again. Dr. Markham's test confirmed my feelings and my home test. I'm pregnant."

Fear stabbed at Susan. She heard Lily's distant voice warning of Maureen's vulnerability, and just as distantly her own saying, "That's wonderful."

Kellen smiled, obviously delighted for Maureen. "Congratulations. How does Niles feel?"

"Somewhere between bewildered and ecsatic." Maureen's happiness trilled in her voice. "Can you both come over for a thrown-together meal? I've got to let off steam, and I think Niles does too. We'd like you both to share our celebration meal."

"We'll be there," Susan said. "When?"

"In about an hour." Maureen turned and started out the door. "Very informal. Come as you are."

When the door closed, Kellen said, "I don't think we should tell them tonight what Lily said."

Susan nodded.

It was after nine o'clock when they finished eating, and Susan insisted on helping Maureen wash and put away the dishes and utensils. While they had been at the table, Niles had told them that he would be leaving

Wednesday for a week at the company's home office in St. Louis. He'd been appointed chief engineer on a major project, and there were many details to review. He asked Susan to look in on Maureen and Bridget from time to time.

Now, in the kitchen, Maureen said, "I'll have the car all next week, and I'll be able to follow any leads we come across."

Susan wanted to tell Maureen of her visit to Lily's townhouse, but knew tonight was not the time. Yet she couldn't permit too much time to pass.

"I'm sure," she said, "we'll come up with some new leads."

"I hope so. It seems to me that we're just gathering bits and scraps of information."

"No, Maureen. What we've discovered so far isn't vague. We're starting to see a pattern in the infant deaths, we're correlating them, and—very soon, I think—we'll be able to put everything together and know what to do."

"I already know, Susan." Maureen's face became harsh and taut. "We have to confront that woman. We have to tell her we know she's responsible for the deaths of all those babies."

"Maureen, we can't do that! We don't really know for sure."

"I do."

"Maureen, you're overreacting."

"Am I? Well, maybe so, but I have two lives to protect. If the situation was reversed, you'd be impatient. You'd want to know the answer."

The words hurt. Susan sucked in her breath. She wanted to scream at Maureen: I'm closer to the answer than you know, and in getting that close I almost had my mind blown apart. But she remained silent, feeling both vulnerable and wary.

Maureen made a choking noise deep in her throat

and turned away. "I'm going to protect Bridget and the
new life forming in me. I'd like your help, Susan, but if
I must, I'll do it alone. I swear I will."

Susan gently stroked her friend's back, feeling the
knotted muscles which corded it. "You've told me you
have an aunt and uncle living up in Apopka. Why don't
you take Bridget and move in with them for a while, at
least while Niles is in St. Louis?"

"I will if we don't come up with anything else. But I
want to see that woman receive her just dues. I want to
make her suffer like she's made so many others suffer."

Walking home from the library the following afternoon, Susan ignored the pristine sharpness and brilliant coloring of the campus. Everything was blurred
and gray in her mind, the result of the sentiments
Maureen had exhibited the previous evening.

When they had returned to her apartment after the
meal, she had told Kellen, who'd shaken his head,
saying it was possible Maureen might be introducing a
new problem. Susan wanted to think that her friend
was the same unruffled, complacent woman she'd first
met when moving into the apartment complex; but
several times during the day she had admitted to herself
that Kellen might be correct.

The light was growing dimmer, and she shivered.
When she came out from under the trees she saw a
cloud bank rising in the southwest. She scowled, feeling
concentric waves of irritation rippling through her,
because this evening she wanted to visit the city library.
There was an off chance their reference files held new
information.

As she walked past, she glanced at the Neilson
apartment. She saw no movement on the other side of
the glass patio door, then remembered they were going
to one of the area's malls for a meal and to shop for
odds and ends Niles needed for his St. Louis trip.

The storm lingered just above the southwestern horizon as if deciding whether to move eastward, toward the coast, or creep southward, staying over the arid central portion of the state. It made no rumbling sounds, did not vibrate with the reflections of internal streams of luminosity. The mass merely squatted over the flat lands beyond the St. John's River, growing darker and plumper. Only the scent of distant rain implied that it carried with it anything other than fluffy vapor.

Susan wasn't hungry, so she decided to wait until she returned home from the library before fixing herself a sandwich. Wanting to get away before the storm moved in, she hurriedly washed her face, brushed her hair, and applied new makeup.

After she closed the front door behind her, she glanced upward toward the clouds to see how far, if at all, they had advanced.

At first, because it appeared so graceful silhouetted against the graying sky, she didn't recognize the bird that was circling slowly on outstretched wings above the apartment complex. Riding the high air currents with the soaring elegance of an eagle, it spiraled upward in slow circles. At the top of its climb it hesitated as though seeking something of interest on the ground below it, then, with wings rigid, it swooped earthward in a speed-gaining dive. Just above the apartment rooftops it pulled out of the plunge to spiral upward and resume its slowly circling hover. She was surprised to recognize the bird as a pelican. For a moment longer, she continued to follow its maneuvers, pleasantly surprised at the fluent flight of such an ungainly bird, hardly wondering what could attract the bird to the apartments so far inland.

The storm had finally made its decision. It moved with a plodding heaviness eastward. When the blackening clouds passed over the St. John's River a succession of cascades drenched the earth. Like fiery communications between them, lightning forked from cloud to cloud, followed by the reverberations of thunder.

Tom Andrews stood at the sliding glass door of his apartment looking at the gray curtain of rain that had drawn itself between his building and the one on the far side of the swimming pool. The illumination from the recreational area lights on the tops of their slender poles was filmy, almost obscured, giving the impression the lights themselves were attempting to hide in this night that had come too soon.

He looked at his wristwatch. It was twenty minutes after eight. A feeling of frustrated anger aimed at the storm flowed through him. Laurie was due to arrive in ten minutes, after finishing her nursing shift at the hospital. Tonight was the night she'd finally agreed to come to his apartment, and all his instincts told him the evening was to be an overwhelming one he'd long remember, but now its promises were endangered by the storm. She might not want to drive through it. Tense, expectant, he waited for the telephone to ring.

He was about to turn from the door when he thought he saw a small portion of the storm's darkness shift near the outer edge of one of the hazy ovals of light. It wasn't so much a movement as a restlessness in the dark, as if a very small section of the night had become more opaque that the area around it. He squinted, saw nothing, and, shrugging, started once more to turn back to the living room. But from the corner of his left eye, he saw the stirring again, this time a definite movement. He stood still and directed his complete attention on the spot. Vaguely, he could just make something lingering beyond the outer fringe of the watery illumination.

He turned, went swiftly across the room to a table lamp, and turned it off, then hurried back to the door.

He told himself it wasn't nosiness, but well-grounded curiosity to see what, if anything, would be out there in this storm.

With the lamp out, the reflections of the room behind him were no longer superimposed on the glass. The splotch of blackness made a precise movement, quitting the spill of light to move back into the darkness. But Tom's eyes were accustomed to the night now, and before it disappeared he suddenly recognized the form's contours.

It was a woman out there in the rain-lashed darkness.

He was unable to put together details, but he was certain she was dressed in black and seemed taller than average. She might have black hair, but that was a supposition because of the way it shined from the rain's wetness.

He could no longer see her; there was absolute stillness in the dark where she had disappeared; yet he had the unsettling suspicion that she was still there, just outside the reach of the light. Without being certain why, he received the impression that she was waiting for someone. In the opposite building there was only one darkened apartment, and he wondered if she was waiting for its occupants to return. He didn't know their name, but he knew they had a small baby. But why didn't she wait in her car? Surely she had one.

He looked at his watch again. If it wasn't so close to Laurie's possible arrival, he'd call to the woman and invite her to wait inside his place, but he didn't want anyone, particularly a strange woman, in the apartment when, or if, Laurie arrived. He'd carefully created the mood he wanted for this night, and he didn't want it destroyed.

Finally, with a last look out into the night, he shook his head, drew the drapes, then crossed the room to turn on the tape player and the table lamp.

* * *

As Susan had expected, the city library held no more information on Lilith than was in the college library's book stacks. The librarian told her that additional material might possibly be obtained through the county library exchange program, but she frankly doubted any of the other libraries possessed more than was available here.

Sitting at a table in the reference room, disappointed in spite of having known what to expect, Susan idly leafed through a copy of a book someone had left on the table, *Flora of Florida*. She wasn't very interested in the subject, but outside the rain was still falling hard. Still, she wasn't really reading; she was thinking and remembering.

Pelican . . . storm clouds . . . pelican and storm clouds . . . over the apartments. A pelican! A pelican was one of the creatures into which Lilith could transform herself, according to the book.

"Oh, my God!"

The words burst from her, ricocheting through the silent room with a sound too great for the book-lined walls to muffle. Around her, heads jerked up and startled faces pointed at her.

Susan was on her feet, wanting to apologize, but too unsettled to do more than look incredulously around the room. Then, without thought, she whirled and all but ran from the room, feeling pairs of startled eyes following her as she hurried through the reading lounge and the lobby.

The rain was cold. It slapped her face and whipped her shoulders, clutched at her hair and stung her bare arms, its wet little pellets determined to dig and slice their way into the very core of her body. Halfway along the walkway to the parking lot, she lost her breath and was forced to gulp in a mouthful of rain in order to regain it.

And while she ran, screaming inside her was a voice, distorted with hysteria, sending its soundless plea out into the night. "Stay away! Stay away! Don't come home yet. Keep Bridget away. Please! Please!"

She coaxed the Escort to a heedless speed through the crystalline shroud of rain. Forms without shape blurred through her peripheral vision, but floating before her in the rain-ravaged fan of the headlights' illumination was the marble face of a baby. Bridget's face. Screaming.

When she swung into the apartment's parking area, the rain had slackened, but it still rattled on the car's windshield and hood. She made no attempt to find her assigned space but pulled into the first available one she saw, tromping on the brakes too hard and coming to a jarring halt, hitting the curb with the front wheels. Leaving her purse on the seat and the keys in the ignition, she shoved open the door and pushed out into the rain.

She ran up the walk, her heels sounding off-toned and deadened on the wet concrete. Around her the rain hissed on the lawn and ahead of her the pool area was bathed in an amberish, mystic illumination. The Neilson apartment was dark.

She stopped, feeling the vibration of her rib cage from the thudding of her heart, the quivering in her fingers. She wanted desperately to draw in a deep breath, but could manage only short, rapid gulps. While she fought to impose order on her mind and body, around her the night shifted the same way the darkness had in Lily's townhouse the previous morning.

Pulling aside a coil of wet hair that had fallen down her forehead, Susan took a step forward, then tried once again to draw in a deep breath, this time succeeding. The stirring of the air accompanied her, beginning to circle around her in a counterclockwise direction, and not too far out in the rain was the muffled sound of movement as though things that did not belong there were positioning themselves in the rainy blackness.

That was when she felt the other presence, off somewhere to her left in the direction of the pool. Whatever it was, it felt massive, giving her the insane sensation that it was occupying a large portion of the pool area. Yet she could see nothing, as if whatever it was was hiding on the far side of the darkness. A cold spot formed between her shoulders, then began to uncoil and trickle down her spine, and she swallowed, forcing back the bile rising in her throat.

She began moving sideways toward the sliding door of the Neilsons' dark apartment, holding her eyes on the place where she thought the presence was located. The stirring air increased its motion and the sounds behind it became more delineated: the flapping of ghostly wings and clawed paws stalking through the saturated grass. She stepped onto the concrete slab in front of the door, hesitated, then turned to face the pool. As she did, she saw movement, what appeared to be a black silhouette against the blackness of the night.

She looked around. In the building on the far side of the pool, windows glowed with a weak yellow light through the rain, and on either side of her misty yellow shafts spilled from the neighboring apartments. She was not alone. All around her were people who would at least come to their windows or doors if she screamed. Confidence seeped back into her.

She did not know what was out there in the darkness. Maybe nothing. But yesterday morning had bludgeoned her emotions. The sculpture show had turned impressions into reality. Unthinkable suggestions were now acceptable; she was willing to concede the existence of phantom creatures inhabiting the world. That reaction had brought her here from the library, placed her between the aberration out there and the door to the Neilson apartment. Yet her intellect refused to believe that what was coming toward her existed. Nothing had been confirmed, it said. Everything, until otherwise proven, was illusion or hallucination.

She knew she should say something, but her throat muscles were constricted, too taut to force out any words.

The silhouette didn't move.

"Who are you?" She heard the words as if they were not her own, as if it was not her voice speaking over the hissing of the rain and what might have been the distant rumble of thunder.

The shadow-thing said nothing. But now, where the face should be, two round discs glinted like tiny reflections of green and red lightning.

"Tell me who—or what—you are."

No sound came from the unmoving image, but the discs began to glow with a pulsing red hue, pointed straight at her. Whatever was outside the circle of spinning air drew closer. Vibrating against her eardrums, the pounding of her heart became the only sound audible to her.

"Damn it! Tell me who you are!"

Something white rushed out of the darkness, diving slantwise between her and the figure, circling, then disappearing back into the night. It had moved too fast to be defined, but Susan was more than half certain it resembled one of the fowl she'd seen perched on a pedestal at the sculpture show and in Lily's townhouse.

She looked at the windows glowing with light. Her confidence increased. In her veins adrenaline surged. She stepped to the edge of the concrete slab.

"You're not going to get in this apartment, if that's

what you want," she called. "I'm not alone. Look around. See the lighted windows? There are people behind them. People who'll come if I scream."

The two discs remained aimed at her, but she thought she detected a stiffening of the figure.

"Look around, damn it!" She stood still for a moment, forcing herself to return the stare of those round discs. "Okay, I'm going to do it. I'm going to scream."

Her movements were exaggerated, easily defined, as she sucked in a deep breath, knowing the thing in the night would see it.

With a squawking sound, the fowl-like creature dove past her again, so close she could feel the slipstream of air behind it on her face. Startled, she fell back a step and gasped, her lungs losing the breath she'd drawn.

But over the hissing of the rain came the sibilant release of another's breath. The red circles flared. Very slowly, the thing took a step backward, then another. Susan could feel the hate surrounding it, the loathing like a physical extension of it. An isolated roll of thunder rumbled directly over her head. The rage reached for her, escalating, entwining about her until her flesh cringed from its touch. The atmosphere swirled faster, then faster yet, becoming a maelstrom of whirling air. Susan heard the invisible wings beating against the air, the phantom paws moving away through the grass. And then, partially blurred by the whirling air, the figure itself faded away.

The air was quiet, heavy-burdened and wet with the summer heat and falling rain. No hint remained of the loathing and hate which had churned in it minutes before.

Suddenly an automobile's headlight beams reflected in the rain between two of the apartment buildings, not illuminating the area but creating a momentary glow that added dimension to the blackness. With a squeal of wet brake linings, a car stopped, a door slammed, and hurrying footsteps sounded on the concrete walkway leading from the parking lot. The footsteps were fast, making a spiky sound on the walk, the sound of a woman hurrying through the rain. Susan saw a woman, shoulders bent, huddled beneath an umbrella, heading for the building on the far side of the pool.

Susan stood looking out into the now-empty night, at the woman who continued on to a sliding door, which a man opened when she stepped onto the concrete slab before it. Susan's mind only marginally assimilated the visual images. She was emotionally drained, but she could not help but wonder if the figure with its glowing eyes had not sensed the approach of the woman under her umbrella, and if that, as much as Susan's show of defiance, had driven the creature back into the rainy night.

Another car door slammed.

Susan shuddered, then stepped out into the rain and hurried to her front door. She was on the stoop before she remembered that her keys and purse were in the car. Frustration adding its assault on her nerves was more, she feared, than she was capable of handling.

A light flicked on in the Neilson apartment.

She was past thinking. Reaction was setting in and she'd be unable to hold at arm's length the fear soon to descend on her.

She ran down the walk to the car. Giving no thought to her actions, she got in, started the engine, and backed out of the parking space.

As she left the complex's entrance, she said out loud, "God, Kellen, be home. Please, please be home."

Tom Andrews came up a long tunnel from sleep to wakefulness, and when he arrived wasn't certain at first where he was, because it was dark and his senses immediately relayed to him a succession of the pleasures the night had provided him. At his side, Laurie moaned in her sleep and turned her blonde head on the pillow so her face was visible. More awake now, he slowly moved his eyes lingeringly over the clean symmetry of her splendidly proportioned features, and for the first time in his recent memory thought he had found the woman with whom he'd like to share a relationship more substantial and expressive than a singles bar's short-term acquaintanceship.

At first he wasn't sure if he heard voices if it was some memory attempting to penetrate his reflections. But then, over the subdued murmur, a single voice rose, trilling upward in choked cries that pinnacled in a shriek, and he knew what he was hearing was no memory.

He flung the sheet from him, levered himself out of bed, giving no thought to disturbing Laurie, and padded barefoot to the bedroom window. There was another scream as he pushed the curtain aside. Across the pool, an apartment was ablaze with lights. He saw people huddled, some on their knees as though kneeling over something, and others standing looking down.

"What is it?" Laurie was at his side.

He nodded at the lighted apartment. "Something's happened over there."

Laurie pulled the curtains farther apart. "My God, those are paramedics. Someone's in trouble."

She allowed the curtain to drop and hurried to the chair on which her clothes were neatly folded.

"What are you doing?"

"Going over there. Maybe I can be of help."

"Laurie, don't get involved."

"I'm a nurse, Tom. I'm obligated."

He watched her run for the apartment's door, still buttoning her uniform blouse.

He got into a pair of slacks, slipped a sport shirt over his head, and started for the door to follow her. Then he stopped. If it was a medical emergency, there was no help he could give; in fact, he'd more than likely be in the way, told to please move back to give the paramedics room to work. He went to an end table on which a package of Benson and Hedges lay and shook one out. After lighting it, he walked slowly through the sliding door to stand outside on the concrete slab to watch and wait.

Only a few minutes later, he saw Laurie come out of the apartment. He watched her walking slowly around the pool. Her shoulders were slumped and her arms hung limply at her sides in positions he recognized as defeat.

He said nothing when she stood in front of him, not even when he saw the wetness of tears on her cheeks, knowing she would speak when the effort was not too great.

"There was nothing anyone could do," she finally whispered. "Nothing. The little tyke was already dead when the medics arrived."

"A baby died?"

She nodded. "Another SIDS victim."

"Jesus!"

Laurie closed the space between them and thrust herself against him. Her sobs were gentle, but came from far down inside her, where the deepest emotions smolder. He put his arms around her shoulders.

"Why can't we find out the cause of SIDS, Tom? Why?"

"I don't know, Laurie." He stroked her back. "I don't know anything about medicine."

"He—he was—was such a—cute little fellow, Tom. And only two months old. Raymond . . . that was his name . . . he really never knew he had a name, did he?

They—they just moved in here four days ago."

"Easy," he whispered. "Easy, Laurie."

She pressed her face tighter to his chest. He looked over her head at the pool area, and as he did, for some reason, the sight of the dark-clad woman he'd seen standing in the rain reformed in his mind.

20

STORM-TOSSED DEBRIS LAY SCATTERED ON THE LAWN AND across the parking area. Dried palm fronds torn free by the gust of wind resembled overused brooms carelessly discarded by an uncaring maintenance crew. Reminders of the storm remained high above the earth as well, where wind currents tore at white clouds, ripping loose frayed streamers that were eventually shredded into a high-altitude mist. The sun remained hazy, as though unwilling to make an effort to burn away the overcast.

It was difficult for Susan to dress. Her fingers were thick, too fat and clumsy to hold a comb and brush. Worst of all, her mind refused to function, remaining shriveled in the uncomprehending mass it had formed itself into the night before. Finally conceding there was nothing more she could do, she left the bedroom without looking at herself in the mirror, fearing what she would see might crumble her resolve to face the day.

Kellen was spooning instant coffee into two mugs. He looked up and smiled, but it was a lopsided movement of his lips and she knew the brief two hours of sleep they'd managed had done neither of them any good.

"I'm not going to say good morning," he said.

"No, don't."

She sat on a stool at the small serving bar and watched him pour hot water from a yellow teakettle into the mugs, and then squinted at the steam rising from them. Kellen sat on a stool beside her, not saying anything, studiously watching the steam rise from his own mug. They were talked out, she supposed. Unthinkable possibilities and consequences had been reviewed again and again; extraordinary speculations had been examined and discarded.

A frosty apprehension told Susan that if Kellen hadn't been home, she might have become immersed in a mental darkness from which recovery would have been a long time coming. When she'd arrived here last night, even instinct had deserted her; her muscles were operating reflexively, forcing her plastic limbs to respond in erratic movement. From the moment the image had faded away behind the whirling air currents until she'd become aware of being curled up on a sofa beside Kellen with his arm around her, all she could recall was the wonderful sight of the lock of brown hair falling over his left eye as he opened the door to her frantic knocking.

She reached over to lay a hand on his. "Thanks."

He took her hand, squeezed it gently. "Thanks for coming when you needed help."

"God, I did, didn't I?"

"Yes. I'm sorry I wasn't there."

"I think you were—in spirit."

He released her hand and took up his mug, trying a quick sip of the still-steaming coffee. It was too hot, and he set the mug down. "What do you plan to do now?"

"Tell Maureen and Niles. They have to know."

He nodded, made another attempt at the coffee, and once again set the mug down.

"She'll insist it was Lily out there," Susan said. "She's more than half convinced Lily is some kind of supernatural being."

"What do you think?"

"I—Oh God, I—I don't know, Kellen." She hammered the bar top with a clenched fist. "I just don't know."

"I know."

She looked at him. "You think Lily is something supernatural—a demon?"

"I—" He shrugged, then shook his head. "No, I guess not."

She continued to look at him, not wholly believing his half-hearted denial.

"For the sake of discussion," he said, "if she does possess powers beyond our comprehension, why would she direct them at you and Maureen and Bridget?"

"Me because I'm sure she knows I told Sam he was getting too involved with her. I think her pride and assurance were shaken. Maureen because she's helping me, and because I'm certain Lily knows Maureen thinks she's a demon. I think because Sam and I looked into her actions, Lily has declared a vendetta against me. She must know I'm continuing to investigate the baby deaths, and it probably enrages her."

"Then you think it was her last night?"

"Like I told you last night, Kellen, I didn't see any features, nothing really, only a black silhouette. I can't even swear it was a female figure. But, yes, intuitively I think, I feel, it was her."

He looked at her intently, not bothering to brush away the tumbled lock of hair. "If she really is involved in the baby deaths, and if it was her last night in front

of the Neilson apartment, it means she was after
Bridget and you drove her off."

"I stopped her," she said slowly, "but it might have
been the appearance of that other woman that drove
her off."

"But it still means that if she's after Bridget, you're
in her way."

"Yes, I guess so." Then she told him about the
sculpture's face resembling Bridget's, and the hate
coming from Lily's car when Susan had followed her
that night to the apartments. "So, if I did drive her off, I
guess it wasn't the first time."

Kellen said nothing for a moment as he turned his
mug slowly between his fingers, then asked, "She just
suddenly appeared, didn't she? From nowhere, so to
speak."

"Yes. Sam said she was a vagabond."

"Here and there," he mused. "The book you found
in the other room, *The Unexplainable Explained*, said
the infant deaths were scattered throughout the world."

"But over a long period of time, a long, long period
of time."

"Yes."

"What are you thinking?"

"Nothing for sure," he said thoughtfully. He got up
and walked toward the living room. "I'm going to turn
on the morning news, okay?"

She nodded.

The fanfare preceding the news was finishing.

"Another baby died last night from what has been
diagnosed as Sudden Infant Death Syndrome," an
emotionless voice said. "The infant boy was discovered
in his crib by his mother a few minutes after two
o'clock this morning at the Village Green Apartments.
The family had moved into the apartments only four
days ago, coming to the area from Huntsville, Ala-
bama. Efforts were made by paramedics to revive the

child, but a spokesman said the infant was already dead when the paramedic team arrived. This is the thirteenth infant death attributed to SIDS in the past two months in this area, with a proportional increase reported from Orlando and Jacksonville. County and state health departments, we are informed, are working on various theories, but as yet no reasons for this sudden epidemic of the mysterious infant-killer has been discovered. Moving on, the Board of County Commissioners—"

Kellen, who had not moved away from the radio, turned it off. Susan sat staring at him, a terrible boiling inside her rapidly gaining in intensity, a burning torment threatening to numb her.

"It came back," she whispered. "Whatever it was, it was after a baby—and it came back."

"When you kept it away from Bridget."

"Oh my God, Kellen. I—I doomed that baby."

"No!" He crossed the room and grasped her shoulders. "No, you did not! You did not. Whatever it was, it had decided on that area, maybe those apartments themselves—*if* the thing you saw is what killed the child."

Susan felt hysteria vibrating inside her, tremors ricocheting along her nerve lines.

"Hold on!" Kellen was shaking her gently but forcefully. "Don't let go. You've no reason to blame yourself for this death, no reason to associate yourself with it. Use your intelligence, Susan. Think the situation out. Maybe what you saw didn't kill the baby. Maybe it was all a horrible coincidence."

His words channeled themselves through the turmoil in her mind. She clutched desperately at them, accepting the solace they offered. She nodded. "I'm all right."

"You sure?"

"Yes . . ."

He dropped his hands. "What about Maureen?"

"I've got to get to her. No, *we've* got to get to her. If she heard that, she could be in a frenzy."

"Let's go."

She followed Kellen in her car, wishing he'd drive faster, knowing he was going as fast as the early morning traffic permitted. All of her composure had not returned, she knew, for she had the surrealistic impression that she was following him through a ravaged land.

When they pulled into the Village Green parking lot, she suddenly realized that Maureen would not be home. This was Wednesday morning. Niles was leaving on the seven-thirty flight for St. Louis. Neither Susan nor Kellen had remembered that during the minutes following the news cast.

"She won't be here," she said, getting out of the car.

"I know. I remembered too."

Susan looked at her watch. It was seven thirty-five. In twenty-five minutes she had to be at the library. Kellen saw the glance at her watch. "Look, you go to work. You were off day before yesterday. I've a light schedule today, so I can stay to be with Maureen. Hugh Wallace can fill in for me. I'll phone him from your place."

Suddenly all she desired was to find a hidden place to go where her nerves would cease screaming, where the pain threatening to fill her head would go away, but looking at Kellen's concerned expression, she knew that if such a place existed, she could not desert him or Maureen to find it.

While she brushed her hair and changed into another dress, Kellen called to make arrangements for his replacement to cover him for the day.

He drove her to work, quickly kissing her before she got out of the car, promising to phone her when Maureen arrived home.

Although the woman said nothing, Susan was aware that Marge Anderson was struggling not to ask questions; she also knew that she was permitting herself to drift away from the library activities around her, subconsciously seeking that remote place where healing would occur.

She was watching a ray of sunlight slant through a window, then melt away into the gray of the morning when the telephone on her desk rang.

She picked it up before the first ring was completed.

Kellen's voice was low-pitched and slow, as though scattered thoughts were making it difficult for him to speak. "I'm at your place," he said. "I just came back from talking with Maureen."

"How's she taking the news?"

"She's upset, naturally, but not as much as we anticipated." He paused. "Actually there was a kind of calmness about her."

"Oh, that's good."

"She really gave the impression of being—well, I guess, you could say determinedly calm."

"Did you tell her everything that happened last night?"

"Yes, of course."

"God, I'm glad she accepted it so easily. She has some deep strength, I think."

"I think you both do."

"What did she say?"

"Not a whole lot, but I received the distinct impression that she had planned for something like this." He paused again. "Did you know she has an aunt in Apopka?"

"Yes."

"Well, she's going to take Bridget up there. They're going to stay with her aunt and uncle."

"I suggested that she do that, but she refused."

"Then she's changed her mind. She's packing now. I think she expects to be gone by noon."

"Oh?" She glanced at her watch. "I'll try to get out

early for lunch. Will you pick me up? Maybe I can talk with her before she leaves."

"All right."

She left her desk ten minutes early. Kellen was waiting for her, his Toyota in the No Parking space.

He handed her a blue envelope when she got in the car. "Maureen's gone, but she asked me to give you this."

The envelope was unsealed; she took from it a sheet of corresponding blue notepaper. As Kellen eased the car down the campus driveway through the noontime choke of cars, she read the letter aloud.

Susan:
I know this will come as a surprise to you. I'm taking Bridget and going to Apopka while Niles is in St. Louis. My Aunt Corliss and I have never been close, but whatever tensions might arise, I'm certain I can handle them better than the ones which would nag me in the apartment. I know I'm being selfish, that I'm running out on you, after my "gung-ho" attitude. I still think Lily is to blame for the infant deaths, but I must protect my daughter and the new life forming in me. I'll phone Niles from Apopka, and I know he'll agree with me that this is the best action to be taken. If it takes forgiving, please try to forgive me, Susan. But if you had two lives to protect, you might behave the same way. I hope we remain friends.
                                                        Maureen

Susan held the note in her lap. "She's saying a lot, but she's leaving a lot unsaid. She gives no address in Apopka, as if she doesn't want me to contact her."

"Maybe she doesn't want you to. It sounds to me as if she's making a clean break for a while from everything around here."

"That's not like her, it's out of character. She was very 'gung-ho' about placing the blame on Lily."

"But as she said, she's got two lives to think about, and if she actually thinks Lily is Lilith . . . well, I can understand her taking off." He turned into the apartment's parking lot. "This afternoon I'll phone Niles's company and find out at which hotel he's staying. Then tonight we can phone him. Okay?"

"It will have to be, I guess."

She prepared tuna-fish sandwiches for lunch. Once again Susan felt she was becoming hemmed in with abstractions. Although Kellen accepted Maureen's reasoning as given in the note, Susan could not correlate her friend's sudden flight with her past, almost fanatical resolve. She had the odd sensation of watching Maureen through a sheet of flames as the other woman walked along a path that zigzagged across a darkened landscape.

When she was getting out of Kellen's car back at the library, he asked, "Do you want company tonight?"

She did, but she knew that she would not be the best of companions, that she needed time by herself to smooth away the jagged edges that were serrating her emotions and splintering her thinking. She hesitated before answering.

Kellen reached over and took her hand. "You want to be alone, don't you?"

She nodded. "Upset?"

"No. Maybe it wouldn't hurt me to sit in a darkened room and do some thinking. I won't promise not to phone you, though."

Summer classes were nearing the end of their term, which meant a stirring of activity in the library as examinations drew nearer. For more than half the afternoon, Susan assisted students whose anxieties had suddenly surfaced as term-paper deadlines approached.

By late afternoon, the veil of haze which all day ha
smudged the sun began to thicken. At five o'clock, whe
Susan stood on the library portico, the gathering darl
ness had lowered and started a slow pulsation. The a
was stifling, soggy. She drew a deep breath and coul
all but feel the dampness clinging to the insides of he
nostrils and coating her throat. Surrounding the l
brary, the silence of the nearly deserted campus was a
oppressive as the air, accentuated by a distant rumb
of what might have been homeward bound traffic or th
grumbling approach of faraway thunder. She disco
ered that she was holding her breath standing very stil
as if waiting for something of vital importance t
occur. At that moment she had the disconcerting sensa
tion that in some way time was running out.

Kellen's blue Toyota pulled into the No Parking spo
Without questioning his reason for coming, she hurrie
down the steps and across the wide concrete apron.

"What are you doing here?"

"I didn't think you'd make it to your place before th
rain came, and I wanted to tell you Niles is registered a
a Holiday Inn. I've got the address and phone numbe
I'm going to call him tonight."

"You?"

"Yes. I want you to pull back, at least for tonigh
Relax. Niles and I get along fine, and I don't expect hir
to be hesitant in telling me about Maureen."

She knew he was right and smiled.

The storm was constructing itself directly overhead
When she got out of the car at the end of the walkway t
her building, the overcast had gathered into ponderou
clouds, heavy with the rain filling their dark interior.
Kellen did not turn off the ignition, only gave her
quick pat on the left thigh while saying he'd see her th
next day.

No rage rode this storm, unlike the one the nigl

before. Tonight's storm churned indecisively overhead, incapable of sustaining its wind beyond flustered gasps which did no more than rattle the rain against the windows like rapping fingertips. Its infrequent thrusts of lightning were smothered in the rain it had allowed to fall too quickly from its ill-formed clouds.

Not hungry, but telling herself she should put something on her stomach, Susan mixed a can of chunked ham with a daub of Miracle Whip, added a teaspoon of pickle relish, and spread the result between slices of toast. Frowning at the sandwich, she told herself her eating habits were atrocious.

While she munched the sandwich and sipped ice tea, she leafed through the books she'd brought home from the library. She had refused to construct even a web of hope on the information contained in the volumes, but here and there she found a sentence or a paragraph which she jotted into a notebook.

An hour later she sat reading the jottings. There was nothing helpful. Disgusted, she pushed away from the table, stuffed the notebook into a desk drawer, and slammed it shut. She threw the uneaten remains of the sandwich in the garbage.

Her disgust quickly passed. It was only ten minutes to nine, too early to go to bed, yet a weariness settled on her as she stood listening to the rain, now also hearing thunder to the east, out over the beaches. In the pit of her stomach something clenched.

She went to the front window to look across the empty pool area at the dark Neilson apartment. The emptiness of it touched her nerves, and as much as she fought to keep it away, the feeling that in some way evil was involved with the rain and was moving through the night settled on her. She gave an involuntary shudder, then turned from the window. Tomorrow, she told herself, the distortions could begin all over again, but

for this evening she chose to be a recluse from fea
Tonight she was going to push the outside world awa
and keep her mind dormant.

A few minutes after ten, she turned off the bedsi
lamp. Sleep was very close. Her mind was not skippi
from thought to thought: it was eager to accept the re
awaiting it. She rolled onto her left side, feeling herse
drift into the welcoming darkness.

A great booming noise echoed around her, darti
back and forth between the walls, hammering at t
ceiling, losing some of its power, then being rejuv
nated with another crashing roar.

Suddenly Susan was sitting straight up in bed, u
aware of waking, the sound reverberating in her hea
staring wide-eyed at the window, which was a blazi
rectangle of fiery illumination. Jagged streamers
green and blue and amber, like tiny lightning bolt
slashed with a reptile hissing across the room, bringi
with them the stench of things burning, weaving into
latticework of flame exploding in the darkness.

She tried to scream to relieve the tension whiplashi
out of control through her, but contracted muscles ha
already closed her throat tight, and only a gurgling ga
escaped her lips.

Howling in its race around the building, the wi
drove curtains of rain against the flaming windo
reflecting the lightning flames in repeated images. S
had the terrible impression the window was a huge fly
eye staring unblinking at her with its multiple facets

She pushed herself against the headboard, diggi
her heels into the mattress, feeling the muscles of h
legs trembling with the exertion. She could hear t
gulping sound of her breathing and feel the pumping
her heart as terror and choked-off air sent it into
spasm of desperate beating. She wondered if she ha
gone insane, if this nightmare fantasy was occurri
only within the convulsions of her mind.

Then the storm stopped, abruptly.

The interweaving streamers of fire were gone from the room, the ricocheting thunder was replaced with the air conditioner's murmur, and the watching fly's eye was only a gray, water-streaked rectangle in the room's darkness.

She sat staring at the window, having the sensation she was seeing it through a veil. Slowly she swung her feet off the bed, wanting to stand up so she could run if it all began again, and was preparing to push herself to her feet when a blackness framed itself in the window. She clawed away a tangle of hair that had fallen over her eyes to see a dark silhouette against the night sky, hovering just beyond the pane. The thudding of her heart sent tiny trembles down her arms and into her fingers. The silhouette beyond the window moved closer, taking on detail. She felt sweat running down her face, soaking her body. Then she recognized it.

With wings stretched and beating like oars holding a boat steady in a rapid current, a bird fluttered at the window. It was the living creature from which the marble sculpture had been modeled. She could feel it looking at her through the water-spattered glass, studying her, and while she sat helpless before its stare she felt the tension gaining force within her, hearing the point where terror would consume her.

The laugh was clear, a crystal-pure tone in the storm-cleaned air. When she first heard it, it trilled with subdued mirth, then slipped into a mocking harshness. It taunted her derisively in a woman's rich contralto voice, becoming, the longer it went on, the cruel laughter directed at one on whom an obscene practical joke had been directed. The laugh became touched with dementia, taking on the ludicrous tones of a mechanical laughing woman on a carnival midway. Finally, in desperation, she clamped her hands over her ears to try to cut off the flood of insane sound.

Then suddenly, as though riding a current of night air, the voice soared away.

At the same time, the bird outside the window disappeared.

Sluggishly the foundations . on which reality was constructed began to reform. She dropped her hands from her ears to dig her fingers into the mattress on either side of her. Finally the terror drained away, and as it did rationalization seeped into her mind.

She looked at the window, still hearing the insane laughter, but now understanding that the horror she had just experienced had not been an attack on her body but on her senses, that it had occurred to frighten her, to demonstrate to her the skimpy defenses she possessed against the power she and Kellen and Maureen were challenging.

When she lay back down on the bed, she knew sleep would be denied her.

21

IT WAS EARLY FRIDAY MORNING. JUST OUTSIDE THE WINDOW a mockingbird was twittering and yodeling in the morning's young light.

"Maureen, I don't understand, I swear." Corliss Hatcher stood at the bedroom door looking at her niece, who was snapping shut the clasps on an overnight bag laying on the bed. "You just don't seem to be thinking in a way I can comprehend. Honestly."

"I guess it must seem that way, Aunt Corliss. I know it was a shock to you and Uncle Will for me and Bridget to pop in here without so much as a phone call, but you know I do appreciate you agreeing to let us stay until Niles returns from St. Louis. But I've discovered I forgot to take care of a few things in Melbourne. I'll be back tomorrow."

"Honey, you know having you here is no problem. We're delighted that you and Bridget have come to visit us. But the trip seems to be too much on the spur of the moment. Your uncle and I have the feeling you're running away from something. What is it? We know you and Niles haven't fought, the phone call from him last night proved that. Can't you tell us what's wrong?"

Maureen looked at her aunt. She knew that the woman's concerns were valid. Since she and Bridget had arrived Wednesday afternoon, she'd given only vague answers to both her aunt's and uncle's queries, afraid to admit the true reason for her unannounced visit. Instead she'd told them of an apartment in which the plumbing had gone bad, of the tearing out of wall sections to reach broken pipes, of no vacant unit in the apartment complex into which she could move while repairs were undertaken.

Her aunt took a slow step into the room, then another. She grasped the footboard of the bed. "Maureen, we've never been close. I don't know why, and I don't want to analyze that right now, but though you've tried very valiantly to hide it, Will and I have picked up the vibrations of fear coming from you." She looked down at her hands, at her knuckles, which stood out like white blisters. Then she lifted her head and stared straight at her niece. "Are you afraid for Bridget, Maureen? We've heard of the epidemic of infant deaths in the Melbourne area. Have you brought her here to get away from them?"

Listening to her, Maureen felt ashamed. "Yes, that's why I'm here."

"Honey, why didn't you tell us that? Why this dumb story of an uninhabitable apartment? It's only natural, Maureen, for a mother to protect her child. My God, that's nothing to be ashamed of."

"But the cause of all the deaths has been diagnosed as SIDS, Aunt Corliss. It's something that can't really be protected against. I thought you and Uncle Will would think I was batty for running away from something as nebulous as that."

"Oh, Maureen, Maureen. I could feel insulted that
you had no more trust than that in your uncle and me."

"Please don't. I've got to admit that I've been feeling
paranoid. I just couldn't stay alone in the apartment. A
baby died only two doors away Tuesday night. It—well,
it sent me over the edge, and I had to get Bridget away."

Corliss nodded. "I understand. I only wish you'd told
us."

"I do too."

Again Corliss nodded, this time at the overnight bag.
"Do you have to go back down there?"

"Yes. I fled so fast, there're things I didn't do, like I
said. I want to go to the bank to get some cash. I want to
ask a friend to keep her eye on the apartment. And I
can see I didn't bring enough clothes." She shook her
head. "I guess I was terribly mixed up. Maybe I still
am."

"Maureen, don't think of it that way. You mustn't
doubt your actions. Now, not only are your uncle and I
quite capable of taking care of Bridget for twenty-four
hours, we'd love to. It will bring to life some fond
memories of when your cousin Ethel was that age." She
laughed. "I think I can still change a diaper and dish
out baby food. Don't fret. She'll be safe here."

"I know, Aunt Corliss. That's why I brought her
here."

"Well, I guess you'd better be on your way."

"Yes, you're right. I'll be back about noon tomorrow."

In her playpen, set up in the living room, Bridget was
occupying herself with a yellow plastic ball, listening to
the bells jingle inside it as she rolled it across the pen's
flooring. Maureen looked at the play pen and the toys in
it, knowing that she'd forgotten nothing, that her
packing had been very complete.

She took Bridget up in her arms, nuzzling her nose
against the child's. Bridget giggled.

"You're going to behave like a lady, aren't you, for Aunt Corliss and Uncle Will?"

Bridget giggled again, putting her fingertips on Maureen's lips.

"Okay. That's a promise, isn't it?"

The giggle became a coo.

"Of course she's going to be a little lady," Corliss said.

Maureen squeezed Bridget to her breast. Her breath caught with her sudden, desperate desire to never let go of the tiny body pressing against her. She'd felt so sure on Wednesday, when the plan had constructed itself in her mind, but now, with Bridget so close, so much a part of her, doubts and hesitations were tunneling through her resolve. She gave a silent cry. No! She must do what must be done. She dared not falter.

"You'd better go, Maureen," Corliss said softly. "Time is moving. Now don't give her a second thought; your uncle and I are experienced baby-sitters, and she's going to be much more comfortable here than being hauled around in a car in this heat."

"I know." Maureen placed Bridget back down in the pen. She pursed her lips and made a kissing sound at her daughter. "See you tomorrow, honey."

It was one-thirty when Maureen drove slowly past the complex where Lily lived. It had been easy enough to find from the descriptions Susan had given of it. South from it, a quarter of a mile or so, there was public access to the beach where she planned to park. Then she'd walk along the beach to the complex, make herself familiar with her enemy's home territory.

She found the access and drove into the ill-defined parking area, being careful to avoid the loose sand, its deep ruts stark indicators of cars that had sunk to their hubcaps.

After locking the car, she placed a wide-brimmed

yellow hat on her head, threw a short beach coat over her left arm, and dropped the car keys into her beach bag. Walking toward the beach, she experienced the odd sensation she was entering a new, unknown dimension.

Susan stood listening to the telephone in Apopka ringing. Kellen was sitting on the sofa watching her, folding and unfolding the slip of paper on which he'd written the number Niles had given him.

"Hello." The woman's voice was slightly breathless, as though she'd hurried to the instrument from a distant part of the house.

"Mrs. Hatcher?"

"Yes."

"I'm Susan Rutledge, a friend of Maureen's in Melbourne."

"Oh?"

"May I speak with her, Mrs. Hatcher?"

"She isn't here, Miss Rutledge. She returned to Melbourne early this morning. She had several things to take care of, she said." Corliss Hatcher was guarding what she was saying. "She doesn't plan to return here until noon tomorrow, so maybe you can contact her at her home."

"Her apartment's dark, Mrs. Hatcher. I'm a neighbor."

"Oh, well I'm sure she'll be there before too long. She had quite a list of things to do."

"It's almost nine o'clock."

"Oh? Well, certainly she'll be finished with what she planned to do very shortly."

"Did she bring Bridget with her?"

"No, Bridget is here. Maureen didn't want to haul the child around in the heat."

Susan looked out the dining-area window at the sky that was darkening much too fast. "Mrs. Hatcher, may

I ask what was Maureen's attitude—was she nervous or uptight?"

"No." The answer was immediate, but the voice hesitated for an instant. "No, she was composed." Another hesitation. "Do you know why she came here, Miss Rutledge?"

"Yes, and I'm happy she did. With Niles away and what's happening here, I think Maureen showed good judgment."

"Her uncle and I do too."

"Well, thank you, Mrs. Hatcher. I'll watch for lights in her apartment."

Kellen stopped fidgeting with the paper slip. "She's here in Melbourne?"

"Yes."

"What for?"

"To do a few things. Her aunt didn't seem to know what they were."

Kellen got up and crossed the room to stand beside her at the window. "Why don't I like the sound of that?"

"For the same reason I don't."

"She wouldn't, would she? My God, Susan, she wouldn't try some act against Lily. Maureen's too all-together, too self-possessed."

"Like I've told you, she's been losing that. She's become desperately fanatical concerning Lily. She's hidden it from everyone but me. I don't think even Niles suspects."

"Where would she be?"

As Susan started to shake her head, she heard it, an isolated cry in her mind. "Lily's!"

"What?"

"Lily's. There's a storm coming, Kellen. She might be at Lily's, to try to stop her if she starts to leave the townhouse."

"Oh, Christ!"

"Let's go there, Kellen! It's the only possibility."

The storm had moved in silently, stealthily advancing from the west, approaching without lightning flares or drum rolls of thunder. Now, as they drove along the coast, it unleashed a fury, opening its bulging undersides to deluge the earth.

Kellen shook his head. "I can't see. The wipers aren't worth a damn in this waterfall."

"Just keep going, Kellen. We've got to get to Lily's place. We've got to."

Maureen was sweating. The coolness of the night air was an illusion. Where she stood, under the dripping leaves of a stunted oak tree, the air was thick and cloying; she felt she might be breathing beneath the surface of a great black-watered lake. Her lungs were struggling in an effort to fill themselves to their required capacity, and failing. She leaned against the rough trunk of the tree, steadying herself as a wave of disappointment swept over her. Suddenly common sense was begging her to walk down the driveway, go back to the Dodge, and drive away. But then defeat would replace disappointment, and self-contempt would follow that.

Bridget was safe, so her plan to confront Lily must not be cast aside because of the vagaries of nature. Actually, nature was siding with her. It had sent the storm. When Lily came out to drive in the rain . . .

But Lily had not come out. Her garage door was open, and Maureen could see the black Oldsmobile dully shinning in the cave-like gloom. Ten minutes before, she had arrived at the conclusion nothing was going to come of her idea, but there still remained the off chance Lily would respond to the storm.

No lights showed in the windows of Lily's unit, nor

did any sound come from the townhouse. There was only a stillness that was unnatural, like the hush in a crypt.

She was huddled under the tree when the explosion came. As if the entire universe was disintegrating, a crash of whitish-green brilliance sizzled through the air. Trees and bushes and the looming building across the parking area were washed out, disappearing without a trace in the fireball. It jabbed at her eyes like slashing knife blades, instantly blinding her. The shock sucked the breath from her lungs. Thunder crashed, jarring the foundations of the earth, shaking water from the branches over her in a drenching cascade. She screamed, not realizing it, and dropped to her knees, quivering as she pressed herself against the tree, throwing her arms around it. From the far side of her blindness, she heard the wind rushing in, ruthlessly driving the rain before it. It jerked and twisted the small oak as though determined to uproot it. Maureen screamed again.

With a spectacular display of light shards, her sight returned, and she stared into the curtain of rain stretched between her and the townhouse building. The one unit in which there had been lights was dark now, so she saw the building as a towering wall.

She pushed herself to her feet, holding on to the oak until she felt her muscles firming, then stepping out on to the pavement. Without the concealment of the foliage, she felt exposed, more vulnerable than at any time in her life. Whimpering, she took a step, discovered that her legs were functioning solidly beneath her, then took another. Her clothes were like a rough mold, sticking to her. She squinted against the needle jabs of wind-driven rain.

She saw the blank, dark rectangle of the front door to Lily's townhouse. She took a step toward it, her right hand clenched into a fist, prepared to hammer on the paneling.

Then, high up in the darkness, a crackling noise erupted, like a mountain of cellophane being crumpled. She looked up. Thousands of tiny lightning bolts were snapping back and forth across the black sky, criss-crossing so closely that they wove a nearly solid canopy of pulsing flame.

She stopped. To her right she saw the silhouettes of the entrance pillars. An inner voice screamed at her to go to the car, to escape this place that was a caldron in which an unholy power was shimmering. She looked at the closed townhouse door again. No! No, she couldn't leave. Behind that door was the creature who was stirring the caldron.

Suddenly the fiery web in the sky brightened, washing the entire surrounding area in a garish flood of red-tinted light. For an instant, Maureen distinctly saw Lily standing between the pillars, legs spread, her hands on her hips. She saw the scornful smile on the woman's lips. And she saw her eyes. They were as red as the burning heavens, but more intense, reflecting the internal flames of a terrible, searing hate. The sky sizzled. Red flame vomited from it, and Lily was gone. The rain-clogged darkness was empty.

Maureen cried out, her thoughts blurred as if the rain was seeping into her brain. Her fingers felt hollow and brittle as she spread her right hand on her abdomen where the new life was forming.

A gust of wind sideswiped the Toyota, and the light car staggered to its left though Kellen fought the wheel to hold the vehicle in the driving lane.

"I don't think Lily would go out in a storm like this," he muttered. "If Maureen's there, she's only getting herself drenched."

"But we can't take that chance."

"I know. I know."

The car started down the slope of the high-rise bridge into Indialantic. Half way to the bottom a surge of rain billowed around it as though trying to swallow the shuddering vehicle. Kellen was compelled to slow the car until it was no more than creeping through the night.

Susan stared at the rain-opaqued windshield. Every fiber in her body felt overdrawn, strumming with the tension of building fear, instinct telling her that Maureen had plunged into a dark abyss of horror.

Her voice was brittle from the dryness in her throat and mouth, when she asked, "Can you go any faster?"

Maureen's legs had become unsteady again. Wisps of flame, reminding her of St. Elmo's fire, darted back and forth across the driveway between her and the entrance, snipping at her eyes. They didn't appear malevolent, though, and she was certain she could twist her way through them without receiving more than one or two trivial burns.

She had to try. She had to admit defeat for now and get to the car. Around her the darkness seemed to shift as if it too was preparing itself for some kind of convulsive outburst.

"Damn you, Lily!" she screamed. "Damn you."

She walked in the direction of the car. Somewhere to her right she heard laughter, harsh and trilling, but then it was swallowed in a sizzling sound like cold water on a hot skillet. Ahead of her the fireballs multiplied, began darting faster, crisscrossing, leaving streamers of flame behind them, weaving in and out until they formed a glittering cocoon.

Maureen cried out as she stopped, and then imagined she heard the echo of it from some place far off in the darkness. The rain clawed at her face, trying to shred the flesh from her cheekbones and brow with its skeletal, cold fingers. She covered her face with her hands, hearing her gasps and sobs muffled behind them. Where were the complex's tenants? Dear God, couldn't they hear the unnatural sounds, see the reflections of the exploding lights? Or was it all happening only inside her mind?

The snarl was loud. It penetrated her consciousness. The final warning of a predator about to attack.

She dropped her hands, but saw nothing, only the darting fireballs. But now she realized the barrier was slowly moving up the driveway in her direction. She took a step back. From behind her came the clicking of clawed paws on the asphalt of the parking lot. She whirled. There was nothing there. Then she smelled it, the same odor that had been in Susan's apartment that night Susan had saved Bridget. Yet Maureen's desperate, swinging eyes found nothing in the darkness.

She felt her lungs, then her throat, and finally her open mouth forming a scream, but what she heard was only a moan, gasping and choked, a sound destroyed by terror. She watched the fireballs fan out, forming a semicircle around her, and from some remote but still functioning portion of her mind came a frayed thought telling her everything that was authentic and substantial was being cut off from her.

That was when she saw it. It was floating, a darkness which had dislodged itself from the night, drifting, bobbing, almost indolent in its movement, so gauzy it could have been an illusion created in her struggling mind. She glanced away. But the night grew tighter and she received the impression that all dimension was gone from the world, that even time itself was losing itself in the depthless night.

High overhead lightning etched streaks across the sky. Thunder rumbled.

She watched the rippling area of darkness become

more defined, a shape occupying several square feet of the night. It lingered in front of a clump of shrubbery as if giving her a chance to examine it, then began to drift slowly across the parking area toward her.

Maureen took a step back. Thoughts tried to pour through her mind, but it would not accept them. The blackness drifted closer, hesitated once more, then resumed its movement in her direction, growing larger as the perspective changed. Suddenly she knew something terrible was about to happen.

There were no more hesitations. The blob of blackness moved with a steady determined drift toward her. When it was only half a dozen feet from her, scattered pieces of memory drew together in her mind long enough for her to recognize it.

She opened her mouth to scream, but before her fear-tautened muscles could force past her vocal cords the breath required, a sticky substance packed her mouth with what might have been cotton, then trickled down her throat to stuff it full. Little tendrils of it wiggled up her nostrils. For an unbelieving instant, she stood staring straight ahead as the realization that her breathing was cut off exploded in her mind. Reflexively she arched herself, at the same time clawing at the blackness. Her hands passed through the mass as they would through smoke, touching nothing, feeling nothing firm brush against her skin.

She fell to her knees, frantically clawing her fingers into her mouth in a desperate attempt to pull out whatever was jamming it. There was nothing there. Her mouth was empty.

She was only barely cognizant of collapsing to her left side, but even as she did she rolled onto her back, her feet digging for purchase on the hard slippery asphalt as she tried to slither away from the hovering blackness. It followed her for the few inches she was able to move, hanging over her like a sooty cloud undisturbed by the still-falling rain and wind eddies.

She felt muscles collapsing inside her, flesh softening. Far away, at the outer edges of her consciousness, she felt her heels beating on the pavement and her fingers clawing at her sides.

Then the darkness began rushing toward her, a total, all-around darkness that her paralyzed mind knew was the last one she would ever see. The minutes of terror and pain were ending. With bulging eyes, she stared up at an oak branch that was already lost in the descending darkness.

As the final blackness wrapped her within its folds, for a tiny fraction of an instant, she saw red eyes watching her.

22

THE PASSING OF SEVEN DAYS HAD DONE NOTHING TO RELIEVE
the burden of oppressive sorrow Susan had carried
since Maureen's death. Instead, the passing time had
intensified the horror. More and more Susan believed
that much of the responsibility of her friend's death
belonged to her, no matter that the medical examiner
had proclaimed it was caused by a ruptured heart
artery. During each day her conscience had become
more weighted with this bitter notion, until now it
constantly flogged her with the terrible sensations of
guilt. And under that sorrow was the dreadful knowledge that Lily had killed Maureen. She knew it. And
knowing that, she knew she must confront Lily.

Susan was alone in the library's reference room this
Friday afternoon. From her desk drawer, she took the
notes she had brought with her from home. Somewhere
in them there had to lay a clue, no matter how small,
and she had to find it.

Niles Neilson's gaunt face moved through her memory, a mask of sorrow and uncomprehension, the features of a man living alone in an apartment that must seem indescribably empty. Bridget was still with Maureen's aunt and uncle in Apopka. Niles had wanted to keep the baby with him after the funeral, but Susan and Kellen had convinced him to let her stay with the Hatchers, telling him she would be better cared for by them until his equilibrium returned.

Maureen's funeral had been quiet, attended by some of the Village Green residents and Niles's coworkers. Comparing it with the crowded memorial service conducted for Sam, Susan could not help but feel an appalling sadness that her friend had touched so few people.

She looked again at the description of Lilith in her notes. Two bold words thrust into her consciousness. *Hebrew myth.*

Of course! Dear God, of course.

A place to start. A place to seek advice.

She dug out the phone book from the bottom desk drawer and looked up the address of the local synagogue.

She glanced at her watch. It was two-thirty. She thought about phoning, but instead pushed herself to her feet, looked around the empty room, then hurried to where Marge Anderson was sitting behind the main desk.

"Marge, I've got to leave. It's something personal, something concerning Maureen's death."

Marge looked at her quizzically, seemed about to make a comment, then waved a thick hand. "Go ahead. I'll get a couple of extra hours out of you next week."

Rabbi Jacob Cohen leaned back in his desk chair, his left arm resting on the chair's arm. His right hand touched the thin sheaf of papers before him on the desk, his long, slender fingers, the fingers of a violinist or pianist, Susan thought, tapping an improvised rhythm on the top sheet. His dark eyes stared over her right shoulder at some distant place in a time long vanished.

They sat for a time in silence. Finally the rabbi's fingers became still. He shook his head and drew a long breath, then blew it out through pursed lips, as though reaching a decision which for a while had hung in precarious balance. Slowly he leaned forward, resting his forearms on the desk, and picked up the papers in both hands.

"What you have here, Miss Rutledge," he said, "is a proposition that is so impossible, it could almost be possible." His voice was low and well-articulated, and held her attention more than would a stentorian tone. "You have built a solid case to show that this woman, Lily, might be what you think, but, as you concede, its roots are in myth; so, consequently, in the eyes of the law, what you have is merely a six-and-a-half-page supposition. I fear the authorities would call it a product of an overzealous imagination."

"Do you think that? Are you diplomatically saying that I'm slipping around the bend, Rabbi?"

"Of course not. Of course not. But from what you've told me, you've been under a lot of physical and emotional stress during the last few weeks. You have lost two very close friends under circumstances that are not only mysterious but gruesome, so you have every right to be shaky." He looked down again at the notes she had given him. "But can you honestly believe that a woman who never existed committed these crimes?"

"Yes, because I think she did exist. I think she still exists. I think that because her story is so full of terror, it has been classified as a myth as a precaution against hysteria. Sam, I know, became infatuated with her.

Something happened between them, and she became Lilith and turned viciously on him. The myth says she chooses a man to live with for a while, then becoming tired of him, moves on to a new one. In Sam's case, I'm certain it was more than boredom on her part that caused her to kill him. Maureen was killed because she was seeking proof that Lily is Lilith—and because she was pregnant."

"All religions have these kinds of myths, Miss Rutledge. Ours, yours, Islam. They are the darker side of our beliefs."

"They are the darker side of life, Rabbi. But we see that every day, don't we? We know most myths and legends have their origins in actual happenings."

"It's possible, you know, that the origin of this myth is within a myth itself."

"I realize that, but I believe that whatever her origin, Lilith does exist." She endeavored to keep an indication of contention from her voice. "I'm going to continue trying to prove it, Rabbi. I must."

"I wish I could give you the help I think you came here seeking, Miss Rutledge, but it's beyond my ability. I admit I have heard the story of Lilith. I have also heard of the golem. But if either exists, I have never seen documentation to prove it one way or the other." He shuffled the papers in his hands, as if reluctant to hand them back to her. "All I can say is that this woman, who you say calls herself Lily, does seem to be an enigma. I would ask you to be careful, if you go on with your investigation."

"I will. Thank you for your time, Rabbi Cohen."

He stood up. "Thank you, Miss Rutledge, for a more than interesting hour."

He remained standing until the office door closed behind her, then quickly looked around the office. He saw nothing unfamiliar, but the sensation which had grown during the last minutes of the conversation with Susan Rutledge remained.

During that time, and even now, he'd felt another presence in the office. From a place in a corner something had been watching them and listening to their discussion. It had moved once, shifting position ever so slightly toward the Rutledge woman, causing no more than a passing ripple in the draft of air conditioned air.

Then suddenly it was gone, like an illusion exposed to the bright light of reality. He felt buoyancy return to the room's atmosphere. For a short time longer, he continued to stand, with his fingertips spread on the desktop, directing his concentration to suppressing the subtle apprehension nipping at his senses. Then he sat down and leaned back in the chair, hands folded in his lap, brows drawn together in a scowl. Something was definitely wrong. The rabbi began to worry about Susan Rutledge.

Susan sat at the writing desk in the apartment's living room, the six and a half pages of her jottings spread before her. She had stared at them so long that the writing was blurry, squiggly lines on the white paper. She shook her head, then closed her eyes and sucked in her lower lip. The door chimes rang. Startled she looked up, trying to hold on to her concentration, but losing it when the chimes rang again.

Kellen stood on the stoop holding two white sacks that exuded the aroma of Chinese food. He held them up. "When you didn't come out of the library at five, knew you were off doing something, and assumed you hadn't eaten, so I brought this." A boyish smile played hesitantly on his lips.

She stepped back. "Come in. I never could resist a man bearing Chinese food."

Other than her breakfast mug of coffee and a can of Diet Pepsi for lunch, this was the first she'd eaten all day. She was absolutely astounded how delicious the chow mein and egg rolls tasted. It had seemed, recently, that her taste buds had lost their sensitivity. When they were finished, Kellen helped wash the dishes. Watching him put the plates in the cupboard, Susan thought how good it was to have someone to share an evening with, then wondered if it would ever happen permanently.

Later, in the living room, she asked, "Have you heard anything from the Review Board about your proposal?"

"Not yet. Probably next week." He took a hurried glance at the notes still laying on the desk. "Have you see Niles?"

"Not for the last couple of days. I think he's spending all his time at the office."

"That's good, I guess. I wonder when he plans to bring Bridget home."

"Not for a while, I hope."

They were silent for a long moment as the sorrow which had been their companion since Maureen's death made itself felt. Susan could not pretend to feel other than she did, but she dug deep to find a tiny pool of levity from which she drew a lighter mood.

"Do you have any more meals to deliver tonight?"

"No." He immediately sensed what she was trying to do. "Business is slow tonight."

"Then why don't you spend some time here?"

"I could, I guess. How long?"

"Oh, as long as you want."

"I might want to stay all night."

"I wouldn't object. I'd be an accommodating hostess."

"How accommodating?"

"You're too old to have to ask."

He laughed, then closed the distance between them
and put his arms around her, pulling her tight to him.

Another summer storm moved ponderously through
the night. Susan had awakened when the wind howled
around the building and the thunder rattled the windows. Now she stood looking through the smeared glass
of the bedroom window at the rain slanting across the
darkness. Meager gray highlights spattered the flimsy
water curtain, adding a touch of density to its veil. She
had the impression that out on the other side of the
window the night was cold, that the rain and the
darkness would be unforgiving.

"What are you doing?" Kellen's voice, slurred ever
so slightly by sleep, came from the bed behind her.
"You could get a chill from the air-conditioning, standing there with nothing on."

She felt the tiny goose pimples on her, and nodded,
but wondered if they were from the crisp air or from
the dismay at the sight of the storm. She let her gaze
run once more through the darkness, then turned from
the window. All her intuition told her death was racing
through the storm in a black Oldsmobile to claim a
helpless baby.

Kellen pushed himself erect to sit leaning against the
bed's headboard. "You're letting the storm get to you,
aren't you?"

"No, not the storm, but what's out there in it."

"Lily?"

"Yes." She took her robe from the foot of the bed and
slipped into it, cinching the belt tight around her waist,
then sat on her own side of the bed. "I'm sorry if I woke
you."

"I don't think you did. I think it was the storm."

She looked at the rain striking the window, persistent
and rhythmic. "Maureen died during a storm like this."

"Oh, Susan, baby. Don't dwell on that, please."

"I can't help it. We know Lily killed her. Oh God, if only that damn fallen tree hadn't been blocking the road, we could have gotten there . . . maybe we could have saved her, Kellen."

"Easy, hon, easy. You're reopening a bad wound. Leave it heal. We don't know if we could have, and, honestly, we don't really know if Lily murdered her."

"Yes, we do! Don't play the devil's advocate with me. We both know Maureen was out there to see if Lily went out in the storm, and Lily caught her watching. Maureen was doomed. Remember that threat Lily made when I was in her apartment."

"Yes, and we've also both accepted the fact that the police and sheriff's department would laugh us out of the county if we told them about Lily." He shook his head. "The authorities have what they consider a perfectly reasonable explanation of what happened, and they're not about to change it."

"Except they've no explanation as to why she was out there alone at night."

"Which, I guess, they don't need, since they don't think a crime was committed."

She stood up. "The next storm that comes through when I'm free, I'm going out there."

"Susan!"

"I am, damn it! I owe it to Maureen and Sam and all the babies."

"All right, honey. But when you do, I'm going with you."

Almost a week passed before the next storm thrust its way over the northwestern horizon. Kellen was waiting for Susan when she left the library on the sodden Thursday afternoon. After she got into the car, he told her a line of thunder storms was moving southward. If the radio was correct, they were due to strike the area within the hour.

Thirty minutes later, Kellen pulled well off the pavement of Highway A1A, fifty yards south of the entrance to the townhouses. The storm was approaching faster than predicted. They could see it blackening the northwestern sky.

Time was sluggish, creeping at an abnormally slow pace, stretching the passing minutes into hours. Then all too suddenly, the waiting was over. Raindrops splattered on the windshield. Kellen pushed himself erect behind the steering wheel. "To coin a phrase, this is it."

Susan nodded.

Following the first drops, there was a space of time when nature huddled silently, preparing itself for the onslaught the black clouds were bringing with them. Then the wind swept down the highway with naked fury, recklessly driving a looming precipice of rain before it. The Toyota shivered, the metal of its hood and roof resounding with the determined hammering of solid streams of water.

"We won't be able to see her, if she does come out," Kellen said.

"Pull up closer to the entrance."

Kellen turned the ignition key and was preparing to press down on the accelerator when a flare of light tore a hole in the now-black night.

"That's got to be her! Those have to be her headlights." Susan leaned forward, squinting through the rain-blemished windshield.

The Toyota's engine sputtered, died, then caught. In that moment of hesitation, a black car plunged from between the pillars onto the highway, its rear end fishtailing as it swung north, lunging toward the wall of water erected across the roadway by the storm.

Kellen jammed the Toyota into gear. This time the engine roared and the little car jumped forward. Susan watched the taillights of the Oldsmobile becoming dimmer as the powerful car buffeted its way into the storm front.

"She's getting away!"

"I know, and there's nothing I can do. We're no match for that tank she's driving."

"Oh, Kellen—"

"I'm sorry."

Susan leaned back in her seat. She suddenly felt frail and cold.

It was a silent drive back to the apartment. Kellen, reading her mood, said nothing, allowing Susan to battle depression. He stayed only long enough to drink a mug of coffee, but it was nearing midnight when she finally made the decision to go to bed, very much aware that sleep was going to be elusive.

She thought of the seven o'clock news broadcast the next morning. Would it report another infant death?

23

SHE WANDERED DOWN THE HALLWAY THE NEXT MORNING, having the ghastly sensation it was a catacomb's tunnel through which she walked. She had missed the seven o'clock news; she would try for the seven-thirty broadcast on another station. Her thoughts were a constant and conflicting round of ideas.

The storm-cleansed atmosphere allowed the sun to display itself at its most brilliant. Carrying hints of green from the foliage of the parking area, light flowed through the windows, filling the apartment with a cozy warmth that seemed out of place, given her mood.

She had just turned the burner under the teakettle to its high setting when the telephone rang. With a choked cry, she whirled around to face the instrument, her nerves recoiling from the sound slicing painfully through the weariness clinging to her. When she took the first step in the direction of the ringing phone, the muscles in her right leg threatened to crumble under her. Her hand trembled as she lifted the handpiece.

"Susan." Kellen's voice was unrestrained in her left ear. "Did you hear the early news?"

"No." She held her breath.

"There was no mention of a baby's death during the night."

"Kellen, that's wonderful." But instead of the complete satisfaction she should have experienced, an unsettled feeling claimed her. Maybe it was a diversion, maybe Lily had seen them waiting for her, so maybe she had made the drive last night only to show them she could not be caught.

"What are you thinking?" Kellen's voice seemed to convey a frown.

"Maybe," she said slowly, "she saw us waiting and just took the drive to taunt us."

"Yeah, maybe." There was a sound in the telephone like breath being exhaled slowly. "I'm going to see you this evening, aren't I?"

"If you want to, and I hope you want to."

He laughed. "I want to."

She had forgotten to make a sandwich to bring to work, and surprisingly she was hungry when noontime arrived. She looked at the sandwich truck parked in front of the administration building, thought of the dry, ersatz-flavored sandwiches it offered, and decided to go home to make her own. She wanted more than yogurt.

High masses of clouds moved westward, their edges frayed and misty-looking in the noontime sun. She walked along the campus path, counting her steps, 120 per minute.

When she arrived at her apartment, she was sweaty. Her skin itched and felt feverish under the damp fabric of her dress, and she was touched with a mild dizziness. The air-conditioned air seemed overly cold, pricking her entire body as it wrapped a layer of chill around her. She looked at her watch, calculating the time, deciding she had twenty minutes to squeeze in a shower and lunch before starting the walk back to the library. She decided to only towel off and put on a fresh dress.

At the bedroom door, she stopped. Something was not as it should be. She stood in the doorway, slowly looking around the room, deliberately dividing it into zones, studying each one of them carefully. Nothing was missing. Nothing was moved. Each and every item was exactly as it had been left this morning: the cosmetic jars and bottles on the dressing table, the robe more on the floor than on the foot of the bed, the closet door held open by a hurriedly kicked-off shoe when she decided to wear another pair at the last moment. The room was precisely as it had been when she'd walked away from it four hours before; yet her senses, if not her mind, were alerted to a difference. The strangeness of the situation, and her inability to resolve it, unconsciously caused a tautening of her muscles. For a moment longer, she hesitated, then, attempting to ignore the small squirming in her stomach, stepped into the room.

She thought she might shudder, but her nerves neither cringed nor snapped as she stood looking around once more from this new perspective, feeling the squirming in the pit of her stomach subsiding. She was in a very familiar place, an intimately familiar place, and there was no need for her to be haunted. Yet it, whatever it was, was still in the room, still teasing her senses, still encroaching on her consciousness.

Then she defined it.

So ethereal as to be nearly nonexistent, it floated on the air, undefined and vague, but with just enough substance to give it presence. She drew in a slow, deep breath. The scent of roses, blended with lilac and jasmine and a hundred other perfumes she couldn't

ecognize, caressed the membranes of her nose. She let
out one breath and drew in another. The aroma became
more definite, and she could almost believe she was
standing in the middle of a flower garden that stretched
onward and onward to eventually lose itself beyond the
horizons. For a moment Susan stood without moving,
then expelled the breath she was still holding, frowned
and shook her head.

If she permitted her mind to dwell on the scents and
their origins, her thoughts would become as garbled as
they had been when she'd arisen that morning, she
cautioned herself. Undoubtedly the air conditioner was
pulling them into the room from somewhere, another
apartment or an outside air current.

Acting on an impulse, she went to the window and
looked out. Beyond the glass, sunlight built a solid-
seeming brilliance that for a second or two concealed
the strip of lawn and the black asphalt of the parking
lot. She blinked. Fringed with flares of yellow and gold,
everything came into focus, and she looked out on the
immaculately groomed lawn. There was nothing there
which would generate the scents.

Reaching behind her shoulders for her dress's zipper,
she started to turn away from the window. During this
movement she saw it, from the corner of her right eye,
on the far side of the parking lot—a subdued shining
blackness on the light-swallowing asphalt.

Lily's Oldsmobile. Black and silent and brutish.

Susan dropped her hands, forgetting the zipper, and
leaned closer to the window, squinting against the
searing sunlight. Sitting behind the steering wheel,
looking out the car's side window, Lily returned her
stare. The distance and the sunlight acted as a diffusion
screen, so she couldn't make out the expression on the
black-haired woman's face, but she was certain there
was a tautness in the jawline and that the almond-
shaped eyes were burning.

Susan felt a hairline split opening in her composure.
She was being held prisoner by those eyes on the far
side of the parking lot. A sudden dizziness, accompanied with a clamminess inching upward along her
body, sprinkled droplets of sweat across her forehead.
She tried to reach up and wipe them away, but her arm
was too heavy to move. A breathless little moan escaped her lips. All at once her muscles went flaccid,
seeming to hang loose under her flesh, and she found
herself standing utterly helpless, unable to elude whatever power was reaching through the noontime heat to
strip her of her humanity and will power. She wanted
to scream in anger and desperation, but the distant eyes
would not allow it. All she could do was stand mutely
shuddering while the working portions of her mind
cringed before the hatred that was rampant beyond the
window.

Then Lily turned her head away, and though Susan
knew it was impossible, she thought she heard the
black-haired woman laugh, the same laugh that had
ridden the storm winds outside this window so many
nights ago. A moment later, the Oldsmobile inched
forward, then rolled smoothly in the direction of the
parking lot entrance.

Long after the car disappeared, Susan could do no
more than draw in several lung-filling breaths. The
aftereffects of those glaring eyes still held her immobile.
Then, suddenly, energy flowed back through her. She
felt her muscles flexing as they once more took control
of her rigid body. With a moan of thankfulness, she
turned from the window.

More than once during the afternoon, she felt herself
on the verge of disintegration, with her heart suddenly
accelerating in bursts of violent hammering, clogging
her breath in her throat, as a vision of the black
Oldsmobile flashed through her memory.

She moved through the hours of work by note, forcibly keeping her thoughts solely on the surface of her mind.

Evening came early. When she left the library a few minutes after five, a gray overcast hung above the earth, sullen and tarnished-looking. Kellen wasn't waiting for her. There was a motorcycle in the No Parking zone. She was a tiny bit disconcerted that she felt a touch of relief that he wasn't waiting, but she wanted to be alone to realign the fears and doubts so tightly packed in her brain.

When she arrived at the apartment, the overcast was several shades darker and had put on weight. Convective summer storms were normal, several a week, she had been told, but this summer they were more frequent, everyone was saying. She refused to permit herself to think that there was a correlation between that and Lily.

Half an hour later, the rain arrived. It was a steady rain, the kind, that carried the sweetness of foliage reinvigorated and washed clean. She idly thought that she might benefit by going out into it, that the untainted water would cleanse her of emotional mold.

It was while she was brushing her hair that she became aware the twilight was deepening too fast and, listening closely, she heard the rain falling with a new vigor. After another few minutes, she heard the growl of thunder, bass-voiced, but still far away. She laid the brush on the dressing table and walked slowly to the window to watch the sky darkening as a layer of black clouds scuttled eastward beneath the overcast. A brief reflection of lightning on the trees beyond the parking lot turned them for an instant into a chiaroscuro of brilliant flame and bottomless shadows. The thunder was louder, closer.

Susan looked at the hurrying clouds, calculating that

they would be over the beaches in a matter of minutes
but listening to the slower approach of the thunder
knew it would be much longer before the center of th
storm arrived there.

In a fury of action, she pulled an old pair of slack
and a blouse from the closet, then her raincoat. But
toning the coat, she ran down the hallway and throug
the living room to the telephone. Overhead anothe
bombardment of thunder rumbled through the rapidl
deepening darkness.

On her first attempt, her finger slipped from th
button on the phone, and mumbling, she was forced t
punch out Kellen's number again. She stood listenin
to the repeated ringing on the other end of the line
seeing through the window the darkness sprawlin
around the apartment complex. She heard the rai
become a firm drumming on the windows and acros
the roof. After nine rings, she hung up, stood lookin
uncertainly at the telephone, then turned and hurrie
to the door.

The center of the storm was still behind her. Th
Escort's headlights ricocheted from the streams o
water already glutting the darkness, while the street
glinted as though sheathed in a coating of oil-drenche
ice. She was driving too fast, but she had to reach he
destination quickly, because the darkness and the rai
were trying to plant objections in her mind.

The full fury of the storm trailed her down Highway
A1A. At the entrance to the townhouses, instead o
driving past to park on the side of the road, she turne
in. Switching off her headlights, she backed the car int
one of the visitor parking spaces assigned to Lily'
building. Lily's garage door was closed, and she instinc
tively knew the black Oldsmobile was behind it.

It was too dark to see her watch, and she didn't wan

to turn on the interior light, but she judged that within ten or twenty minutes Kellen would be ringing the door chimes at her apartment. She bit her lip.

A rending crash, sounding like an immense sheet of fabric tearing, shook the Escort in the same instant as a bluish ball of fire raced along the driveway and through the parking area. Susan heard herself screaming as the flaming light pierced her eyes and the sound blasted her ears.

In the black, silent world in which she suddenly sat, intuition sent a frantic twinge through her recoiling muscles. Her blind, deaf brain reacted and began to function. She groped for the key in the ignition, turned it slowly as her foot pressed down on the gas petal. She felt the shiver of the car when the engine started. Then, as instantly as it had disappeared, her sight returned. She saw the rain-opaqued windshield and through it the distorted image of the black Oldsmobile passing in front of the Escort. She gave a hopeless little cry of frustration.

Lily's car was gaining speed down the driveway, already almost to the entrance.

Frantically, Susan jammed her foot down on the accelerator. The little car jumped forward, skidded when she twisted the steering wheel, then plunged after the glowing taillights in front of it.

Lily turned north on A1A, heading the big, black car directly into the storm. Susan followed. She kept her headlights off, using the tail lights ahead of her to guide by. She knew it was foolish and dangerous and dumb, but it was a desperate chance she had to take in hope Lily would not see her. Somewhere in her, the apparatus that sent adrenaline streaming went into motion.

Lily was not driving as fast as when Susan and Kellen had followed her, yet watching the red points of light, Susan suddenly felt that she was racing along a ghostly road in a land that did not exist. She glanced out the side window hoping to see a familiar landmark, but the rain and the darkness had sheathed the Escort with a filmy mass which refused to relinquish even a glimpse of what lay beyond it.

Up ahead, the Oldsmobile's taillights angled to the left, and she knew Lily was traveling the short route to Melbourne Beach. Instead of speeding up, though, the Oldsmobile was slowing. Susan eased her foot off the accelerator. The small car shivered in a whirl of wind, immediately slowing to less than twenty miles per hour. Ahead, the taillights brightened momentarily, then dimmed and moved off to the left. Lily had applied her brakes and turned into the entrance of one of the riverside housing developments. Susan slowed the wind-buffeted Escort until it was no more than creeping through the hammering rain, and came to the concrete arch through which Lily had gone. She turned in. No red glows pricked tiny holes in the darkness ahead of her.

Once she and Sam had driven through this area of 200-thousand-dollar homes, and if she remembered correctly there was only this one road which wound in a serpentine course through the development, eventually returning to exit here at the entrance. If she waited, Lily would have to return to this point and she could confront her, but if she waited, and Lily was here to—

"Damn it! No!"

Susan pushed down on the gas pedal. The road divided not too far inside the archway. Not knowing exactly why, she followed the left branch. It curved farther to the left, then gently swept to the right.

Their yellow glow smeared and diluted, lighted windows passed her. Barely crawling through the waves of rain, the car advanced inch by inch along the black surface of the road. She had the sensation of feeling time rushing by her, like a physical thing riding the whipping wind, and was forced to tighten the muscles in her right foot to keep it from tromping downward on the pedal beneath it.

The road began a moderate curving to the right. As she carefully turned the steering wheel, the sky erupted overhead with a sheet of arching fire, sizzling and crackling. Forked tendrils of flame lashed downward to hiss around the car and skip between the houses. Her eyes snapped shut and her foot automatically tramped on the brake. The car, rocked by the wind, stopped, then instantly filled with the rattle of rain suddenly renewing its fury.

She had no conception of how long she sat with her eyes squeezed shut, but when she opened them again it was to complete darkness, and she realized the lights in the house windows were gone, that the power had been disrupted. Her hands were trembling on the steering wheel, but she knew she had to move the car forward. She nudged the accelerator.

The black bulk almost slipped past on her left, but blackness dully sheening within blackness caught her attention. She braked to a stop and squinted through the semi-transparency of the side window. Lily's automobile set next to the curb.

At first she wanted to jump out of the car and rush to the Oldsmobile, to see if Lily was inside, to run up to the front door of the house she could see as a dark bulk behind tossing shrubbery silhouettes. But as she laid a hand on the door handle, rationality wedged its way into her, cautioning her, telling her to remain in the car, that outside she would be powerless against whatever forces were prowling through the rain.

With a whimper of frustration, she jammed the Escort into reverse, backed it into an angled position in the middle of the road and turned on its headlights.

Nothing moved in the fan of light. No dark shapes. No round discs of glowing fire. Only light-splashed emptiness.

She felt it then, reaching toward her through the rain, the same malignant hate that had been directed at her twice before. It found its way into the car and curled around her, tightening like bands of heated metal that sent sharp spikes into her nerve centers. As before, all defenses crumbled within her, so she felt herself trembling helplessly, unable to erect barriers around her senses.

When another dome of lightning arched across the heavens, a gasping moan escaped her lips as the sizzling light drowned her brain in shards of careening brilliance.

She heard the engine of Lily's car starting, then heard it roar. Unable to see through the light still whiplashing inside her head she could only hear the other car, but its engine noise filled the night, grew in volume, then suddenly rushed away to be swallowed up in the storm.

When her sight returned, the Oldsmobile was gone.

Kellen's Toyota was parked in the space beside her assigned one, and as the Escort's lights swept across it, she saw him sitting in it. All the turbulence in her mind turned to happy confusion. She fumbled off the ignition, pushed open the door, and heaved herself out into the rain. Through the downpour, she saw Kellen moving around his car toward her.

"Oh, Kellen! Kellen!" Unaware that she was moving, ignoring the rain drenching her face and dragging her hair over her eyes in heavy, snarled strands, she hurried to meet him.

His arms were strong, warm, and protective as they folded around her. "You were out chasing her, weren't you?"

"Yes." She snuggled as best she could against him. "I

tried to phone you . . . but you didn't answer. I was going to tell you . . ."

"Hush. We'll talk about it where it's dry."

On the way up the path, she pressed so hard against him that twice their feet entangled. Never in all her life had she wanted to be so close to anyone as she did to this man at this moment, half running, half stumbling through the nighttime rain.

Each of them had toweled their hair and faces dry, and Susan wore a blue towel bound turban-like around her head.

They were sitting on the sofa, with only one light burning in the room. The storm had wandered eastward and a wan moon was hesitantly casting a pale light on the soggy earth.

For more than an hour they had been talking about the evening and the appearance of Lily in the apartment's parking lot. Suddenly, not wanting to search any longer for explanations, not wanting to even continue with any kind of deliberation, Susan moved close to Kellen, who placed his left arm around her shoulders, drawing her tightly to him. "I've been thinking, Susan. I think I should move in with you, or you with me, at least until all this is over. I'm afraid you might be in danger, and I'd feel more comfortable if—well, if I were near you."

A very special warmth caressed her. She remembered the thought she'd had of someone with whom to share the evenings, and knew Kellen was the one. But not under these conditions. Not this way.

She turned her face up to his. "I'd like to live with you. I'd like to live with you for a long, long time, Kellen, but I want to be able to give all of myself to you . . . and under these conditions it would be impossible. You understand, don't you?"

"Yes, I think I do."

She reached up and pulled his face down to hers, placing her lips on his. She put the feeling of wholeness she was experiencing into the kiss, passing it on to him until she became aware of his body duplicating the surge of eagerness beginning to strum in hers.

When her lungs felt empty of air, she pulled her head back. "Will you make your offer again when this is over?"

His arm around her shoulders tightened. "I'm going to make a much more important and lasting offer."

24

SUSAN AWAKENED IMMEDIATELY TO THE SOUND OF THE alarm. It was the second time she had awakened, and this time she lay quietly after turning off the beeping signal, watching the pearly sunlight that streamed through the window as it nudged away the shallow bits of nighttime gray that lingered in the bedroom's corners. An hour before, Kellen had left, returning to his apartment to shave and change clothes. Rolling on her back, Susan yawned, then stretched, enjoying the luxury of the slow, lazy warmth that spread through her as her night-cramped muscles loosened.

She glanced at the clock again. Six fifty-eight. Languor instantly fled. She sat up, swinging her legs over the side of the bed, and grabbed her robe. It was almost time for the seven o'clock news. And she had to hear if Lily . . . if Lily . . .

Shrugging into her robe, she hurried down the hallway, wondering if Kellen would be listening to the broadcast. When she switched on the radio, the tinny musical fanfare that introduced the news program was on its final notes. All the warm lassitude she had felt in bed she now felt seeping from her as she waited for the announcer's voice.

"Dear God," she whispered, "don't allow it to have happened."

The broadcaster made no mention of an infant's death.

She'd done it! If Lily was the killer of babies, last night Susan had thwarted her.

She dressed hurriedly, but with care; for though no celebrations could be held, it was a day during which gratefulness would be in order, and she wanted a sparkle, a tiny flourish, in the manner she went through it.

She was heading for the front door when the telephone rang. It was Kellen, she knew, calling to say he'd heard the news this morning.

There was almost a schoolgirl's lilt in her voice when she uncradled the instrument and said, "Hi!"

"Miss Rutledge? Miss Susan Rutledge?" It was a well-modulated voice, one that she instantly remembered having heard but could not immediately place.

"Yes."

"This is Rabbi Cohen, Miss Rutledge. We talked a few days ago, in my office."

"Yes, of course, Rabbi."

"Miss Rutledge, I must apologize for two things. First, for phoning you at what I know is an inconvenient time, and secondly for permitting you to leave my office with what must have been an unfavorable impression."

"The time isn't inconvenient, Rabbi, only somewhat surprising, and you were probably right to be skeptical about what I said."

"No, Miss Rutledge, I wasn't, and that's why I called you this morning."

Some of the day's sparkle dulled inside her. "Lilith?"

"Yes."

"You've found documents to substantiate my belief?"

"Well, let's say I'd like to meet with you as soon as possible."

He wasn't being cryptic; Susan sensed he was reluctant to discuss the subject on the telephone. "Well, I could be at your office in thirty minutes, Rabbi. I'll have to call the library to tell them I won't be in."

"This won't jeopardize your job, will it, Miss Rutledge? I could come to the library, but I think we should have some privacy when we talk."

"I'll be there, Rabbi Cohen. And don't worry."

Another lie, she thought as she hung up, to be told to Marge Anderson. She stared out the window at the now-lusterless sunlight, wondering how many more times the woman would accept them graciously.

There was a trace of censure in Marge's voice when she inquired why Susan would once again not be coming to work, but the peevish tone faded when Susan explained that she had papers to go through for Sam's parents. She added that she was going to assist Niles Neilson reach a couple of decisions. The lies came easy, much too easy.

Just as she was ready to hang up, Marge said, "Oh, by the way, Susan, your new contract is here. Should I keep it in my desk until you get back?"

"If you think I'm reliable enough to keep on staff, yes. I'd like to sign it."

"You are. You're just passing through a bad time right now. I've been hoping you'd sign it."

Rabbi Jacob Cohen was not a relaxed man. He leaned forward in his chair, his forearms on the desk, his long fingers toying with a small, flat box that was covered in black velvet, with gold at its corners. Susan saw a procession of emotions moving through his dark eyes.

Showing her to a chair, the rabbi had apologized again for the inconvenience he was causing her, but it was obvious to Susan that he considered this meeting to be of great importance, too consequential to wait until a more convenient hour. She said nothing, waiting for him to speak.

Finally, still holding tight to the box, he said, "I was too *modern* the last time we talked, Miss Rutledge. I ignored the fact that in mankind's long struggle we sometimes push aside what our forebears took to be self-evident truths. If it couldn't be seen, touched, or smelled, it didn't exist. If it did exist, we would feel threatened or intimidated, so therefore we ignored it. Turn your back on a problem, and, lo, it isn't there."

Susan slid forward on the chair. "You're talking of the debunking of ancient myths?"

"Yes."

"Of Lilith, in particular."

"Yes." He turned the small black box around in his fingers. "As you said at the time, many legends and myths have their beginnings in events occurring so many millennia ago they are unremembered. But that does not mean that the events did not happen, or that the myths are not based on facts."

"I still believe that."

He looked at her directly then, and she saw sadness in his eyes. "Yes, Miss Rutledge, it is more than possible—at least in some cases."

"What made you change your mind?"

His eyes moved away from hers, and, as they had before, looked at some distant place beyond her shoulders. "It's still difficult for me to admit, but I think when you were here before, there was a presence in this office with you, and not a friendly one. After you left, I still felt it. Something had been watching us and listening to us."

"My God, here too!"

"What do you mean?"

She told him of the times she'd felt a presence: in her apartment, in the restaurant, in the night.

For a long moment after she finished talking, he continued to stare at that faraway place behind her, finally slowly nodding his head. "Then it is more than possible she does exist."

"Rabbi Cohen, are you telling me you believe me?"

"I believe what you have told me, yes. I know that what you've experienced is not illusion." He looked straight at her. "But also, Miss Rutledge, I think you are in danger, great danger. That is why I was so anxious to talk with you."

"Danger? From Lilith?"

"From whatever was in the office with us, from the thing you've seen and felt at other times and other places."

"You seem hesitant to say it is Lilith."

"I'm only hesitant to admit she exists, as a person, an entity. I admit there is evil here in the area."

Susan wet her lips. "I understand, Rabbi, but I'm going to continue thinking of that evil as Lilith, as the woman Lily. I've seen her in action."

"In action? In what way? What do you mean?"

Still sitting on the edge of her chair, Susan told him of the two times she'd followed Lily in her car and of the hate she'd felt. Both times, she said, she was convinced she'd prevented an infant's death. Then, knowing what she was saying would sound like a description of an hallucination, she related her confrontation with the thing at the Neilson apartment, and how later that night a neighbor baby had died. Then, wanting to press her point farther, to try to make him completely understand, she told him of the sculpture show and her visit to Lily's townhouse.

Rabbi Cohen listened hard, his fingers tightening on the black velvet box, muscles delineating themselves along the angle of his jaw. When she finished talking he drew a deep breath and nodded.

"Very well," he said. "I've got to admit my intellectual perspective is being pulled all askew, as I imagine yours has been already, but I believe you, Miss Rutledge."

"Thank you."

He dropped his voice as does one when speaking in confidence. "Since last we talked, I've spent time reviewing copies of ancient writings sent to me by friends. It is believed that Lilith became a handmaiden of Satan during her stay in the Garden, and as such she scoffed at the bucolic serenity of the Garden and relished the carnal lewdness of her secret master. After she was banished, she dwelt for a time with Satan, plotting with him to destroy the Garden. When she made her attempt to kill the sons of Adam and his second wife, Eve, God appointed guardians to drive her away should she return and try to enter Eden again. Though the Garden is gone, the guardians still exist."

"Guardians? Who are they, Rabbi? What are they?"

"Their names are Senoi, Sansenoi, and Sammangelof. They are angels, Miss Rutledge." He turned the small box in his fingers. "Through the millennia, when called upon, they have come to stand between Lilith and those she would destroy."

Susan's hands began to tremble and she clasped them in front of her. "I've read that epidemics of baby deaths have occurred throughout history. If Lilith killed all those infants, where were the guardians? Why do they allow it to happen?"

"They must be sent for, Miss Rutledge. They are not

permanently on watch, and even they cannot penetrate the darkness where she dwells to destroy her. They can only send her back into that darkness."

Her throat was dry, the words harsh-sounding, when she asked, "How—how are they sent for?"

The expression on Rabbi Cohen's face was a dovetailing of a smile and a frown. "I'm afraid there's no eight-hundred number you can phone, Miss Rutledge." The frown became dominant. "We're dealing with a situation born in antiquity, a time when mankind was young and impressive and dwelt in shadows. Ceremonies and rituals were as much a portion of existence as the seeking of food."

"You're saying a ritual must be performed to send for the guardians?"

"A small one, yes." The corners of his mouth slid upward in a controlled smile. "No brimstone, but perhaps a little fire."

Something stirred far back in Susan's mind. Disbelief, or just unease? "Is it complicated?"

"No. Remember, it comes from a time before the human mind became the complex thinking organ it is today. In fact, it may seem very naive and infantile to you."

"*I* must do it?"

"Yes. You're the one Lilith has made herself known to. You are her personal enemy."

Susan nodded. Somehow she had expected this.

Rabbi Cohen set aside the small box and took a manila folder from his desk, opened it, and removed a sheet of heavy, brown, parchment-like paper. With his fingertips, he pushed it across the desk to her. "These are the ritual instructions."

She looked at the paper. A short paragraph, neatly scripted in ink browner than the paper, was centered on the sheet. The words spoke of darkness, of a triangle of flames, and ended with a short prayer or incantation, she didn't know which. She'd study it later.

She looked back at Rabbi Cohen. "This is it? This is all?"

He smiled. "I'm sure it's been streamlined since its inception, but those are the essentials of the summoning." He nodded at the paper. "This is a copy of the ritual instructions, which are kept in the archives of a very ancient, very hidden sect. I had to call in several promises, and make a few, before my request was passed on to them."

Rabbi Cohen replaced the sheet of heavy paper in the folder, closed it, and handed it to her. "Take it. Perform the ritual as soon as you are able."

"Thank you. But what about you, Rabbi? Certainly Lilith knows about you. You said you felt a presence here in the office the last time I visited you."

He leaned back in his chair. "I've thought about that, and I've taken precautions. I've sent my wife and baby son to visit friends in Tampa—a task, I assure you, since I couldn't tell her why I wanted her to visit a city she doesn't particularly care for. Myself, well, perhaps I'm wrong, but I don't feel Lilith will attack me directly. I think she considers me a harassment, but one which, until she destroys you, she can ignore—and considering that your two friends died so violently, I'm convinced she is determined to destroy you. Also, the channels through which I made my request are circuitous and well-protected."

"Still, you're taking a chance."

"It's possible, yes. But I feel I'm a part of this situation now, a major part, and I must help you, no matter what the risks."

Susan felt both grateful and embarrassed. "Thank you, Rabbi."

"Now, Miss Rutledge, for the other reason I wanted

o meet with you so quickly." Again he took up the
little black box. He undid the tiny clasp, hesitated a
brief second, then lifted the lid. "This came with the
ritual instructions, and during the time until the guard-
ans arrive, if they should, I want you to have it."

He turned the box so she could see its contents. Lying
on velvet as black as the exterior was a small medallion,
approximately the size of a silver dollar. She thought it
was silver, but a gray patina covered it, as if polish had
not been applied to it for many years. The design was
mostly obscured beneath the grayness, but she could
discern three robed figures standing close together.
Around them were symbols and what might have been
letters from an alphabet she didn't know.

"It's an amulet, isn't it?" she asked.

"Yes. The figures are Senoi, Sansenoi, and
Sammangelof."

"Why do you want me to have it?"

"Because it may offer you the protection I think you
will need. If this is not a mere myth we are dealing with,
but a dark side of reality, since Lilith has apparently
declared a personal vendetta against you, I feel she'll
soon attempt to destroy you."

He pushed the box toward her. She lifted the amulet.
It was surprisingly heavy for its size and felt warm, as if
from an inner heat. She felt that she was holding an
object that belonged to two very different worlds.

She replaced it in the box. "Thank you again."

"Let's hope it works. Keep it with you at all times."

"How will we know when the guardians arrive? Will
Lilith just disappear?"

"To be truthful, Miss Rutledge, that is another question I can't answer. We have taken a step into the
unknown."

Shortly after that she left, promising to stay in touch.

* * *

She could, she supposed, go to work. Almost half a day remained, but throughout her body there was an influx of vitality she did not want to spend in the library's restrained atmosphere. She looked out at the swimming pool. No one was around. A few minutes in the water would work off the excess excitement strumming at her nerves. Humming a tuneless air, she quickly changed into her swimsuit.

The water was warm when she dove into it, too warm to enjoy. Below the surface, its tepidness streamed along her body as if seeking a way to suck the bursting energy from her, but she swam half the length of the pool underwater before surfacing.

She came up in the shallow end of the pool, her nostrils filled with its chlorine smell, her eyes watering. Bouncing off the shimmering surface, the sunlight nibbled at her face. She drew a deep breath, then blew it out with a snort, at the same time shaking her head, clearing her nose and ears. Wondering if she could still perform a backstroke, she gave a little kick, flipped onto her back, and began stroking her arms in slow, easy arcs.

She didn't know how far she'd gone when the shadow swooped across her. It was small and fast-moving, and she might not have noticed it had it not passed over her face, briefly blurring the sun. Two strokes later the darkness swept over her again, this time slower, almost loitering. Curious, she looked straight up, saw nothing, then roamed her gaze around the sky. There was only a brassy emptiness from which the noontime heat had leeched all color. Then it was there, coming from her left, spiraling down with sail-like wings extended to sweep across the pool and slowly rise to make a graceful turn. A pelican circled directly over her.

Languor shredded from her mind as nervousness blossomed within her.

It was the pelican she'd seen that night outside the Neilson apartment. It continued to circle above her, each revolution of its spiral dropping it closer to the pool. Its neck was pulled back, its head nestled protectively against its body, but she was certain its eyes were scanning her, roaming along the length of her body as they might that of an oversized fish.

The pelican glided lower, and now she could see its eyes, watching her with a hard and brittle stare. She saw rage and hate in that stare. A quick chill raced through her.

Almost leisurely, the pelican spiraled upward in a graceful loop, hesitated, then suddenly folded its wings to its sides and plummeted down, straight toward her.

Her mind did not react; instinct thrashed her legs and arms, rolling her to the left and driving her toward the pool's bottom. She felt the scream in her throat. Ahead, through the blur of water, she saw the wavering sheen of the metal ladder leading out of the pool.

The pelican hit the water to her left and a little behind, the sound of the impact resounding underwater like the smashing of a great glass window. Reacting, her legs kicked in replenished desperation, pushing her body in the direction of the ladder. Through the hair weaving before her eyes, she saw her clawed fingers opening and closing like the tenacles of an underwater creature's antenna. To her left, a black shape rocketed to the surface. She kicked with renewed fury, thrusting her arms forward to what seemed an impossible length.

By the time her fingers closed around the bottom rung, her lungs were begging for relief, sending little spurts of pain through her chest. She drew her feet together and placed them on the bottom rung between her hands. For a moment, she hung doubled there, her head just below the water's surface, her lungs begging her to draw in a deep breath, while she wondered if, and where, the pelican was waiting for her. The muscles in her arms and legs bunched for the final thrust upward.

With all her strength, she pushed with her legs and pulled with her arms. Her head broke the surface in an eruption of foam, water and hair streaming down her face, partially blinding her. She clung to the ladder, feeling her heart move into her throat.

Then, from beyond the mass of wet hair, her alerted senses picked up the awareness of eyes watching her. So intent was the stare that she felt it bordered on the physical. When she lifted her right hand to free her eyes from the tangled hair, her fingers were quivering. To her right she heard a clicking sound, like fingernails tapping a hard surface. She swung her head in its direction. Her mouth opened and closed as she gulped for air and tried to scream at the same time.

No more than a dozen feet from her, focusing their red stare on her, were two glowing eyes. They burned from the face of an animal she could not at first identify. For a long minute they stared at one another, and then, though she had never seen one, she realized the animal might be a jackal.

Beneath a long snout, thin lips pulled back to expose long, viciously curved fangs. Long strings of saliva hung from them. A tongue, speckled black and crisscrossed with what might have been scars, lolled from the open mouth. She could smell the creature, even a dozen feet away; her nostrils pinched at the stench of accumulated filth buried in its shaggy fur. The stink of decomposing meat on its panting breath made her want to gag. It stood solidly on four spread legs, its head lowered, snarling.

Her legs were becoming numb, her knees threatening to buckle. Panic grew in her. In the noontime sunlight, in the swimming pool of an overcrowded apartment complex, she was being held helpless by an animal of the wild.

Down in the bottom of the jackal's throat a low rumbling commenced, while its eyes narrowed slightly, intensifying their glow. It took a pace toward her. Its lips drew back farther, exposing more of the two oversized, drooling fangs, and the stomach-churning stench drifted closer. It was preparing to drive her back into the pool.

She descended one step on the ladder. Inside the ball of fear her mind had become, a kernel was still working. Four feet from her, the jackal stopped, its head swinging from side to side as though it was undecided as to its next move. The growl took on a wet, gurgling tone. Foam bubbled from its lips. It took another slow pace in her direction.

With a cry, Susan swung her right arm, sending a shower of water into the brutish face. The jackal hunkered back a step, the growl abruptly changing to a snort. She splashed again, then again, spraying water over the concrete decking and drenching the animal, which retreated to the outer edges of the concrete. She saw the steady glow flicker in its eyes, then lose a degree or two of vividness. Cautiously, she pulled herself up a step, all the time swinging her right arm, keeping a continuous wave of water arching between her and the jackal.

What she was doing, she knew, was only a temporary solution. Soon her arm would tire. When that time came, she'd no longer be able to maintain the barrier of water between her and the agitated beast, that was now prowling back and forth in a half circle beyond the reach of the spray. Fearful of taking her eyes from it, she nevertheless looked quickly around the pool area. The apartment buildings appeared as vacant as long-emptied structures in a ghost town. The world had shrunk away, leaving the chairs and tables in a nether land of torrid heat.

The awkwardness of her position placed an added strain on her right shoulder that ran down through the muscles in her arm, which was tiring faster than she thought it would. With a fast shift, she clutched the handrail of the ladder with her right hand and commenced splashing with her left. It was cumbersome. She saw the awareness of her problem in the animal's eyes, and watched it advance a step or two, then cease pacing to sit facing her, preparing to wait until her exhaustion became an ally of its own predator's patience.

How long, she wondered, could she last in the midday heat, with her strength being siphoned away by the water and sun and tension? If she swam to the shallow end of the pool, she'd be able to stand in only waist-deep water, out of reach of those terrible curving fangs, thus fighting only the heat.

She stopped splashing, grasping both handrails, shifting her feet on the step in preparation to thrust herself through the water away from the ladder. She drew in a deep breath and tightened her leg muscles.

The jackal tensed, its back stiffening, and turned its head away from her. A moment later, Susan heard a distant car door slam, a man and woman laughing. The jackal looked back at her, its eyes widening, expanding until they were marbles of fire burning through wisps of matted hair. Returning their stare, her chest heaved spasmodically. She grasped for control, for a sanity she felt being torn from her.

All at once the jackal stood, then, without another look at her, loped toward the opening between two of the apartment buildings. She watched it disappear.

When it was out of sight, she pulled herself from the pool and ran to her apartment. The couple strolling

along the walkway from the parking area were too
engrossed with themselves to glance in her direction.

Twilight was a long time coming, and when it arrived
it lingered. The real world reclaimed the pool area; the
chairs were occupied with people and the tables held
drinks and ice buckets, along with an occasional bag of
snacks.

After she had stopped shaking, Susan had returned
to the poolside and spent the afternoon in a web chair,
not really seeing the people around her. She had copied
the prayer Rabbi Cohen had given her onto a piece of
note paper and managed to memorize it. It was short,
rather simple, not filled with elaborate, esoteric
language, and she wondered about its effectiveness. Unfolding the note paper, she reread the little
plea.

Oh, Senoi, Sansenoi, Sammangelof, wherever thou
wand'rest, hear me. I beseech thee.
Thy powers are required.
Lilith is here.
She ties the cord of death about our babies while
they slumber in their beds.
Come deliver them from her, and drive her back
into the waste and desolation that is her realm.
Come, oh guardians of the innocent, and re-
establish the authority of heaven here upon the
earth.

Kellen had phoned, saying that tonight he had to put
the final touches to the revision of his presentation,
asking if she would be all right. She'd assured him she'd
be fine, but had told him nothing of the pelican and
jackal attacks.

* * *

Susan stood in the middle of the apartment's living room, looking at the three candles affixed to the saucer with their own drippings. She had placed them on the floor between the coffee table and the writing desk, far enough apart for her to kneel among them. She didn't know if they were adequate, but the instructions called for three flames and these candles were all she had. Did the guardians, if they really existed, use the flames as beacons to guide them to the person summoning them? She shook her head. She didn't know. There was too much, she realized, that she didn't know. She closed her eyes and drew a deep breath. The pelican and the jackal had warped all the dimensions of her thinking.

In the air conditioner's draft, two of the flames fluttered back and forth like inquisitive insects searching the darkness of the room, and the third flickered as though reluctant to lend its light to the proceedings. Lying in the middle of the triangle was the amulet given her by Rabbi Cohen.

She stared at it. The round piece of metal, sending off shards of reflected light from the wavering flames, looked so tiny there on the floor, so insignificant, that suddenly she felt vulnerable and apprehensive. How could that little circle of alloy be protection from the fury of a demon? A tingling moved along her body. Never in her life had she felt so alone. Her whole being, her very existence, depended on mythical beliefs, on three supernatural beings whose names she could barely pronounce, who probably existed only in mythology.

While she looked at it, the amulet seemed to glow for an instant, as if attempting to convey a message of comfort and power. She felt her thoughts shifting, becoming firmer. She remembered Sam and Maureen and the babies, and, squinting her eyes at the radiant metal, knew that no matter how strange and foolish the action she was about to perform might be, she was going to do it.

She glanced at the kitchen wall clock, just managing to see it in the spill of candlelight. It was ten minutes until twelve. Midnight was the witching hour, and, though the instructions did not specify any set time other than darkness, she wanted to receive every bit of assistance that could be given her. She slowly moved her eyes through the darkness, feeling, as she had for the last fifteen minutes, that she was inside a great black cube which had no place in actuality.

Unconsciously, she wiped her hands on her hips, drying the film of dampness coating her palms. Carefully, she stepped into the middle of the triangle of candles and sank to her knees beside the amulet.

The nap of the carpeting gouged little indentations into her knees. Around her the darkness was taking on a life of its own, becoming more and more cavernous. The air conditioner turned itself on, pumping a stream of cold air across her, sending a shiver through her and causing her, for the first time, to realize she was sweating. Rivulets of moisture were running down her spine and her eyebrows were wet with droplets from her forehead.

In the light of a candle, she looked at her wristwatch. Midnight. Her tongue was thick and dry, but she ran its tip around her lips, which felt cracked and stiff.

She looked down at the amulet, drew a breath. "Oh, Senoi, Sansenoi, Sammangelof, wherever thou wand'rest, hear me, I beseech thee."

Something smashed against the large front window, followed instantly by a beating on the one in the dining area. A popping, crackling sound echoed through the apartment, and a second later an orange streak of fire sliced out of the darkness, sizzled once around the triangle of candles in a tight loop, then snuffed out the candle that had been flickering. When it was gone, the darkness became deeper and more opaque. Phantoms moved in it. A foul smell of unwashed animal bodies, rotting vegetation, and escaping swamp gases polluted the air.

It was Lilith! Susan was certain. It could be nothing else.

Lilith knew about the summoning and had come to stop it. Susan's mind groped for the remaining words of the prayer while her right hand groped for the amulet. After what seemed an eternity of time, her clawing fingers closed around the warm metal. She picked it up and extended her arm before her, moving it back and forth through the candlelight, not certain if the face of the amulet was turned toward the darkness, not knowing if it should be. There was a hiss. Something rushed through the darkness, and the medallion was jerked away from her as though pulled by an unseen string.

Frantically, she snatched it up again, taking a firm hold on the warm metal, searching with her fingertips for the face of it.

A renewed thudding, like wings furiously beating against the glass, came from the rear window.

She spoke the words. "Thy powers are required Lilith is here."

Over the cry of her voice, she heard a sniffling, then a snarling growl at the front door, followed by a furious scratching as if powerful claws were attempting to dig through the wooden panel. A terrible weight threw itself against the door, shuddering it on its hinges.

She pointed the face of the amulet in that direction.

With a viper-like hiss, the stream of lightning fire again sizzled through the darkness of the room exploding one of the remaining candles. Hot wax spattered her bare thigh, burning her in a half a dozen tiny places. Writhing nerves drove a scream up into her throat, but she managed to clamp her lips against it.

She held tight to the amulet.

"She ties the cord of death about our babies while they slumber in their beds."

Behind her, the glass in the rear window shattered, and the flapping of wings hammered on her eardrums.

"Come, deliver them from her, and drive her back into the waste and desolation that is her realm."

It was then she saw the form outside the front window, a blackness in the black of the night, watching her. She could see no detail, but she knew what it was.

"Come, oh guardians of the innocent, and re-establish the authority of heaven here upon the earth."

In the dining area, the battering of the wings against the broken window ceased abruptly, and the snarling at the front door dribbled away to a whimper. Beside her, the last candle flame swelled to create an oasis of pale illumination.

But the figure at the window remained, ominously still.

Susan was shaking with the abuse her mind and body had under gone. She had to gather all her energy into the effort of holding the medallion, now warmer and heavier. Her memory was faltering, but before it lost its contents completely, she put together once again the words of the prayer. This time there were no interruptions when she recited it.

As she stared at it, the figure at the window began to fade. It shifted position, drifting back from the window, then like smoke in a windless atmosphere, slowly dissolved into the nighttime darkness. Yet she received the impression of something nebulous floating out there, like the thing she and Sam had seen that night on the stoop. She continued to hold tight to the amulet. Slowly she became aware of an absolute stillness, a complete lack of sound that excluded even her own rapid breathing.

She lowered her arm and looked down at the round disc cupped in her palm. It had worked. The little piece of metal had constructed a barrier around her, holding the fury of Lilith at bay. She wondered if the prayer too held the power attributed to it, if out there in the nighttime heavens three angels had heard her and seen the light of the candles.

She could only wait.

25

THE DINING AREA WAS DREARY. THE SHEET THAT SHE HAD
hung over the broken window reduced the already glum
morning light to a hueless gloom, an eerie blend of gray
and withered white. She sat staring down at the full
mug of coffee on the table before her, knowing it had
become cold, but also aware that if she drank it the
sharp taste might assist her in unscrambling the
thoughts that had tumbled through her mind since the
attack. Finally her stare moved from the coffee mug to
the shards of glass sprinkled on the floor, and vaguely
she wondered if the maintenance people would create
an issue over the shattered window.

Behind her, still in the middle of the living-room
floor, were the stumps of the candles. Along with the
glass pieces, they were the sole evidence of the horror
and terror that had invaded the apartment during the
night. As Susan continued staring at them, the dull

sheen of the glass segments blurred and she felt a strange separation occurring as her mind divided itself into a half that questioned the whole affair and a half that partially believed and was determined to confront Lilith again.

Then, slowly, the cocoon of numbness unpeeled from around her. In three swallows she drank half the mug of cold coffee, then carried what was left to the sink and poured it down the drain. While rinsing the mug under the hot water faucet, she stared out the window above the sink at the flat expanse of gray sky, and then at the earth reflecting that gray. Across the parking lot, the row of shrubbery was without dimension, appearing to be a theatrical flat hastily erected to conceal a land shrouded in bleakness. Susan shook the excess water from the mug and placed it in the drainboard rack to dry.

By the kitchen clock it was twenty minutes until nine. On the campus, in the library, in all the stores and offices throughout the area routines of life were starting. She was not a part of it. She felt remote, far away from the world she had occupied all of her life. For an eerie few moments, she felt like an orphaned soul.

At nine o'clock, she dialed Rabbi Cohen's office at the synagogue. He answered on the second ring.

"I did it," she said, instinctively knowing he'd recognize her voice. "Last night I performed the summoning ceremony."

He did recognize her, and simply asked, "How did it go?"

She found it was impossible to find the words to describe what had occurred the previous evening.

"Miss Rutledge—?"

"I'm sorry, Rabbi. I—"

"Something happened, didn't it?"

"Yes."

"Bad? Frightening?"

"Yes." Her thoughts fell into a cohesive pattern. "The amulet works."

Now was the rabbi's turn to hesitate. "She came? Lilith came?"

"Yes, I'm sure it was her."

"Tell me about it, Miss Rutledge. Please."

Describing the happenings of the night before, she discovered, wasn't difficult after all. The few intervening hours had smoothed the edges of the original terror and disbelief.

When she finished, Rabbi Cohen's voice was clogged-sounding as he said, "It is more than a myth, then. Thank God, you're safe, Miss Rutledge."

"Thank you. But, Rabbi, if the amulet works, the percentage for the success of the prayer is high, don't you think?"

"It would seem so."

"But you're not sure."

"No. My certainty in many things is being battered at the moment, Miss Rutledge." He hesitated, and Susan heard him draw in a long breath before he spoke again. "Do nothing more for now. Let me try to obtain more information, which will probably take a day or two. Keep the amulet with you at all times."

She asked, "If the prayer did work and the—the guardians respond, how long will it be before they arrive?"

"I can't say. I don't know. Miss Rutledge, you must take great care. I fear you're facing forces beyond mankind's comprehension. Do I sound irrational?"

"No, Rabbi, not when you look at my apartment."

Noon came and went and became early afternoon, then midafternoon, while Susan wandered through her apartment, occasionally reading from her notes or studying the three figures hidden beneath the gray patina on the amulet. Outside, the blurry gray of the morning steadily darkened to a mottled slate.

In the middle of the afternoon, two maintenance men came to repair the broken window. When they left, she found it impossible to pull her attention away from the glass and the gathering darkness in the sky. Trees and shrubs hung limp, weary, and darkly brooding in the unnatural dusk.

She stood looking out the repaired window at the bleak-colored view, hearing over and over in her mind Rabbi Cohen saying, "Do nothing for now."

The advice was well meant and correct, she knew, and her senses told her to heed it. But there were so many whom she would never forget. Their memories called for action. Sam, who she'd come so close to loving. Maureen, so excited about the new life commencing in her womb, and who left behind a motherless Bridget and a wifeless Niles. There was Jetta Ashley, who had ended her life and taken away the one of her unborn child, and the pyschologically broken husband, blaming himself for her death. And then the babies, nearly a dozen of them in the area, whose new lives had been ended before they even knew what living was. And finally, like ghosts on the periphery of her memories, the innumerable infants who had died in mysterious epidemics throughout history.

She shook her head. It was impossible for her to "do nothing more now." She possessed the amulet. Last night it had proven its power. Lilith was helpless before it; so the advantage was now with her and she must exploit it. She could combat Lilith on equal footing. And if those guardians came, why then certainly their combined force would be too much for the demon-woman.

Around four o'clock she dressed in jeans and an old blouse, then pulled a brush through her hair. Where she was going, and what she was going to do, needed no lengthy session before a mirror. She put the amulet in the pocket of her jeans.

A few minutes before five, she stood at one end of the living room, gazing around the apartment, studying the familiar furnishings but feeling no affinity for them, seeing them in the drab light as muted swatches of random color. This was her home, but she had no sensation of belonging.

It was exactly ten after five when she locked the front door after her. It was too early by at least an hour, maybe an hour and a half, but she wanted to be gone before Kellen phoned or came by.

She drove neither fast nor slow, keeping pace with the evening traffic. By the time she turned south on Highway A1A, the sun had given up its struggle with the overcast, and the early twilight was melting into the darkness that was creeping in from the ocean, coming closer with each breaking wave. There was nothing in her life to compare with what might happen tonight, no way to prepare herself.

At the townhouse complex, she parked in a visitor's space assigned to the building north of Lily's, but from which she could easily see both Lily's front and garage door.

The inside of the car began to feel steamy and close. Susan rolled down the window, and immediately the stickiness of the sea air joined the humidity to coat her skin with a gummy dampness. Her stomach threatened to become squeamish, and the steady acceleration of her heartbeat was starting to make itself felt.

The roll of thunder was a surprise, for there had been no lightning. She wondered what Rabbi Cohen would think if he knew she was here and what she planned. She wasn't as surprised when the rain started as she had been with the thunder, but damned herself for not bringing her raincoat.

Driven before an increasing wind, the rain increased

in force. Heavy drops rattled against the side of the car
away from her, allowing her to keep the window beside
her open. Somewhere on the other side of the decora-
tive line of crotons and ixora, lightning rippled. Its
accompanying thunder was closer, and she realized this
was a rapidly moving storm.

Two things happened simultaneously. Susan saw
movement in front of Lily's unit, a dark form hurrying
through the rain in the direction of the closed garage
door. And a whipping draft of wind curled a stream of
rain through the car's open window. It splashed in her
face, blinding her, going up her nose and down her
throat. She gasped and blinked, running a hand frantically across her eyes. When her vision cleared, she saw
that Lily's garage door was open. No lights showed, but
she could make out movement beside the dully gleaming shape of the Oldsmobile.

"No, damn it, not this time!" Fumbling briefly, she
unlatched the car door, and when it swung open,
jumped out into the storm.

The rain's frenzy hit her as she ran along the driveway, drenching her, reaching inside her with an explosive coldness to drive the breath from her and spasm
her muscles, but still she ran.

The red brake lights of the Oldsmobile flared, casting
ruby-red shadows into the rain. She heard the engine
mumble as though in protest at being started, then the
roar as full power surged through it. A thin plume of
white smoke rose, dyed red by the tail lights.

"Lilith! Lilith, I'm here!"

Susan's knees all but buckled as she came to an
abrupt halt behind the car.

"Lilith, you're going nowhere tonight! Nowhere! Do
you hear me?"

The Oldsmobile's engine bellowed. The brake lights
went out. Susan watched the curving black metal and

gleaming chrome rush directly at her like a maddened creature lunging from its lair.

Her feet slipped on the wet asphalt, but she managed to thrust herself to her left in an awkward leap. She whirled, digging the amulet from her pocket, and, holding it cupped in her hand, raised her right arm to point the three engraved images at the head and shoulders framed in the car window.

"Lilith, see what I have! I'll follow you. I'll keep up with you again, and I'll stand between you and any baby you try to harm. Do you hear me?"

The head turned to face her. A gasp rushed from her lips, and she felt the breath knocked from her. She was staring into the features of something not belonging to this world, or any other. Red eyes pulsed from the bottoms of deep wells sunken into the skull above jutting cheekbones. The face from which they burned was a thing of sharp angles and taut planes, with the skin stretched so tight it appeared on the verge of splitting open, a face long dead and mummified. A squeal escaped her, but she kept the amulet pointed at the thing behind the Oldsmobile's steering wheel.

Her arm began to tremble.

The world began to disintegrate, roaring in agony. Thunder crashed and rolled among the buildings, shaking the ground beneath her feet.

Her muscles fought to hold her arm up and rigid.

Beneath and above the thunder Susan heard a terrible snarl, contorted and vibrating with hate. Susan opened her eyes. The Oldsmobile's door was open and the driver's seat was empty.

The rain beat at her, each drop like a tiny fist hammering at her body, driving through the material of her blouse and jeans to pummel her flesh. Frantically, she squinted into the flooded darkness, desperately trying to locate what was out there growling so savage-

ly. The sound came again, off to her right and somewhat behind her, between her and the Escort. The car's
safety was taken from her.

A woman laughed, the mocking laughter that had
filled the stormy night outside her bedroom window. It
came from where the snarling had sounded. She felt
herself weakening, and begged herself not to panic. She
whirled around to look at the windows of the other
occupied units in the building, seeking a place of
refuge. The windows were all dark. They stared out on
the parking lot with a blind, uncaring emptiness, and
she seemed to sense a chill coming from them, as if the
building itself was turning its back on her.

And she knew, at that moment, that this was how
Maureen had died, alone, with a terrible horror coming
at her from out of the night, while the world looked the
other way.

Lightning sent a streamer up the driveway and exploded in a fireball just beyond the Oldsmobile, sending a fan of sizzling fragments spraying through the
darkness. A few of them hissed on the wet pavement at
her feet.

She tried to point the amulet in the direction of the
laughter, but her arm and hand were trembling so
strongly that she couldn't control them and simply
allowed her arm to hang at her side, the amulet
clutched in her quivering fingers. The snarl sounded
again, replacing the laughter. It was closer. Her confidence vanished. Last night, not only the power of the
amulet, but the walls of her apartment, had surrounded
her, adding their protection. Now, at the mercy of the
storm, she felt renewed terror twist her brain. Primal
instincts took control. With a choked cry, she turned
and ran.

The rain became more furious, a cataract of wind-
whipped water. It lashed her shoulders like a whip,

forcing her on and on. She ran without thought, not knowing where she was headed, only wanting to be away from the snarling thing in the darkness and the disembodied laughter. She rounded the building. In the lee of its walls, there was a slackening of the wind and rain, and she slowed her pace. Maybe she would have time during a moment of calm to reassemble herself.

But carried on the wind, the snarl, still murderous in intent, came around the corner of the building. Then she heard the too familiar clacking of the beast's claws on the cement walkway along which she had come. Even in the rain-drenched air, she smelled the fetid stench of the creature.

"No!" She screamed in spite of herself as shock and terror tore anew at her.

She sprang forward, lunging away from the protection of the building, back out into the wind. Only vaguely was she aware of a swimming pool as she ran past its restless water, hearing behind her the snarl and clacking claws of the creature as it drew closer, gaining on her with each stride she took.

Suddenly she spotted handrails and wooden steps descending to the beach. Without hesitation, she grasped one of the rails and, not looking to see what was at the bottom, vaulted down the short flight of steps. When she struck the sand, her feet rolled out from under her and her momentum threw her forward to her hands and knees. The amulet slipped from her fingers. Whimpering, she clawed through the sand until she found it, then crabbed away from the bottom of the steps, and stood up. Wet sand clung heavily to her, wanting to pull her back down to all fours. With a sand-caked hand, she brushed aside the mat of hair over her eyes, then fearfully looked at the steps to see if the animal had followed her down. They were empty. She swung her head from side to side, but saw nothing on the beach with her. She was alone.

This time the woman's laugh was guttural. Instead of soaring on the wind, it sank beneath it to rasp on Susan's ears.

Lily was standing at the top of the steps. Then Susan saw the two slices of flame that were her eyes, gleaming in the semi-silhouette of the head, and knew it was not Lily but Lilith who stood there staring down at her.

Thunder roared back and forth across the heavens, rumbling like a distant artillery duel between two great armies. Suddenly, as though the earth and sea were vomiting up all the rotten things from their depths, the air was filled with the stench of corruption. A vast force shouldered its way along the beach, sending out streamers of malignancy too powerful for the rain to wash away.

At the top of the steps, Lilith raised her arms, reaching high, appearing to fondle and caress the boiling clouds rushing toward the sea. Though her hair must have been as wet as Susan's, it whipped around her face in long black ribbons like a cloud itself scurrying for a distant place.

A holocaust of lightning struck. A great bolt tore away the night, ripping the heavens wide open, sending a great tide of blinding light along the beach and out across the tumbling waves. Over the stomach-turning stench which had come with Lilith, there was the smell of burning ozone.

Susan cried out. Even as she raised the amulet, her leg muscles collapsed, dropping her to her knees. The lightning explosions were painful to see, and she covered her face with her gritty hands. All around her, she heard the air rushing in a maelstrom of wind and the wild broken cadence of the waves pounding the beach. She remained crouched, bent forward with her face buried in her hands, lost in a black and white void

while sensations began weaving themselves into functional patterns, feeling the sand-encrusted metal of the
amulet scratching her cheek. Thank God, she still
possessed it.

Through the echoes of the thunder, she thought she
heard a whirring above her, then a flapping noise.
Suddenly she remembered the sound of wings beating
against the apartment's window the night before. She
dropped her hands and glanced skyward.

The rain cut at her face, but through matted hair and
squinted eyes, she saw the outspread wings of a bird.
Black silhouettes against the boiling clouds, they were
stretched to catch the wind. She moaned. Clearly the
bird was taking a position from which to attack.

Her fingers tightened on the amulet. Cupping it in
her hand, she forced her arm up, pointing the face of
the medallion at the bird.

A curdling screech came from above her. The bird
was swooping at her, its wings stroking the wind with
powerful sweeps steering it directly at her kneeling
body. Suddenly it veered away, its wings flapping
furiously, its red eyes glaring at the metal disc in her
hand. Emitting a shriek of rage, the bird plummeted
past her, then, still screaming its fury, soared upward to
vanish into the rain.

Gasping, she struggled to her feet, spread her legs to
retain her balance, and looked in the direction of the
steps.

Lilith was gone.

Susan didn't move. Around her the night pulsed
silently, as though regaining its strength after the turmoil of lightning and thunder. She felt an unnatural
warmth in the palm of her right hand and looked down.
The amulet was glowing faintly. It was working! It had
protected her from the attack of the huge black bird
and was hold Lilith beyond its barrier of power. Now it

was Susan's turn to go on the offensive.

That was when she saw it.

Very slowly, placing one paw deliberately before the other, it was coming down the steps. She didn't know what it was, but she knew it wasn't the jackal. This was a sleek animal, moving with the rhythm of a feline. But like the jackal and the pelican, it possessed fiery, blood-red eyes, now staring straight at her. It was halfway down the steps, descending them leisurely, giving the impression that behind those glowing eyes its brain was enjoying the anticipation of what was to come. It reached the bottom and did not hesitate, but, without breaking stride, started to cross the sand toward her. Its eyes sought hers and locked onto them.

Memories tumbled over themselves in her mind. The red, burning eyes. They all possessed them: the pelican, the jackal, this creature . . . and Lilith. A passage from the reference material wedged its way into her memory flow: Lilith can assume the forms of the jackal, wildcat, pelican, or kite at will, along with, some sources believe, a species of long-extinct fowl.

A vile taste flooded her mouth. Inside her head, the pounding grew louder. Coming toward her was the wildcat transformation of Lilith.

She took a step backward, then another, slowly, feeling the uneven sand with her toes before putting her weight on her foot. Even had she wanted to, she could not have pulled her eyes away from the wildcat's face: they were held helpless by the animal's unblinking stare. She couldn't lift the amulet.

"This is how you killed Sam, isn't it?" she cried. "You turned yourself into one of these creatures and tore him apart on the beach."

The big cat hissed, baring its fangs, but underneath the animal noise, she thought she detected a sound like the expulsion of human breath in a deep-throated

:huckle. Lowering itself until its belly grazed the sand,
he beast scurried around her to take a position be-
ween her and the water.

"You can't hurt me, Lilith." Her voice shook, but
vas surprisingly clear. "You know I have the protection
>f the amulet."

Again the creature hissed, this time raising a forepaw
is it might to brush the words away.

Quickly Susan bent down and scooped up a handful
>f wet sand. Neither woman nor beast moved. The rain
;wept around them in waves and the heavens rumbled
n continuous pain. Their eyes remained locked. Final-
y, just as the tremulous motion in her stomach threat-
ned to move upward to squeeze her lungs, the red eyes
>roke contact to wander up and down her body,
;tudying her as though curious about this woman who
`aced it with such determination. Then it ceased its
:xamination, and along its sleek body muscles tensed
ind bunched in preparation for movement. Susan saw
what was happening, and, with a cry, threw the handful
>f sand at its burning eyes and raised the amulet.

She was too late. The animal yowled and sprang at
1er. Even though she was prepared, she stumbled as she
leaped to her left. The extended claws of the animal's
right paw gouged her right shoulder. There was an
instant of pain, then horror as the fingers of her right
hand opened, dropping the amulet. She whirled to see
the wildcat crouched, ready to attack again. Out of
desperation, she backtracked toward the water. With a
hissing snarl, the beast lunged, this time for her face,
but in its fury it misjudged the distance and the
instability of the sand. Susan's backward spring as the
wildcat launched itself carried her just out of reach of
its slashing paws. Susan turned and raced for the surf,
driving through the eddies and currents that clutched
and tugged at her legs. She waded out until a wave

rolled over her head, then, bracing herself, turned to face the beach.

The wildcat was gone. So was the amulet. There was no sign of its glowing circle on the sand. Either the surf had buried it beneath the sand or sucked it out into the sea.

An incoming wave struck her shoulders and rolled over her head. Her feet skipped along the sandy bottom. She windmilled her arms in a furious effort to retain her balance, managing to keep her head above the water without swallowing any. The ocean's salt in the gouges on her shoulder spread a mesh of pain down her arm and across her back. It was impossible to brace herself against the relentless shoving of the waves, and she stumbled forward another step. Through the smudge of rain and seawater blurring her eyes, the beach appeared empty, but she knew Lilith was watching, planning, gathering herself for a new assault. And she had no defense, now that the amulet was gone. At that moment, with a terrible knowledge, Susan knew Lilith could never be destroyed.

They came, then, all of them, out of the rain, riding the wind that suddenly howled along the narrow strip of sand, filling the air with their putrid stench. While like alabaster, but smeared as if with soot, they whirled along the waterline to form a barrier through which she knew there was no passing. The creatures were those Susan had confronted on their pedestals in the nonexistent sculpture show and in the gloom of Lily's townhouse and riding the whirlpool wind in front of the Neilson apartment. But now there was life in them. Through the hissing rain and slapping surf, she heard their guttural snarls and squawkings.

A wave, bigger than the others, thundered down on her, lifting her from her feet and somersaulting her across the bottom. Her wounded shoulder scraped through the tumbling sand in the undercurrent, creating a chaos of pain through her entire torso.

When Susan struggled to her feet, she was standing in water only up to her knees, her feet sinking into shifting sand. The creatures had disappeared.

Susan heard the hiss of rage before she saw the woman. Lilith was halfway up the beach. Susan felt the inhuman rage, like an aura, surrounding the woman who, dressed in night-blending black, stood with her arms folded across her breast and her legs spread in a solid stance. Through the dark hair half hiding the other's face, almond-shaped fires burned in their bottomless wells.

Around them, the wind howled in its own demonic fury and the rain ferociously pummeled the earth, but neither woman moved. Then, only faintly descernible in her peripheral vision, Susan became aware of things moving, coming nearer. She was certain she saw a light. It was no more than a tiny fan of bluish-gold, but her eyes absorbed it and sent it hurrying deep into her turbulent brain. She felt the shadows disappear inside her, was suddenly aware that the tightly closed grip of terror on her mind was being pried open. A moment later, there was an instant of pure warmth as all her fear washed away.

The sea gave her a final shove, but this time it was more of an urging push, an encouraging stroking of her back. She took a tentative step forward, then another, with the ocean nudging her on. She stopped when the water still swirled around her ankles, and, though she wasn't sure, she thought Lilith took a halting step backward before she looked upward at the storm clouds scuttling eastward.

The bluish-gold fan of light began to swell, arching upward while extending across the beach, quivering and throbbing like a miniature aurora borealis between the dunes and the water's edge. From within it a low humming commenced, like a dynamo building to full power. The colors brightened.

From the corner of her eye, she caught movement and sensed Lilith had taken another step backward.

The arc of light grew in brilliance. Its pulsing slowed, becoming almost a solid plane of color and moving toward the two women. Although it grew no louder, the humming became a steady flow of sound, and around her Susan felt the storm-punished air trembling from this new assault of sonic waves. They had no affect on her, but off to her left she heard a hissing, and looking quickly in its direction saw Lilith standing braced on spread legs, her hands raised before her in a defensive position. A stab of elation jabbed at Susan. For the first time, she was seeing a fracturing of the woman's menace.

She looked back at the radiant light. Long robes whipping in the wind, three tall, ethereal figures moved down the beach. Their approach was neither fast nor slow, just a steady oncoming advance. Though she could not distinguish their faces, she sensed the eyes of the three were focused sharply on Lilith.

Suddenly the night was filled with movement. While she watched the approaching figures, great forces shifted and the darkness trembled as it might if somewhere out in the void towering mountain ranges were tumbling. The center figure raised its arms. Tiny bolts of light sizzled from its fingertips. Immediately the rain doubled its fury and just as instantly the beach was transformed into a quagmire through which runnels of water rampaged toward the choppy surf.

Susan became aware of the voice then, rising on the wind in a keening cry.

"Damn you . . . Damn you . . ."

She cupped her hands around her eyes to protect

hem from the rain and looked at Lilith. Through the
eil of rain and darkness, she saw Lilith slowly raise her
rms toward the racing storm. She stood that way,
gnoring the punishment she was receiving from the
ain, reaching higher and higher for the hurdling cloud
lass.

The three figures moved closer, fire bolts streaking
rom the fingertips of their own raised arms weaving a
veb of golden-amber illumination between the women.

Lilith's form began to alter. At first Susan thought it
vas a trick of the rain and the weaving bolts of light,
ut the transformation continued and she came to
ealize that it was not an optical distortion. Lilith's tall,
tatuesque outline swelled. Susan watched her curves
hift position, the upstretched arms thickening into
blongs, the long legs melting together. When the
hanging ceased, the form remained where it was,
waying in the wind; then suddenly the oblongs which
ad been arms spread, and Susan saw they were wings.

"No," she whimpered. "No . . ."

Her mind tried frantically to reject what she was
eeing, but her eyes watched a huge bird spread its
vings to the wind, hesitate, then soar up into the rain,
piraling in circles that became wider and wider the
igher it ascended.

Far to the east, blossoming up from beyond the
orizon, a sheet of lightning flared to bathe the clouds
nd the ocean with an uncanny reddish glow. Long
vings spread, the bird was silhouetted against the fiery
background, then the fan of light slowly receded to the
orizon. The bird was gone.

She would never be sure, but as the bird became lost
n the boiling sky, Susan thought she heard a wailing
cry.

Shaking, Susan sank to her knees in the surf, unaware
of the water pulling at her. It was over. Everything was

done. Even the ethereal figures of the three guardian
were gone.

Abruptly the wind fell to a cooling breeze. The rai
slackened to no more than a gentle summer drizzl
The storm's thunder and howling were silent, only th
remembered sounds of a time that was past.

Six Weeks Later

SUSAN WALKED BRISKLY ALONG THE CAMPUS PATH. SHE WAS experiencing a mood as near to pure happiness as she had felt for a long time. From out of the north a steady evening breeze carried a tantalizing hint of autumn coolness, and her body was responding, her muscles working smoothly.

Unashamedly, she held out her left hand, her fingers spread, and looked at the ring. It seemed to wink at her in the evening light as if sharing her mood. It wasn't a large diamond, but its meaning was large. She had been wearing it for two weeks, and it felt comfortable on her finger. During the Christmas holidays, she and Kellen planned to have a small ceremony, then spend four days in Montego Bay on a honeymoon.

Kellen and Niles were standing beside the pool when she rounded the corner of a building. In her stroller, Bridget was playing with a stuffed bear. How well, Susan thought, Niles had assumed the double burden of child care and work. It had been nothing less than a quantum shift in his life style. During the day, Mrs. Collingsworth baby-sat Bridget. She was an elderly neighbor who had adopted Bridget as a grandchild. At times Susan wondered if the kindly widow might not be spoiling Bridget.

Niles was ready to wheel Bridget into their apartment for her evening feeding. "I'd like to stay and talk, Susan, but twenty minutes ago I switched from provider to housekeeper. Why don't you both come over later and we can have a chat." He looked down at his daughter. "Since Bridget isn't much of a conversationalist yet, I'll have her in bed."

They said they'd do that.

They pulled two web chairs to the stoop in front of Susan's apartment. Although Kellen had not moved in, he kept some clothing and personal items here. After the marriage they planned to live here because of its proximity to the campus. He'd no longer require all the space he now occupied, Kellen said, because all of his projects would be replaced with only one. When Susan had asked, "Which one is that?" he'd answered, "You."

"Rest yourself." He grinned. "I've got daiquiris in the refrigerator."

"Are you always going to spoil me like this?"

"No promises."

When they each held a chilled glass, Kellen looked out at the pool, then up at the sky, finally back down to his drink.

"Okay, what's bugging you?" she asked.

As if a sudden cramp had struck his neck, his head gave a little jerk. "Nothing."

"Come on. You're good at a lot of things, but acting isn't one of them."

He nodded. "I think you should know, but—well, I don't want to upset you. You've come such a long way since that night."

In spite of herself, she felt an unnatural chill from the cold glass she held in her fingers move up her arms. "What?"

"Do you remember that man we met at the townhouse when we pretended to be apartment hunting? The one whose wife drowned herself? His sister was with him."

"Yes. Glenn Ashley."

"That's him, yes." Kellen took a slow sip from his drink. "I saw him this afternoon in the supermarket. He recognized me, and we talked."

"Oh?" The chill was up to her shoulders now and moving across them. "How is he?"

"Recovered, I guess. His lease runs out at the end of the month and he's going up north, he said. Probably to spend some time with his sister and her husband."

"Well, that sounds encouraging. So why are you so twitchy?" She felt her breath catching.

"He mentioned Lily. In fact, I take it she was the main topic of conversation around the complex out there for a while."

"Go on . . ."

"Damn it! I shouldn't have brought this up."

"Yes, you should. Now, tell me, please."

"Okay." He drew a deep breath. "None of the residents knew, of course, what Lily was—is —whatever. To them, she was just a woman who stayed to herself and suddenly disappeared. I guess it's still that way. Even with Glenn. But one day, he saw a truck in front of Lily's townhouse, and the resident manager was directing the loading of the truck with her furniture. They talked."

"And—"

"Well . . . The manager had received a cablegram from Madrid telling him to dispose of the furniture as he desired, except for a wooden chest in the bedroom. That was to be put in storage, with the name of the storage company sent to her in care of general delivery in Madrid. When Glenn asked, the manager said he didn't think Lily was living in Madrid, that she'd indicated it was merely a stopover point on the way to her new home."

As much as she suddenly wanted to not listen, Susan forced herself to fix her attention on what Kellen was saying.

"None of her sculptures were there. Only the pedestals." He glanced quickly at her, then stared at his drink. "The people who live there think she took them all with her. They found a lot of dead plants and flowers and dried-out palm fronds in her bedroom, like a garden gone to rot. It seems many of the people who live there think she was some kind of crime queen and had to leave fast, because either the law or other criminal elements were after her."

Susan set her unfinished daiquiri on the cement beside the chair, stood up to walk slowly to stand beside the swimming pool. A moment later, Kellen was at her side.

"I shouldn't have said anything. I'm sorry."

"No, don't be. I've the right to know." She leaned against him. "I knew she wasn't destroyed. Rabbi Cohen said the guardians couldn't do that—only drive her away. She is Evil, Kellen, and Evil has existed since the beginning and will be with mankind forever. It is the dark, lurid side of nature, but a portion of it nevertheless, like the unseen side of an object being reflected in a mirror. But Lilith is recognizable and can be combated."

"Probably."

"What do you mean, probably?"

"Susan, honey, she's been traveling the world virtually undetected since time began, coming and going as she pleases. She can continue to do that. What's to stop her?"

"Old knowledge renewed. Determination. Because her existence is such a terrifying thing, it's been hidden, rightly or wrongly, in an obscure myth. It's different now. Some people, key people, know that she's real —and they know what to do about her. They, in turn, will make it known to others that she is truly out there in the night, one of the terrible mistakes that happened during creation."

Kellen squinted at the sun's reflections on the pool's surface. "I wonder why she allowed herself to become known here."

"I don't think she allowed it, it just happened."

"How?"

"Because of Sam, I think. The questions he had concerning her, and his seeking answers to them, seriously irritated her, because Lilith supposedly can control the man who she chooses to be hers while living in an area. But she found Sam was not easily dominated. Then I began nosing around, and then Maureen became involved. It was an intolerable situation for her; she tried to frighten Maureen and me away, but when we continued gathering information, she knew she had to kill us to protect herself. When she accomplished that, she'd disappear as she always had. Until this time, her stay in a community, I'm sure, ended when people began to question the number of unexplainable deaths, before, in partial desperation, they sought answers in the metaphysical."

"I have to admit, you make it sound logical, but do you honestly think she can be held at bay?"

"No . . . not entirely, Kellen, no more than any recurring tragedy, like . . . well, you know, tidal waves, erupting volcanoes, hurricanes. But I've been told by Rabbi Cohen that the warnings about her have been sent out along certain channels. There's some kind of underground network, I gather, that links various sects and groups and scholars; so while the scientists and the medical people shake their heads in puzzlement and defeat over the unexplainable infant deaths, there'll be others alert and waiting for her arrival, prepared to drive her away. As tragic as they were, I know, the deaths of the babies here will not have been the useless horror they appear."

He put his arm around her waist and drew her to him. "I think you're right, Mrs. Atgood-to-be."